THE FAMILY CARNOVSKY

The Family Carnovsky

BY I. J. SINGER

Author of *The Brothers Ashkenazi*,
Yoshe Kalb, etc. Translated by
JOSEPH SINGER

New York
THE VANGUARD PRESS, INC.

Manufactured in the United States of America by
H. Wolff Book Manufacturing Company, New York, N.Y.

Library of Congress Catalogue Card Number: 68–8089

Standard Book Number 8149–0003–8

Designer: Ernst Reichl

To Genie

BOOK ONE *David* 1

BOOK TWO *Georg* 117

BOOK THREE *Jegor* 263

BOOK ONE *David*

1

The Carnovskys of Greater Poland were known for being stubborn and contrary but nevertheless were considered sages and scholars with minds like steel traps.

Their genius was reflected in their high scholarly foreheads and their deep-set and restless black eyes. The stubbornness and contrariness exuded from their noses—powerful, oversized noses that jutted from their lean bony faces with a mockery and arrogance and seemed to say, "Look, but don't touch." Because of this stubbornness, none of the Carnovskys became rabbis, although they easily could have; instead, they turned to trade. For the most part they became appraisers in the forests or rode the rafts down the Vistula, often as far as Danzig. In the small shacks that the raftsmen built for them on the floating logs, they carried Talmuds and books of law that they studied with a passion. This same stubbornness led them to take a strong interest in mathematics and philosophy, and even in books printed in German. Although they were merely well-off, they married their sons to the daughters of the richest families in Greater Poland. David Carnovsky was picked off by the daughter of Leib Milner, the biggest lumber merchant in Melnitz.

On the very first Sabbath after the wedding, when the new bridegroom had been escorted to the house of worship, he managed to antagonize the rabbi and the town's ranking citizens.

Although a native of Greater Poland, David Carnovsky, the Hebrew scholar and grammarian, recited the chapter of Isaiah in the Book of Prophets in a Lithuanian accent and with such grammatic precision that the Hasidic Jews in the house of prayer became irked. When the prayer was over, the rabbi let the young man know that here, in *his* domain, this form of Hasid-baiting was not looked on with favor.

"You must understand, young man," the rabbi pointed out maliciously, "that we hardly consider the Prophet Isaiah to have been a Litvak, and certainly no enemy of Hasidism."

"On the contrary, Rabbi," David Carnovsky said, "I can prove that he was indeed a Litvak and an anti-Hasid as well."

"Where is your proof?" asked the rabbi smugly as the influential citizens listened with curiosity to the dispute between him and the young stranger.

"It's simple," David Carnovsky said. "If Isaiah the Prophet had been a Polish Jew and a Hasid, he would have been unfamiliar with the rules of grammar and his writings would have reflected the erroneous Hebrew used by all ignorant Jews and Hasidic rabbis."

To be so badly shown up by a callow youth before his whole congregation was something on which the rabbi had not reckoned, and from great vexation he began to stammer and to attempt a rebuttal. But his words were incoherent and only increased his panic. David Carnovsky gazed mockingly at the rabbi.

From that day, the rabbi feared the stranger. The affluent Melnitz Jews, who occupied the choice place near David Carnovsky and his father-in-law at the eastern wall of the house of worship, weighed every word they addressed to the sharp-tongued young man. But when, during one Sabbath, he introduced heresy into the house of worship, the rabbi and the town leaders came out openly against him.

It happened during the reading of the Torah, when the worshipers turn their heads from the eastern wall and, facing the lectern, silently repeat the section of the Pentateuch after the reader. David Carnovsky, replete in his new prayer shawl that he wore draped not over his head but across his shoulders as befitted an anti-Hasid, was also silently reading from his Pentateuch when the book suddenly slipped from his hands. He bent to pick it up, but his neighbor, a Jew who seemed to consist of only a prayer shawl and a beard, anticipated him. He swiftly pressed his lips to the opened Pentateuch in apology to it for having fallen and was about to return it to its owner when he realized that he had kissed words such as he had never seen in any Pentateuch. They were neither Hebrew nor Yiddish. David Carnovsky held out his hand for his Pentateuch, but the Jew who was only prayer shawl and beard turned it over to the rabbi to examine. The rabbi quickly scanned the book, turned to the title page, and grew red from shock and indignation. "Moses Mendelssohn's Pentateuch," he cried. "Moses Dessauer's *Biyur!* It is a blasphemy against God!" A great tumult and commotion erupted in the house of worship.

The reader rapped his hand against the desk to remind the congregation that they were in the midst of a prayer. The rabbi himself began to pound on the lectern for attention, but the men rumbled and seethed. For all the "shushes" and "well nows" and raps on the lectern, the din only grew louder. Seeing that no one was listening to him anyhow, the reader quickly raced through the required section of the Pentateuch, and the cantor, without his customary trills and quavers, concluded the additional service. As soon as they spat out the final *"Aleinu"* against the strange idols, and even before the prayer was properly ended, the house of worship began to buzz like a beehive.

"Moses Dessauer's forbidden book!" the rabbi seethed, pointing to David Carnovsky's Pentateuch. "Such a thing has never been heard of in Melnitz . . . I will not permit the words of that Berlin apostate in *my* town!"

"Moshe Dessauer, may his memory be blotted out," the Hasidim raged.

The unlearned Jews cocked their ears trying to determine what had happened. The Jew who was only prayer shawl and beard skimmed through the house of worship like an animated feather duster. "The minute I saw it I knew there was something wrong," he announced for the hundredth time. "I sensed it immediately!"

"A fine son-in-law you've bought yourself, Reb Leib!" the influential citizens chided the town magnate.

Leib Milner was confused. In his prayer shawl with its silver collar, with his white beard and gold-rimmed glasses, he was a picture of well-bred dignity; he could not comprehend what all the fuss was about. A son of leaseholders whose wealth had been recently acquired, he knew nothing of the Torah outside of the daily prayers. Somehow the word *"Biyur"* had reached his ears, but what sort of beer this was or what it had to do with his son-in-law was beyond him. "Rabbi, what's going on here?" he pleaded.

The rabbi angrily pointed to the Pentateuch. "You see, Reb Leib, this Moses Mendelssohn of Dessau brought shame upon Israel!" he shouted. "He led Jews into apostasy with his blasphemous Torah!"

Although Leib Milner still did not understand who Moses of Dessau was, he gathered from the rabbi's tone that he had been some sort of Jewish missionary who had led his son-in-law astray. He tried to restore peace in the house of worship.

"Men, my son-in-law, long may he live, obviously was not aware of the context of this book," he said. "It isn't fitting that Jews squabble in a house of worship. Let us rather go to our homes and make the Sabbath benedictions."

But his son-in-law had no intention of going home and making the Sabbath benediction. He pushed his way through the crowd toward the rabbi. "Give me back my Pentateuch," he said. "I demand that you return it."

The rabbi had no intention of returning the Pentateuch although he really did not know what to do with it. If it had been an ordinary forbidden book and this had not been the Sabbath, he would have ordered the beadle to light a fire in the stove and to burn the impurity before the entire congregation as the law directed. But this *was* the Sabbath, the blasphemy had been printed together with the Torah, heresy alongside the Holy Word. Still, he did not want to return the book to its owner. "No, young man, it will not see the light of day again!" he cried.

Again Leib Milner tried to intercede. "David, my son-in-law, what does a Pentateuch cost? I'll buy you ten more expensive Pentateuchs! Forget about it and come home."

But David Carnovsky was adamant. "No, Father-in-law," he said, "I will not let him keep this Pentateuch; not for anything in the world!"

Leib Milner tried another approach. "David, Leah is waiting at home for your benediction," he said. "She'll perish from hunger."

But David Carnovsky was so embroiled in controversy he didn't even remember his Leah. His eyes blazed. He was ready to take on the world for his convictions. At first he demanded that the rabbi show him even one word of heresy in the book. Then he began to quote the Torah skillfully to show that the rabbi and the influential citizens neither knew nor were capable of understanding even one word of Moses Mendelssohn's writings. He then fell into such a rage that he claimed that Rabbi Mendelssohn, blessed be his memory, possessed more Torah, wisdom, and fear of God in his little toe than the rabbi and all of his congregation together.

With this statement, the young stranger went too far. The fact that he had defamed the rabbi and the pious Jews and that in a house of worship he had called a heretic "rabbi" and blessed his memory so severely tried the patience of the Hasidim that they seized him by the arms and escorted him to the door. "Go to hell along with your rabbi, may his name be blotted out!" they cried after him. "Go to that Berlin convert, cursed be his memory!"

And David Carnovsky did just that.

Although he still was entitled to a long period of board at the home of his in-laws, he did not want to remain in a town in which he had suffered such humiliation. His father-in-law pleaded with him, promised that they would leave the house of worship and pray at the synagogue, where the men were more modern and progressive. He would even form his own quorum at home if David insisted. Leah, David's wife, begged him not to take her away from her parents' house. But David Carnovsky was adamant. "I will not spend another day among these savages and ignoramuses," he insisted, "even if you offer me a roomful of gold!"

In his anger, he called the men of Melnitz every name he had learned in his worldly books: benighted denizens of the Dark Ages, idolators, asses.

Not only did he want to abandon the town that had so disgraced him, but all of Poland, which was steeped in darkness and ignorance. For a long time he had been drawn to Berlin—the city in which the sainted Moses Mendelssohn had once lived and from

which he had spread his light across the world. From early childhood, when David Carnovsky had studied German from Mendelssohn's Pentateuch, he had been drawn to that land across the
border that was the source of all goodness, knowledge, and light.
Later, when he was older and helped his father in the lumber
business, he often had to read German letters from Danzig, Bremen,
Hamburg, and Berlin. Each time he did this, a strange feeling of
sorcery came over him. The *Hochwollgeborn* that preceded each
name breathed of great nobility and grace. Even the colorful postage
stamps bearing the portrait of the strange Kaiser evoked within him
a longing for this alien yet familiar land. Now he saw an opportunity to fulfill this longing. He proposed to his father-in-law that he
pay him the balance of the dowry, which would allow him to reset-
tle across the border.

At first Leib Milner would not hear of it. He wanted his children
and his sons and daughters-in-law by his side. His wife, Nehama,
stopped up her ears to drown out such talk. *That's all she needed—
to let her Leah go to some foreign country! They could offer her the
moon and the stars—she wouldn't agree to it . . .* She shook her
head so vigorously that her long earrings whipped her cheeks. But
David Carnovsky persisted. With a torrent of words, with erudition
and logic and a flurry of arguments, he harangued his in-laws. Leib
Milner could not long bear up under such pressure, but Nehama
wouldn't capitulate so easily. *No and double no!* she insisted. *Not
even if it should lead to a divorce!* But at this, Leah herself in-
terceded. "Mama," she said, "I will go wherever my David will tell
me."

Nehama hung her head and burst into tears. Leah clung to her
mother's neck and cried with her.

As usual, David Carnovsky got his way. Leib Milner paid him the
entire dowry, some twenty thousand rubles. With the same persua-
siveness, David convinced his father-in-law to go into business with
him and to ship him lumber to Germany on rafts and wagons. Nehama baked batches of cakes and cookies and packed innumerable
bottles of juice and preserves, as if her daughter were going off into a
wilderness and needed to be provided with the good things of life
for years to come. David Carnovsky trimmed his beard to a point,

put on a derby and a jacket cut to the knees, bought a top hat for Sabbaths and holidays, and ordered a frock coat with silk lapels.

Within only a few short years David Carnovsky managed several notable achievements in the strange city in which he had settled. To begin with, he learned a fluent German, the German of lumber tycoons, bankers, and officials. Secondly, he prospered in the business and became an important member of that industry. Thirdly, he completed a course of the Gymnasium from textbooks, a goal to which he had long aspired. And fourthly, because of his knowledge and erudition, he made the acquaintance of the leaders of the community in the synagogue in which he prayed—not raggedy Eastern Jews but the distinguished descendants of long-settled German Jewry.

His elegant apartment located in the front of the house on Oranienburger Strasse became a gathering place for savants and scholars. The walls of his study were lined from ceiling to floor with books, for the main part old prayer books and rare volumes that he purchased from the book dealer, Ephraim Walder, on Dragonerstrasse in the Jewish quarter. Not only the rabbi of the synagogue, Dr. Speier, but other scholars and learned men—librarians, seminarians, and even the aged Professor Breslauer, the oldest member of the Theological Seminary—all gathered here to discuss the Torah and the wisdom of Israel.

When, after three years, his wife Leah bore him his first son, David Carnovsky gave him two names: Moses, after Moses Mendelssohn, a name by which the boy would be called up to the Torah when he grew older; and a German name, Georg, a corruption of his father's name, Gershon, a name with which he could go among people and use in business.

"Be a Jew in the house and a man in the street," the father of the circumcised child exhorted his son in both Hebrew and German, as if to make sure the infant understood.

The invited guests nodded their heads in approval.

"Yes, yes, my dear Herr Carnovsky," said Dr. Speier, stroking his tiny beard that was as thin and pointed as a pencil, "ever the golden mean. A Jew among Jews and a German among Germans."

"Ever the golden mean," the men agreed, and tucked the snowy napkins beneath their high stiff collars in anticipation of the feast to follow.

2

Leah Carnovsky's greatest joy was to hear her child praised—especially when someone remarked on the boy's resemblance to his father.

Although in the five years since the birth of her darling son she had heard countless such compliments, she longed to hear them again and again.

"Look, Emma," she said, and drew her maid away from her work to look at the boy as if for the first time. "Isn't he the sweetest thing?"

"Certainly, Mistress."

"The image of his father, isn't he, Emma?"

"But of course, Mistress."

Like all women, Emma knew that mothers loved to be told that their offspring resembled their fathers, but in this instance no lie was necessary—little Georg was the image of David Carnovsky. His burning black eyes were prematurely framed by brows that were too thick and too sharply etched for a child. The stubborn and arrogant Carnovsky nose jutted prematurely from the childish face. His hair, which his mother would not allow to be cut, was actually blue in its blackness. Emma tried to find some trace of the mother in the boy but it was not easy. Leah Carnovsky had light brown hair, a pale skin, gray eyes that occasionally changed to green, and a quality of feminine goodness in her rounded face and figure.

"His mouth is exactly like the Mistress's," Emma said finally, to indicate at least a trace of the mother in the boy.

But Leah would not concede even that. "No, the father's mouth," she insisted. "Look for yourself, Emma."

The women began to examine the boy, who was hard at play astride a wooden horse. The youngster became aware of the women's inspection, felt his own importance, and stuck out his tongue. Emma was offended. "You fresh little devil!" she reprimanded him.

The boy's swarthiness reminded her of Satan. Leah Carnovsky felt such a surge of maternal rapture at the boy's impudent gesture that she hugged him to her bosom and showered him with burning kisses. "Joy, happiness, treasure, my prince, may I suffer your every pain, my sweet little Moshele," she cooed and pressed the boy's head to her bosom.

Little Georg tried to tear loose from her arms and kicked his legs against his mother's lap. "Let me go, Mutti, I must go to my horse!"

He didn't like it when his mother kissed him so passionately and tweaked his cheeks. He liked it even less when she spoke strange words that he did not understand and called him by unfamiliar names. Besides, everyone called him Georg. Only his mother spoke so strangely. He could not bear it. "I'm not Moshele, I'm Georg!" he corrected her angrily, for which Leah rewarded him with kisses on both his eyes. "Bad boy, wicked boy, obstinate Carnovsky *akshun,* Moshele, Moshele, Moshele," she murmured.

To mollify him, she gave him a chunk of chocolate, although her David had given strict orders that the boy should not be given sweets. The lad bit into the chocolate and in his delight forgot about the despised name. He even let his mother kiss him as much as she liked.

When the wall clock in the dining room struck eight, Leah took the boy to bed. Emma offered to do it but Leah would not give up this pleasure. She washed the chocolate from his hands and face, took off the sailor suit, and dressed him in a nightshirt that reached to his toes. Setting him astride her neck, she carried him from one door-post amulet to the other so that he might kiss them before going to sleep. Little Georg kissed the amulets. He did not know what they were but he knew that if he kissed them, good angels would come to his bedside and watch over him the whole night through.

Besides, the amulets were sheathed in small, shiny tubes that he enjoyed touching. But when his mother began to read the bedtime prayer with him, he was overcome with laughter. The Hebrew syllables seemed even funnier than the Yiddish words and he repeated them in reverse. He grew hysterical with laughter when his mother cast her eyes to the ceiling and drew out the phrase, "God is one." She reminded him of a fowl drinking water and he began to cluck like a hen, transforming the holy words into a chicken's "cut, cut, cut, cut . . ."

Leah Carnovsky grew pale. She was afraid that the good angels whom she had summoned to guard over her child's bed—Michael on the right, Gabriel on the left, Ariel at the head, and Raphael at the foot—might take revenge upon the boy. "Don't do this, my child," she entreated him. "Repeat after me, my treasure: 'With your whole heart and soul.' "

"Belebebeche chelelecheche," the boy said, and shrieked a loud, piercing laugh that penetrated to all the rooms of the apartment.

Despite her fear of the blasphemy, Leah could not contain herself and burst out laughing. She felt that she was sinning but she could never resist joining in when someone laughed, and she laughed until the tears came. But soon she reminded herself that her David was liable to hear her in his study and she knew that he hated laughter. Besides, he was entertaining important visitors, and she muffled her face in Georg's pillow.

"Go to sleep! Go to sleep!" she admonished the overstimulated boy and kissed him from head to toe. First, his every finger, then, his every toe. Finally, she turned him over on his stomach and planted a kiss on his very bottom. "Sweet as honey," she sighed.

After covering him and begging God's forgiveness for the boy's foolish antics, she headed for the dining room, exhausted from the maternal emotion and the laughter.

"Emma, tea for the gentlemen!" she ordered.

Rearranging herself and fixing her hair, she went into her husband's study to serve refreshments to his guests. Only men were present, all of them senior to her husband by many years. They wore black knee-length coats and snowy linen. Most of them wore glasses.

One patriarch wore a tiny skullcap and smoked a long, porcelain pipe that made him look like a small-town rabbi; but at the same time he spoke a very elegant German and was a professor.

"Good evening, Herr Professor!" said Leah, blushing.

"Good evening, my daughter, good evening," said Professor Breslauer, his ruddy, childish face shining among the thickets of snow-white hair and beard.

Afterwards, she greeted the other men who, although they were dressed like gentiles, were clean-shaven, and spoke German, retained the appearance of Yeshiva students. But their manner was very worldly and they addressed Frau Carnovsky with exaggerated politeness.

"Good evening, gracious lady!" they said, bowing awkwardly. "How are you?"

Each of them took a tiny skullcap from his pocket, put it on to make the benediction over the food, and promptly put it back. They made the benediction very quietly, barely moving their lips, except for Professor Breslauer, who intoned it aloud. And just as loudly he complimented Frau Carnovsky on her homemade strudel. "Ah, you're a master baker," he said. "Such genuine Jewish strudel I haven't tasted in sixty years. You have a clever wife, Herr Carnovsky."

The men nodded agreement. The only one to outdo Professor Breslauer's compliments to Frau Carnovsky was the rabbi, Dr. Speier. Stroking his beard, he commended not only her strudel but her beauty as well. "The praiseworthy Frau Carnovsky surpasses the proverbial Woman of Valor. Because of the other it is written that her grace is deceitful and her beauty is vain and only her virtues are praised. But the esteemed Frau Carnovsky is that kind of valorous woman whose grace and beauty are not deceitful and vain but go hand in hand with her moral virtues."

Professor Breslauer beamed. "You are a real ladies' man, my dear Rabbi Speier," he admonished him, wagging a finger roguishly. "Be careful I do not tell your wife. . . ."

Everyone laughed and enjoyed the repartee, which was a welcome respite after the Torah and the wisdom. But not the host, David Carnovsky. Although he was younger than the others and his face still reflected energy and vitality, he could not abide idle chatter. He wanted to tell his guests about a rare volume he had found among the trash at Reb Ephraim Walder's bookstore and he could not bear time wasted chatting with a female. "I want you to know, gentlemen," he interrupted, "that I have located a remarkable old *Midrash Tanhuma*, published in the year—"

Leah left the study. About *Midrash Tanhuma* she had nothing to say. Besides, she knew that her David did not like her to linger in his study when he entertained distinguished visitors. To this day she did not speak a good German. She made errors and interjected expressions from Melnitz and caused her husband great embarrassment. Therefore she hurriedly left the room, somewhat ashamed of herself. Despite all the extravagant compliments, she felt like a servant who has finished her tasks and been dismissed.

The chandelier in the dining room cast dark shadows and Leah was filled with a deep sorrow when she sat down to darn her husband's socks. Although she had lived for years in this strange city, she was still as lonely as when she first came. She still longed for her parents' house, for her girl friends, for the town where she had been born and raised. Her husband treated her well. He was faithful to her and provided her with all the good things, but he had little time for her. During the day he was occupied with his business; at night, with his books or his guests with whom he discussed Torah and wisdom. She understood neither his business nor his Torah. Her neighbors were strangers to her and Leah did not know to whom to turn in her loneliness. She seldom went out with her husband. Only during the holidays they went to the synagogue together; he in his top hat, she in her holiday finery and jewelry. They strolled slowly, arm in arm, and on the way they met other couples walking with festive calmness and serenity. The men tipped their hats, the women nodded. But that was the extent of it.

Although she was companionable, good-natured, and liked to laugh, Leah could not make friends with the respectable ladies from the synagogue. She felt alien among them and afraid. And just as alien to her were the prayers of the cantor in the synagogue. Although they were said in Hebrew, they sounded as if they were spoken by a priest. And just as un-Jewish to her were the choir and

Dr. Speier's sermons. Rigid and icy, the rabbi spoke with an assumed fervor and broad gestures that were incongruous with his stiff face and figure. He also used a highly exalted German full of flowery phrases and quotations from German writers and philosophers, seasoned with verses from the Scriptures and excerpts from prayer books. The women of the synagogue were enthralled with Dr. Speier. "How divine he is!" they gushed. "Don't you find it so, Frau Carnovsky?"

"Yes, of course," Leah agreed, but she did not understand a word of what she had heard. Neither did she understand the prayer book in German translation, which did not transmit to her the flavor of Jewishness. The synagogue, the holy ark, the Torah, and even God Himself seemed alien in this luxurious, churchlike edifice. Just like her mother back home, she was eager to indulge her familiarity with her beloved God and to call Him "Papa." But she dared not do this in the heathen palace that seemed more like a bank than the Lord's house.

David Carnovsky was very proud of his synagogue and its distinguished congregation. Not only did its leading members treat him as an equal, they had even made him an officer of the synagogue's board of directors. From time to time they gave him the honor of helping the reader remove the Torah from the holy ark and replacing it after the reading. In addition, he pointed with the silver fescue to the proper page during the reading. The men pressed his hand afterward, as is the custom, and greeted him with a "Good Sabbath," and David Carnovsky felt highly exalted because of these honors. After the Melnitz house of worship and its boorish worshipers, it was to him a great achievement to win such respect from the honored old citizens of Berlin—the magnates, scholars, and men of enlightenment—and he wanted Leah to share in his glory and to feel proud. But Leah felt uneasy with her husband's friends—uneasy and lost.

She felt even more uncomfortable during their visits to Dr. Speier's house, to which they were occasionally invited. The rabbi's wife was very pious, even though her husband was a reform rabbi. She not only prayed three times a day but kept washing her hands and making benedictions over each glass of coffee, each sweet and fruit. She was a great student of literature and, like her husband, quoted writers freely and recited poetry from memory. A native of Frankfurt and the product of generations of rabbis, she was steeped in erudition that she showed off like a scholarly male. Because she was barren she never discussed children, but spoke of the wisdom and learning of her great-grandfathers, the rabbis. She was also familiar with the genealogy of all the better Jewish families, not only in Frankfurt and Berlin but throughout the whole country. She knew who stemmed from whom, who was betrothed to whom, and how much everyone was worth. Her guests were just as distinguished and wellborn as she. They were for the main part elderly women who were no longer interested in fashion, pregnancies, and child-bearing and spoke of engagements, dowries, wedding gifts, and family trees. The rabbi's wife dominated the conversation. She pontificated rather than spoke, frequently quoting her father or grandfather. "As my late grandfather, the famous Rabbi of Frankfurt, once remarked in his famous Sabbath of Repentance sermon . . ." she said every other sentence.

Leah Carnovsky had nothing to say regarding her ancestors, who were leaseholders in obscure Polish villages. In order to get a word in, she occasionally tried to describe some of her son's antics but the rabbi's wife wanted no part of such talk. Leah Carnovsky breathed freely when she left the rabbi's house. "David," she begged her husband as they walked home, "don't take me along on these visits again, David dear."

David Carnovsky flared up at her: "For God's sake, speak German!"

German to him signified light, culture, Moses Mendelssohn, and the highest form of Jewishness, while Leah's jargon reminded him of the rabbi of Melnitz, the cult of Hasidism, of stupidity and ignorance. Besides, he was afraid to be mistaken for an inhabitant of Dragonerstrasse. Only after they came home did he lecture his wife sternly. For the hundredth time he prompted her to remember her position. She was no longer some insignificant little housewife from Melnitz but the wife of David Carnovsky, a friend of old Berlin families. He could not go visiting by himself like some aged roué who was separated from his wife. They had to go together, as was fitting and proper among people of standing. She had to accustom herself to converse with educated people and to associate with respectable ladies. She also had to improve herself and read as he did, so that she would not disgrace him. Above all, she had to improve her speech, her grammar, and always speak German instead of that Melnitz Yiddish that crippled her pronunciation. She had to acclimatize herself to this new world just as he had. No one could possibly detect that he was a stranger. Leah listened to her husband's complaints and accusations and did not know what to say in her own defense. She felt wretched.

As usual when she was depressed, she wrote long letters in a homely Yiddish to her parents, to her sisters, to her brother in America, to relatives, to her girl friends back home, and poured into them all her sorrow and longing.

David could not understand how his wife could find so much to write. True, he also wrote a lot, but only concerning important matters—business correspondence, orders for lumber, or scholarly commentaries. What possibly could fill the letters of such a simple woman was beyond him. Still, he said nothing to her but, examining a page out of curiosity, chuckled at her errors in spelling and ran his warm, tanned hand over her silky hair. Leah nuzzled up to him with her soft, feminine body. "David, love me," she pleaded. "Whom else have I but you?"

Caught up in the emotion of love, Carnovsky forgot wisdom and respectability. But one thing he did not forget was his German. Even in moments of greatest ecstacy he whispered endearments to Leah in that language. She was offended; his words of endearment in that strange, guttural tongue were repugnant to her. They did not contain the true flavor of love.

3

Solomon Burak's discount store on Landsberger Allee was crowded and noisy. Women of every age and appearance—old, fleshy German women with heavy, dark hats festooned with flowers and ribbons; scrawny workers' wives with clinging children in hand; young blonde girls dressed in sweeping, colorful gowns and carrying parasols—all crowded the large store that was jammed with goods from floor to ceiling—underwear, linen, stockings, aprons, satin wedding gowns, veils, shapeless maternity dresses, swaddling clothes, even shrouds for corpses. The salesmen and sales-women—slick, agile, black-eyed and black-haired—worked with re-markable speed to serve the hordes of customers. They measured swiftly, figured quickly, packed feverishly. "Next, please, next!" they prodded the women who stood in line ready to buy.

At the cashier's desk sat Frau Burak, who took in money and gave change. Her soft fingers bedecked with rings skillfully added the banknotes and sorted out the coins. Her lips, set in a perpetual smile directed both at the customer and at the money, kept whispering, "Thank you! Thank you!"

The most agile, lively, and slick of all was the proprietor of the store himself, Solomon Burak. Lean, fair, and dandy in a light checked English suit, a red tie, and a silk handkerchief tucked into the bosom pocket of his jacket, and with a large ring on the index finger of his right hand, he looked more like a German comedian or circus performer than a Jewish storekeeper. He spoke a racy, Berlin-accented German, ripe with the flavor of the big city; but his energy and nervousness unmistakably labeled him an immigrant from the East.

"A ducat more, a ducat less," he said to his salesmen and saleswomen, "as long as there is action. I like things humming!"

This had been his policy from the very first day when, still a youngster, he arrived from Melnitz and with a pack on his back peddled goods throughout German villages. This same policy he employed later when he opened a small women's-wear credit store on Linienstrasse in the Jewish quarter. And it was still in effect now that he had long since left the Polish-Galician neighborhood and worked himself up to a huge establishment on Landsberger Allee. He liked the routine of the business—the buying, the selling, the manipulating. He dealt in huge lots, the larger the better as far as he was concerned. He also purchased out-of-style merchandise, damaged goods, remnants of bankruptcies and fires, anything that was cheap. And he sold as cheaply as he bought. He sold goods for cash, on credit, and on the installment plan. And although he was no longer located on Linienstrasse and his clientele was entirely gentile, he did not try to conceal his origin as did most of the Jewish merchants in the neighborhood. His Jewish name was inscribed in huge letters on his sign. Neither did he embellish his store with flaxen-haired salespeople as did the other Jewish merchants in an attempt to conceal their own Semitic background.

On the contrary, he employed his and his wife's relatives whom he brought over from Melnitz. He thus reaped a double benefit—he provided needy people with a livelihood and was able to have trusted employees, his own flesh and blood. The younger ones, those already familiar with the latest fashions and the German language, he employed in the store. The older ones he sent out to collect the installments.

The other Jewish merchants in the neighborhood who were long-settled and assimilated were irritated by Solomon Burak. They were not so much annoyed that he brought down prices and sold cheaply as that he had brought the Jewishness from Poland to Landsberger Allee. They could not bear the name "Solomon" that he had spread in such blatant letters across his sign. They regarded it as typical Jewish impudence calculated to antagonize the gentiles.

"Why 'Solomon'?" they demanded. "Wouldn't the family name by itself suffice? And if you insist on having the first name too, why not only the initial 'S'?"

Solomon Burak laughed with derision at his neighbors. He could see nothing wrong with the name Solomon, nor could he understand their objections to his foreign-born sales force. In the coarse German that he had learned as a peddler, spiced with a mixture of Melnitz Yiddish and Hebrew, he proved to his outraged neighbors that he did better with his "Solomon" than they did with their gentile decoys with which they tried to masquerade their heritage. His name might be Solomon but the gentile women and girls came flocking to him because he sold for a few pfennigs less.

"How does the saying go? 'Impure may be Moshe, but his pfennig is kosher'. . ." he laughed.

He did not spare his coreligionists, neither his fellow merchants, nor the manufacturers from whom he purchased the huge lots of goods, nor even the bank directors from whom he borrowed large amounts on interest. He told them that even though they were long-settled and Germans for many generations back, they were despised by the gentiles every bit as much as he, the stranger, and as were all Jews—and because of this, they needed to feel no superiority to him, Solomon Burak.

"How does the saying go? 'Fritz or Horst, man hates the Jew but likes his purse!' " he concluded with a rhyme, and rubbed his hands to indicate that there was nothing else to be said on the subject.

The black-eyed Berliners who envied the upstart's blondness shook their heads ruefully. Although they were well aware that he spoke the truth, they did not like to hear it from the lips of a former peddler who had so quickly moved up to Landsberger Allee. They were uneasy because of people like him, who with their names, conduct, and business tactics caused the gentiles to lump them, the long-settled and German-assimilated Jews, in the same category. They were afraid because of these recent arrivals who resurrected the very Jewishness that they, the old settlers, had for so long masked and concealed.

"Well, let us talk no more about it," they said, anxious to leave such a painful subject.

But Solomon Burak wanted very much to talk about it. Just because they did not like these matters he brought them up at every opportunity. In the same vein he also interjected Jewish expressions when speaking to the manufacturers and bank directors who squirmed at any reminder of Jewishness. Solomon Burak employed his bilingual speech not only toward Jews but also used it in the store whenever some irksome customer annoyed him too much.

"This is the very latest fashion à la *Kolomeye*," he jested with severe gravity. "*Simchas Torah* model number thirteen. . . . Isn't that right, Max?"

Just like his store, Solomon Burak's apartment was in a constant ferment. It was filled with relatives, friends, acquaintances, and, above all, people from Melnitz. As soon as some woman came to Germany to consult a famous specialist, or when a couple was in transit to America, they first made a stop at the apartment of Shlomele Burak, who called himself Solomon here. They lingered at his house for days, even weeks on end. They dined at his table and slept on his sofas. Solomon Burak himself made fun of his tumultuous household. Hotel du Bedbug, he liked to call it, but he spoke not to discourage visitors, only in the spirit of fun. "Live and let live," he would say to his wife when she occasionally tired of the constant stream of guests.

One of the guests who infrequently dropped in at the "hotel" was Leah Carnovsky, who came from the same town as Solomon and Yetta Burak.

When her husband was home Leah did not visit the Buraks, for David Carnovsky wanted no truck with boors from Melnitz. He wanted to forget the years on the other side, to wipe them from his memory. The very fact that he was himself a foreigner made him want to avoid contact with other foreigners. Besides, the Buraks had not been his equals on the other side either. They were paupers and illiterates, and Carnovsky, the scholar and aristocrat, had a strong aversion to their kind. The first time the Buraks dropped in uninvited and Solomon, cigar in mouth, became too familiar with David and slapped him on the back, Carnovsky shook him off with such vehemence that the other understood never to come again.

"I have nothing in common with this trash," David said afterward to Leah, "and you should avoid them too. They are not fit company for the wife of David Carnovsky."

Because of this, Leah stayed away from her friends. But when David went to Bremen or Hamburg on business she grew so dejected in the empty apartment that she stole away to the Buraks to see a familiar face and exchange a friendly word. Yetta and Solomon Burak always greeted her with great affection. "Reb Milner's little Leah!" Yetta exulted and clapped her hands. "Solomon, Shlomele, come look who's here to see us!"

Solomon-Shlomele laughed gleefully. "Yom Kippur must have come out on Rosh Hashonah this year if Frau Carnovsky herself has condescended to visit Solomon Burak," he said teasingly.

At the same time he conducted himself with the exaggerated politeness he learned to employ toward ladies in the cheap dance halls he once frequented; helped Leah remove her long coat and took her parasol.

"Has your husband gone out of town?" Yetta asked as she exchanged kisses with Leah.

"Yes, Yettele," Leah said, embarrassed because she had to visit her friends in secret.

Solomon made a joke of it. Running to the stove, he tested it to see if it was still standing, in accordance with a Melnitz proverb that said: When an exalted visitor comes unexpectedly, the stove is liable to fall apart. Yetta, who since her marriage to Solomon constantly supervised his conduct and bridled his excesses, put a stop to his antics. "Shlomele," she chided him, "Solomon, let the stove be."

Leah burst out laughing. She was overcome by homesickness and nostalgia. She felt relaxed and wanted to laugh—to laugh aloud. Yetta only awaited the apportunity to laugh with her. Pleased at the reaction to his joke, Solomon felt compelled to go on. "How is the Passover turkey?" he asked Leah Carnovsky.

Leah was puzzled. "The Passover turkey?"

"I mean Herr Carnovsky," Solomon explained. "Is he still puffing himself up?"

Now he had gone too far and Yetta gave him a piece of her mind. "Shlomele," she said, "don't forget yourself. Go tell the girl to bring us something to eat."

Leah ate the poppy cakes, the horn-shaped rolls, and the bagels that reminded her of home. She tasted the honey ball and jam and beamed. "A real treat," she said. "Just like in Melnitz."

The apartment filled with people. It was always open house at the Buraks'. The gentile maids did not even ask who was calling; they admitted everyone. Not only did relatives come; so did all kinds of brokers and agents; secondhand clothes dealers from the Jewish quarter in need of a loan; ailing people on their way to visit spas or specialists; fathers of old maids accumulating dowries; distinguished paupers; ordinary spongers; victims of fires—Solomon Burak turned no one away. "A ducat less, a ducat more, live and let live," he said, counting out the bills swiftly.

There was always something cooking in the kitchen. The gentile maids whom Yetta had taught to cook such Jewish delicacies as kugel and carrot stews were busy stuffing fish and slicing noodles, baking poppy-seed cakes and honey balls, and continuously serving refreshments. The subject most often talked about was Melnitz. Everything that happened there was known in this apartment: who had grown wealthy and who bankrupt; who had died and who married off a child; who had been united through marriage with whom; who had fallen victim to a fire; who had already gone off to America and who was planning to go. Leah Carnovsky drank in the conversation, her cheeks aglow with happiness. She was home again. The whole town and its people paraded before her eyes. From time to time she reminded herself that she had stayed too long and made an attempt to go but the others wouldn't let her leave. "In just a minute I'll let you go, Leah," Yetta said, holding her friend's hands.

Leah needed little urging. She wanted to make up for all the torturous visits to the rabbi's house, for her lonely and regimented existence. Here she could speak freely, behave naturally, talk about dresses and cooking, and boast about her child and hear Yetta repeat *her* children's clever remarks. Most important, she could laugh, laugh at every trifle as she had in her parents' house. When the table was set with familiar dishes, Leah's happiness was complete. "Look here—noodles and fish broth," she cried. "Real Melnitz noodles and fish broth!"

The guests savored both the homely dishes and their host's ripe anecdotes about his travails at the hands of the gentiles and the village dogs until God helped him work his way up to a point where he could enjoy life, thanks to the patronage of the stupid German dolt. From the gentile Germans the conversation veered to the Jewish Germans who, just like their Christian counterparts, looked down on foreigners and wouldn't give a dying Polish Jew a drop of water to drink.

"Who could ask for a better example than the Posen Jews, who were once Polish themselves and now snub other Polish Jews?" a guest said indignantly.

"Are the others any better?" asked Solomon Burak. "As soon as they climb the social ladder they won't give us a tumble!"

Yetta realized that her husband was again treading on dangerous ground and, as usual, tried to restrain him. "Shlomele, don't talk so much or you're liable to swallow a fish bone, Solly dearest."

Solomon-Shlomele took a sip of the Passover Slivovitz that he liked to drink all year round and waved away the mention of all Germans, both gentile and Jewish, along with the Posen Jews and all the rest. "Let them all go to hell," he said. "They'll yet tip their hats to Solomon Burak or my name isn't Shlomo."

Ecstatic at the thought of Germans tipping their hats to him, he turned on the green phonograph with the large horn and played a cantorial hymn from home, "Because of Our Sins," a new record he had bought at Ephraim Walder's bookshop on Dragonerstrasse. The phonograph wailed to the Almighty God; it groaned, cajoled, and wheedled like a child to its father. Leah felt the same reverence she had as a girl when her mother took her to the women's synagogue during the High Holy Days. Although she did not understand the Hebrew words, they stirred her with their homelike flavor, their lament and solemnity. This talking machine brought her closer to God than did the cantor and the choir at her husband's synagogue.

"Dear God," she whispered familiarly, "sweet dear Papa. . . ."

4

True to his principles, David Carnovsky made certain that his son was raised a Jew at home and a man in the street. But to his Christian neighbors, Georg was merely another Jew.

The courtyard of the great apartment house on Oranienburger Strasse was not especially large, but it was extremely lively. The front apartments, in one of which the Carnovskys lived, were spacious. Few children lived here. But the apartments facing the courtyard were a world apart, small, congested, and filled with children. The garbage bin that stood in the yard was large; cats and dogs swarmed around it. Through the open windows could be heard the sounds of women screaming and girls singing. Here and there a sewing machine clattered and a dog barked. Frequently an organ grinder came and played love songs and soldiers' ballads. From all sides women thrust their heads out of windows. The children were thick as flies, especially around the garbage bin.

Among all the flaxen-haired, pale-complexioned, blue-eyed, and snub-nosed children, Georg was the only black-eyed, black-haired, and dark-complexioned one. And although he lived in a front apartment, he was always with the children in the courtyard. Their fairness made his swarthiness even more conspicuous. And just as conspicuous was his seething and fiery nature. Whether they played soldiers or cops and robbers or hare and hunter, he put too much fervor into the game. He was the absolute master and issued orders about how the games should be played. The other children obeyed him. But Georg not only issued the orders but punished those who

disregarded them. With eyes ablaze, cheeks flushed, he dominated
with Carnovsky bullheadedness the blond lads with the brush hair-
cuts and the girls with stiff pigtails and freckled, soft throats. His
hands plucked from the circle of children those who spoiled the play
or did not move quickly enough to suit him. "Oh, those girls are
ruining everything!" he raged.

At first the offended girls only mocked his swarthiness. "Black
raven!" they jeered. "Black ape!"

Georg meted out punishment on the spot. The girls burst out crying and ran to their mothers. One aroused mother came down the
stairs and pricked little Georg with a sewing needle. "You fresh
little Jew!" she shouted. "Don't you lay your sheeny hands on my
baby!"

Georg opened his eyes wide the first time he heard this word.
Although his mother made him kiss the door-post amulet at night,
although his father had already taught him his Hebrew alphabet, he
did not connect these things with being a Jew. He assumed that all
children were made to do the same. He therefore ran to his mother
in great confusion. "Mutti," he said indignantly, "the children in the
courtyard called me a Jew. . . ."

Leah stroked his velvety hair. "Don't let it disturb you, my child,"
she said. "They are bad children. Don't play with them. Instead,
come with me to the park where you can play with nice children."

But this did not satisfy Georg. "What is a Jew, Mutti?" he asked.

"A Jew is someone who believes in one God," she explained.

"Am I a Jew, Mutti?"

"Of course."

"And what are the other children in the courtyard?"

"They are Christian."

"What does Christian mean?"

Leah thought it over. "Christians are those who don't pray in
synagogues but in a church," she finally said. "Our maid, Emma, is a
Christian. Do you understand, child?"

Georg understood, but he could not comprehend why he should be
called a Jew, and a fresh Jew at that. He understood it even less
when he grew older and the children in school told him that he was
a Christ-killer. When the time came to study religion, he and some

other boys were told to leave the classroom. Although pleased at being freed from his studies for a while, he was also ashamed and confused. The gentile children quickly enlightened him. "A Jew does not have to learn about Jesus Christ," they told him, "because the Jews crucified Jesus. You are a goddamned Christ-killer."

Again he ran to his mother. "Mutti, what is a Christ-killer?"

With concern, and choosing her words carefully, Leah Carnovsky told him that the gentiles served a God made of wood who hung on a cross with nails driven into his hands and feet. The Christians claimed it was the Jews who had crucified their God.

"Is this true?"

"God is one," Leah replied. "He is in Heaven and no one can see Him—so how could men hang God?"

Georg laughed at the children who could believe such nonsense. But the fact that adults who knew everything could believe this too, even the teacher of religion, Herr Schultze—this was beyond him. But since his mother avoided further discussion of the subject he went into the kitchen to talk it over with the maid.

"Emma, you're a Christian, aren't you?" he asked the maid, who was ironing the master's shirt collars.

"Certainly," Emma said. "Catholic."

"What is Catholic?"

"Well . . . not Protestant is Catholic . . ."

Georg still did not understand. Taking down a rosary that hung on a nail over her bed next to a photograph of a soldier, Emma showed him that Catholics had such rosaries and that the Protestants did not. From the beads hung a brass crucifix.

"What is that?" Georg asked.

"Our Lord, Jesus Christ," Emma said piously.

"Is that your God, Emma?" Georg asked.

"Yes," replied Emma. "There He is on the cross, nailed to it."

Georg tried to repeat his mother's argument that since God was mightier than man He would not allow Himself to be hanged, but Emma objected violently. "Don't you dare speak that way about Our Lord, you little fiend!"

By this time Georg realized that he would learn nothing from her and wanted to know only one thing more; did she consider him, Georg, a Christ-killer too?

"Of course. All Jews are," she said. "That's what the priest himself told us in church."

She had personally seen during Easter services how the Jews had perpetrated this deed. The Lord Jesus in His white robe, with a crown of thorns upon His forehead, walked in front carrying a heavy cross upon His shoulders. The Jews with the long thick beards were beating Him until he bled. Others spat at Him. If Georg didn't believe her, she would take him along to church some Sunday and prove it to him.

One Sunday, without her mistress's knowledge, she did take him. His black eyes agape, Georg looked at the high stained-glass windows, the candles, the choir boys in their white surplices. But mostly he stared at the huge figure of Jesus carved from stone and painted pink. The wounds in His breast dripped blood. Georg also noted the women kneeling at His feet, the kindly bearded men with the halos around their heads, and the bad men with the wicked eyes and crooked noses.

"Emma," Georg whispered, tugging at her dress, "who are they?"

"Those are the Christ-killers, the Jews," she said.

Georg hated these people, especially the one wearing a long red robe—the kind worn by hangmen in children's books—and an earring in one ear. But he still could not understand why the boys said that he, Georg, was a Christ-killer. Getting nowhere with the women, neither his mother nor Emma, he went to the one who knew everything in the world. "Father," he said quickly, running directly to his study from the church, "why did the Jews crucify the Lord Jesus?"

David Carnovsky was shocked. At first he demanded to know who had told Georg these things. Later he warned that a small boy must not speak of such matters. But Georg would not be dismissed with evasions. Since earliest childhood he had pulled dolls apart to see where the legs grew from; broken whistles to see where the sound came from; torn open watches to see why they ticked, and locomotives, to see why they ran when wound. He loved to ask

"Why?" when he did not understand things around him. "Why?" he would ask sharply, "why is it so?"

Nor did he allow his father to put him off this time. He wanted a definite answer as to whether or not the Jews had actually crucified the Lord Jesus. And if so, why? And why did the children say that he, Georg, had done it? Even the adults, the women in the courtyard, said it and called him a Jew and a sheeny.

David Carnovsky, realizing that subterfuge was useless, talked to him as one man to another. He spoke at length about Judaism and Christianity, about good people and bad, about educated, intelligent people who loved peace and friendship and about the wicked and stupid ones who sought only hate and conflict. He concluded by counseling Georg to look for friends among the good and intelligent children and to be a good person and a good German.

"The children say that I am a Jew, Father," Georg said.

"You are that in the house, child," David said, "but in the street you are a German. Do you understand now?"

Georg did not understand and David had no choice but to tell him that he was still too young for such things and that as he grew older they would become clearer. Georg left his father's study dissatisfied and shaken in his absolute faith in the wisdom of adults.

He realized that not only his mother and Emma did not know much, but neither did his father. He was confused about the names the children in the courtyard called him, but since he could not defend himself against his tormentors with reason, he used force each time they called him a dirty Jew.

He had no intention of going to the park with his mother where the well-behaved children played. He was drawn to the courtyard because here, even if from time to time he was called "Jew," it was possible to play freely and without supervision, to run wild, to stand on one's head, to hide behind the garbage bin, or to listen to the street organ. And when Kurt, the janitress's son, became his closest friend, his status grew so much that no one in the courtyard dared call him "Jew," or even "Black Raven."

Kurt was the oldest of the children in the courtyard and the most respected. Partly it was because his widowed mother was the janitress and could either chase the children with her broom or let them continue their games; partly because Kurt and his mother shared their basement apartment with a hotel porter who came home wearing a uniform with brass buttons and gold stripes. Originally the friendship between Georg and Kurt had begun because of chocolate. Georg always kept a piece in his pocket that his mother gave him secretly and he let Kurt bite off as much as he wanted, whenever he wanted. Afterward their friendship ripened to a point where they sealed it in blood.

From that time on, a sweet life began for Georg in the courtyard. Kurt took him into the little cubicle where he kept rabbits and guinea pigs that leaped about in the hay, cocking their ears and squealing. He also allowed him to feed the parrot with the shedding colorful feathers and large crooked bill. No one dared call Georg names any more. Only the mother of a pampered girl with whom he had once fought continued to call him a fresh little kike, but Georg became accustomed to this as one becomes accustomed to every evil, and it ceased to disturb him. He no longer went crying to his parents. Nor did he go to them later, when a second and even more urgent event shattered his childish innocence.

Observing the rabbits and guinea pigs, he saw the little creatures mating, and this made a vivid impression upon him. But rather than ask his parents about it he turned to Kurt, who explained it to him in the bluntest possible terms.

Georg was astounded. When Kurt told him that people did the same and that this act produced children, Georg's senses reeled. "Go on, you lie!" he said angrily to his friend.

He could not believe such things, especially about his own mother and father. But Kurt only laughed at him and swore that it was true. He had seen it with his own eyes at night. His mother and the hotel porter who lived with them did it. They assumed that he, Kurt, was asleep, but he was only making believe and he saw everything. Georg thought about this for several days and finally believed Kurt. Many things he had seen before and not understood and asked his mother to explain now became clear to him. His mother had fooled him. Only Kurt told him the truth. Now he had even less faith in grown-ups and in his parents. Disillusioned, he began to go his own boyish way.

5

Like every stubborn person, David Carnovsky resented others who were stubborn. Georg was constantly at odds with his father.

David Carnovsky had his son instructed in two areas, the worldly and the Jewish. From early morning to late afternoon Georg attended the Sophien Gymnasium, named after Princess Sophie, where he studied secular subjects. For the afternoons his father engaged a candidate rabbi, Herr Tobias, to instruct the boy in matters of Judaism, the Scriptures, the Hebrew language, Jewish history and grammar. Georg hated both studies, the secular and the Jewish, and brought home terrible grades.

David Carnovsky fell into a rage each time he saw Georg's report card. A self-taught man, he felt that his son should be thankful for the good education he was providing him, should study with enthusiasm and reward him, his father, with the best possible grades. But Georg was not only ungrateful but did everything possible to avoid studying. David could not accept the fact that his child, a Carnovsky, should not be eager to learn. It was obvious to him that the boy had inherited the bad traits from his mother.

"See the fine grades your son brings home," he said to his wife, emphasizing the fact that it was *her* son who was the poor student.

Leah flushed angrily. "Why *my* son all of a sudden?" she asked. "He is as much yours as mine."

"All of my family were scholars," David said smugly.

Even more vexing to him was the fact that his only son had a good mind, a Carnovsky mind, but simply refused to apply himself.

At first David spoke to the boy kindly, as the sages advised. With compassion and logic he proved to the youngster that it paid to study. Excluding the fact that education was a good thing in itself and separated the man from the beast, there were also practical considerations. Georg needed only to look around the courtyard. Who was it that lived in the front apartments, dressed well, and were respected by everyone? The educated people, of course. And who lived in the cramped flats, worked hard, and were respected by no one? The common people, those without education. Therefore it was clear as two and two equaled four that he, Georg, must make sure that he belonged to the world of the respectable, the affluent, the educated. He must apply himself to his studies and not associate with a janitress's son who was bound to grow up an ignoramus, a pauper, and a man without hope or promise. "Do you understand what I am saying to you, Georg?" David asked.

"Yes, Father," Georg said.

But he did not understand at all. The life of the poor people in the courtyard seemed infinitely more attractive. For example, there was Herr Kasper, who lived in the corner of the courtyard and drove a large freight wagon. He was a very powerful man and always jolly. Each time he passed in the huge van harnessed to the large dray horses he took his children along for a little ride up on the driver's box. Above him lived Herr Reinke, a police official who sometimes wore a uniform and at other times civilian clothes. From the band of the green hat that he wore when dressed in civilian clothes, a little feather stuck out. His large, yellow mustache curled upward, his arms were covered with tattoos of anchors and girls, and he also played a clarinet. His son told the children that his father occasionally allowed him to play with his revolver.

Herr Jeger, in the attic apartment, stuffed animals and birds, all kinds of owls, stags, foxes, wild ducks, and peacocks. His children always brought down pretty colored feathers from birds' wings. And even the janitress who lived in the cellar kept rabbits and guinea pigs and had a parrot. Sundays she had guests and everyone sang and danced.

Georg envied these people, especially their children. Even though their fathers beat them occasionally with their belts, they were free to play unsupervised, to run, to be away from the house for hours on end, to swim in the summer and skate in the winter. Their mothers did not hover over them as did his mother, or tremble over their every move. They were also permitted to keep pets. Every boy but he, Georg, had a dog.

Georg felt like laughing at his father. He would have gladly traded all their spacious rooms along with the elegant furniture and everything else for a room with rabbits and guinea pigs such as Kurt had.

David often made his son come to his study to greet his distinguished guests. They were very friendly toward the boy, especially Professor Breslauer. Pinching Georg's cheeks like a doting grandfather, he asked him for what career he was preparing.

"What will you be when you grow up, lad—a banker, a merchant, perhaps a professor? Study hard and you will achieve everything. As Reb Elisha Ben Abijah said: 'He who studies as a child can be compared to ink on a fresh sheet of paper, but he who begins studying as an adult can be compared to ink on a worn sheet of paper that has no substance.' Do you understand?"

Georg felt even a stronger revulsion toward education after seeing these men. With their beards and spectacles, their tiny skullcaps, and their pedantic language, they seemed ludicrous. If this was the result of studying hard, he would resist education with all his might. Anxiously he waited for Kurt's whistle that was the signal to meet in the cubicle in the cellar.

There, in the dark among the rabbits and guinea pigs, he and Kurt planned quite different careers. At first they decided to become policemen with helmets and uniforms and swords strapped to their sides. Later they found out that it was even more fun to be sailors, to wear bell-bottomed trousers and a blouse with a low-cut neck, and to sail the seven seas. Later still they discovered that the finest thing of all was to become a lieutenant in the army and to wear silver epaulets, polished boots, a gray cape, and a monocle. Preparing for this great adventure, they goose-stepped through the cubicle, lifting their legs high to the great terror of the rabbits and guinea pigs.

Faced with the realization that he could accomplish nothing with

kindness, David Carnovsky began to deal with his son harshly. He
scolded him and sent him away from the table to eat in the kitchen.

But to Georg, this was not punishment. Eating in the kitchen was
much more fun than sitting in the dining room and listening to his
father pontificate. Besides, Emma told him stories about soldiers and
sailors she knew.

It was much worse when his father beat him for bringing home
poor grades. From fear, the blood would drain from Leah's face.

"David, what are you doing?" she would cry. "Do you forget that
he is the apple of our eye?"

"He that spareth the rod, hateth his son; but he that loveth him,
chasteneth him betimes," Carnovsky quoted from Proverbs to demonstrate to his wife that he was only trying to help their child. With
force he tried to compel his son to love his studies and his teachers,
but Georg was just as determined not to love his studies and certainly not his teachers. More than any other subject, Georg detested
German history that was taught by Herr Kneitel and the Hebrew
grammar and ethics that he studied at home with Herr Tobias.

From the first day Georg met Gymnasium teacher Kneitel, a mutual dislike formed between the two. The teacher liked to address
Pupil Carnovsky by not only his German name but by the Jewish as
well. "Georg Moses Carnovsky," he would enunciate pointedly.

The gentile boys were delighted. "Hey you, Moses," they repeated
to him, although he could hear distinctly the ringing voice of Herr
Kneitel.

Because of Herr Kneitel, Georg hated history. Rather than pay
attention to the teacher's words, he drew caricatures of him. Professor Kneitel was enraged at the boy's ignorance. The few other Jewish students were well versed in German history, much more so than
their gentile classmates. From long experience Professor Kneitel
knew that the Jewish pupils were always the best and that they
had to be the best because of the characteristic demands of their race.
He was certain, therefore, that this alleged ignorance of Georg
Moses Carnovsky was not due to any stupidity but to an unwilling-
ness to accept his, Professor Kneitel's, teaching. And he considered
this a personal affront. He gave Georg the worst grades, sent him

out of the room, gave him punishment homework, compositions to write about war leaders and heroes. One time, he even sent for David Carnovsky to come to school.

It happened after Georg had circulated a very comical sketch of the teacher through the class, and one pupil in the front row could no longer contain himself and burst out laughing at the very instant that Professor Kneitel was passionately describing the campaigns of his favorite hero, Arminius the Cherusci. Herr Kneitel immediately launched an investigation and snatched up the offending piece of paper. After he had examined it through his glasses, he flushed not only on his parchmentlike cheeks but up to his shining bald pate. He saw an apparition with a huge naked skull with two hairs draped across it. Exactly two. The Adam's apple was unusually prominent; the cuffs were flying. Herr Kneitel could not believe that this obscenity was intended to represent him; it was much too horrible. But underneath was written a very funny poem constructed around his name. This was too much. To burlesque his name, Kneitel, the honored name that boasted judges, preachers, and even a general in the family! . . .

He virtually shook with indignation. "Who did this?" he screamed.

"I did, Herr Professor," Georg confessed immediately.

"Georg Moses Carnovsky," the professor said, drawing out the name, "I've been waiting for something like this!"

First he gave him two blows with the ruler across the knuckles. Then he placed him under lock and key until evening. And finally he sent for his father to come to school.

David Carnovsky put on his Sabbath coat, as was his custom when visiting people of importance, and combed out his tiny beard. When Professor Kneitel showed him the caricature that Georg had drawn of him, Carnovsky grew incensed. A stolid, earnest man, he despised all forms of drawing and painting and considered it wasteful nonsense, especially caricature. He was shocked when he saw government officials and prominent people lampooned in the newspapers. It transcended the limits of decorum and good taste. "Disrespect, Herr Professor," he said, "a shame and a disgrace!"

"That's exactly what it is, Herr Carnovsky, a shame and a disgrace," Herr Kneitel rejoiced.

David Carnovsky grew even more infuriated when Herr Kneitel showed him the doggerel scribbled beneath the drawing. "No, Herr Professor, I can't listen to another word of it," he said. "This is too base to repeat. Too base and dastardly."

"That's precisely what it is, Herr Carnovsky, base and dastardly," the professor said, seizing upon the phrase as a hound seizes a bone.

In his most precise German, David Carnovsky excused himself to the teacher and expressed his views about the younger generation that knew neither gratitude nor good manners. As many quotations from Proverbs, as many wise observations about the value of education and of proper behavior as he could cull from memory, he translated into a faultless German for Professor Kneitel. The professor replied with precisely as many quotations from German philosophers and writers.

"I am very pleased to have made the acquaintance of such an honorable and erudite man," Professor Kneitel said, pressing his sweaty palm against the warm dry hand of David Carnovsky. "It only pains me that the son does not follow in the foosteps of his father. It has indeed been a pleasure."

"The honor is all mine, Herr Professor," David Carnovsky replied, bowing deeply. "And you may rest assured that my son shall be meted his proper punishment."

He was true to his word. He flogged his son to the limit of the boy's endurance.

"So you'd make scribbles during your study period, would you?" he roared. "You'd write poems about your teacher? Here are your scribbles! Here are your poems!"

But the incident only raised Georg in his schoolmates' estimation, both for the drawing and for the instant admission of guilt.

For a while Petchke, the class poet, tried to stir up trouble with Georg. He couldn't bear the fact that he had been supplanted as the class hero. When, during recess, the boys traded cheese and ham sandwiches, Petchke warned them each time not to trade with Georg. "Moses from Egypt cannot eat pig meat," he mocked.

But Georg did not take this lying down. He composed a derogatory poem about the class poet that made everyone laugh. Petchke realized he couldn't get the best of Georg with his tongue and resorted to force to teach that Moses a lesson. The whole class formed a circle to watch the fight. Although Petchke was taller and had longer arms, Georg was broader and huskier and wouldn't let his opponent put him down. Neither boy gave in and the only result of the fight was a patch of black hair from Georg's scalp left in Petchke's hand and a snip of Petchke's military bristle between Georg's fingers. After that, the boys' anger subsided and they made up.

But Georg kept up the conflict with Professor Kneitel. Under no circumstances would he pay attention to the history lessons. Out of spite, he even applied himself to the other subjects, especially to mathematics, until he was among the first in the class. Herr Kneitel was furious. He lost his composure altogether when Georg asked him provocative questions in class. He tried to impress upon Georg how important it was to remember all dates concerning kings and princes and to be familiar with the lives of military leaders and patriotic writers. "Who the poet would understand must visit the poet's land," he concluded his little sermons with a quote.

"Why, Herr Professor?" Georg would ask with assumed gravity, to the great delight of the class.

Herr Kneitel was sure that the boy's impertinence was due to his heritage. That was the way the members of his race were, either too humble, like the other Jewish boys in the class, or too arrogant. In the midst of one dispute with Georg, he tried to hint at the reason behind such behavior. He told the class the story about the merchant from Alexanderplatz who had a habit of answering every question with another question. When asked why he answered everything with a "why," he replied: "Why shouldn't I ask why? . . ."

Herr Kneitel, who never told jokes, laughed heartily at his own. The pupils, who were well aware of whom he was referring to in his mention of the merchant from Alexanderplatz, flushed, but Georg did not not lose his composure. "Herr Professor, that joke was printed in last year's calendar," he said, showing off his worldliness.

The boys roared with laughter.

Georg showed no more enthusiasm for his lessons with Herr Tobias at home. He hated the grammar, the Scriptures, and, above all, *The Chapters of the Fathers* by which David Carnovsky set such store.

Georg did not personally dislike Herr Tobias. A weak and beaten man, he knew that most of his pupils were given to him out of charity and studied with him reluctantly. He was timid and quiet and his soft, sad eyes pleaded only for compassion; but his lessons made no sense whatever to Georg. Try as he might, he could not figure out why he must commit to memory the difficult grammar of a dead language, as well as the ethics of a religion for which he felt nothing but revulsion.

He despised the guttural words, the square, big-bellied Hebrew characters, and the grammar, which was even more involved than the Latin *plusquamperfectum* at the Gymnasium. Because of this he hated Herr Tobias too, even though he pitied him.

"Hear my son, the instruction of thy father, And forsake not the teaching of thy mother," Herr Tobias chanted in a wailful tone, "For they shall be a chaplet of grace unto thy head, And chains about thy neck."

Georg yawned right in his face.

The eternal warnings about choosing wisdom and good deeds over evil and wickedness disgusted him. He hated the writers of *The Chapters of the Fathers,* the rabbis with such names at Halfata Ish Kafar, Hananie, Natai Harbli, and the rest of that crew. He imagined how they must have looked—full-bearded and wrathful, demanding of people only drudgery and constant exertion.

"Funny people," he remarked in the midst of the lesson.

"Who, Georg?"

"Those rabbis Halfata and Harbli," Georg said.

Herr Tobias' soft black eyes grew even softer and more pitiable. "Beware!" he chastened his pupil. "One dares not speak thus of saintly men."

"Why not, Herr Tobias?" Georg asked, puzzled. To this Herr Tobias could make no reply and only sighed despondently.

"Well, let us go back and repeat again," he pleaded, his eyes one concentrated mass of sorrow; "let us begin with Solomon's Proverbs. . . ."

Georg realized that the hour was over and, like an arrow shot from a bow, dashed to the courtyard.

Although he was attending the Sophien Gymnasium, he still kept up a friendship with Kurt. In the musty cubicle that stank of mold and sourness, with its small barred window that faced the courtyard and permitted little light, the boys spent their happiest hours. They fired toy pistols and read crime novels that Georg was not permitted to read at home. Here Georg could also draw with chalk on the walls the most outlandish caricatures of Herr Kneitel as well as drawings of fat naked women with mammoth breasts. Kurt told him all sorts of fascinating things that he had seen taking place between his mother and the hotel porter in the one-room flat they shared.

When Georg became thirteen, his father sent him to Rabbi Speier to prepare him for his confirmation. With an affected fervor that was incongruous with his icy exterior, Dr. Speier lectured Georg Carnovsky on the responsibilities that would be his when he crossed the threshold from boyhood to manhood. As soon as he, Georg, uttered the prescribed words, his father would cast off all his son's burdens and he would become personally responsible for his own deeds. Therefore two paths lay open to him, as God had informed the Jews through Moses: "See, I have given you life and death, good and evil. It is up to you to choose your life's path."

Dr. Speier had already given this lecture to hundreds of boys. He could give it in his sleep and wanted only to get it over with as quickly as possible. But with Georg it did not go as smoothly as usual. When he suddenly began to address Georg by his middle name, Moses, as he would be called up to the Torah, the boy corrected him. "My name is Georg, Herr Doktor."

The rabbi raised his finger in warning. "Georg you are to the world, my son," he instructed him. "In the synagogue you are Moses."

"I am always Georg," the boy insisted.

Dr. Speier was forced to give the boy several minutes more than he usually allowed for such occasions. With feeling, he told him of the torment the Jews had suffered for their belief in the Torah and concluded with the observation that Georg should be as proud of his name as of belonging to the faith of Moses.

But as usual Georg asked his customary question. *"Why* should I be proud, Herr Speier? Why?"

Dr. Speier's icy face turned brick red. " 'The fear of the Lord is the beginning of knowledge. But the foolish despise wisdom and discipline,' " he quoted from Proverbs to chastise the boy. "Do you remember what was written there, Moses?"

Georg replied sharply that he did not remember such nonsense. His words bristled with obstinacy and spite. The mockery seemed to exude from the jutting Carnovsky nose. Dr. Speier stopped to consider the unusual circumstances. A product of generations of Germans, there was not a doubt in his mind that the key to the boy's character could be found in his Eastern origin from whence emanated all of Jewry's bad traits. But he said nothing. He also kept from showing his anger even though it raged within him, reminding himself that anger did not befit an erudite man.

"Good day," he dismissed the boy to indicate that their meeting was over.

When David Carnovsky learned of the incident he flew into such a temper that he even forgot his beloved German and began to scold his only son in the same Yiddish words that his father had used to castigate him. He predicted that the boy would grow up a no-good, a convert, a criminal, and everything evil.

"Only a shoemaker will I make of him!" he threatened. "So help me God!"

6

After fifteen childless years following the birth of her son, Leah Carnovsky, to her amazement, found herself pregnant again.

She was as thrilled as would be any barren women whom God had suddenly remembered. Although she had already given her husband a fine boy, Leah's inability to conceive made her ashamed before him as if she had a deformity. Her mother, sisters, and all her female relatives were celebrated for their fecundity. And her long spell of childlessness pained Leah all the more because her life was so empty. She had not been able to adjust to the alien city. The longer she lived in it the more isolated she felt. Her husband grew ever more absorbed in his business and cultural pursuits and Leah lavished all her maternal affection upon her only child. She tried to feed him, to dress him, to prepare him for bed, even to bathe him just for the chance to fondle his flesh. But to Georg this was an affront to his manhood. Ever since Kurt had explained the facts of life to him, he was ashamed to let his mother see his maturing body. The older he grew, the more he avoided her, and she suffered. "Rascal, one kiss let your mother give you," she would plead, "at least before you go to sleep."

"I'm not a girl," Georg sneered.

Without her husband's permission Leah consulted specialists in Berlin about her barrenness. On her annual visits to Melnitz she poured out her grief to her mother who, smug in her own prolificacy, proposed various homemade remedies. She even had taken her daughter to a neighboring town to ask the great Wonder Rabbi there to intercede with God in her behalf.

Having abandoned all hope although she was only in her early thirties, Leah's pregnancy made her delirious with joy. The first stirrings of life in her womb dispelled all feelings of futility. Her whole existence became centered around the being she was about to bring into the world. Well before her time, she began to knit little shirts and sweaters for the baby and hugged them to her burgeoning breasts as if they were things of flesh and blood. The first time the baby kicked, a feeling of such exquisite rapture came over her that she closed her eyes. "David, I'm so happy I'm afraid—God forbid—that I will miscarry," she said. "May the evil eye only spare me."

To David Carnovsky, both her joy and her anxiety were incomprehensible. "You'll go to your grave a female," he said with disgust.

Her husband's callousness offended her and she asked God that He bless her with a child of her own sex, a daughter who would understand a mother's heart and respond to affection. She pictured the dresses she would sew for her, the braids she would weave in her hair. The consuming adoration she developed for the unborn being inside her smothered her passion for her son. She watched over him as closely as before and worried about his appetite, although he ate as for two, but the close attachment she had formed toward him was lost forever. She suddenly began to feel ashamed before him, as if he were some strange male and her growing belly was the result of an indiscretion by a woman of her age.

"Why are you staring at me, Moshele?" she would ask, blushing, and hide her belly with her hands.

"The things you imagine!" Georg would snort, furious because she had guessed his feelings.

At fifteen, with his mother about to bring a new life into the world, he felt more than usually restless, lost, and tense. He suddenly seemed to sprout as if overnight. He grew slimmer; his downy hands became bony and masculine; an Adam's apple jutted out from his rounded throat, and soft black hairs blossomed on his cheeks. His voice began to change. One minute it was deep and manly, the next, girlish and shrill. Often, in the midst of a conversation, to his great humiliation he began to crow like a rooster. His former composure and self-assurance gave way to a clumsy bashfulness. Worst of all were the pimples that erupted all over his face. The more vigorously he scratched them, the thicker they sprouted. At night he dreamed strange dreams.

His schoolwork deteriorated from day to day. His father wrangled with him and reproved him. He didn't have a friend in whom to confide. Kurt had been apprenticed to a saddler and came home only on Sundays. Georg greeted him warmly but Kurt remained aloof. His hand felt oddly rough and callused and smelled strongly of leather, paint, and glue. His way of talking was strange too, the clipped, measured words of one who has assumed the yoke of maturity and has no more time for foolishness. This sobriety, blending an acceptance of his new standing in life with a kind of importance from working for a living, accentuated the chasm between them, the apprentice and the student from the wealthy family. Without a word the friendship between the two boys faded forever. Nor were Georg's gentile schoolmates at the Sophien Gymnasium his friends. They enjoyed his baiting the teachers; they went with him to streets where the prostitutes promenaded and fled with him when the girls approached, but they seldom invited him to their homes. Only one, Helmut Kalbach, went out of his way to seek his friendship but Georg took no pleasure in the relationship.

Approximately the same age and in the same grade at school, Helmut was a plump-bodied orphan who lived with his widowed grandmother on a government pension. He was a timid and sentimental boy. His soft blond hair formed golden ringlets like a girl's, his delicate, white hands always smelled of scented soap. The boys at school had nicknamed him Fräulein Trude. From the very first, Georg felt uncomfortable around Helmut. He didn't like his plush-covered albums with photographs of his late parents, romantic verses, dried wildflowers and butterflies. He was disgusted when Helmut sat at the piano and picked out sad, melancholy tunes. His language was priggish and precise. When Georg was rude or used a coarse phrase, Helmut blushed. You couldn't even insult him by calling him an idiot. It was no fun being with him. Worst of all was his possessiveness. He went into jealous rages when Georg was friendly with other boys. He sulked, glowered, and wrote him spiteful notes on perfumed pink paper. All this seemed to Georg not only very funny but also somehow queer. He would avoid Helmut for long periods of time, but Helmut always forgave him, gave him presents, and was thrilled to make up again. This flattered Georg's vanity and made him feel important and masterful, proud that he could control another's happiness and despair. In the face of his father's scorn and his own feelings of inferiority, it was comforting to be fawned over and idolized. For a time, Helmut's doglike adoration would give him satisfaction but soon he would tire of it. After a couple of days his friend's dainty manners, white hands, and plump body that seemed so incongruous in men's clothing would get on Georg's nerves.

He felt worst of all when his mother went to Dr. Halevy's Maternity Clinic with his father to await the baby's birth. Although his mother's pregnancy had relaxed his parents' supervision, it had also stirred his blood.

Women had begun to congregate in the house. Despite David Carnovsky's objections, Yetta Burak came often. She bustled about and teased Georg because he would no longer be the only child. She also brought along her daughter, Ruth, a girl Georg's age whose ripe breasts strained against her jacket that was tightly fastened with gold buttons from neckline to waist. When Yetta Burak introduced her daughter to Georg he turned red without knowing why, grew angry at himself and at the girl, who undoubtedly must have noticed the blush. "Georg Carnovsky," he croaked, trying to make his voice deep and resonant. He thrust out his hand quickly and drew it back even more abruptly to run back to his room.

His mother stopped him. "Is that the cavalier you are?" she asked laughingly. "Ask Fräulein Ruth to your room and entertain her for a while. I've got some things to talk over with Frau Burak that aren't for you children to hear."

Mumbling under his breath, Georg invited Ruth to his room.

As they were leaving, Yetta Burak remarked to Leah: "They make such a lovely couple. . . ." She said it quietly enough, but Georg heard and grew even more irritated and embarrassed.

As restless as he was, Ruth was calm. She talked, laughed, and measured herself against him to see by how much he was the taller. Later, she tried to waltz with him. Feeling her warm female softness and hot breath so close, Georg danced badly and felt his palms grow sweaty. He tripped over his feet while she grew more sure of herself. After she left, Georg felt relief mixed with a mounting sense of tension. He went to visit Helmut, who as usual was delighted to see him.

Helmut speculated about the coming baby. "What would you prefer, Georg, a little brother or a sister?"

Georg was in no mood to discuss it. For his part, he could do without either. Babies were very queer things; they screamed and made noise. Helmut couldn't understand this attitude. He would have given anything to have a baby sister to cuddle; a soft little angel with blond curls. He had never had any brothers or sisters.

Suddenly tears welled up his eyes and he gripped Georg's hand. Georg tore free. The touch of his friend's hand repelled him. Helmut trembled. "Promise me you'll always be my friend, Georg," he pleaded.

"But I am your friend," Georg said.

"I always feel you'll drop me and get other friends," Helmut sobbed, "and I love you so dearly!"

"You're an idiot," Georg said.

Suddenly Helmut leaned forward and kissed Georg on the cheek. Deeply disgusted, Georg pushed him away. Helmut fell on his back and his nose began to bleed. Georg became frightened. He took his time about leaving. He wanted Helmut to revile him, even to hit him, but Helmut only cried. Feeling very guilty, Georg ran from the house, certain he would never come back. He was confused, ashamed, frustrated. He roamed the streets. He wandered into Linienstrasse, ablaze with the garish lights of nightclubs and taverns. Streetwalkers accosted him and made lewd suggestions. But he kept to the streets. When it grew late, he went home. His parents were out. He went to the kitchen to Emma, the maid who had been with the family for years. She was sewing lace on a pair of ladies' drawers. Her full bosom bristled with pins and needles. She felt the boy's burning eyes on her.

"What's the matter?" she asked and laughed coarsely, showing her gums.

"Nothing," Georg said nervously.

Emma's jutting bosom shook and all the pins and needles shook with it. "You want something to eat?"

"No."

"Then what do you want, *Junge?*"

He said nothing.

She flicked his nose. "Mommy went to get a baby from the 'tork?" she taunted him.

"You think I'm such a fool?" he said with irritation.

She laughed. "I thought you still believed in storks."

He glared at her. The laughing woman, her billowing bosom, her fleshy neck, the curving hips that threatened to burst through the fuzzy dress—everything provoked him. His eyes were aflame.

"You're a good-looking boy, Georg," she said suddenly. "Big and dark like your father, but the pimples on your face make you horrible."

He didn't know what to say. Emma laughed. "Yes, you're a disgusting slob. I've noticed it for a long time when I change your sheets. . . ."

"If you call me that again I'll slam you one!" he said, using language he had heard in Kurt's house.

"You pup," she taunted, "just you try it!" She laid her sewing aside and stood up to challenge him. He began to scuffle with her. He felt the firmness and heat of her ripe body, the great strength of her limbs. In an instant he had her pinned.

She did not stop laughing, squirming, and taunting him. "Disgusting slob," she said through pouting lips.

Suddenly Georg caught a glimpse of her bare thigh where the fuzzy dress had hiked up during the struggle. It was fat, pale, and round, his first view of forbidden female flesh, and he felt the blood rush to his head. "Well, who is stronger?" he breathed hotly.

Emma made no effort to cover up. "Slob," she goaded him, "hot-blooded pig."

Suddenly she pressed him to her with such a fury that Georg lost his breath. Just as in the old days when she bathed him, she began to pull off his clothes. "You clumsy devil," she warned him, "you'll stick yourself on the pins."

In the coarsest terms and calling things by their rightful names, she showed him how to conduct himself in his first sexual encounter. "You pig!" she cried, alternately kissing and biting him. "You clumsy goat!"

When Emma replaced the pins in her bosom and again began to sew the drawers, Georg was left dumfounded. Ecstacy, regret, exultation, and disgust all struggled within him simultaneously. He felt a great wave of love for the woman who had given him so much pleasure, along with a deep sense of shame. From his forbidden reading he knew that women cried after committing such sins and he wanted to comfort her, as a seducer should his victim.

"Emma," he stammered, "I'm very sorry. Really."

She shrugged as if he were addled. "What kind of gift will you buy me because of the new baby?" she asked matter-of-factly.

He didn't know what to say—he had never bought a gift for a woman. Emma suggested that he give her the money that he would spend on the present and she would pick something out for herself. He emptied his purse and all the marks and pfennigs fell into her hand. She tucked the money into her bosom. "Thanks," she said with indifference.

As if nothing had occurred between them, she returned to her sewing. Her face looked dull and placid as a cow's that, having fulfilled her annual obligation, returns to her grazing. Georg did not know what to do. The ways of the female sex puzzled and provoked him. Emma told him to run along. "Go to sleep, Georg. I've got work to do."

Making up his bed for the night, she gave him a few things to understand. To begin with, he was to tell no one what had happened, not even his closest friends. Secondly, he must not go to streetwalkers as other stupid boys did because it was a waste of money and a danger to his health. If he turned his allowance over to her she would be very good to him. "Agreed, *Junge?*"

"Yes," he mumbled.

When Leah Carnovsky came back from Dr. Halevy's Clinic with

a little girl, just as she had hoped, she found her son a changed person. His face was smooth and clear. His eyes, freed from their burning frenzy, were calm and serene. And just as calm and relaxed was his behavior. He even kissed her willingly and also kissed his new baby sister. With a mother's perception Leah realized that something had happened to change her son and she was disturbed, but she said nothing about it. Her attention was completely taken up by the new baby.

David Carnovsky detected the same change in his son. Georg was sedate; he even began to apply himself to his schoolwork and brought home excellent grades. His father was puzzled.

"A strange boy," he said to his wife, "a little crazy, I'm afraid."

"I'd love to see him grown up already," she said and cast her eyes piously toward the ceiling.

7

The faded, crumbling buildings on Dragonerstrasse in the old secondhand clothes dealers' quarter that the gentiles mockingly called Jewish Switzerland contained many stores, markets, butcher shops, guest houses, and houses of worship.

On gory, dripping blocks butchers cleaved sides of meat that bore Hebrew stamps testifying that the animals had been slaughtered according to ritual law under the supervision of eminent rabbis. Elderly Jewish matrons whose wigs seemed incongruously youthful on their creased, toil-worn faces carefully watched the butchers lest they cheat on the weight or try to pass off anything but the strictly kosher product. Although these women were poor, they paid higher prices for their meat than the Jewish matrons in the better neighborhoods because they had no faith in butchers who trimmed their beards, spoke German, and were under the supervision of rabbis with shaved faces. They were reconciled to paying the extra few pfennigs for the assurance that the animal had been slaughtered by neighborhood butchers—Polish or Galician Jews from home who, here in the new country, had altered neither their mode of dress nor their customs and were supervised by rabbis also recently arrived from the other side.

In guest houses and restaurants that prominently displayed Stars of David and bore signs boasting that the food was not only delicious but also strictly kosher and that its honored patrons could expect courteous service, waiters wearing silk skullcaps rushed about serving Jewish delicacies to the patrons at the closely packed tables.

The most popular dishes here were chopped liver, stuffed intestine, pickled spleen, stewed carrots, and noodles with consommé and fowl. The diners were mostly secondhand clothes dealers who bought up old clothes in affluent neighborhoods or peddlers from the East who had left their wives and children behind. Their packs and the rags they had bought lay heaped on the floor beside them. The other diners included bakers who specialized in Jewish bread and pastry; tailor journeymen temporarily stuck in the neighborhood; emigrants without the funds to continue their trips to America; women who had come to consult Berlin specialists; and sundry *shnorers.* The elderly patrons said grace, made benedictions over the food, and squabbled with the waiters about their checks. The younger ones laughed, talked business, sang, and played cards and dice.

The neighborhood groceries and bakeries displayed all kinds of white bread, egg cookies, homemade black bread, and flat rolls of every kind—with onions, with poppy seeds, and with caraway. On the red-painted and peeling Emperor Franz Josef Hotel hung a sign announcing that its proprietor, Reb Herzele Vishniak from Brod, gave his guests royal treatment and was very reasonable with his rates for a room or a bed. He also catered weddings, providing the rabbi, the beadle, musicians and jesters, as well as the most delectable foods and wines—naturally, all strictly kosher.

From the small synagogues, houses of worship, study houses, and quorums compressed between the stores and stalls emerged elderly Jews with phylactery sacks tucked under their arms; Jews wearing velvet Galician hats and long beards; Jews with derbies pushed back on their heads and trimmed beards; Jews with long sidelocks, with medium sidelocks, and with short sidelocks. From an open window floated the chanting intonations of a Hebrew teacher delving into the mysteries of the Torah with his pupils. Leaning against lampposts alongside their wagons were teamsters, street urchins, and loafers smoking and spitting into the filthy gutters. A tall, big-bellied policeman in a helmet and a Kaiser Wilhelm mustache plodded majestically along the pavement strewn with paper, manure, and rotted vegetables. The loafers saluted him and respectfully promoted him in rank: *"Guten Tag, Herr Kapitän . . ."*

"Tag . . ." he responded negligently from a corner of his mouth and continued his beat, his eye fixed on man and doorway.

Reb Ephraim Walder's bookstore, pressed between a secondhand clothing store and a tailor shop, was noisy and congested. A green phonograph with a large horn raucously moaned the hymn, *Kol Nidre*. On it prospective buyers tested out the new Yiddish records. Pious Jews bought prayer shawls, ritual fringes, prayer books, phylacteries, and door-post amulets. Elderly women bought Yiddish storybooks about highwaymen, princesses, and miracle workers as well as hoary accounts of Dreyfus' incarceration on Devil's Island, books of poems, and song lyrics. Boys in non-orthodox garb browsed through dog-eared volumes of Sherlock Holmes that could be borrowed. Things sold here included skullcaps, Sabbath candles, Hanukah candelabra, brass Passover ceremonial plates, marriage licenses, printed forms, white linen robes, and black covers for coffins.

Among the shabby neighborhood people stood a figure dressed in the latest fashion: Solomon Burak, who had taken time off from his business to steal down to Dragonerstrasse for a look at the latest Yiddish records. He played one after another and deeply relished the prayers and chants. He skipped from the mournful *Kol Nidre* chant to a breezy Yiddish theater ditty about an elderly man with a frisky young wife to a moralizing dirge about the destruction of the Temple. He lifted his hands piously during the rendition of *Kol Nidre,* snapped his fingers in accompaniment to the theater piece, and shook his head in sorrow at the dirge. But he became completely enraptured when he played the record about Little Izzy who was going back to the glorious land of his ancestors. Although it had never occurred to him to leave Landsberger Allee, the spiritual appeal contained in the lyrics moved him, and he accompanied the phonograph with genuine emotion:

"Izzy, little Israelik, won't you please come home
To the glorious land where you stem from . . ."

Later, when he played a wedding tune, his feet grew so restless that he began to sway, to the great amusement of the youngsters in the store.

"Miss Janet, Miss Janet, do I dare.

Ask you a dance with me to share?"
he said teasingly to the proprietress of the store.

Miss Janet, a prim spinster whose only interest was the French romantic novels that she had to constantly lay aside to sell a woman's prayer book or a bundle of ritual garments, lifted her frizzy dark head from her beloved book and opened her preoccupied myopic eyes wide in surprise. "What did you say, Herr Burak?"

Solomon Burak abandoned his burlesque German for a familiar Yiddish: "I would like to dance a wedding tune with you, Miss Janet. Don't you think it's high time already, my dear Fräulein?"

Miss Janet grimaced. She hated to be teased, particularly about her spinsterhood. And just as heartily she despised the records her customers were forever testing. They shattered her concentration and destroyed the mood created by the novels in which crinolined ladies accepted homage from velvet-clad cavaliers. But she did not show her displeasure to Solomon Burak. For one, she was too well-reared; secondly, he was a good customer who bought every new record and did not haggle as did the others. And Miss Janet put up with his manners, which she found deplorable and unbefitting a gentleman. The moment he left she again buried her nearsighted eyes in the tightly printed pages. Stuck away in Berlin's ugliest street, she was lost somewhere in a world of parapets and honeyed phrases. Because of this she called herself Janet, although her name was really Yentl.

In an upstairs room by a narrow staircase sat her elderly father, Reb Ephraim Walder, for whom the store was named but with which he had no connection. All the holy and secular books, prayer shawls, religious paraphernalia, and records were Janet's concern, her means of earning a living for herself and her father. He, Reb Ephraim, was immersed in the sacred rare old volumes and manuscripts that were stocked in unpainted cases from the hole-riddled floor to the beamed ceiling.

Tall and lean, with a long face, a full gray beard, and long hair; with a threadbare cotton skullcap on his head and a large pipe in his toothless mouth, he sat among his holy books, stray pages torn from prayer books, dusty parchments, and precious manuscripts, and pored and searched with a magnifying glass. Near him on a large wooden table strewn with papers stood an earthen pot containing sharpened goose quills and a saucer of paste with several worn brushes. With the paste Reb Ephraim fixed torn pages, glued edges, and patched torn parts. He used the quills to mark corrections on the margins or with small, curving Hebrew characters to fill in the parts of the text that had been torn out or burned. He preferred goose quills to ordinary steel pens and obtained them from a neighborhood poultry dealer. He sharpened them lovingly with a penknife. His handwriting seemed more Arabic than Hebrew. Every letter was embellished, elaborated, and adorned with all kinds of appendages and squiggles in the style of a scribe copying the Torah.

Professor Breslauer from the Seminary was a frequent visitor here. He did not like to visit the Ghetto; still, he had to come because there was not a sage in all Berlin the equal of Reb Ephraim Walder. Others came too—distinguished rabbis, historians, and researchers in Judaica. Dragonerstrasse was enthralled each time dignitaries from the fancy Western sector of town appeared—not only Jews but even pastors and gentile professors who came to consult Reb Ephraim about Jewish theological matters. Because of this, even the policeman accorded the old gentleman respect and saluted him when he saw him in the street.

But he seldom got this opportunity because Reb Ephraim rarely went out. From long before daybreak until well past midnight he sat among his books and manuscripts. A small kerosene lamp illuminated his table by day and by night, since the dusty windows that were also barred faced the murky courtyard and allowed little light. Alongside his table stood a small iron stove into which Janet constantly fed wood and coal to warm her father's ancient bones. On this same stove she also prepared their meals, usually lean and tasteless chicken soups, the kind made by women who are loveless and barren. Mostly she boiled tea there that the old man liked to drink, many glasses at a time with a tiny lump of hard sugar held between his lips.

Professor Breslauer and the other dignitaries were anxious to remove Reb Ephraim Walder from the Ghetto. They argued that his daughter could continue to run the store on Dragonerstrasse while they moved to a light apartment among decent people where Reb Ephraim would not have to keep a lamp burning all day and ruin his eyes. In addition, all the books and manuscripts were being destroyed here, ravaged by the dust and the mice. They also needed to be put in order and catalogued. But Reb Ephraim Walder would not hear of it.

"No, Rabbi Breslauer," he said, "it's best that I live out my years on Dragonerstrasse the way I've always lived."

His books were his whole life. He would not sell his treasures to the libraries and museums for all the money in the world although the offers were frequent and generous. On the contrary, whatever profits accrued from the store he invested in rare volumes. The book dealers in Lemberg, Warsaw, Vilno, and Berdichev knew that Reb Ephraim in Berlin was an avid collector of rare volumes, and they always notified him when they came upon a particularly precious item. Neither did he allow anyone to handle his books. One could examine whatever volume one wished in his presence but it could not be taken out of the house. As for cataloguing—what for? He remembered every one of his books. He was not only well versed in the Talmud and in the thousands of commentaries and treatises but also in all the philosophical works.

Another frequent guest here was David Carnovsky.

For one, he bought old books, those of which Reb Ephraim had more than one copy. David Carnovsky was always eager to buy a precious volume, especially one dealing with philosophy. Then again, he enjoyed talking with Reb Ephraim; actually, not talking but listening, for there was nothing about philosophy or Judaic wisdom that the old man did not know.

"I know, Reb Carnovsky," he frequently remarked, "I can show it to you in my books."

With youthful agility he scaled the ladder and pinpointed the proper volume among the thousands stacked there. He dusted the book with a turkey-feather duster and glowered angrily at the bookworms that were destroying its edges. "Villains, Reb Carnovsky!" he vilified the tiny creatures. "About them King Solomon said: 'Little devils can work immeasurable harm.' "

Presently he forgot the worms and beamed like a child as he

looked at his treasures. He loved to talk about them, to tell the history of each book and manuscript, and while doing so he displayed such erudition that David Carnovsky became enraptured. He listened without interruption. Only when Reb Ephraim's throat grew parched and he summoned his daughter for a glass of tea did David Carnovsky get a chance to ask him something.

"Reb Ephraim, what's happening with your own writing?"

Reb Ephraim quickly gulped down the remaining tea. He loved to talk about his manuscript and particularly to be asked to read a portion of it. He gave the desk drawer a powerful wrench, since it had stuck for more than fifty years, and took out two thick, densely written manuscripts that were sewn together with wide, crude stitches along the spines.

These were his life's works that he had begun writing many years before when he first came as a boy genius from Tarnopol to the Theological Seminary in Berlin. But he was far from finished. The more he wrote, the more extensive the manuscripts grew. They were written in two languages. One was in Hebrew, with its elaborately carved characters and an embellished title page that was inscribed *The Book of Knowledge.* This was a work that reorganized nearly the entire Torah, beginning with the Scriptures and including the Babylonian and Jerusalem Talmuds. With extraordinary logic and remarkable ingenuity, Reb Ephraim cleared up all the errors and inaccuracies that had been perpetrated in transcribing the Torah throughout the centuries. Although hundreds of scholars had already undertaken this task, Reb Ephraim maintained that enough remained to be contributed to the effort, and he had devoted his life to it with no end even in sight.

"The old scholars are to be envied, Reb Carnovsky," Reb Ephraim observed, pointing to a yellowed, faded print that hung from a rusty nail over his table. "Rabbi Moshe, the son of Maimon or, as the gentiles call him, Maimonides, had time for everything—for medicine, for learning, for philosophy, for community work, even for debates with Arabic scholars and government officials. We present-day people are in comparison, alas, worthless. . . ."

Reb Ephraim's second manuscript was written in German, with pointed Gothic characters and ornate capital letters at the beginning of each chapter. This work was aimed at the gentiles, for Reb Ephraim was convinced that all the Christian hatred for the Jew was based on a lack of understanding of the Jewish Torah and scholarship. Once initiated into the treasures of the Torah, the eyes of the gentiles would open to its true light that would illume their minds and hearts.

"If only I live long enough to finish it, Reb Carnovsky," Reb Ephraim said feelingly. "God forbid that I be forced to leave it undone."

" 'You will reap the fruits of thy labor,' " David Carnovsky said, quoting the Scriptures as was his custom.

Reb Ephraim took a pinch of snuff from his horn-bone snuffbox to clear his brain and settled down to read a portion of his life's work. David Carnovsky cocked his head attentively to pick out the short sentences afloat in the vast sea of quotations that crowded every page. He nodded in agreement with Reb Ephraim's brilliant revelations. Reb Ephraim turned up the flame of the kerosene lamp and his fine face glowed with saintliness. The warm, reddish flame lent his pale face and gray beard a kind of patriarchal piety that the faces of old men reflect by melting candlelight at the closing services on the Day of Atonement.

The same spiritual glow also bathed the virile, sharply etched features of David Carnovsky. After a day of haggling, wrangling, scheming, and bearing up under the vulgarity of gentile porters and draymen, it was a delight to listen to the venerable Talmudic scholar.

This divine light fell too on Methuselah, the old tomcat that lay curled up in a ball in the corner and listened with cocked ears to his master's sonorous voice. The tomcat was blind from old age, but although he did not see, there was nothing wrong with his sense of smell, and he diligently hunted out the mice and destroyed them without mercy, for which Reb Ephraim was extremely grateful. He kept the cat close to him, gave him the tough pieces of meat that he himself could no longer chew because he was toothless, and did not let his daughter chase the animal from the house. Janet detested the mangy old tomcat and wanted only to get rid of him. "Scat, Beelzebub!" she would yell and brandish her broom.

But Reb Ephraim protected his pet. "Fie, it isn't proper to chase an old man," he said jestingly. "Is it not written in the Torah: 'Ye shall adorn the face of the patriarch'?"

"That refers to a person, not to a cat," Janet said.

"What do we know about a cat, my child?" Reb Ephraim asked. "The Ecclesiastes says that man is no more exalted than an animal."

Janet lowered her broom although she did not agree. The people in her French novels were noble, elegant, and chivalrous and she could not comprehend how her father could equate them with a blind tomcat. Still, she listened to him. She had no one else—no mother, sisters, or brothers. Years ago, when she was still young, there had been someone—a young man who had come to study at the Theological Seminary and who often came to discuss learned matters with her father. He had been handsome, with blue eyes and a closely trimmed blond beard. Janet had fed him, pampered him, and darned his underwear. She had dreamed that one day he would ask for her hand, but once when they were alone he had behaved abominably, unlike the cavaliers in her novels. He had pushed her down on the floor on top of the books that lay scattered there. She had torn loose and tearfully denounced him to her father. The disgraced young man had fled from the city and become a missionary, and from that day on Janet would have nothing to do with men. Her father became the only person in her life.

She now left the house as seldom as he did. All day she sat in the store and, in addition, had to cook, clean, wash, darn socks, sew, and repair. Only her novels helped her forget her spinsterhood.

It was worst on the Sabbaths and on the holidays when the store was closed. Reb Ephraim did not pray at the synagogue except during the Fearful Days, and the pious Jews in the neighborhood were contemptuous of him. The old-fashioned rabbis from the other side hinted that he was a secret heretic and a disciple of the false Messiah, Sabbatai Sebi. Why else would he be visited by the enemies of Israel from the West Side? Although he knew of his reputation in the neighborhood, Reb Ephraim was undismayed. A true disciple of Reb Moshe, the son of Maimon, he knew that service to God lies not in joining a quorum of porters and peddlers but in an intelligent understanding of the divinity. On the contrary, the rabble that

mooned and wailed when it prayed and called God Papa and Sweet
Father, as one might address an idol, further separated the man of
wisdom from the pure divinity. And their rabbis were no different—
ignoramuses with whom a scholar must not associate. Janet, who
was devout, God-fearing, and afraid of Gehenna, did not work on
Sabbaths and holidays, and it was then that the full wretchedness of
her existence came over her. Although twenty years had gone by, she
still loved the blue-eyed young man who had so grievously insulted
her. She tried to picture him at his worst, when, frantic, flushed, and
full of lust, he had flung her to the ground. She also thought about
his leaving the Jewish faith and becoming a missionary. But the
blacker she tried to paint him to herself the more appealing he
emerged. This enraged her and made her cry over her miserable existence, her dead mother, brothers, and sisters and, above all, her
wasted years as an old maid. Mostly she cried at night, lying in her
dead mother's bed across from her father.

"God in heaven," she blurted out in her torment.

It hurt Reb Ephraim to hear his daughter cry. Although he knew
that nothing in mortal life mattered; that all human pleasures, joys,
and passions were mere vanity and folly; and that only wisdom was
eternal as was the deity, still he pitied his daughter who cried in the
night. He could not console her, for he knew that she would not
understand his explanations. She was only a foolish female to whom,
unfortunately, the ways of wisdom were hidden, and who existed
merely by instinct, as did a cow. For a moment he pondered the
ways of the divinity that endowed a man with animal understanding
along with the capacity for human sorrow, but presently he sat up
and said to his daughter in the darkness, "Don't cry, Yentl, it is
senseless, my child."

Janet cried even harder.

Reb Ephraim felt a weakness in his body and, putting on his cotton robe and slippers, strolled out into the courtyard. Through the
courtyard gate a gentile girl came, leading a soldier to her cellar
room. The soldier looked at the old man with the long flowing beard
and the cotton skullcap and shattered the night with his laughter.

He wagged his fingers under his chin to simulate a goat's whiskers
and bleated mockingly: "Me-eh-eh, sheeny, me-eh-eh . . ."

8

David Carnovsky did not turn his only son over to a shoemaker as he had often threatened.

At twenty, Georg was graduated from the Gymnasium and with honors. For the graduation ceremony David Carnovsky ordered for his son a frock coat, a starched shirt, a top hat, and patent-leather shoes. The stiff collar seemed especially white against Georg's swarthy, masculine face. David Carnovsky put on the Sabbath coat and top hat that he wore to the synagogue. As usual when faced with a situation in which she was unsure of herself, her German, and her manners, Leah Carnovsky did not attend. All the members of the faculty were dressed in their finest. Among the dignitaries were several high-ranking military men and even an elderly, half-paralyzed princess leaning on a cane, a granddaughter of Princess Sophie for whom the school was named. Professor Kneitel held himself ramrod-stiff in his outmoded frock coat and excessively high collar. The long tails of his coat swayed and fluttered at his every bow and scrape before some prominent visitor. The school principal, Hofrat Briehe, the terror of the teachers and students alike, danced attendance on the distinguished guests, and the thick lips that all year spewed venom and abuse upon one and all now dripped honeyed phrases. The faculty's servility delighted Georg. The thought that he would soon be free of Kneitel, Hofrat Briehe, and all the other tyrants left him exhilarated and impatient.

"Hofrat von Shithead doesn't know when to let up," he whispered to a colleague.

"We're going to celebrate at the Gipsy Cellar tonight," his friend said. "Come along, there'll be some real hot girls."

When Georg came home in the frock coat, top hat, and with his diploma in hand, Leah spat three times to ward off the Evil Eye.

"Well, David," she beamed, "didn't I tell you the boy would turn out well? Now you'll have great satisfaction from your son."

But her prophecy did not come true.

Like any good businessman, David Carnovsky wanted his son to attend business college. He had bought at a bargain an apartment house in the north sector of the city, a large house densely populated by factory workers and laborers in the Neukölln district, and he wanted to pass along to his son the traditional *Torah and Srorah* —a spiritual and a material inheritance that would survive him by one hundred and twenty years. However, Georg had no urge whatever to attend business college. He considered engineering, architecture, even painting—anything but a commercial career—and David Carnovsky was aghast at the thought that his son should select occupations that were so alien and unbefitting a Jew.

"It's only to spite me that he's doing this!" he raged to his wife. "That renegade! I won't waste my money on such foolishness! I want results for my investment!'

After weeks of pouting and wrangling, a compromise was reached. Georg gave up his plans for engineering, architecture, and painting; his father abandoned his hopes for a business career, and George enrolled for—of all things—a course in philosophy. David Carnovsky was not entirely satisfied.

"Rabbi Zadock said that the Torah must not be used as a mattock," he complained. "The Torah goes well only with *Srorah*— business. . . ."

Still, he did not oppose Georg too strenuously because no matter what, philosophy was a science close to his heart. He conceded another point. His apartment house needed a manager since he lacked the time to care for it himself and he appointed Georg to collect the rents and to manage it in return for a small salary.

With a sense of paternal importance David Carnovsky took from his wallet a thick sheaf of hundred-mark bills that were smooth and crisp, as he liked his money, and passed it over to his son to pay for a year's tuition at the University as well as to purchase a suitable wardrobe. "When I was your age, my father, may he rest in peace, didn't give me any money," he observed as he always did when comparing his son's position with his own. "And that's why you must study diligently and work hard too—*Torah and Srorah*. . . ."

Georg neither studied diligently nor worked hard.

Like a suddenly liberated slave, he yearned only to shuck the years of parental and scholastic supervision and to be free.

At first he grew inordinately fond of fine clothes and ordered several custom-made suits tailored in the latest style, as well as ties, gloves, a silver cigar case for the cigars he was now able to smoke, and even a silver-monogrammed cane. This quickly squandered the tuition money and Leah secretly slipped him the extra money he needed to pay the University. But although he paid for his tuition he missed more classes than he attended.

After his passion for clothes abated, he turned to carousing.

Like every young student, he sought out the company of older students who included him in their gatherings at a beer hall where they had a room with a fantastic Latin name set aside for their exclusive use.

Although they were all Jewish and could not belong to Christian fraternities, they behaved at these gatherings like true German students. They did not fence or fight duels but they did sing gay student songs and often bawdy ones about women and wine and they drank beer from huge steins although most of them had no taste for it. They also employed the traditional manner of initiating a newcomer —the "fox"—into their society. Carnovsky was no exception. First he was smeared with flour and ordered to eat a bowlful of peas from the floor without using his hands. Then he had to deliver a philosophical lecture on the subject of Aristotle and beer with sausages. When that was over he was forced to drain a brass boot that was filled to the brim with beer. The students also gave him a nickname, Hippopotamus, in allusion to his uneven teeth. He was very proud of this name. He drank more than necessary at these gatherings and also did his best to sleep with as many waitresses and shopgirls as possible to maintain his reputation as a true German university student. He quickly got to know all the bars, cafés, and pastry shops around Unter den Linden where couples liked to meet. Like the other young men-about-town, he went on a nightly prowl around the department stores at closing time when the girls came out, to try to snare a desirable companion for the evening.

"Are you free tonight, *Schatz?*" he would ask, linking arms with the girl before she even had a chance to respond.

Tall, well-dressed, with black hair and black eyes, a rarity among the fair-haired and blue-eyed young men, he was seldom turned down. His very white and uneven teeth laughed easily between the full red lips and the girls found his patter amusing. His extravagance overwhelmed them. He treated them not only to beer but even to wine, and if a girl with a sweet tooth humbly asked for a second portion of apple strudel, he ordered it for her willingly. Accustomed to the parsimony of the fair-haired young men, the girls assumed both from his behavior and his appearance that he was a stranger. To flatter him, they speculated that he was a Hungarian, an Italian, a Spaniard—anything but a Jew.

Mocking himself, Georg would say, "I am Prince Karno from Moroccan Persia on the Indian Ocean and the North and South Pole by the Tigris and Euphrates Rivers. Do you know where that is, sweetheart?"

The girls did not know and were embarrassed to admit it. But they were fascinated nevertheless. His jokes made them weak with laughter. His warm brown hands seemed to give off life and lust as if they were charged with electricity, and they stirred the pale and anemic shopgirls to passion. His incredible success with women made him popular with the older students and they sought his company at their drinking bouts. But just as he had tired of clothes, Georg also grew bored with these gatherings. Although he sang all the stanzas of *Frau Wirtin* and drank more beer than he could hold, he could not relax because of the unspoken anxiety, the fear of one's identity that seemed to hover over the long table and cling to the very walls of the room. One sensed a conspiracy to avoid the mention of one's descent before the waiters and servants, as if it were some sort of defect, something to hide. Special care was also exercised to keep away from the shabby and wild-haired coreligionists from Russia who had come to Berlin to study. The black-haired and black-eyed students from the West avoided these black-haired and black-eyed students from the East even more than they themselves were avoided by their fair-haired colleagues. They wanted as little contact as possible with the "beggars" and "nihilists" who, with their Asiatic Semitism, stirred up the Jewishness that they, good Germans who happened to be of the Hebrew faith, had worked so hard to conceal.

As usual, that which was forbidden attracted Georg and he began to fraternize with the "Russians." The more his comrades cautioned him, a native German, about consorting with outsiders, the more he gravitated toward them.

"The wolf is drawn to the forest," his friends remarked pointedly, emphasizing the fact that Georg was not the product of an old-established German family but the son of Polish riffraff.

These ragged strangers were not as strained and inhibited as were the Jewish students from West Berlin. They wore their identity easily and proudly and bore themselves in a free and open manner. As a rule they liked to clown and to play practical jokes. They existed on a piece of herring and a glass of tea and thought nothing of it. Georg Carnovsky was intrigued by this attitude and became close friends with a student named Judah Lazarovitch Kugel, whom his colleagues called Bardash, a phrase he used on all occasions.

The German-Jewish students were particularly repelled by this fellow because of his preposterous family name and his provocative first name that recalled the betrayer of Jesus. He was the poorest, the shaggiest, the most ragged of all the "Russians," but at the same time the most energetic and fun loving.

Ungainly, with a wild mop of hair that seldom felt a comb, always in need of a shave, with a broad Slavic nose and devilish eyes, and speaking a horribly mutilated German, he was in love with the world, with himself, with his outlandish outfits, and even with his nickname.

"Bardash, kiddies!" he roared, meaning that everything was hogwash; that one must take nothing to heart but live and love and enjoy the world.

Older than most of the others, he made no plans for the future but remained a professional student wandering from university to university, where he listened to all viewpoints impartially and never matriculated. He had studied natural science in Berne, law in Basle, classical literature at the Sorbonne, and sociology in Liége, and now he was taking philosophy courses in Berlin.

"Bardash!" he said to friends who jeered at his eternal changes of curriculums and at his wanderings. "Rejoice, my children!"

He said the same thing on the first of each month when he visited the Aid Society to collect his monthly allotment from Kommerzienrat Kohn, who reprimanded him for his dress, his manners, and his general behavior.

Kommerzienrat Kohn felt scandalized when his coreligionists from the East came for their monthly stipend. His full, silver side whiskers bristled with indignation. In his lapel he proudly wore the medal that His Majesty the Kaiser himself had bestowed upon him for his philanthropic activities. He was justifiably proud of his wealth, his charity, and his standing. He felt affronted by these ragamuffins who spoke such broken German and contaminated it with Yiddish phrases. Everything about them disturbed him—their clothes, their unshaven faces, their unkempt appearance. They never saw the inside of a synagogue; they did not know about Sabbaths and holidays; they ate food that wasn't kosher. They were also corrupted politically. Kommerzienrat Kohn had even been told on good authority that they either dreamed foolish notions about setting up a Jewish state in Palestine or incited revolutions and even terrorism among the workers. To his absolute horror and indignation, he often read inflammatory articles in the newspapers about these foreign agitators whom the gentiles tended to equate with him as stemming from one and the same kettle of fish.

"Your attitude is monstrous, gentlemen," Kommerzienrat Kohn would exhort these students. "What a Christian can do, a Jew cannot. If anything, we must set an example for the other races. As the wise Talmudic sages put it, 'Each Jew bears responsibility for the other.'"

More than anyone else he tried to reform Judel Kugel.

"Benedict Spinoza was a philosopher too but he combed his hair every morning and dressed neatly, if poorly. You are disgracing our people with your disgusting appearance! What will the gentiles say?"

"Bardash!" Judel Kugel replied.

Kommerzienrat Kohn's clean-shaven chin between the snowy white side whiskers turned livid from provocation. "Don't jabber that barbaric jargon at me!" he growled. "I don't understand one word of it!"

What vexed him most was the youth's omission of his title. "I am Herr Kommerzienrat," he raged. "Mind you, I don't care a fig about the title itself, only about you learning proper manners. . . ."

Judel Kugel accepted the few marks from the irate philanthropist with an unwashed hand and didn't even bother to thank him.

To this messy, happy-go-lucky youth Georg Carnovsky attached himself with all his customary fervor. Whether this was because he was despised by all the respectable people—which always appealed to Georg's perverse nature—or because of the fellow's tremendous appetite for life that exuded from him through all the rents and wrinkles of his garments, was something Georg himself could not tell. He only knew that he liked him, liked his looks and the humor that shone out from the irreverent eyes; he even liked the word "bardash."

He accompanied Judel to the café where the "Russians" waged their eternal discussions while downing oceans of tea.

No one there took Judel's words seriously, although he entered into every discussion. "Windbag, where's the logic in it?" earnest youths in eyeglasses who were eminent logicians demanded. "The logic—where is it?"

"Bardash!" Judel Kugel always said. "Let it be without logic so long as it's good."

Although Georg did not understand the discussions, he sided with his friend. He was particularly pleased with him when, following the debates, he began to sing Ukrainian, Russian, and Yiddish songs in a deep and chesty bass.

Georg also visited Judel's room that he rented from the shoemaker, Martin Stulpe, in the poorest section of Berlin near the Stettiner Bahnhof.

This room, which was both a cellar and not a cellar, since only a few steps led down into it, was small and narrow and seemed even smaller because of Judel's bulk. It did not have a separate entrance, and to reach it one had to walk through the room in which the landlord repaired the shoes. A sign with a large, yellow riding boot on it swayed to and fro before the front door at the slightest breeze. The smell of wash, frying lard, leather, and cobbler's glue hung heavily in the air. The steam rising from Frau Stulpe's boiling laundry clouded the photographs of wild-haired and bearded Russian writers and revolutionists that Judel Kugel had clipped from magazines and pasted on the walls of his room. The guitar that hung from a nail above his iron bed dripped moisture. Most of the time Judel would be fussing with his teapot—the only possession that he carried from country to country—and boiling tea for himself on the kerosene stove.

Although the room was damp and decrepit, Georg enjoyed his visits. Judel introduced him to the shoemaker Stulpe and his family, who were impressed by Georg's elegant dress and manner.

"A Russian too?" Herr Stulpe asked.

"No, a true *Berliner,* Herr Stulpe," Judel said laughingly. "No Cossack, this one."

The neighbors in the courtyard considered Judel a Cossack because of his size, appearance, and bushy hair. They pestered him for explanations of Cossack customs regarding horses and lances. Judel told them all kinds of fairy tales that they accepted as gospel truth. The courtyard seamstresses were fascinated by him and followed him into dark corners at night to sample a bit of Cossack love-making. Judel played his guitar and sang melancholy Russian ballads for them while they dreamed of his birthplace among the Siberian steppes. . . .

As usual when Georg came to visit, Judel put up the teapot to treat his friend to a glass of tea. Georg had no urge, however, for Judel's muddy tea and instead invited him to Pupp's beer hall down the street.

"But I don't have a pfennig to my name," Judel said. "You'll have to treat me, Kraut."

"Shut your Russky snout, Bardash," Georg said in a freehanded manner that proved he was so intimate with an older student that he could even insult him.

In the tavern, the men from the neighborhood sat at tables drinking beer and puffing on pipes and cheap cigars. From a corner came the lusty sound of a favorite ballad.

> *"Frau Wirtin hatte einen Major*
> *der trägt an seinem Schmock*
> *einen Trauerflor.*
> *Er kannt es nicht vergessen*
> *das ihm die böse Syphilis*
> *die Eier weggefressen. . . ."*

They spoke a street jargon here that was almost foreign compared to the German Georg heard at home Some of the men brought their wives, who knitted incessantly. The men did not order beer for them; they sat and stared like cats watching people drinking milk. When, finally, one of them could no longer contain herself and smacked her lips too loudly, the husband remembered her presence and said in a lordly manner, "Only one sip now, mind you . . ."

"But of course, dearest," the wife said, and quickly gulped down the swallow her husband had magnanimously left in the bottom of the stein. "Ach, good beer! Thank you!"

The tavern owner, Pupp, whose big belly was too large for the small tavern, served all his patrons personally. *"Prosit, meine Herren,* drink up! It's good beer," he said, lauding his own product.

For this, the men bought him a round although he was the boss. Pupp gulped it down in one swallow and gave the men a round on the house. The men returned the gesture and ordered more beer for him and for themselves. And so it went on and on. Judel laughed heartily. "You're a funny bunch, you krauts," he said with delight. "Even when you drink, you figure out every drop."

Georg felt hurt. Although he had nothing in common with these people, Judel's remarks about "krauts" somehow upset him and he felt called upon to defend his countrymen. "They have to figure every drop. They're poor people."

"Bardash!" Judel said. "In Russia the people are even poorer but there when you drink, brother, you drink 'til you haven't a shirt on your back!"

Judel's father, a village cobbler, had wanted to make a shoemaker of him but he had refused to settle for such a life and took to the road without a groschen to his name. Wearing his father's old jacket and boots, he made his way to Odessa to study and to try to make something of himself.

He had already done many kinds of work: shined shoes in the street; tutored at the home of a wealthy colonist; been a coke burner at a lumber camp; helped a Tatar village peddler carry his goods; prepared high school students for examinations; helped a cattle dealer drive cows to slaughter; been a longshoreman on the Black Sea; consorted with revolutionists; spent time in prison; and attended various universities of Europe.

Georg sat with his mouth agape listening to the adventures of the unkempt youth whose lack of responsibility and penniless condition he envied. Judel looked over the people in the tavern and for no reason at all began to laugh. "Come with me, comrade, we'll hit the road together," he suddenly said. "I'm sick of everything around here."

"But what about school?" Georg asked.

"To hell with it! And you can say the same. Believe me, it'll be more fun to go off together."

Georg knew that he would not go wandering off with his friend. This was too much, even for him. But he neglected his studies as much as Judel did. Every day he vowed to take himself in hand, to study and do his work. But every day he had a hundred other, more important things to do. He still could not cope with freedom after so many years of discipline and restriction.

He was restless. He took things up and he dropped them; he changed friends as he changed sweethearts, always seeking something different. When he stopped carousing and applied himself to his studies he did so with all his heart. He then vowed to work hard and to be sober and moderate, as befitted a student of philosophy. But as soon as he began this new regime he quickly tired of it and ran off again to the taverns, the shopgirls, the loafing, and the hell-raising.

Just as he neglected his studies, he also avoided his parents' house. Although David Carnovsky had no knowledge of how his son was doing, since he neither had the time to find out nor did the University inform him, he somehow felt that Georg was not bringing home

sufficient knowledge and wisdom for the money he had invested in
him. An enlightened man and a kind of philosopher himself, he
would have enjoyed discussing with his son some of the lofty concepts taught at the University and gaining insight into the latest
developments from the world of thought. He was also eager to look
at the work his son was doing and at his classroom notes, but Georg
had nothing to say or to show him. David Carnovsky prodded him
with a verse from the Torah: " 'When the Jews grew sated, they
transgressed!' I didn't have it as easy as you, my boy."

He would have liked a reckoning. He would have liked to know
what good it did a young man to run wild, to drink beer, and to hang
around with bums and God knows whom else. He also wanted a
report on the condition of the house Georg was supposed to be managing. Georg always had trouble with the accounts. He never got
along on the small salary he had been allotted, often borrowed from
the rent money, and was always in debt. Every Saturday night when
his father balanced the accounts Georg offered some new excuse.
David Carnovsky looked at his son with his black piercing eyes; his
sharply etched nose seemed to exude scorn.

"I detest lies," he said. "There is nothing in the world I hate as
much as a lie. I demand an accurate accounting."

Georg could offer no accounting, either for his behavior or for
the money. Therefore he avoided his parents' house.

He often spent his nights on the leather sofa in the little office set
aside for him in his father's apartment house. Although this sofa had
broken springs and his bed at home was soft, he preferred to sleep
here because there was no one to check up on him, no one to
care when he slept or got up. He could even come in at dawn after
a night on the town or bring up a girl friend. The janitress, Frau
Kruppa, wagged her finger at him in mock reproof each time she
swept up his office and found a stray hairpin or a ruffled garter. She
herself was far from old and the men in the courtyard still made
eyes at her when she swept the yard. It irked her, therefore, when the
young student brought home loose women—surely, prostitutes—
one after another, when she herself would have been quite willing to
go out with him. "Out raising hell again," she said roguishly and
clicked her tongue. "Watch out or I'll tell the old man. . . ."

As usual after a night of hard drinking and sleeping late, Georg got up with a headache and a hangover. Sitting there with his elbows propped on his knees, he felt a strong revulsion for his wasteful existence, for his deceitful treatment of his parents, and, most of all, for himself. He realized, finally, that his father had been right all along—he was bound to come to a bad end. . . .

9

In Solomon Burak's usually cheerful apartment, the phonograph no longer played gay Yiddish theater tunes as it once did.

This was not because Solomon Burak's business was going badly. On the contrary, he had recently enlarged not only his store but also the sign bearing his name, to the distress of his German-Jewish neighbors. It was said on Dragonerstrasse that Solomon Burak himself did not know how much he was worth. Still, neither he nor his wife Yetta was content.

What good was their money to them when their daughter Ruth was pining away from love for Georg Carnovsky, who did not even know she existed?

She had loved him since their first meeting. She took every opportunity to accompany her mother to the Carnovskys, allegedly to see Georg's sister, Rebecca, of whom she was so fond. But Leah knew that the girl was infatuated with her son. She saw it in Ruth's eyes, and in the love she lavished upon the child whom she fondled by the hour, transferring to the little girl the passion she felt for her brother. Yetta Burak did not try to hide her feelings. Each time she saw the two young people together she said: "What a handsome couple."

Leah could not understand why her son avoided Ruth. "Why are you so rude to her?" she asked. "Such a fine, pretty, educated girl. What do you have against her?"

Georg was puzzled himself. Ruth was everything his mother said. Her eyes were velvety black, soft and full of love, especially for him.

She was cultured, played the piano, and knew all the operas. But she did not excite him as other girls did. The billowy softness of her ripe curves was more maternal than virginal. She was a mother through and through, from her stolidity to her excessive love of children. Her bosom was also too large and puffy, making her look even shorter and fatter than she was. Although he was normally attracted to voluptuous women, Ruth's rounded bosom left him as cold as would the breast of a mother nursing her baby. He could not work up a passion for the plump and placid girl whose piteous eyes begged him to love her, to marry her, and to beget her with a flock of children. Her softness, sweetness, and goodness reminded him of the strudel his mother baked for the Sabbath. Although her obvious devotion boosted his ego, it also smothered all desire for her. He had even concocted a secret nickname for her—Madame Rebbetzin.

Ruth did everything she could to make Georg want her. She read the latest books in case he should decide to discuss literature; she came to his house often on the pretext of giving Rebecca piano lessons. She put all her emotion into the mournful chords that she directed toward Georg's room, and through Chopin's Nocturne bared her deep longing for him. Leah Carnovsky wiped away a tear at the girl's anguish crying out from the ivory keys. It reminded her of her own youth and of the years forever gone.

She kissed Ruth's soft hair and the girl hungrily snuggled up to Leah's bosom. Even David Carnovsky, deep in some ponderous volume in his study, heard the haunting chords and wondered how two boors like the Buraks could have produced such a talented daughter. The only one unaffected was Georg himself. The moment he found out that Ruth Burak was visiting, he ran from the house.

"Where are you off to?" his mother said. "Don't you see we have a guest?"

"Yes, yes," Georg said innocently. "But I haven't a moment to spare. I'm sure Fräulein Ruth will excuse me. Won't you, Fräulein?"

And he smiled ingratiatingly to persuade Fräulein Ruth to excuse him, which naturally she did, the tears welling up in her eyes.

Feeling a complete fool for coming, humiliated by Georg's indifference and embarrassed by Leah's pity, she hurried to leave before her tears began to fall in earnest.

"Good-by," she blurted out and ran downstairs, vowing never to return. She even determined to stay away from the street where he lived. But in a few days she felt herself drawn to the apartment again, to every room, to every piece of furniture. She envied Georg's neighbors who lived in the same house and could see him every day. Berating herself for her weakness, disgusted with her lack of pride and filled with shame, she crawled back to Oranienburger Strasse for another glimpse of her beloved. Even if he avoided her and offered transparent excuses to run away, she treasured the short moments she could be near him, hear his voice, see the smile on his swarthy face and the sparkle of his eyes.

For hours before the visit she primped and fussed in front of a full-length mirror, wondering what kept him from wanting her. Sometimes she thought she was ugly, awkward, and frumpish and she didn't blame Georg for his indifference. But soon she began a more detailed examination, feature by feature. She compared herself quite objectively to other girls, to her friends, and she decided that she was much more alluring and desirable. She fell in love with her own image. She stroked her hair, admired her soft downy arms, grew ecstatic over her legs, and even fondled her full, milk-white breasts. Filled with self-admiration and tingling with a warm, moist rapture, she could not understand how any man could resist her. She was convinced that if only he would take the time to look at her closely and see her full-blooming, ripening beauty, he would fall to his knees before her and cover her with kisses. But the fact remained that he did not bother to look at her and ignored her shamelessly. Even on those rare moments when she did manage to spend some time with him, she grew so distraught from her deep feelings for him that she behaved like a tongue-tied ninny.

Before she left her house she rehearsed what she would say and how she would say it. But when they came together she forgot all her plans and gaped at him like a lovesick schoolgirl. Georg enjoyed her discomfort and assumed an infuriatingly patronizing manner. Ruth felt a contempt for herself that flustered her even further, and to conceal her confusion she launched into an involved discussion about music, a subject in which she felt superior. But Georg refused to be serious and maintained his mocking tone.

Lying in bed, Ruth berated herself over her gaucheness. She recalled every word that was said—each of his mocking questions, each of her halting replies. Now she thought of clever retorts but the damage was already done. She had exhausted every means of attracting him. She read up on the psychology of sex, wore the most enticing clothes she dared, used the recommended perfumes, and dieted to lose weight, especially from her bosom. She paid particular attention to her grooming and wore her hair differently each time. She also begged God to grant her the beauty and wisdom that she needed to win the one she loved. She spent restless nights tortured by an emotion with which her innocent mind was not equipped to cope.

"Tell me what to do, God!" she cried.

Her parents shared her anguish. "I don't have a word of advice to give the girl," Yetta sighed, lying next to her husband. "She's wasting away before my eyes. . . ."

"And for whom? A nothing, a lout," he muttered.

He was even more indignant than his daughter that anyone would have the audacity to reject her. Such fine, decent, good-looking, and intelligent children as his could not be found anywhere—not even in a royal household. And she, Ruth, was the best of the lot!

When Yetta had first told him about his daughter's infatuation, Solomon Burak felt both hurt and exalted. On the one hand, it disturbed him that his daughter had chosen, of all people, the son of the haughty and insolent David Carnovsky. On the other, he felt a certain thrill because his life would again be linked with that self-appointed aristocrat. Like any successful businessman who believes in the power of money, Solomon Burak was certain that he could overcome any of young Carnovsky's objections with a large enough dowry, whether the boy's father approved of the match or not. He was prepared to turn over to the young man a huge sum of money, more than he could afford; to heap presents on the couple, and to furnish a house for them as only Solomon Burak could. Convinced that he would win out, he relished the prospect of

forcing David Carnovsky to become his in-law. To bring things to a
head, Solomon Burak arranged a great party to celebrate Ruth's
graduation from the Academy, to which he invited all the merchants
with whom he did business as well as all of Ruth's friends. He engaged a cook from the finest Jewish restaurant and hired an army of
waiters and servants. The apartment was filled with flowers. Ruth's
piano teacher, a dignified gentleman with an artistic beard and a
great shock of hair, was present to add a cultural note to the festivi-
ties. The new grand piano that was Ruth's graduation present
gleamed with an ebony glow in the brightly lit parlor. Among those
invited first had been Leah and young Georg Carnovsky. Solomon
Burak planned that while Ruth and her teacher performed on the
piano he would tactfully take Georg aside for a man-to-man talk.

"A ducat more, a ducat less," he would say, "as long as you two
will be happy and have a good life together."

But Georg never showed up. Everyone was there, even Leah
Carnovsky, but the one for whom the whole thing had been intended
merely sent a long, congratulatory telegram. After the guests had
gone, Ruth began to cry.

"May he be buried a hundred feet deep!" Solomon Burak swore,
trying to console his daughter. "Just you wait, I'll find you a bridegroom a thousand times nicer and better-looking. Just leave it to
me!"

To spite the Carnovskys, he was prepared to sacrifice all he had to
find the most eligible husband in all Berlin for his daughter. If she
wanted a businessman, he would get her the biggest. If she wanted
an educated man—a lawyer, a doctor, even a professor—he would
arrange it.

"Don't cry, silly girl," he soothed her. "No daughter of Solomon
Burak need ever cry. . . ."

But Ruth wanted to cry. She did not want a big dowry or expensive gifts or even a professor—she wanted Georg. "What can I do if
he doesn't love me?" she wailed to her mother.

To this, Yetta had no answer.

Solomon Burak tried letting the matter run its course. He was
sure that time, the best cure for all ills, would take care of this prob-

lem too. To get his daughter's mind off her troubles, he threw a series of large parties to which he invited the gayest and most attractive young men in Berlin's Jewish community.

Dancing with his wife, he would say, "Well, Yetta, what's happening? Anything yet?"

"No, Shlomele," Yetta would say anxiously, keeping in step with him, "nothing at all. . . ."

When Ruth began to lose her appetite and the will to go out, her father decided to do something that went against his grain and did not befit a man in his position. Without a word to Ruth or his wife, he decided to face David Carnovsky and to talk things out with him frankly. Finding it inconceivable that a young man could reject a girl with Ruth's attributes, Solomon laid all the blame on Georg's father, that arrogant, stiff-necked snob. It was he, the self-inflated ass, who prevented the match because the Buraks didn't measure up to his standards. Like any experienced merchant, Solomon knew that the best way to triumph over an enemy was to buy his friendship. Without telling anyone, he put on his most conservative dark suit and black shoes and, feeling very solid and respectable, went to David Carnovsky's house on Oranienburger Strasse.

Shaky and worried, unlike his usual self, Solomon Burak walked up the painted stairs to David Carnovsky's apartment. He even lingered for a few moments before the door, like a poor relative coming for a handout. Finally he rang the doorbell. He was ready for any humiliation for the sake of his daughter. Waiting in Carnovsky's study, he lit a cigarette, took a few puffs, ground it out, and lit another. From all sides books faced him, books and more books. He didn't believe that in a lifetime anybody could read a tenth of the books collected here, and he was convinced that Carnovsky bought them not to study but out of false pride and the need to show off. Still, they filled him with a kind of awe and a feeling of inadequacy.

When David Carnovsky came in with his brisk stride, his neatly trimmed beard, and spotless frock coat, Solomon bowed too deeply, realized his *faux pas* and, from confusion, bowed once more. Carnovksy was polite but reserved. The tilt of his sharp nose displayed the contempt he felt toward one beneath him. Although he knew Solomon Burak's name, he pretended to have forgotten it. "I . . . believe we've met. What is the name again?"

"Solomon Burak, originally Shlomo," Solomon blurted out "A townsman of yours . . . that is, of your wife's, Leah's. . . ."

"Of course, of course, Herr Burak," Carnovsky acknowledged. "How can I be of service to you? Do sit down."

"I'd rather stand, Herr Carnovsky, if you don't mind. As we say among us merchants: 'Better to stand on one's own two feet than to sit badly' " . . . and he laughed nervously.

Not even a hint of a smile crossed Carnovsky's icy features. Stroking his abbreviated beard, he waited for the visitor to come to the point. Solomon was crushed. He always found it easier to express himself with a joke.

He cleared his throat several times, swallowed, and began to speak.

Rambling, adding irrelevant details, repeating himself often, quoting what he had said to his wife and what she had said to him, becoming more and more entangled and often straying from the subject, he finally managed to communicate to David Carnovsky the reason for his visit.

During the whole time Solomon Burak was speaking and despite a strong temptation to shout: "Get on with it!" David Carnovsky did not utter a single word. Although the frequent "So I said to my wife and she said to me" tried his patience, he remained silent because he subscribed to the theory that a Talmudic scholar must listen and not interrupt.

Only after Solomon Burak had finished describing his daughter's qualities and had clapped his hands boldly, as if having succeeded in emerging from a deep morass, did David Carnovsky begin to stroke his beard and to examine his visitor from head to foot, as if seeing him for the first time. He had ascertained what Burak wanted from his first few sentences.

"What is it you actually want, Herr Burak?" he asked in a cool voice.

"I want you not to stand in the way of my daughter's happiness, Herr Carnovsky," Solomon Burak said. "A ducat more, a ducat less, it can't be a matter of money, since I'm ready to go all the way for the sake of my child."

For a moment David Carnovsky said nothing. His custom was to consider every matter with deliberation, although what Solomon Burak now proposed was simply out of the question. To link his family with an ignorant boor from Melnitz, and a former peddler at that, was preposterous, and David pondered the best means of letting Burak know that such a match was impossible. For a moment he thought to say that a Berlin university student was not a Yeshiva boy from Melnitz and that here a father had no say in such matters. The best lie is often the truth, it occurred to him. But soon he decided that it would not be wise to reveal to Solomon Burak that he had no control over his own son. "No, Herr Burak," he said firmly, "what you propose cannot be."

"Why not, Herr Carnovsky?" Solomon Burak asked too quickly. "Why not?"

"First of all, my son is still in school. Secondly, a man must be established financially before thinking about marriage. That's the way things are done in this part of the world."

Solomon Burak waved his hand impatiently. "Don't let that part of it disturb you for a second, Herr Carnovsky. I'm prepared to pay for your son's tuition and board and everything else besides."

"Thank you, I am quite capable of supporting my own son," David Carnovsky said frostily.

Solomon Burak felt that he had committed another *faux pas* and he tried to correct it. "Herr Carnovsky, I didn't mean to imply that you needed anyone's help. But in my house your child would be like one of my own. . . ."

"Thirdly," Carnovsky continued, ignoring the other, "my son is still young and has plenty of time to think about marriage. At his age a boy must study, only study, and not fill his head with other things."

Ever the businessman, Solomon Burak brought the matter around to the subject of money. "Herr Carnovsky, I'll make your son a very rich man. . . ."

"No," Carnovsky replied.

"He'll be a big man in Berlin. I've got thousands of friends in the city. I'll get him the best job available. Leave it to me. When Solomon Burak wants something, nothing can stop him."

"No," Carnovsky said again.

Solomon Burak hooked his thumbs in his vest pockets. "I'm not good enough for you, is that it?" he asked with a crooked smile.

"What are you trying to force me to say, Herr Burak?" Carnovsky asked.

Solomon Burak took several puffs on the cigarette and threw it into the ashtray. He came up so close to Carnovsky that he almost stepped on his feet and said thickly: "Listen, if it was up to me only, I would never come here. I'm a proud man too. I made my fortune with these two hands and I don't have to back away from anybody. But since it concerns my daughter's happiness, my self-respect doesn't mean a thing, not a thing."

"I don't understand what you are trying to say," Carnovsky mumbled.

"I'm an ignorant man, a common man, and I don't try to hide it. But my daughter is educated. She is bright, refined, and decent. You can be ashamed of me all you like, but never of her. For her I'd do anything in the world, even crawl before you, Herr Carnovsky, even beg. Because she is my baby. She is unhappy. She cries!"

Carnovsky remained polite but unmoved. "I am sorry for your daughter, Herr Burak, but it isn't my fault. Everyone must stick to his principles."

Solomon Burak left Carnovsky's study without even saying goodby. As he was leaving, Leah invited him into the dining room. Although she hadn't heard anything the men had said, she guessed the reason for Solomon Burak's visit and she was deeply ashamed. She herself had no objection to her son marrying Ruth Burak. On the contrary, she pitied the girl. Nor did she consider the Buraks in any way inferior. Her own father had been neither a great scholar nor an aristocrat.

"Shlomele, at least have a glass of tea before you go," she urged him, embarrassed beyond words.

Solomon Burak could not wait to leave the apartment. "I might contaminate one of Carnovsky's glasses," he said. "Please let me go."

When Ruth found out what her father had done she got into bed, buried her face in a pillow, and refused to get up. Her father caressed her and pleaded with her at least to look at him. "I did it for you, child. Please forgive me!" he cried.

"Leave me alone, don't even look at me!" she cried, sobbing into the pillow. "I don't want to see anyone! Not anyone!"

She was so filled with shame and humiliation, she wanted to die.

10

The apartments in David Carnovsky's house in the workers' quarter of Neukölln were narrow, crowded, and noisy. From the closely set windows issued a constant din of sewing machines, screaming children, barking dogs, and bickering couples. On Sundays a retired veteran of a military band blew martial calls on a bugle.

The only apartment that was somewhat larger and quieter, its shades lowered even in the daytime, belonged to Dr. Fritz Landau. It was located within the courtyard gate on the ground floor so that his patients would not have to climb stairs.

The children always tried to peek into the doctor's apartment to see what strange things went on inside. For one, Dr. Landau was a Jew, the only one in the house, and it was interesting to see how such people lived. Secondly, his patients stripped naked and the children were eager to see how their stern fathers and mothers looked without clothes. The boys were particularly anxious to see naked women, but Frau Kruppa, the janitress, drove them away with her broom.

Like every servant, she felt demeaned to be a janitress in a house inhabited by paupers. The fact that a doctor lived among this riffraff elevated her status somewhat and she chased the youngsters who dared to disturb him. *"Jesus, Maria, Kreuz Sakrament!"* she screamed angrily, "don't make a commotion around the doctor's window, you snots, you pig snouts, you lousy scum!"

The only thing that marred her janitorial admiration of the doctor was his lack of punctuality with the rent, a habit unbecoming a professional man and one she could not equate with a person of his standing.

One time when Dr. Landau still had not paid his rent by the end of the month Frau Kruppa suggested to Georg that he remind him, as he frequently did the other tenants whose rents were always overdue.

A few evenings later Georg Carnovsky visited Dr. Landau's apartment for the first time. A sign on the door said to walk in. In a room off the narrow corridor an old woman stood at a stove and stirred in a pot from which dense clouds of steam rose. A long, hard bench, the kind seen in village taverns, extended the length of the corridor. Over it hung signs cautioning the waiting patients to abstain from smoking, to keep quiet, and to enter in proper sequence. Other signs advised that spitting spread tuberculosis and that alcohol and tobacco poisoned the human system.

The old woman mumbled from out of her boiling pot: "Herr Doktor's office is to the right. Knock first."

Georg Carnovsky knocked and walked in. A middle-aged man with a copper-colored beard and wearing a white smock was standing in a corner washing his hands in a basin of water. Without turning around he said in a deep voice, "Undress, undress!"

Georg smiled. "I am Carnovsky, the landlord's son. I've come for the rent and I am quite healthy."

Dr. Landau quickly dried his hands, smoothed his fiery beard, and regarded Georg from head to foot through his thick lenses. "Whether you're healthy or not, young man, is for me to determine. That's something you can't know by yourself."

Georg's brisk and businesslike manner quickly evaporated. Dr. Landau smiled at him artlessly. "So it's money you want, is it? That's nothing new. Everyone wants it. The question remains, however: Where does one get it?"

"It was my understanding that you had a large practice, Herr Doktor. I often see patients lined up outside your door."

"Neukölln patients have lots of diseases but few marks," the doctor said quickly. "Sometimes I have to give them money myself."

Georg merely stared at him. Dr. Landau took his hand as if he were already an old friend and led him to a table on which lay a small tray filled with money, mostly paper marks, with a sprinkling of silver and even a few pfennigs. "You see, young man, my patients put their fees here, whatever they can afford. That's my principle. If someone needs money, however, he takes some out instead." He laughed.

Bringing his thick lenses close to the tray, Dr. Landau began to total the amount clumsily, like one unaccustomed to handling money. "Whatever it comes to, that's how much you'll get," he said.

Georg felt even more ridiculous in his role as landlord. "It doesn't really matter, Herr Doktor," he said. "It can wait."

Dr. Landau did not stop counting the small change, at the same time paternally asking Georg his age and his course at the university.

"I'm not only a rent collector, I'm also a student of philosophy," Georg said proudly.

Dr. Landau was amused. "The worst profession a young man could possibly choose."

"Why so, Herr Doktor?" Georg asked with surprise.

Again Dr. Landau took Georg's hand and led him to the bookcases that lined the walls. "Here are all the philosophical works from Plato to Schopenhauer. During the several thousand years between the one and the other nothing new has been added. This science does not progress; it stands in place, tapping in the dark like a blind man. Now, over here you see books on medicine. Every volume brings new developments."

Although he was an indifferent student, Georg felt called upon to defend his field. "You speak like a physician, not a philosopher, Herr Doktor."

"I spent years on that trash," Dr. Landau said, "and I regret the waste of time."

Georg tried to say something else but Dr. Landau interrupted him. Taking out an old illustrated medical book, he pointed with an iodine-stained forefinger to a page. "You see, only a few hundred years ago court physicians treated the kings and princes with black-magic potions and incantations. Now we have the X-ray machine and the microscope. What did philosophy accomplish from Athens to Königsberg?"

Before Georg could answer, Dr. Landau led him into an adjoining room. "Elsa! Elsa! Let this young man look through a microscope and see what a microbe looks like."

In a small room filled with jars and bottles of every hue and color, a young woman in a white smock stood pouring a fluid from one test tube to another. She looked up at Georg with large, intelligent brown eyes. "Papa, you didn't even knock!" she said with mock severity.

"I beg your pardon a hundred times over," Georg said, bowing. "I am Georg Carnovsky."

"Elsa Landau," the girl said, putting down the test tube and smoothing her hair that was the same shade as her father's coppery beard. After focusing the eyepiece of the microscope, she showed him the microbe on the slide. "Do you see those little blue streaks? That's the tuberculosis bacillus. Keep your other eye open and you'll see better."

"Well, Herr Philosopher, this is something that can be seen. Try to see the categorical imperative," Dr. Landau said.

Elsa tried to quiet her father. "Papa, let the gentleman look."

But Dr. Landau would not be silenced. "A young person can either help humanity or busy himself with nonsense. Neukölln doesn't need the categorical imperative, young man, it needs hygiene and medicine. Right, Elsa?"

Georg looked into the microscope with curiosity. With even greater curiosity he studied the doctor's daughter. Against the snowy whiteness of her smock her hair seemed especially fiery. Her brown eyes were serene, wise, and penetrating. The smile she directed at her father was full of tolerant amusement, filial love, and admiration.

No amount of urging could persuade Georg to accept the pile of money that Dr. Landau had scraped together. "For heaven's sake, there's no rush about it, Herr Doktor!" he protested. "I'll come back when you're less pressed for money."

He wanted an opportunity to come back again to the girl whose coppery hair glowed in the gathering dusk.

"I was very pleased to meet you and so forth and so on," Dr. Landau said. "And, as I said, give up that worthless philosophy and take up some useful work."

Elsa was appalled. "Papa, is that the way to talk about someone's profession?"

"The egg does not teach the hen, Dummkopf!" Dr. Landau said, and cuffed his daughter lightly to let her know who was boss.

"Stupid, but I love her anyway," he remarked to Georg as if to an old friend.

"In your place, Herr Doktor, I would do the same," Georg said.

Elsa smoothed her hair in embarrassment and put out her warm hand to Georg. "It was very nice meeting you, Herr Carnovsky, and *auf Wiedersehen.*" And she turned back to her test tubes and slides.

Although her words were conventional for the occasion, Georg treasured them as if they were something quite special. He could not forget the warm touch of her fingers. Although he had a date with one of the shopgirls he didn't keep it, and for the first time since coming to the University, he did not go out for the evening.

Early the next morning he got up from the leather divan, washed and dressed carefully, and with his briefcase full of books started for the University.

Frau Kruppa was in the midst of sweeping up the courtyard. "What's wrong, Herr Kandidat?" she asked, her female curiosity aroused. "Up so early?"

Georg went into a small café on the corner and ordered breakfast. Chewing the crips rolls, he watched the sidewalk.

When he saw her come out of the courtyard gate carrying a briefcase, he quickly paid his check, left his customary excessive tip, and ran to catch up.

"Good morning, Fräulein Elsa," he said in a normal voice, as if the meeting had been accidental. "I believe we're headed in the same direction?"

"I am going to attend an autopsy at the charity ward, Herr Carnovsky," Elsa said smiling. "In any case, we can go as far as Unter den Linden together."

From that day, a new existence began for Georg Carnovsky. Instead of accompanying his cronies to bars and taverns, he attended classes each morning. Rather than prowl around department stores in the evenings trying to pick up shopgirls, he came back to the house to visit Dr. Landau. Later, he began to haunt the medical school to wait for Fräulein Elsa and to ride home with her.

One rainy day, having gotten soaked from the long wait, it suddenly occurred to him to transfer from philosophy to medicine in order to be near her. "You know," he said to Elsa when she finally came out, "I believe your father is right. Philosophy is really a silly occupation. Don't you agree?"

"I wouldn't know. I know nothing about philosophy," she said, "but personally I wouldn't trade medicine for anything in the world."

Georg took her arm. "Won't you have a glass of wine with me? It's terribly wet outside. We'll go in someplace and toast my new profession."

"But no strong wine, Herr Carnovsky. I'm not accustomed to drinking and my father is opposed to all alchohol."

In a cozy corner of the small pastry shop, under the glow of the dimmed red lamp that had been lit to offset the darkness of the overcast day, Elsa's brown eyes sparkled. After the first glass of wine the color mounted to her face. "This is the first time in my life I've drunk wine," she said, enjoying her indiscretion.

"Will you take off your hat, Fräulein Elsa?" Georg asked.

"My hat?"

"I want to see your hair," he said. "It reminds me of fire. . . ."

She smiled and took off her hat. "You have strange notions for a philosopher."

"An ex-philosopher, you mean. Come, let's drink to my new profession."

When they were outside, Georg asked to carry the black box that she was holding. She was reluctant, but he insisted.

When they arrived at her laboratory she took back the box and opened it. The blood drained from Georg's face. A skull looked at him through gaping eye sockets. The stench of death and decay assailed him, although the skull had been boiled and scrubbed clean. Elsa put it in a basin. "Not feeling well, Herr Carnovsky?"

"It's nothing, Fräulein Elsa, just the shock of seeing that thing. . . ."

"Look, the blood has drained from your face." She held a vial under his nostrils. "Sit down and inhale. This will make you feel better."

Georg tried to compose himself but the harder he fought against it, the worse his nausea became. The odor of death and rotting flesh made him reel. Worst of all was the shame he felt before the girl. "Not the best start for a prospective doctor," he quipped weakly.

"It doesn't matter. Lots of people begin this way. Here, drink this glass of water."

She undid his collar and wiped his sweating brow. Standing over him, her coppery hair brushed against his face but Georg didn't even feel it. He could only see the freshly boiled skull staring at him with hollow sockets.

For the next few days he was ashamed to see her. He had mixed feelings about a girl who carried a skull around in a box. But a few days later the nausea and shame were replaced by a deep longing for her, and with Elsa at his side he went to enroll in the medical school.

When Leah Carnovsky told her husband that their son had switched courses, he went into a frenzy. "I'm through with that no-good!" he roared, crashing his fist on the table.

Not that David Carnovsky had anything against the medical profession. On the contrary, like all respectable Jews, he valued it as a highly desirable calling. He also knew that Rabbi Moshe, the son of Maimon, and other distinguished Jews had devoted themselves to the science of medicine and that it had given them access to royal courts and allowed them to serve the Jewish cause. But he no longer believed in anything his son undertook, that worthless idler who squandered both time and money. "It will last from Purim to Passover," he said to his wife. "I won't give him another pfennig."

As usual, Leah defended their son and persisted until David agreed to give him one more chance. Ranting and grumbling, David again opened his wallet and handed over to his wife several crisp new banknotes to pass along to their son, since he himself was reluctant to face him. "He will as much be a doctor as I will a wet nurse," he said to Leah. "You mark my words."

Georg took to his new studies with such determination that David

Carnovsky grew uneasy. On the one hand he felt proud that his son had finally come to his senses. On the other, he could not completely forgive him for making him a liar.

"Well, what do you say to the boy now, David?" Leah asked triumphantly. "He's studying and working hard, may the Evil Eye spare him. Like a new person altogether."

But David would not let her have any satisfaction. "I'm not convinced yet. Who knows how many times more he'll switch back and forth?"

"Bite your tongue," his wife said anxiously, ever afraid of tempting fate.

II

Like all the workers in the neighborhood, Dr. Fritz Landau got out of bed before daybreak and woke his daughter. "Up, lazybones!" he said, pounding his fist on the door.

The first thing he did was wash from head to foot with cold water. Since there was no bathtub in the old-fashioned apartment, he washed at the kitchen sink, to the great disgust of his old maid servant, Johanna.

"Herr Doktor should be ashamed of himself," the old woman complained each time anew. Dr. Landau's fleshy body, red from scrubbing, shook with laughter. "Silly old woman, how many times have I told you a naked body is nothing to be ashamed of? That's something stupid people have thought up."

Old Johanna waved him away with disgust. "Ach, the nonsense you babble," she mumbled and shielded her eyes to avoid looking at the slippery male body.

When he was finished, the doctor forced his daughter to take a cold bath too. "You can't get out of it," he warned, combing out his dripping beard. "Do it or I'll drag you in here by your hair."

No matter how cold the weather might be, Elsa did as she was told, fully aware that her father was quite capable of carrying out his threat. From the time of her mother's death in her early childhood until she was a grown girl he had washed her daily from head to foot. He would be doing it still if she would let him. As far as he was concerned, there was nothing improper about it. Therefore she hurried to the kitchen sink and the old woman again closed her eyes. All nudity, even female, repelled her.

"He is crazy himself and he makes her crazy too," she muttered. "Such goings-on I've never seen in my whole life. . . ."

Dr. Landau drew on a coarse homespun shirt, velvet trousers, loose-fitting, thick-soled shoes, and a velvet jacket. Hatless and with a thick cane in hand, he went out for his morning stroll with only a glass of water to sustain him. Elsa, also bareheaded and in loose-fitting clothes, was forced to come along.

"Faster! Faster!" he prodded her when she fell behind. "And swing those arms. So!"

The whole neighborhood knew the odd couple. Housewives carrying shopping baskets greeted them and men hurrying to work tipped their hats respectfully. *"Grüss Gott, Herr Doktor. . . .* Splendid morning, Herr Doktor. . . ."

"Morgen, Herr Jerge; Morgen, Frau Beitzholz; Morgen, Herr Knaule," responded Dr. Laudau, calling each one by name.

Others addressed him not as Herr Doktor but as Comrade Doctor. "A fine, good morning, Comrade Doctor. Did you sleep well, Comrade Doctor? Rested up, Comrade Doctor?"

"Morgen, Comrade Albrecht. How goes it, Comrade Witzke? *Morgen,* Comrade Miller, *Morgen, Morgen, Morgen,"* Dr. Landau said over and over again.

The men smiled proudly because the doctor called them Comrade. They were proud that he belonged to their party and attended meetings at Petersile's beer hall.

"Nice chap," they said to one another.

"And Comrade Elsa is a fine girl too."

Dr. Landau raced through the streets. "Don't slow up!" he warned his daughter. "And don't breathe through your mouth, *Donnerwetter!* Only through the nose, the nose, the nose!"

Precisely one hour later he turned back toward home. Now they met the children on their way to school with schoolbags slung over their shoulders.

"Good morning, Herr Doktor, good morning, Fräulein Elsa."

"Morgen, you rascals, *Morgen,"* Dr. Laudau said, tickling the youngsters' bellies with his cane. "Whose kids are you?"

"I am Karl Wendemayer. My father is the shoemaker."

"Oh, yes. I sliced your windpipe when you had diphtheria," Dr. Landau recalled. "You're a real rascal, you are. . . ."

"Herr Doktor stuck a spoon down my throat," a stout little girl piped up, "it hurt. . . ."

"Stick out your tongue," Dr. Landau ordered her. "Don't be ashamed, silly goose. So!"

The children laughed at the one who had to show her tongue in the street and Dr. Landau laughed with them.

"No playing around the garbage can, now!" he warned, brandishing his cane, "and don't you dare breathe with your mouths, you germ-swallowers! With your noses . . . so! . . ."

Laid out on the smooth unpainted table was the breakfast old Johanna had prepared—dark bread, honey, milk, and various raw vegetables: carrots, cabbage, and lettuce. Dr. Landau did not permit any ham or coffee on his table, and certainly no beer, which he considered poison.

He vigorously chewed the chunks of raw cabbage, urged Elsa to eat, and at the same time yelled to Johanna to close the door to the kitchen from whence the odor of frying lard came drifting in. Johanna was the only member of the household who refused to eat what she called "grass." She had to have her ham, her pork cutlets and coffee, but Dr. Landau could not stand the smell of frying meat.

"How many times have I told you to close the door when you're frying that stuff? I don't want to inhale those disgusting smells. They're poison, poison, poison!"

"I've been eating it for more than sixty years and I'm still healthy," Johanna said spitefully.

"That's for me to determine," Dr. Landau said, and threw off the velvet jacket to put on his white smock. Elsa helped him into it and at the same time picked the crumbs and shreds of vegetables from his beard. Dr. Landau washed his hands at the kitchen tap and boiled his instruments on the stove while old Johanna grumbled because he was messing up her kitchen. To her, the boiling of instruments was another of the doctor's eccentricities. Precisely at eight o'clock, long before most of his colleagues began their working day, Dr. Landau started seeing his patients.

The reception room was filled with neighborhood people—mothers with babies, pregnant young women, retired workers. In the kitchen that faced the reception room Johanna was busy with her cooking and washing. Although Dr. Landau repeatedly ordered her to keep the kitchen door closed for hygienic reasons, he could not get her to do so since she enjoyed gossiping with the waiting women about their ailments and about the doctor's habits. Dr. Landau saw one patient after another.

"Don't be ashamed," he scolded his women patients who were too shy to undress. "There is no shame in being naked . . . no shame . . . no shame . . . no shame . . ."

He got furious when a patient smoked a pipe in his presence. He could not understand why men smoked, swilled beer, and ate sausage and ham. To him these habits were the root of all sickness and he grimaced whenever an elderly man came to him with stomach trouble. "Man!" he exclaimed in his North Berlin accent. "What do you expect from your stomach when you go on abusing it? You stuff it with meat, drown it with beer, and smother it with smoke so it growls, belches, fills with gas, and stinks like a garbage can."

He talked to the women just as bluntly. He blamed all their ills on the fried foods they ate, and the grease, fat, sweets, coffee, and alcohol they consumed. The women heard out his accusations silently and asked for medicines, but Dr. Landau shook his head. Dumb geese! First they polluted their bodies with poison, then they wanted to wash it away with some colored water! He would not prescribe that hogwash on which the quacks and pharmacists grew rich. There was no miracle potion to serve as a cure-all; the way to health lay only through adherence to the rules of hygiene—proper diet, regular breathing, cleanliness, fresh air, and pure water.

"Use water, clean, pure water from the tap, not filthy, colored swill from the pharmacy!" he roared. "Do you understand?"

Only in exceptional cases did he prescribe potions, pills, or powders. But even then he did not write prescriptions but issued the medicines ready-made from the glass cabinet in his office or ordered Elsa to make them up in the laboratory.

"Don't pay me!" he growled at his patients. "Put it on the tray and keep moving, keep moving, others are waiting!"

The local doctors were up in arms because he allowed the patients to pay as much as they could afford. The neighborhood pharmacist, Magister Kurtius, was his mortal enemy. He slandered Dr. Landau at every opportunity and swore that he was not an accredited physician but a charlatan, a seducer, a quack, a defiler of Christianity, and a socialist agitator who was against the Kaiser, the *Vaterland*, and the church. But the more he railed against him, the more the neighborhood people flocked to Dr. Landau's office.

Elsa assisted her father although she was only a medical student. She vaccinated the children, gave injections, swabbed throats, took temperatures, tested blood pressures, and helped out in any way she could. Dr. Landau also made her listen to patients' lungs and hearts, and tap and probe both male and female bodies. "Put away that god-damned stethoscope and use your ear instead!" he growled at her. "The ear is a doctor's finest instrument. . . . Like so!"

After supper he frequently went to Petersile's beer hall where his fellow Party members gathered. Herr Petersile put a glass of milk before him and gave him all the newspapers and magazines to which he subscribed. Dr. Landau sipped the milk, after which he wiped his red mustache and began reading the newspapers that put him into a terrible rage. "Scoundrels! Villains! God-damned slaves of the Kaiser!" he bellowed.

The guests at the other tables nodded in agreement. They were proud of Herr Doktor who lived in their quarter, talked their language, believed in their cause, and frequented their beer hall. "*Prosit,* Comrade Doctor!" they toasted him. "*Prosit.*"

"*Prosit,* you beer-swillers and smoke-swallowers," Dr. Landau said, and again dipped his mustache in the milk.

The crowd laughed with delight at Dr. Landau's aversion to tobacco and alcohol. People from adjoining tables gathered round to hear his views on politics. He became overwrought, waggled his beard, gesticulated wildly, hurled imprecations, and preached loudly to one and all. He reviled his opponents, the money-bags, the secret police, the Junkers and Kaiser's ass-lickers. The men whinnied with laughter at his ripe language and colorful invective.

Although the Party leaders did not entrust him with any responsibilities because of his incendiary nature and impractical views, they enjoyed his diatribes and laughed along.

They did, however, make use of his daughter, who lectured the workers' wives on feminine hygiene and child rearing. Herself a virgin, she taught the women their conjugal and maternal responsibilities. The women took her seriously—some even sought her advice about their marital and domestic problems and told her their intimate secrets. She also conducted a children's group to whom she explained the economic and political facts of life. The young working girls were proud of the doctor's daughter who championed their cause; the young men were all secretly in love with her.

But the one who loved her most was young Georg Carnovsky, even though she gave him no encouragement. Like a rear wheel that can never catch up with the front one, Georg fruitlessly pursued Elsa, who always left him trailing hopelessly behind. His ego was crushed and he felt humiliated and beaten.

Since early in their friendship, when he had made such a fool of himself by almost swooning over a skull, he had felt this inferiority in her presence and he could not rid himself of it no matter how he tried. He felt it whenever he was with her—in the laboratory, in the dissecting room, everywhere.

Like all young medical students, he affected a flippant, cynical air in the presence of death but he could not rid himself of his aversion to decay and formaldehyde, which nauseated him and penetrated deep into his being. He chain-smoked, trying to smother the nausea that welled up within him.

"Frau Wirtin hatte einen Major . . ." he bawled irreverently along with the other students as they dissected the cadavers.

Elsa Landau neither smoked nor sang bawdy songs when she worked. She barely even spoke. With perfect equanimity, as if she were cutting material for some sewing project around the house, she stood by the blood-soaked table that was strewn with human arms and legs and worked with her scalpel and shears. She cut flesh, separated muscles, blood vessels, and nerves. She was exceptionally skillful at this work and the professors had assigned her to be the prosector and to demonstrate the technique of dissection to the new students. The men students, who were not concerned because their instructor was a girl, joked with her, complimented her beauty, and even made insinuating remarks when it came time to deal with the lower portions of the cadavers. Elsa did not become righteously indignant as would the average girl. She merely looked at the students with her wise brown eyes as an adult would look at obstreperous children and said quietly but firmly, "Come now, colleagues. I see no reason for laughter."

Her bearing was so dedicated and dignified that the young men quickly grew sober and felt unworthy for having differentiated between one part of the human anatomy and another. Although her hands retained their femininity while she skillfully used the instruments and her slim figure was provocative in the white surgical gown and breathed of life amidst all the death, no one had the temerity to address her in the leering tone that was used toward the other girl students.

"Not like this, colleagues, this way," Elsa showed the younger students how to dissect. "And kindly don't blow smoke in my face."

The students did as she asked. All their courage and fortitude was blown out of them along with the smoke in the presence of the quiet and competent girl. Next to her, Georg Carnovsky felt the humblest and most insignificant of all.

Just because he wanted her approval and was eager to show how composed, skillful, and superior he was, instruments dropped from his hands and he made one mistake after another. He could not stop smoking as she would have liked him to do. He needed the smoke to keep down the nausea and to mask his inadequacy. Her calm dexterity unnerved him. He only breathed easier when they left the dissecting room and went out into the street. There, in the fresh air, among people and movement, he was again the male—stronger, bigger, dominating. She reached only to his shoulder. She was slim and delicate and had to look up to him when they spoke. He carried her briefcase, took her arm when they crossed a street, and treated her like a fragile piece of china. She accepted his proprietory manner and smiled up at him girlishly. She laughed at his jokes when they sat closely pressed together in the trolley on the way home.

But his confidence deserted him again when they were back in the murky laboratory from which he could not pry her. She never had time for him, not even in the evenings. While he proclaimed his love, she poured urine into test tubes or analyzed blood, saliva, or menstrual discharges.

"Put away that slop, for God's sake," he fumed. "I am talking to you."

"Why does it bother you?" asked Elsa, who did not differentiate between clean and repulsive matter but was concerned only with its chemical and bacteriological aspects. "As a medical man you must develop a different concept toward these things."

"A medical man! A medical man!" he said angrily. "Right now I'm not a medical man but only a man! A man, Elsa! Why can't you be a woman for a while?"

Elsa laughed at his outburst and looked at him with her wise brown eyes like an adult watching a child's tantrum.

"You men make me laugh—you always have to show off your strength but you aren't such heroes after all. We women aren't ashamed of our weaknesses."

"You don't know what life or love are all about, Elsa. If you have any capacity for love at all, it's reserved for bacteria."

For the hundredth time he vowed to give her up for girls who were uncomplicated, loving, and docile. He would even have preferred to take out Ruth Burak than a girl who made a fool out of him, treated him like a child, and made him miserable. He determined to show her that he was strong and that he could get along without her. But he could not stick to his resolution. On the contrary, the more she bedeviled him, the more he liked it. An evening did not pass that he did not visit her laboratory, with its conglomeration of acrid, repulsive odors.

His reward were the Sundays and holidays when he went hiking with Elsa and her father.

While the people in the neighborhood were still catching up on their sleep after a week of hard work and early rising, Dr. Landau began to nag Elsa to make up their rucksacks for the day's outing. This was his only day of rest and he was anxious to get out of the house before he was called for some emergency.

With canes in hand, rucksacks on their backs, folded raincoats, and tin cups for well water, they set out across country lanes, meadows, and woods. Georg Carnovsky went along, dressed in wide knickerbockers, high woolen stockings, and thick-soled walking shoes. His hair gleaming, he walked along beside Elsa, breathing in the sweet scents of grass, water, and shrubbery. As usual, Dr. Landau told them how to breathe properly.

"Not with the mouth—dammit, with the nose, the nose, the nose!" he growled.

"If you don't stop nagging, we're liable to run ahead and leave you behind," Elsa teased.

"Go ahead! I'm strong enough to make my own way," he answered, and with a deep thrust of his cane into the ground he strode forward to demonstrate his youthful vigor.

Elsa watched him with fondness and admiration. "You sweet, dear, funny *Papachen*," she whispered, and kissed the mouth that was hidden somewhere within the thickets of red beard and mustache.

"Don't get sentimental now!" Dr. Landau said sternly to hide his own feelings.

Striding across the meadow, he stooped often to caress the yellow and white wildflowers and to chase butterflies, grasshoppers, crickets, young frogs, caterpillars, and reptiles lurking in the grass. At times he picked up a mole or a field mouse.

"What exquisite creatures," he said, tenderly stroking the soft pelts. "Look at their eyes, so handsome and wise. . . ."

He knew the whole order of animal species, their nomenclature and habits. He also knew the curative properties of herbs that medical practitioners normally rejected. He squeezed out the juice of fat, reddish oak leaves that peasant women used in poultices for wounds. He crushed camomile flowers that were scalded in hot water and used to treat colds or as a cathartic. He stretched on the ground next to anthills to watch the ants bustle and toil, inhaled the acrid odor they exuded, and lauded the peasants who boiled the creatures for a potion with which to treat rheumatism.

With ears cocked, he listened for every bird call and buzz of an insect. He recognized every creature by its voice. He gently picked up toads and studied them closely through his thick-lensed glasses. The toads were repulsively soft, crusty, and warty and Georg was reluctant to hold them when Dr. Landau passed them along. "The green swamp frogs are pretty but toads are disgusting," he said.

Dr. Landau was offended. "No living creature is disgusting. Isn't that so, Elsa?"

She took the toad, turned it over, studied its speckled belly, its wide mobile mouth and clumsy, jerking legs, and agreed with her father. "I think he's adorable," she said, "particularly his belly."

At the same time another thought occurred to her. "This is a particularly handsome specimen, Carnovsky," she said. "Let's sit down and dissect it together."

Georg took the toad from her hand and put it aside. "Not today, Elsa. For me it's enough that we cut things up all week."

Out in the open field he grew very much aware of her young body.

She became a completely different person there—gay, playful, almost irresponsible. She drew in the fresh air not only with her nostrils as her father had taught her, but also with her mouth and all the strength of her young strong lungs. She petted village dogs who approached snarling but soon succumbed to her. She caressed the wet muzzles of calves who bleated longingly with their heads drawn forward and remarked often how beautiful the world was.

"Don't you agree, Georg?" she asked, calling him by his first name.

Georg burst out in a song that echoed and re-echoed through the countryside. Peasant girls stared out of windows at the odd trio. Dr. Landau's red beard, Elsa's mannish attire, and Georg's pitch-black hair seemed to them alien and curious.

Dr. Landau set a rapid pace, as if keeping time to Georg's song, and swung his arms briskly. *"Morgen,* good people, *Morgen,"* he greeted the peasants standing before their doorways.

When the sun grew too hot, Dr. Landau found a stream in which to swim. Swimming with Georg, he called to Elsa, who was hidden in the bushes, to take off her clothes and join them.

"Silly goose, how many times must I tell you that nakedness is nothing to be ashamed of? Come on in!"

"Later, after you come out," she replied from afar.

Georg floated on his back, swam underwater, and performed all kinds of stunts.

Only after the men were out and dressed did Elsa go in. Georg listened to her splashing from a distance. "Elsa!" he called out, just to say her name. "Elsa!"

The sound echoed endlessly. Her head still wet, her body exuding the scent of fresh water, she laid out the lunch she had prepared— the vegetables, cheeses, milk, and fruit. She bustled about officiously, like a housewife feeding her family. Georg was ravenous.

Elsa plucked the crumbs from her father's beard and threw them to the birds. As soon as lunch was over, Dr. Landau stretched out on the grass and fell asleep, snoring so loudly that his beard and mustache vibrated with every breath.

The huge sky reflected gold, blue, silver. A dark blue line of distant forests stretched across the horizon. Flies and crickets buzzed. The contours of a crumbling castle loomed sharply against the mountainside. The village church steeple glistened in the sunlight. A stork sitting in an old naked tree loudly clacked its bill and cried, breaking the silence. Georg was blissful. He listened to the thousand different sounds that penetrated the silence and wondered if Elsa heard them too.

"Isn't it magnificent?" he asked, taking her hand.

"Yes, Georg," she said and, resting his head in her lap, ran her fingers through his hair. Even when her father woke momentarily she let Georg's head remain where it was. Georg grew uneasy when he saw that Dr. Landau was awake and started to fidget but the doctor merely turned on his other side.

"*Dummkopf!*" he mumbled and soon was snoring again.

Elsa looked around with a dreamy expression and crooned softly. Her voice was soft and soothing, like a mother's rocking her baby to sleep, her eyes grew misty and languid.

"Sleep, little one," she whispered. For a while Georg closed his eyes and gave himself up to the comfort of her arms, but soon he rebelled at the humiliating position and sat up abruptly.

"What's wrong, *Bube?*" Elsa asked, puzzled.

He was infuriated by her patronizing, maternal tone. He would not be treated like a baby, patted on the head, and lulled to sleep. He was a man, not a lap dog. He wanted plain talk between them. Here and now he demanded a straight answer—was she trifling with him or was she serious? Did she love him, damn it, or did she not? If she did, he would speak to her father and they would be married and live together like normal people. If she did not love him, she should say so and let him go.

Elsa let him have his say, looking at him with eyes that were again clear, wise, and resolute. "What is this, an ultimatum?" she asked mockingly.

"That's just what it is," he replied.

Elsa started to put the things back into the rucksacks and gave Georg some good advice. She was always ready to work with him in the laboratory and to go hiking with him on Sundays because she was very fond of him, perhaps even loved him. But this should not stop him from seeing other girls who would make a fuss over him, be properly submissive, and treat him like a lord and master. She realized that men had a need to prove how masterful and domineering they were, that they wanted to feel big and strong and, because of inherent weaknesses, that they must always act heroic. But if he expected her to act like a typical female, he had the wrong girl. She would never be anyone's slave, not of any man living, and this was precisely the reason she would never marry. For her, her medicine, her Party, and her laboratory were enough. She neither had the time nor the urge to become someone's wife.

"Do you understand?" she asked, and kissed his lips.

He was riled and tried to overcome her with masculine tactics. Elsa looked at him with cool deliberation and laughed.

"Silly," she said and laughed even louder.

He felt demeaned and humbled. She always managed to keep the upper hand. To save face, he began to whistle with an assumed indifference. The quiet countryside echoed his bravado.

12

Although the day was bright and sunny, the vast dissecting room at the Institute of Pathologic Anatomy was brilliantly illuminated. On stands affixed to the walls hung various-sized skeletons. Jars of liquid containing human hearts, livers, stomachs, and intestines lined the shelves. Attendants wheeled in male and female cadavers on stretchers and laid them out on the tin-covered dissecting tables.

"Make way, Herren Kandidaten," they kept warning the students who stood around in quiet groups smoking furiously. "Make way!"

From long experience the attendants had picked up much knowledge of anatomy and dissection and were contemptuous of the students who knew less than they. The students moved aside without protest. It was a big day for them—the day when the seniors had to take their final examinations in surgical procedure before they could graduate. What was more important, Geheimrat Lentzbach himself, the chief of surgery, would be present. The students paced nervously back and forth in their white smocks. The guards were just as restless.

"No smoking, Herren Kandidaten, no smoking!" they warned and made sure that the students crushed out their cigarettes.

They knew that although Geheimrat Lentzbach himself smoked during the examination, he did not like his students to do so. A test operation was to him like a real one and one did not smoke during an operation. Besides, he believed that the students should get to know the stink of death. It would do them good. When

he had been a student at Heidelberg he had had to endure this smell
too. The students discarded their cigarettes in the sand bucket. When
Geheimrat Lentzbach approached, the guards drew themselves up
taut as violin strings.

"*Guten Morgen,* Herr Geheimrat," they greeted him with military precision.

"*Morgen,*" he barked, walking past briskly, his head erect.

Although he was already a septuagenarian, he held his slim body
as ramrod-stiff as an athletic young lieutenant. Unlike the other professors who affected beards and flowing pompadours, his snowy
white hair was clipped short in military style and his mustache was
turned up like a hussar's. Otherwise, his energetic face, burned brick
red by the sun and wind, was cleanshaven. The scarred cheek that he
had collected at Heidelberg glowed redder than the other and his
icy blue eyes looked around with undisguised contempt. He strode
through the hall like a general trailed by a retinue of adjutants.

"*Guten Morgen,* Herr Geheimrat," the students greeted him timidly.

"*Morgen,*" he answered curtly, and looked them over like a com-
mander reviewing his troops

Everyone squirmed under his gaze, particularly Georg, for among
the ten seniors scheduled for the final examination he was the only
one with a last name ending in a "sky," a "Moses" in the middle, and
black hair and eyes. Although he had always been treated fairly
by the professors, these unusual factors now made him somewhat
uneasy and he avoided Geheimrat Lentzbach's piercing eyes. He
hated himself for his anxiety, yet he could not control it and it
caused him to make his first mistake when Geheimrat Lentzbach
called his name.

"*Jawohl,* Herr Professor," he responded but, quickly realizing his
mistake, added: "*Jawohl,* Herr Geheimrat. . . .'"

Geheimrat Lentzbach looked at him with a gaze that chilled his
blood. He was very particular about titles. The students were required to address him not only as "Herr Geheimrat" but as "Professor" as well, and although Georg had been quick to correct himself,
Professor Lentzbach was not as quick to forgive the oversight. He

despised mistakes and panic and insisted upon discipline and correctness. He therefore selected the agitated, black-eyed student as his first victim.

"Appendectomy, Carnovsky!" he roared, selecting a cadaver.

The corpse was not in the usual dismembered state to which Georg was accustomed, but was whole—fresh from the clinic. It was the body of a young woman, at most twenty years old, tall, slim, and pallid. Her breasts were small and girlish. It was doubtful that she had ever borne a child; possibly she had even died a virgin. Her waxy features were pretty and symmetrical and bore the dignity and invulnerability of death. She seemed to be sleeping. Georg even imagined that she was still warm to the touch and his hand trembled ever so lightly when he sliced open her belly.

"Steady! And keep those hands still!" Geheimrat Lentzbach barked as he observed.

Georg again felt the queasiness rising up within him from the stench of formaldehyde, death, and decay, and he fought with all his might to control the creeping nausea that incapacitated his nerves and fingers. Cold sweat broke out on his forehead as Geheimrat Lentzbach closely studied both his work and his reactions.

"Calmly and quickly!" he commanded. "Forget that a corpse is lying there and imagine that it is a patient whose appendix must come out. One cannot fumble for even a second at a time like this. One must work calmly and quickly!"

The advice only served to unnerve Georg all the more and he struggled to contain the nausea that threatened to negate all the years of hard work and effort.

"*Jawohl*, Herr Geheimrat," he replied as he struggled for self-control.

The minutes dragged by like hours, like eternities. With superhuman effort he cut into the cadaver, removed the appendix, and showed it to the professor. Glancing uneasily at him, he awaited some word of praise or at least a nod to indicate that he had done a good job, but Geheimrat Lentzbach remained impassive. Georg waited for the professor to dismiss him and to call on someone else. He felt that he must get away from the stench and the tension and

run out for a quick smoke. But Geheimrat Lentzbach was in no
hurry to release him. Like the other professors, he did not like things
to go too easily for his students. He always tried to give them something to remember him by for the rest of their lives before they got
out of his clutches. Without a single comment to the young man
with the odd name about the operation he had performed, he posed
a new challenge to him, one seldom given on such occasions.

"Eye enucleation," he said, which meant that Georg would have
to remove an eye from the body of the young woman with the
opened abdomen.

Georg approached the body and with trembling fingers tried to
pry open the tightly closed lids. He had to use force to get them open
and then he looked into an eye that stared back at him in mild,
pleading appeal. He felt himself grow cold as the eye stared up at
him reproachfully, lamenting its too brief life, its humiliation before
strangers, its loneliness and unwarranted mutilation. His hands
began to tremble anew and Geheimrat Lentzbach hissed angrily:
"Steady! This is an eye, a delicate organ. Stay calm, goddamn it!"

Georg was sure that in another second he would faint, but he
managed to cut out the eye in prescribed fashion. Another student
held the eyeball while Georg severed the muscles that bound it to
the inner tissues.

"Enough!" Professor Lentzbach finally barked and nodded to indicate that the student had passed the examination.

Georg walked away on quaking legs. Although his ordeal was
over and the years of effort had not been in vain, he felt neither
joy nor relief. He was completely indifferent, as if in a daze, and
wanted only to get away as far as possible from the dismembered
body, the stink of death and decay, and especially the corpse's accus-
ing eye.

The fresh air, bright sunshine, and sound of children's laughter in
the street were like a tonic, but the reproachful look in the blue eye
refused to fade. It showed in the face of every passing woman.
He even saw it in the spotless coffee house where he ordered
several cognacs to brace himself. The waitress, who knew him,
smiled at him with her blue eyes, but instead of smiling back as

usual and passing some light remark, he looked up at her with fear.
She reminded him of the young woman lying on the dissecting table.

"What's wrong, Herr Doktor?" she asked.

"Another cognac," Georg replied.

Even that night in the cabaret to which he went with his
friends to drink and forget, he could not rid himself of the vision.
The girls hugged him and let him take liberties. He ordered
glass after glass of wine, sang lustily, and was too noisy and gay,
trying to still the fear within him, but in the midst of all the merri-
ment he again saw the blue eye in the face of a laughing café girl.

At dawn he went home to his cubicle in Neukölln. He lay down
on the divan, wanting to sleep, only to sleep, but instead of sleep a
figure appeared—of all people, his old Hebrew tutor, Herr Tobias,
with whom he had studied the book of the Prophet Ezekiel. Georg
begged him: "Herr Tobias, let me be, I want to sleep. . . ." But
Herr Tobias did not listen, and with a funereal voice went over the
chapter in which God set the Prophet Ezekiel down in the midst of
the valley and " 'it was full of bones . . . and there were very many
in the open valley and, lo, they were very dry. . . . And God said
unto Ezekiel: "Prophesy over these bones" . . . and there was a
noise and . . . the bones came together, bone to its bone, there
were sinews upon them and flesh came up and skin covered them
above. . . .' "

"Herr Tobias, I'm tired, my head aches," Georg pleaded. "No,
Georg, repeat!" Herr Tobias said and again translated: " '. . . and
the breath came into them, and they lived, and stood up upon their
feet. . . .' "

Georg could not understand the difficult words and ran away in the
middle of the lesson to the Friedrich Wilhelm University. But here
he saw the skeletons suddenly come down from their stands in the
dissecting room and begin to march. They were joined by the dismembered limbs and they all united, limb to limb and bone to bone
and became whole again. Before them walked the young woman with
the one blue eye and all the skeletons walked behind her. Georg
tried to run away but they pursued him. They trod over the stone
floors, marched up the stairs and out of the dissecting room, rattling
their bony legs and swinging their bony arms. They gathered by the

thousands, by the hundreds of thousands, by the millions. Their ranks extended as far as the eye could see—a death march beyond all conception. Georg ran and screamed for his fellow students to flee with him and they all raced down the stairs—the students, the servants, the professors, even Geheimrat Lentzbach. He, Georg, ran in front and held Elsa's hand, but the skeletons still followed— swarms of skeletons, vast multitudes. Their bones clacked on the pavement and Georg began to scream in terror. . . .

When he opened his eyes, Frau Kruppa was standing over him, shaking his shoulders. "You devil. . . . It's the afternoon already and you're still having nightmares."

His head aching and his spirit broken, Georg went to see Dr. Landau. "I'm afraid, Herr Doktor, that I was foolish to give up philosophy for medicine. I don't seem to have the guts for it. Certainly not for surgery."

"*Quatsch!*" Dr. Landau said. "A doctor without a heart is a butcher with a medical diploma. Only a person with a heart can be a great doctor. Take my word for it, my young colleague."

Again David Carnovsky put on his holiday outfit for the graduation exercises and again Leah Carnovsky stayed away, still unsure of her German and her manners. Georg wore his frock coat and patent-leather shoes. Professors in robes, bemedaled dignitaries, and high-ranking military leaders were present. Geheimrat Lentzbach delivered a thunderous discourse like a general exhorting his troops to battle, urging devotion to duty and to the *Vaterland*. Georg accepted his medical diploma with the same feeling of relief with which he had graduated from the Gymnasium. He took a brief vacation in a fishing village on the Baltic Sea where the fresh salty air, the sun, and the wind helped wash away the years of hard work, dissections, and disgusting odors of dead flesh.

In August he came back to the city to be among the first to apply for a position in a good hospital. The first street down which he walked found him caught in the center of a military parade.

"Down with Russia! Down with France!" voices cried. "Up with the Kaiser and the *Vaterland!*"

"Victory over the French shall be ours," sang marching soldiers as their hobnailed boots thundered on the pavement.

Flags fluttered, bands played. Men took off their hats and sang *Die Wacht am Rhein* and Georg Carnovsky sang along in his deep bass.

Among the first to be called up to military service was young Dr. Carnovsky, who was assigned to a field hospital on the Eastern Front.

13

Things were grim in the old secondhand clothes dealers' quarter that the gentiles laughingly called Jewish Switzerland.

The Galician Jews displayed Austrian flags alongside the German in their butcher shops, restaurants, and synagogues. Next to the portrait of Kaiser Wilhelm with his pointed, turned-up mustache and spiked helmet they hung pictures of their Austrian emperor with his benevolent white side whiskers and paternal eyes. The largest portraits and the biggest flags hung from the peeling balcony of the Franz Josef Hotel, owned by Reb Herzele Vishniak from the village of Brod. Elderly Galician Jews in alpaca jackets praised their emperor: "A fine old gentleman, may the Evil Eye spare him, a true monarch," they said with genuine affection.

"May God grant him good health," the women added.

Young men called up for military service teased their Russian neighbors. "We'll give your Russky bear a good hiding," they said. "Our boys will teach him how to dance to our tune, just you wait and see."

These were trying times for the Russian- and Polish-born Jews in the Quarter. The tall, big-bellied policeman who for years had patroled the streets keeping everyone under surveillance now went from one alien household to another preparing the people for internment. He arrested all the Jews who were from Russia, although they explained in their broken German that they bore no love for the Tsar whose authority they had fled.

The Galician Jews also asked him not to be harsh with their Russian coreligionists but the policeman waved them aside: "Nothing can be done, neighbor, wartime!"

Nor did the Russian Jews who had moved to fancier neighborhoods fare any better.

Among the first to face official harassment was Solomon Burak. Not only were his salespeople, the relatives from Melnitz, interned, but he himself, an old-established and prosperous merchant, was ordered to report daily to the police station until new decrees were issued. Solomon Burak was furious because he had just laid in a huge stock of goods for the coming fall season, a selection that would have brought mobs of shoppers to Landsberger Allee.

"A plague on the Russian pigs!" he complained. "Of all the stupid times to start a war, right damn smack at the beginning of the season!"

He sought help from his business friends, the bankers and manufacturers, but no one offered to intercede in his behalf.

"Wartime, Herr Burak," they said smugly. "We can't do a blessed thing for an enemy alien."

Cynically aware that favor-seeking was a waste of time, Solomon Burak turned to an old and trusted friend, his money. It had done its customary reliable job in Russia, where bribery was open and accepted. It would also do it here in a country where such practices were supposedly nonexistent.

His wallet bursting, he went to the very top, as experience had taught him, and despite his crude manners and atrocious German managed to get across the message that he was willing to pay for the privilege of remaining unmolested. And to affirm his patriotism he made an extremely generous contribution to the German Red Cross, one so magnificent that the head of the department cooed with delight. He grew ecstatic when Solomon Burak, with infinite delicacy, pressed a plain sealed envelope into his hand.

"Terribly decent of you, Herr Burak," he gushed, glowing with gratitude and love for humanity.

"It would please me no end if you would send me the measurements of the members of your household so I might present them with some samples of my new fall line," Solomon Burak said, and

with a light wallet and an even lighter spirit he went back to his
store.

Since he couldn't ransom his relatives too, he hired gentile girls to
replace them for the duration. But he and his family were exempted
from internment, and with his customary drive he began to prepare
for the coming fall season. When his German-Jewish neighbors
learned of his dispensation they were outraged. And the angriest of
all was his nearest competitor, Ludwig Kadish, who had already
been called up for military service. "When are you going to the
internment camp, Herr Burak?" he asked, seething with patriotism
and indignation.

"Say the *Kaddish,* wash your hands, and eat your matzo balls,"
Solomon Burak quipped, making a play on words on his competitor's name, as well as a sly allusion to the fact that one hand washed
another—even in the *Vaterland.*

David Carnovsky was shocked when he was ordered to report to
the police and told that he would be interned with the other Russians.

He could not rationalize such a thing happening to him—he who
had fled the darkness and tyranny of the East for the culture and
light of the West; he who spoke the purest German; he who was
a respected member of his synagogue; a disciple of Moses Mendelssohn, Lessing, and Schiller; a prominent merchant; a property
owner, and the father of a German officer. Did they actually dare
equate him with the riffraff from Poland and Russia?

The first one he asked to intercede on his behalf was the rabbi,
Dr. Speier. But the rabbi was reluctant even to be seen in the com-
pany of the man whose home he had visited for years to discuss
Torah and wisdom.

"Wartime, my dear Carnovsky," he said coldly. "I can't afford to
become involved."

Nor was Professor Breslauer any more helpful. " 'When cannons
roar, the muses must be silent,' " he quoted.

David Carnovsky went to see Reb Ephraim Walder in the secondhand clothes dealers' quarter. He didn't go there to seek help—

he knew that the old man had no influence. He only went to unburden himself of his disappointment in his good friends, the men of enlightenment.

Passing Grosse Hamburger Strasse where the small monument of Moses Mendelssohn stood, he raised his eyes to the bronze figure of the philosopher who was the reason for his coming to the city of culture and light. *Some generation you have spawned,* he thought bitterly, *a fine bunch of sages and scholars!*

As he neared the Quarter, he passed a group of prisoners being herded by police while men waved their fists and women spat at them. "Kill the goddamned Russians!" they cried. "Beat them to death!"

The prisoners were pelted with rocks and manure. Carnovsky felt uneasy in the midst of the bloodthirsty mob and he walked briskly toward Dragonerstrasse. Austrian flags and portraits of the Kaiser fluttered from Reb Ephraim's bookstore. Janet Walder had apparently laid out a considerable sum of money for these items. As usual, Reb Ephraim sat among his books, searching, studying, and writing.

"Welcome, Reb Carnovsky!" he said, laying aside his goose quill. "I haven't seen you for a long time. Sit down."

"Don't forget that we are enemies," David said with irony. "If you're afraid, I'll leave at once."

Reb Ephraim smiled. "Being afraid is for the mob, not for a student of the Talmud."

David Carnovsky poured out his frustration and disappointment to Reb Ephraim, who was not at all surprised. At his age, having already seen and heard almost all that life had to offer, he accepted everything philosophically—human weakness, ingratitude, even war.

"Since the first conflict when Cain slew Abel not a day has gone by without a war being fought somewhere. That minor philosopher but great sage, Voltaire, brought it out very well in one of his books whose title I cannot at this moment recall, Reb Carnovsky."

With perfect equanimity, as if the world were not in upheaval, Reb Ephraim began to read a portion of his manuscript to David Carnovsky, the latest interpretation that he deemed essential to include in his life's work.

Surprisingly, the only person to stand up for David Carnovsky was his son Georg. Dressed in his brand-new officer's uniform, he went to the police, pushed his way in to the highest ranking official, and pointed out the fallacy of interning a man whose only son was an officer at the front. His intercession had the desired effect.

"Go figure it out," Carnovsky said to his wife, this time not in German but in a homely Yiddish. "Who would have thought of counting on Georg?"

"I always knew the boy was something special," Leah said piously. "I only wish that God will protect him in the dark days to come."

The one hit hardest by the outbreak of war was Dr. Fritz Landau of Neukölln.

"Idiots! Asses! Cannon fodder!" he berated the troops as they marched off singing to the front. "They still sing, those dumb oxes, even as the court lackeys and Kaiser's ass-lickers are sending them off to be butchered!"

"Calm down, Papa," Elsa pleaded, "and don't say those things in front of the patients. They're liable to report you."

"Let them!" he screamed. "I'll tell the truth to the devil himself!"

Like a huge trip hammer, he excoriated the leaders of the Party at Petersile's beer hall when, carried away by patriotism, they supported the war budget. He called them idiots and blockheads who substituted paper for brains and ink for blood. If they had any conception of what a marvelous mechanism the human body was; of the amazing substance of which it was composed; of how ingenious and rational was the construction of every limb; of how cleverly each tissue and nerve was connected; of how efficiently the human heart, lung, eye, and every organ functioned, they could not countenance murder so lightly. But they were crude, callous brutes who knew nothing besides their dirty politics and their inborn Germanic reverence for crowns and epaulets. And this was precisely the reason they could make such an easy transition to butchers and executioners.

Nor did he have a kind word for Georg Carnovsky, who came in his uniform to say good-by before leaving for the front.

"Adieu, Dr. Butcher!" he growled, extending only the tips of his fingers.

Georg tried to appease him. "Hopefully, I will be healing, not killing, Herr Doktor. Don't be angry with me. I didn't start the war."

"You all started it, all of you! You've become a pack of moral bankrupts and murderers!" Dr. Landau raged.

Elsa gave Georg a quite different reception. Although she was by now a qualified physician and worked with her father, she was disappointed because she could not go to the front and envied Georg his opportunity. Caught up in the national excitement, the parades, the martial music, the patriotic fervor and the fluttering flags, her young blood was stirred and her spirit drawn to become part of this grand epic of courage and sacrifice.

"What I wouldn't give to go with you, Georg!" she said, snuggling up to him. Georg was thrilled. His face glowed with the excitement of the early days of war, before its horror and finality set in; his eyes sparkled with the anticipation of the great adventure and Elsa was swept up by the wanton mood that seized all the young people of the day.

"You look damn fine in your uniform," she said.

Dr. Landau could not stand any more. "You're as stupid as all other women," he snarled. "Just like every stupid cow who gushes over uniforms and condones slaughter. It's because of idiots like you that wars begin altogether!"

"Now, now, don't take on so, you funny old *Papachen,* you," Elsa said, and kissed his mustache.

But Dr. Landau was in no mood to be placated and stormed out of the office.

Elsa took Georg's arm and they went off together.

At first she accompanied him to the railroad station to say goodby. Like the other young women sending their men off to the front, she clung to his arm, pressed close to him, and looked deep into his eyes.

"Dearest," she breathed like a smitten schoolgirl.

When the final whistle blew and the conductor began to herd the passengers into the cars, she pressed her whole body against Georg and would not let him go. When the conductor angrily warned that the train was already moving, Elsa impulsively climbed aboard and with gay abandon watched the platform recede in the distance. At every stop she kissed Georg good-by anew and climbed down to take a train home, but every time the train started again she ran up the steps and rejoined him. Like mischievous children, they laughed each time the conductor took their money and grouchily wrote out the new tickets.

In Frankfurt an der Oder they both got off, he to wait overnight for his hospital train, she for the train back to Berlin. They strolled hand in hand in the station but when her train came they again took so long to say good-by that she missed it.

"Funny!" Elsa said as she watched the train leave.

They strolled the streets, completely absorbed in each other. Flags fluttered from every balcony, gay music sounded from somewhere. Officers promenaded with their ladies and young soldiers larked about with girls. Laxity, frivolity, and abandon seemed to exude from every gate and door. A summer shower fell lightly and sprinkled Georg's uniform. For some reason this left them weak with laughter. They walked into a brightly lit hotel beer garden where a female orchestra played patriotic airs and waltzes and couples danced. Georg drew Elsa into the vortex of uniforms and gay summer frocks and she followed his every lead slavishly. Afterward they had wine at their table. Although her father had strictly forbidden her to drink, she now had glass after glass like the other ladies, openly kissed her escort, and drank out of his glass. When it grew late and the couples began to drift out through the foyer into the hotel lobby and up the marble stairway to their rooms, Georg took Elsa's arm and led her to the desk.

"Your worthy names, *bitte*." the desk clerk asked.

"Dr. Georg Carnovsky and wife," Georg said as Elsa nestled closer.

Like two famished beasts they sprang into each other's arms in the small room on the top floor of the hotel while the summer rain pattered softly against the panes and beat gently down on the roof overhead.

The next morning Georg put his head between his hands, awaiting the inevitable outburst. He braced himself for tears, protests, and recriminations, but Elsa was in a fine and pleasant mood.

Like any dutiful mate of a war-bound soldier she helped him into his uniform. Georg was forlorn. "We didn't even manage to get married first, darling," he said guiltily. "We'll take care of it on my very first leave."

"What for?" she asked, arranging her hair before the mirror above the sofa.

He looked at her in disbelief, infuriated by her rejection of the reward he had so generously dangled before her. He assumed that any woman in her position would have seized such an offer.

As always, she had managed to assert her superiority and elude the advantage he had temporarily gained over her.

In the distance, train whistles cried mournfully and echoed through the still morning air like the voices of wounded creatures abandoned to fate. From the street below came the sound of boots pounding on the pavement.

BOOK TWO *Georg*

14

Herr Joachim Holbeck's twin, adjoining, four-story houses in Berlin's Tiergarten Quarter were solid and massive, complete to columns, towers, cornices, balconies, and carvings. Their walls were thick, their windows large, their ceilings intricately carved. The marble stairways were broad, the sculptured angels and seraphim chubby, the ground-floor shop windows huge and dazzling bright. The houses had two entrances each, one for the tenants and the other for servants, delivery boys, and postmen. To beggars, street musicians, and peddlers, even the side entrances were barred.

As solidly as Herr Holbeck had constructed his house, so firmly did Frau Holbeck conduct her household. Everything in the spacious apartment was oversized: the bulky furniture; the rugs and Gobelin tapestries; the brass lamps; and the extensive collection of glassware, porcelain, and ceramics. Even the curtains were heavy and so dense that not one ray of sunlight could steal through to fade the rugs and furniture.

The same massiveness was reflected in the inscriptions in Gothic characters that decorated so many of the household articles, proverbs proclaiming homely wisdom and common sense. They were everywhere, embroidered on towels, carved into the ceramics, and painted on the mugs and steins. The old towels still remaining from Frau Holbeck's trousseau bore such inscriptions as "The early bird catches the worm." On the new towels that Frau Holbeck gave her daughter Teresa to sew was embroidered the legend: "A stitch in time saves nine." The mottoes on the wine goblets were more daring and alluded to wine, women, and song. The velvet cushion on which Herr Holbeck rested his head during his midday nap bore an admonition embroidered in silk: "Just one quarter hour." Even the toilet seat had a velvet cover that bore a rhymed proverb advocating cleanliness.

As solid and conservative as the houses were Herr Holbeck's tenants—affluent, respectable, smug burghers. The one exception was Herr Max Drechsler, an optician who ran a surgical supply store in a corner of one of Joachim Holbeck's houses. The optician, whose every feature and possession glistened—the lenses of his pince-nez, his black hair and mustache, his shoes and rings, his cuff links and tie pin, his shop window and the goods he displayed there —was a Jew, the only one in the two houses. As is often the case when a Jew is alone among gentiles, Max Drechsler distinguished himself by continuously telling jokes to his neighbors. No matter how often he came to Herr Holbeck's apartment, whether to pay his rent or to ask for some repairs, he invariably told jokes, mostly ones concerning a Herr Kohn or a Herr Levy. And although he was always punctual with his rent and kept his store immaculate, Joachim Holbeck considered him too frivolous for his houses and too much of an oddity. It was partly because of his faith, but more so because of his sharp tongue.

However else it may have been blessed, the Holbeck family was not overendowed with humor.

Joachim Holbeck, a stout, good-natured man, avidly bent his square, close-cropped head to hear Max Drechsler's latest anecdote. When, after deep concentration, he finally got the point, he would laugh lustily, occasionally until tears came to his eyes. But most of the time he would miss the point. At the crucial moment when Max Drechsler stopped, anticipating a burst of laughter, Joachim Holbeck merely stared at him with the dull impassivity of a sated cow.

"Yes, yes, yes, that's how it is, Herr Drechsler," he would observe philosophically to squirm out of an uncomfortable situation.

Herr Drechsler's jokes made even less of an impact on Frau Holbeck. She did not even bother to listen. Stout, earnest, obsessed with the responsibility of running a large household and raising children; constantly fussing, darning socks, and patching underwear, she had no patience with such foolishness. Although she was polite to Herr Drechsler, as befitted a woman of her station, she prayed that the dandified Jew would leave as quickly as possible.

Not that she had anything against Jews. On the contrary, she often shopped in Jewish stores because their prices were lower, and whenever her children were sick and the family physician was unable to help she called in a Jewish specialist, since like most Berliners she felt that they made superior doctors. Joachim Holbeck also kept his money in a Jewish bank and bought his securities there. Still, the couple felt uncomfortable around Jews and considered them flighty, like actors whom one admires but avoids socially.

Frau Holbeck had a particular aversion to Max Drechsler because of the nature of his business. Her neighbors had told her that besides selling eyeglasses and thermometers he also provided young couples with illegal birth-control items, and Frau Holbeck, like every mother who had borne her share of stillborn children, was righteously resentful of women who avoided their obligation to suffer and to give birth. In addition, Herr Drechsler displayed in his shop window a large, waxen figure of a naked female wearing only blue glasses, rubber stockings, a surgical brassiere and a corset; and each time Frau Holbeck saw the mannequin she felt ashamed because it reminded her too much of her own body, rendered flabby and shapeless by years of childbearing and rich food. She often wondered why the police allowed such a brazen display. And even though Drechsler's jokes made the Jew the butt, the Holbecks always felt as if somehow they were being mocked and they breathed easier after he left.

"*Ach,* that Drechsler!" Frau Holbeck would sigh.

"*Ja,* that Drechsler," her husband would agree and light another of his fat cigars.

No outer threat was able to penetrate the thick, solid walls of the Holbeck houses in the respectable Tiergarten Quarter. It took the war to do it. First, Hugo Holbeck, the couple's only son, was sent to the Western Front. Then Frau Holbeck stopped serving whipped cream with the coffee. Later she made meat for lunch not every day, as before, but every other day. The decorated porcelain plates began to grow larger and larger as the portions of meat grew smaller and smaller. Then she began brewing coffee from hazel nuts and to spread tasteless jam over the poor, rationed bread. The smaller the portions of food became, the larger grew Herr Holbeck's commitment for war bonds, to which he had to subscribe time and again. Then the tenants began to be late with their rents, as much as months behind. Each morning as he dressed, Joachim Holbeck noticed that his belly was shrinking and his vest growing roomier. He kept tightening and retightening the buckle in back. Their daughter Teresa grew paler and even more fragile, and instead of spending her time sewing and learning domestic chores as a girl of a respectable house should, she began to study nursing in order to obtain work in a military hospital. Finally the war was over and the civil unrest began. A new breed of people appeared in the Tiergarten Quarter, a type never before seen in the neighborhood. They came from the outlying sections, from Neukölln. They came in their ragged clothes carrying red banners and they made such an uproar that it even carried through the thick walls and heavily draped windows of the previously impervious Holbeck houses. Along with the red flags and raucous voices they brought the maladies of the poor—diphtheria, typhus, and dysentery. Worst of all was the Spanish influenza that seeped its treacherous poison through all entrances—both the servant and the family. The first to be infected was the landlord himself, Joachim Holbeck, and within three short days he was dead although Teresa didn't leave his side for a moment.

After the proper period of mourning the widow Holbeck gathered all the account books, stock certificates, war-bond obligations, promissory notes, and calculations that her husband had left her and turned them over to the man of the house, Hugo, who had come back from the front silent and embittered. But he had no inkling of what they were all about. Tall, gangly, extremely fair and pale; wearing yellow boots with high uppers, riding breeches that were wide at the hips and tapered to almost bursting at the knee, a fitted officer's jacket that still bore the mark of buttons and epaulettes that had been torn from it by the soldiers of his platoon, Oberleutnant Holbeck knew nothing about houses, papers, promissory notes, or accounts. The only trade he knew was the one he had been taught so well—that of making war. Now that his usefulness was outlived, he did not know what to do, either with himself or with the houses. He was reluctant to go out into the streets that swarmed with insubordinate soldiers and reckless mobs, and he spent long days at home dreaming of the glory that had been his so briefly and that had been snatched from him prematurely, like a bride kidnapped on her wedding night. He lounged in an easy chair with his long legs stretched out before him, smoked cigarette after cigarette, whistled and played with the dog that had lived the war with him from beginning to end. When he grew bored with the dog, he yawned desperately and polished and repolished his revolver and field glasses, the only items he had salvaged from the war besides a game leg and a lingering cold. From time to time his mother roused him from his indolence.

"Hugo, the stocks must be sold. They keep on falling!"

"So?" he said lazily.

"Hugo, we must collect from the tenants. No one is paying the rent!"

"So?"

"Hugo, the shortage is getting worse. It's impossible to buy a thing in the city. . . ."

Seeing that the man of the house was indifferent to everything, Teresa Holbeck went out to look for a job. Although she had been instructed by her mother in all the domestic skills needed to run a household and even held a certificate from an academy attesting to her homemaking abilities, she took a job as a nurse in Professor Halevy's Maternity Clinic on Kaiserallee.

When Hugo heard the news from his mother he didn't respond with his customary "So?" but added a lusty soldier's curse directed at the pregnant Jew-sows whose bedpans Teresa would have to empty.

Teresa Holbeck blushed. "Hugo? Aren't you ashamed before Mother?"

Hugo stared at his long legs as if seeing them for the first time. Although he was humiliated by Teresa's job, both by the nature of the work and the fact that she would be working for Jews, he said nothing more and remained sitting in his usual stupor while the dog licked the yellow boots to which still clung the familiar odors of blood and gunpowder.

15

Georg Carnovsky also came back from the Eastern Front with a uniform from which the buttons had been torn and with the rank of captain for his services as a regimental doctor in the field. But he did not wear his uniform a single day longer than necessary. Although the barber urged him to have his hair clipped close and shaved at the temples as was the custom among the returning veterans, Georg asked for a regular haircut. He threw away not only the regulation jack boots but even the shoes that still bore the stink of death, decay, and the battlefield.

It wasn't that the smell of blood still bothered him. In the years he had spent in the field, in first-aid stations and lazarrets, he had virtually been soaked in blood and breathed death and decay almost constantly. His hands had amputated mounds of legs, cut open bellies by the hundreds, wallowed in gore, gangrenous flesh, and pus. His ears had heard muffled groans, blood-curdling shrieks and death rattles until they could hear nothing else. His eyes had seen murder, fear, hope, and despair; but above all—death, death in a thousand forms, each no less terrible than the other. He no longer felt nauseated by rotting flesh, but it repelled him as much as ever and he wanted to rid himself of every memory of armies and battlefields. He certainly did not want to talk about it.

His parents were disappointed. As she passionately kissed her son's cheeks, burned an even deeper brown by the sun and wind, Leah's maternal passion came flowing back and she addressed him again as the child she once remembered. "My treasure, my only comfort, my sweet Moshe, Moshele, Mosheniu," she crooned, "tell your mother everything you went through . . ."

David Carnovsky was just as anxious to discuss the war. Having avidly followed in the newspapers the course of battles, the movement of armies, and the military tactics of both sides, he was eager to show off to his son his knowledge of conditions at the front. But Georg wouldn't cooperate. The one hurt most by his attitude was his sister, Rebecca. In the four years Georg had been away she had blossomed into a tall and well-developed girl despite the food shortages. Now, barely fifteen, she had eagerly awaited her brother's return. She never stopped boasting to her classmates about him and could not wait for the day he came back so that she could show him off to her friends in all his military splendor.

"Please, Georg, don't take off your uniform," she begged him. "You look so well in it. . . ."

"I don't want to wear these rags an extra day, child," he said, stroking her thick black braids.

She tore the braids from his hand. She could neither stand being called "child" nor hearing a German uniform described as a rag. It was enough that her mother considered her a child; she didn't want to hear it from a brother who was determined to rob her of her long-nurtured dream of strolling before her friends with an officer for an escort. Even Georg's compliments couldn't assuage her deep disappointment. Besides, he didn't *really* think she was pretty.

Her skin was dark; her eyes large, black, and fiery; her teeth white but uneven; her lips full and red; her hair so black it seemed blue. Her nose, the prominent Carnovsky nose, was too masculine for a female face and at first glance made one blind to her fine eyes and striking complexion. Rebecca hated her face.

"Mother, why couldn't you make me like you!" she cried each time she saw herself in the mirror.

Leah had no sympathy with these complaints. She was so deeply in love with her husband that she considered him the handsomest man alive and she was proud that the children resembled him. "You should be glad you look like your father," she chided the girl. "So dark and alive!"

But Rebecca didn't want to be dark in a city of fair people. She didn't enjoy being stared at in the streets. She didn't want to be called "Gipsy" by her schoolmates. No, she didn't believe it when Georg called her pretty.

"You're mean and I hate you!" she said.

For a long time he looked at this child who within a few short years had matured into a typical female with all the wiles and caprices; then he got up to go to Neukölln.

Nothing had changed in Dr. Landau's apartment. On the long wooden bench mothers with babies, pregnant young women, and retired workers still waited. Old Johanna still gossiped about the women's ailments and the doctor's eccentricities through the open kitchen door.

He opened the door slightly to the doctor's office. Dr. Landau, wearing the same smock with the familiar elbow patches, was thrusting a tongue depressor down a crying girl's throat. Only his beard had less red in it and more gray.

"No crying," he was saying, "no crying, no crying. . . ."

Georg tiptoed in and Dr. Landau looked up with quick recognition. He didn't interrupt his examination but, smiling broadly, continued to swab the child's throat. Only after he had disposed of the stained swab and washed his hands did he speak with his back still turned. "Very pleased to see you, Carnovsky. Very, very," he mumbled. "But the patient must come first, *nicht wahr?* It's the height of the season in Neukölln, grippe and diphtheria."

"I only stopped in to say hello," Georg said. "Is Fräulein Elsa in the laboratory by any chance? I'd love to see her."

"Elsa can be found anywhere these days but in the laboratory," Dr. Landau said, drying his hands on a towel. "At meetings, rallies, demonstrations—everywhere but in the office where I need her most."

Georg was deeply disappointed. He had spent the entire trip to Neukölln thinking up different ways of surprising her. He hadn't even telephoned to say he was coming, so eager had he been to make the meeting a surprise.

"In that case, Herr Doktor, I won't disturb you," he said. "I'll let myself out."

"Nonsense!" Dr. Landau said. "Wash your hands, put on a smock, and give me a hand. That way I can get through faster and we can talk in the meantime."

Tapping naked female backs, swabbing children's throats, and injecting serums, Dr. Laudau asked Georg about his experiences. "Well, Dr. Butcher, how did it go there with the glory and the heroism?" he asked with heavy sarcasm.

He assumed that Georg would take offense and braced himself for a heated debate about militarism, but there was no fight in Georg.

"You were right, Herr Doktor," he said quietly. "The front was a slaughterhouse and we were the butchers. There is nothing to tell."

Dr. Landau dropped his jeering tone and looked at Georg affectionately. He grew serious. What could a young physician do in postwar Berlin? Work in a hospital? Open an office in the Western sector? Or maybe become a specialist, as was the fashion?

As usual, he uttered the word "specialist" with distaste, for he despised the species. Peering down a patient's inflamed throat, Georg mentioned his preference for surgery. "The war gave me a splendid opportunity to operate," he said. "Years in a hospital couldn't give me such experience."

Dr. Landau sneered. "Cut! Cut! Cut! That's all everyone knows. Why shouldn't a young man become an obstetrician?"

Georg looked up in surprise.

Tapping a woman's blue-veined and distended belly, Dr. Landau explained. "After the annihilation the world needs rebirth. What could be better than giving life to new generations? After a harvest, one must sow. Sow, sow . . ."

Georg said nothing. Dr. Landau smiled blissfully. "The most enjoyable part of my practice is delivering babies. The birth of a human being is a great joy to me. When I'm called in the middle of the night to a delivery I run with pleasure."

When Elsa came home that night and saw Georg she flushed deeply. They stood there a moment, silently facing each other. Dr. Landau grew angry. "Are you ashamed in front of me? Kiss each other and get it over with!"

They kissed and kissed again.

"Good! Now let's eat!" Dr. Laudau said briskly. "Eat, eat . . ."

Supper consisted of a small dish of vegetables and a large pitcher of water. Old Johanna no longer wrangled with Dr. Landau about his aversion to meat. Few people in Berlin were eating meat these days. Dr. Landau chewed the inferior vegetables with gusto, noisily drank the water, and didn't stop talking. Elsa tried to contain him.

"Papa, let Georg get a word in. After all, he is the one who has come back, not you."

"You're as stupid as the rest of the Party!" Dr. Landau said. "All you can think about is war and heroism."

"I'm surprised to hear such talk from you, Dr. Landau," Georg said. "You no longer speak like a Party man."

"The war educated me," Dr. Landau said. "They are no better than the Kaiser's lackeys. They supported the war budget and I've washed my hands of them. I have only my medicine now—my old and true friend, medicine."

It suddenly occurred to him that it would be good if the young doctor became a permanent member of the household. At first it was a purely professional consideration. He no longer could cope with the heavy load of patients that had accumulated during the trying months following the war, and Carnovsky seemed to have developed into a competent physician. It was true that the front offered invaluable medical experience. Elsa was also potentially a skillful doctor. Working together, the three of them could show Neukölln a thing or two. From the purely professional aspect his mind wandered to more practical considerations, his daughter's happiness. That Carnovsky loved his daughter was something a blind man could see. He was a fine-looking, strapping young man and seemed fairly intelligent. Elsa also seemed fond of him. What prevented his becoming part of the family? Dr. Landau grew so inflated with paternal concern and so pleased with his solution that he almost put his thoughts into words, but suddenly he was consumed with self-loathing at his bourgeois attitudes. How petty and inane of him to indulge in scheming and matchmaking like some housewife! Furious at this unaccustomed plunge into middle-class sentimentality, he quickly rose from the table, took his cane, and started out on his customary nightly walk.

Elsa tried to tell him about the speech she had made to the workers but he cut her short. "Your place is here!" he roared. "You

belong in the office and in the laboratory. Leave politics to party
hacks who don't know anything else."

She tried to brush the crumbs from his beard but he turned away
and stormed out of the house. "It's my beard!" he shouted, "Not
yours! Mine! Mine!"

As soon as the door closed behind him, Georg drew Elsa close.
"How I missed you, redhead," he whispered, kissing the hair that
gleamed in the lamplight. "Now we can be together always. I'll talk
to your father tonight."

Elsa moved his hand from her face. "No. You mustn't do that,"
she whispered.

Georg let her go as if he had been slapped. "Is there someone
else?"

"Don't be ridiculous."

"Then what's wrong?"

"It's the Party. It takes all of me and leaves room for nothing else.
Nothing, do you understand?"

He would not listen to such nonsense. It was idiotic. Maybe before
the war he could have been taken in by such excuses, but not now.
She belonged to him. It was his right, his due. They would marry,
work together, and later, when they were more secure, she would
have a child.

He hugged her with all the hunger accumulated during the years
at the front. He wanted to subdue her, to make her his again.
"You are mine! Mine only! You belong to no one else!" he said
hoarsely.

He held her roughly and for a while she submitted to him. But
soon she tore free with unexpected strength. "No!" Her eyes were
wide open and spiteful, even contemptuous.

"Elsa, this isn't like you. Have you forgotten the day I went
away?"

"I have forgotten nothing," she said, her face relenting. "I remember it all and I don't regret a thing. But that doesn't obligate
me to marry you and be your slave."

"Is it possible that nothing remains from that time?" he asked.
"Not even a trace of feeling?"

She touched his face. She did love him, of course. She always had and always would, but she was determined not to settle for the empty life of a housewife and a nursemaid. New times were coming and there was important work to be done in Germany. The leaders of the Party had entrusted her with great responsibilities, the kind seldom offered a woman. There was even talk of making her a Party deputy. No, she wouldn't give up such opportunities for personal happiness!

Since force had no effect on her, he tried a softer approach. He spoke of his love, of his years of longing. He even offered to compromise his principles. Although he didn't approve of firebrands in skirts and was convinced that a woman's only happiness lay in marriage and children, he was willing to give in to her whims and not interfere with her outside interests. He was sure that one day she would come to her senses by herself. He was willing to give her his word that he would let her do exactly as she pleased if only she would agree to be his.

She remained adamant. She knew men and their need to dominate and subdue women. And she knew him, Georg, better than anybody. He needed a woman who would be a complete slave to him and a mother to his children. Hundreds of girls would be thrilled with this role, but not she. This was precisely the reason she would never marry. He should make an effort to understand her position.

He refused to hear any more. "Lies!" he shouted. "You don't know the first thing about love and you never will! Before, you loved microbes; now it's demonstrations."

Elsa began to kiss Georg and to teasingly muss his hair. "I love a silly, angry boy," she said as if to a child. "Don't pout, *Bube.*"

He pushed her away roughly. "I'm not your boy and I don't want to hear any more of this *Quatsch!*"

Again he felt debased by the stubborn, redheaded bitch who had used him, then discarded him. The thought that any woman could reject him after being his punctured his ego. Previously, it had been he who had done the rejecting; he whose attentions women had sought; he to whom they had submitted and wept after. Now he was the victim and it was a role he did not savor. "You'll live to regret this," he said, "but it will be too late then, Comrade Deputy!"

At the threshold he bumped into Dr. Landau coming back from his walk. Georg began to stammer to hide his agitation.

Dr. Landau smiled knowingly. "The old, old story that stays forever new," he quipped. "Don't be upset, my young friend. Smile, smile . . ."

Georg forced himself to smile.

"That's better. And take my advice and go into obstetrics. Not all women are crazy. Most of them do marry and have children."

Elsa tried to say something but her father cut her short. "To bed, you silly goose! To bed!"

He put his arm around Georg's waist and held him close for a moment. "If you like, I can give you a letter to Professor Halevy recommending that he take you on in his clinic."

Georg was impressed. "*The* Professor Halevy?" he asked.

"He's an old friend of mine, and although he's a specialist he's a great doctor and a decent fellow besides. A rarity, I might add, among specialists."

16

Following the war years, during which few women gave birth, Professor Halevy's Maternity Clinic on Kaiserallee was again crowded with patients. Although times were bad, jobs scarce, and currency worthless, the returning veterans seemed in a frenzy to marry and propagate. Professor Halevy's clinic was an old-established institution with an equally old and highly respected physician at its head. His abundant mustache and connecting mutton chops were of a type no longer worn except by old family retainers. They resembled two white tufts of cotton. His beaklike nose was traversed by brown and bluish veins. Only his black deep-set eyes retained a youthful sparkle that was incongruous to the worn and wizened face. His hands too were still firm and agile enough to conduct the most delicate operations on the highborn women who comprised the bulk of his practice. In many instances he had delivered the babies of three generations of a single family. His "children," now middle-aged, included some of the most important people in the city—high-ranking leaders in business, the professions, the armed forces, and government.

On the walls of his large office, the windows of which faced a garden, hung many photographs of the professor: alone during his early years of practice, and posing with other distinguished scientists at various medical conventions after he had achieved fame. Among the pictures were large portraits of two persons particularly dear to the professor. One was a photograph of an elderly man with thick hair and beard and a skullcap on the very tip of his crown. This was his father, a rabbi in a small town on the Rhine. The other was a portrait of a young man whose delicate features and eyeglasses did not go with his corporal's uniform. This portrait was draped in black. It was the last one taken of the professor's youngest son who had been killed at the front.

Although it was three years since the head nurse, Fräulein Hilda, had hung the crepe around the portrait, the professor was still unable to look at it without a twinge of sorrow. Even now, as he sat studying an X ray, his eyes darted to the face of his dead son. But hearing Fräulein Hilda's light tap on the door, he quickly looked away as if caught in some shameful act.

"Herr Professor, there is a Dr. Carnovsky calling," she said into his right ear, since his left one was deaf.

"Carnovsky? Who is he?"

"The Professor asked him to come." Head Nurse Hilda smiled as if to negate the fact that the old man's memory was failing. "He's the one with the letter from Dr. Landau."

"Fritz Landau? Oh, yes, of course! From Fritz. . . . Send him in, by all means, Fräulein Hilda."

Accustomed to click his heels in the presence of a superior, Dr. Carnovsky reacted automatically. But soon he reminded himself that he was face to face with a distinguished physician, not his colonel, and he bowed twice, once more than custom dictated, in honor of the elderly gentleman.

"Dr. Carnovsky, Herr Professor," he said deferentially, "Dr. Georg Carnovsky."

"Talk into my right ear, my young colleague," Professor Halevy said. "I'm quite deaf in my left one."

Georg flushed slightly. He wasn't sure whether the old gentleman had used the title "colleague" facetiously. But he crossed to the right side and repeated his introduction. Professor Halevy nodded.

"And how is dear Fritz?" he asked with a smile. "Still roosting in North Berlin and fighting the world?"

The affectionate reference to Dr. Landau put Georg more at ease and he briefly discussed the doctor's practice among the working people of Neukölln. Professor Halevy laughed with delight at his old friend's eccentricities. Even the snowy side whiskers and brown and bluish veins in his hawk nose seemed to be laughing. "A fine physician, Fritz. An excellent internist even in the old days. But he's completely mad. He only wants to fight the whole world."

When Georg began to describe his experiences at the front, the professor couldn't help glancing up at the black-draped portrait and feeling a terrible sense of loss. That so many had come back but not his son opened up old wounds inside him; but presently he reminded himself that envy was an immoral emotion, especially for a physician, and he fixed his eyes on the young man before him.

"What is the main reason you want to go into obstetrics, young man? Is it because you have an inclination for it, or is it because you were able to get a letter of recommendation to me from Fritz Landau?"

Smiling, Georg explained that Dr. Landau had planted the thought in him with his allusion to sowing after the harvest. The professor laughed again. "Good old Fritz! So mad and yet so very, very wise. How very aptly put: 'Sow after the harvest.' . . . That's precisely the case."

Georg enumerated his extensive medical experience in the field and the old man nodded knowingly. "That's all very nice but I don't like mass-production methods, young man. In my clinic I insist on slow and deliberate work . . . slow and deliberate. . . . Come in the first thing in the morning, I'll make the necessary arrangements."

It all happened so quickly that Georg couldn't believe his ears. He had actually been accepted for Professor Halevy's staff, something every young doctor in Berlin dreamed of! He thanked the old man warmly. The professor offered his hand, which was surprisingly firm and powerful for a man his age. When Georg was already at the door, he called him back.

"What is your name again? Carnovsky? I don't seem to recall such a name in our community."

Georg told him about his father, who had given up the chance to become a great rabbi in Poland to emigrate to the city of enlightenment and culture. Even now he continued to study the Torah and holy books that to him, Georg, were a mystery.

Professor Halevy listened with interest. "I am happy to hear that," he said, "because my own father was a rabbi and a Jewish scholar."

He pointed with pride to his father's picture and suddenly turned to the black-draped photograph. "And this is my late son, Emanuel, who was named after my father. He was killed in the war."

Georg offered his condolences. Suddenly Professor Halvey realized that he had done a very foolish thing in revealing such an intimate fact to a stranger and he was enraged at his indiscretion. *Senile fool! Dotard!* he castigated himself, and quickly transposed his anger toward the young man. "Good day!" he barked at Georg abruptly.

He felt a powerful urge to sting him. "You're a good-looking fellow," he said maliciously, "and young matrons prefer to be treated by a fop rather than by an old rooster. . . ."

17

Elsa Landau was elected to the Reichstag as she had predicted and launched her political career auspiciously.

Because she was young, a woman, and pretty, the reporters lionized her. But no matter how hard they tried to get her to comment on love, fashions, and marriage, she skillfully evaded these questions and stuck to issues of importance, thus greatly impressing the newspapermen with her forthrightness, her precise knowledge of government affairs, and of pertinent facts and figures. With her very maiden speech she made her mark in the Reichstag.

Her coppery hair agleam under the strong lights, her slim, youthful, and vital figure erect on the podium, she faced the hundreds of assembled men and scornfully derided those who opposed her Party's views. While the deputies on the left applauded vigorously, the members of the right-wing parties started their usual hooting and jeering. The abuse did not upset her; like a veteran legislator, she adroitly kept her attackers at bay, holding her own against the most experienced hecklers.

Just as she had skillfully dissected corpses in her student days, she now dissected the old and dead world whose dogmas and mores could no longer serve the new Germany. In her spare time away from the Reichstag she addressed mass meetings of workers, demobilized soldiers, and youth groups. She traveled throughout the land and was met everywhere by bands and banners. Neukölln was proud of its Comrade Landau. When the people now met her father on his customary strolls they greeted him warmly and often remarked:

"Congratulations, Herr Doktor, your daughter was mentioned in the newspapers again."

"Don't wear so many clothes, friends," he would scold them. "You're overdressed. Your bodies must have air. Air, air . . ."

He did not want to discuss his daughter's notoriety. He would not even go to the Reichstag to hear her speak. "Idiots! Loafers! Clowns! Numskulls!" he vilified the reporters who publicized his Elsa and made her name a household word throughout Germany.

But the one even more disturbed by the flood of pictures and stories was Dr. Georg Carnovsky. It was imposssible to avoid seeing or hearing mention of Elsa Landau. He saw her in the morning paper at which he glanced during breakfast. He saw her on the newsstands in the streets, on magazine covers in the waiting room of the clinic. Wherever he went she looked at him, her eyes mocking and triumphant.

At first he tried to erase her from his memory. To hell with her speeches and slogans—he had a position that every young doctor in Berlin envied. He would show her, that redheaded bitch, that although she had been his tutor in anatomy he would leave her far behind professionally.

He threw himself into his work with renewed energy; was the first to come and the last to leave.

The years in the field had not all been wasted. There, he had been forced to make swift decisions and to operate under the most primitive conditions, often without anaesthesia or by moonlight. He had performed tasks customarily relegated to nurses and orderlies. This experience now lent him an assurance that transmitted itself to the patients. They had confidence in his skill, they liked his brisk yet sympathetic manner. The nurses admired his speed and dexterity in changing bandages, dressing wounds, and other tasks at which nurses often outshine doctors. Professor Halevy himself took note of his competence and remarked more than once in front of the other doctors, "Nice work, Carnovsky, very, very nice."

Georg was pleased by the professor's praise and redoubled his efforts. Through hard work he hoped to blot out the memory of the one who had hurt him so badly.

But no matter how much he vowed to ignore the front pages that were filled with her speeches and opinions, because he had more important things to read—medical books and articles—he could not resist glancing at the newspapers. Each time he did this, the humiliation came flooding back and rekindled his hate toward her. But fanning the hate also stirred his love, a love that was deep and abiding, all the more so because it was unrequited.

Elsa's notoriety destroyed Georg's peace of mind, his appetite, and his sleep. One day, and hating himself for it, he went to the Reichstag when she was scheduled to speak. He was going there, he told himself, not only out of curiosity but also because of a secret urge to scoff at people who grew so enthused over a girl who had squirmed like a bitch in heat under his belly. Jammed in among the curious who crowded the gallery, he didn't hear a word of her speech, nor did he care to, for he had no interest in what she had to say. He could only recall the one night they had been lovers. Although years had gone by, he remembered every detail, her every gesture and yielding movement of rapturous surrender. He had the wild urge to stand up and announce to one and all that the Fräulein Doktor now being so noble and righteous on the platform had once been his bedmate.

He stood for a long time in the wings waiting for her to come out in order to tell her again what he had said so many times before. Neither her speeches nor the fuss being made over her impressed him. To him, she was the same Elsa and he had every right to call her his, as did any man a woman who has shared his bed. He was no schoolboy to be used and lightly cast aside. He was a man who demanded what was due him.

But when he saw her coming, surrounded by her fellow deputies who were listening to her respectfully, with flocks of reporters and photographers jockeying around her for position; when he saw how proud and blooming and happy she looked, he felt small and insignificant again and realized that whatever he had still hoped for was over forever. He turned back to his work with an even fiercer determination.

The nurses smiled and looked boldly at the brilliant and dedicated young doctor who was so obviously destined for success. But he ignored them all and they were insulted as only women can be when a man ignores them. Georg enjoyed their mortification, of which he was well aware. He took out his resentment of Elsa on her entire sex. He walked among the scrubbed pink and white girls with calculated indifference and watched as they followed his every move and made sure to keep out of his way. He was very strict with them when they assisted him. He savored their feminine resentment and agitation; their nervousness and clumsiness in his presence. The one who suffered most was the youngest among them, Nurse Teresa Holbeck.

From their very first meeting, when she had fumblingly helped him into his smock, blushed furiously, and grown even more distracted by his even, burning gaze, she had been dreading the time they would work together.

Georg, who was quick and impatient, shrugged irritably when she handed him a bottle of ether instead of morphine.

"Morphine," he said through tightly clamped lips.

She became so confused that she gave him a wad of cotton.

"Not ether, not cotton, but morphine," he said, biting off every word. "Morphine!"

When she was through, Teresa ran to her quarters and cried. She hated him for making her look so stupid.

But on the following day when he went back on duty she worried that he would pick another nurse to assist him. He didn't pick another nurse; furthermore, he even apologized for his brusqueness. "That's the front," he said. "War nerves. Surely you didn't let it upset you."

"Of course not, Herr Doktor," she lied, and blushed even more because of the lie.

From that day on, Nurse Teresa felt uneasy. Uneasy when Dr. Carnovsky chose another nurse; uneasy when he selected her.

The other nurses laughed at her. With the intuitive feminine ability to ferret out the subtle relationships between the sexes, they sensed her discomfort in the presence of Dr. Carnovsky and teased her about it unmercifully. Although she tried to deny it, she was a very poor liar. Her every emotion, every change of mood, showed immediately in the extraordinarily pale face and blue eyes.

Nor did she reciprocate when the other girls were malicious toward her.

Dr. Carnovsky began to tease her too, although he was correct and cold to the other nurses. Knowing that she could not stand his burning eyes, he stared at her until her cheeks were scarlet. At times he was patronizing to her, asked her about her boy friends, whether she liked chocolate, and which matinee idol she was infatuated with.

Teresa was insulted. She wanted to tell him that even if she was only a nurse she read serious books and went to the theater not to moon over actors but to enjoy the plays. There were many other things she wanted to tell him, but she was too timid to speak. And although his words were mocking and insulting and his manner infuriating, she longed to hear them. She loved to hear his deep voice, to see his face, to feel his piercing eyes looking at and through her.

"Is Herr Doktor making fun of me?" she asked, although the question was superfluous.

"Where did you get such innocent blue eyes in such bloodthirsty times, Nurse Teresa?" he asked suddenly.

She turned a fiery red from the tip of her cap to the collar of her starched uniform. If the ground had opened before her at that moment, she would have gladly jumped in.

18

No one in Professor Halevy's clinic, neither the doctors nor the nurses, could figure out why Dr. Carnovsky began to go out with Nurse Teresa Holbeck.

The young doctor's career had progressed rapidly. He was called in by Professor Halevy for consultations more often than any of the other doctors and more frequently entrusted with the most serious cases. The patients were thrilled when in the course of an examination they felt on their trembling flesh the touch of his warm brown hands that exuded so much life and vitality. It was predicted that he would go very far in his profession.

"What can he possibly see in her?" the nurses asked one another, full of wonder and jealousy.

Georg did not understand it himself.

At first, when Nurse Teresa showed her love for him so openly, he was more amused than intrigued. Like most young doctors who try to appear older and more sophisticated, Georg grew a mustache that, in his case, made his uneven white teeth seem ever whiter. He also affected a dignified tone when addressing his patients. To Nurse Teresa, however, he spoke as if to a child, and with undisguised drollery.

"How goes it?" he would ask. "Still blushing at everything?"

"No, Herr Doktor," she would say as her face began to glow.

Another time he would be paternal. "You are anemic," he would say. "You should take better care of yourself."

"What shall I do, Herr Doktor?"

"Drink milk. Or better still, get married. That's the best remedy
for anemic girls."

Teresa became one pillar of fire but Georg didn't stop.

"Don't you have any boy friends?"

"Oh, certainly. But nothing can come of it."

"Why not?"

"Because . . . because I don't love any of them, Herr Doktor."

"Love was something for our grandmothers, not for girls in our
time," he said brutally.

His cynicism stung her and made her unusually bold. "You
mustn't talk that way, Herr Doktor."

"Why not?" he asked innocently.

"Because . . . because love is eternal. Love is sacred!"

"You sound like someone in love. Who is the lucky fellow?"

She fled from him.

Ministering to her patients, she seethed with resentment against
the man whom she loved and who treated her so shabbily. The fact
that he had chosen her as the butt of his cruel humor hurt her. She
vowed to demand the respect that was due her as a lady or to avoid
him altogether. But it took just one word from him to again make
her stand by passively and listen to all his taunts.

More than once Georg determined to stop tormenting the bashful
girl. For one thing, it was demeaning. The nurses were beginning to
look at him knowingly. Their glances seemed to say: "We know
all about you, brother . . . we know that there is something going
on between you and one of us. There are no secrets here. . . ."

This could hurt an ambitious young doctor. What was it then, he
wondered, that drove him to torment the girl?

Fair and thin and antiseptic in the fitted uniform that made her
appear even more childish and unattractive, she looked more like
an ungainly schoolgirl than a woman. Her long neck was pale,
delicate, soft, and incomplete, as if still in the process of formation.
Her chin was just as indistinct. And her personality was as colorless as her appearance. She was without humor, always serious, devoid of any wile or artifice. Everything she did or said was artless. More than once Georg told himself to sever this relationship
that boded no one good. But the mere sight of her blushing and

hangdog expression roused in him some need to harass this pale and
submissive creature and he again resumed his teasing, bantering
tone.

One morning when she put a vase of blue cornflowers on his desk
he said, "Lovely flowers, blue and innocent as your eyes."

Although he said it in jest, she took it as seriously as she did
everything else and from then on put fresh flowers on his desk daily.
He grew so accustomed to them that when for some reason they
weren't there, he missed them and felt a kind of emptiness. And
soon he began to miss her as well, her paleness, her gentleness, the
quiet sound of her voice so full of frank adoration.

Mostly it was her docility that attracted him. After Elsa, Teresa's
pliancy was like a balm. He began to find in her qualities of which
previously he had been unaware. The soft neck no longer seemed
weak, but delicate and appealingly fragile. The weak chin now
seemed vulnerable and he wanted to lift it and to make her smile.
Even the lifeless, watery blue eyes acquired a strange warmth. *A
dear, funny thing,* he thought fondly, and continued to tease her
against his better judgment.

One time he had the opportunity to see her in a different light. It
had been a difficult night. A pregnant woman whom Dr. Halevy
had entrusted to his care had died in the early morning hours. Georg
had no cause to feel guilty. The woman had suffered from a heart
condition and Dr. Halevy had reluctantly accepted her as a patient
knowing that her chances of survival were slim and that her death
would reflect unfavorably upon the clinic. Georg had injected her
with serum, had kept her in an oxygen tent, and called on all his
medical knowledge to keep her alive. He was depressed by the tragedy, unnerved and exhausted. He snarled at Nurse Teresa when she
helped him take off his surgical gown and tried to console him.
"Shut up, for God's sake," he snapped at her.

Frightened, she turned to go. "Good night, Herr Doktor" she said,
to relieve him of the responsibility of taking her home.

He took her arm. "Come on, let's walk you home," he said. "I
must be with somebody . . . have a living person at my side. . . ."

Teresa had to half trot to keep up with him. Silently he smoked
cigarette after cigarette. When they came to Tiergarten, he sat down

on a bench. She seated herself at the other end. The sky was deep blue and full of stars. The Milky Way seemed particularly white. A star fell and suddenly vanished. Georg looked up at the vast network of silver islands amid the infinite ocean of darkness and brooded.

How cold, beautiful, and frightening the starlight was! Maybe this light that now fell upon his hands had begun thousands of years before and had raced at unfathomable speeds to finally settle on a solitary bench in a deserted park in Berlin. With the same sublime indifference it now shone on the waxlike face of the young woman who had died in his arms.

How trite and fleeting and insignificant was human life in comparison! But then again, who could tell? Maybe it was all up there just because the human eye saw it that way? For the woman in the morgue nothing remained, no stars, no light, nothing. Georg pondered the eternal mysteries of life and death. Suddenly he remembered that another human being was sitting beside him.

"What are you thinking on this quiet night?"

"I'm thinking that on such a night it would be good to die. . . ."

"Don't talk like a cheap novel!"

She looked at him with eyes as blue and enigmatic as the sky above. They were secretive and strange, as if from another world. He took her hand. "Your fingers are icy," he said idly.

For a moment she left her hand helplessly in his. Then she pulled his fingers to her lips and kissed them. He sat there, stunned. It was the first time a woman had kissed his hand. "What are you doing, child?"

Her eyes looked back at him so light and transparent they no longer seemed alive but like those in a primitive icon, fantastic in size and color.

"You're too solemn," he said. "You must learn to accept things as they are."

She lowered her head. "I know that it's hopeless. I know that I can never be for you. But I ask nothing of you . . . not one thing . . . You aren't angry with me, are you?"

"Why would I be?"

"Give me a child," she said. "I'll go away . . . I'll never bother you again. . . ."

He felt a great surge of pity for her. "Come," he said, taking her hand. "It's cold out here and you're feverish."

Instead of taking her to his place, which would have been so easy, he took her home. In the dark hallway of the solid Holbeck house he kissed her for the first time.

He thought all night about the quiet girl. How much courage it must have taken for her to speak to him this way.

From then on, they began to date openly. The other nurses were furious. "You'd think she's such a quiet one—can't put two and two together. But she managed to fool everybody. . . ."

When David Carnovsky heard that Georg was seeing a gentile girl he was stunned. Many fine matches had been proposed for his son. One of the men who worshiped at his synagogue was a Herr Lippman, a marriage broker who insisted that everyone call him "Doktor." Every Sabbath after services he walked with David Carnovsky and spoke of the advantageous matches being offered his son. While enumerating the traits of the prospective brides, he bent to Carnovsky's ear in a confidential manner and said with great conviction: "My dear Herr Carnovsky, such opportunities don't come up more than once in a lifetime. And mind you, the fathers-in-law I'm talking about are not Eastern immigrants but Germans as far back as you care to go. Take the word of Dr. Lippman on it."

He was telling the truth. Although David Carnovsky was Polish-born, which was a definite drawback, the long-settled Jews of West Berlin wanted to marry their daughters to his son who was a native German and a rising associate of the famous Dr. Halevy. They were prepared to give sizable dowries, to provide a fully furnished office on the Kurfürstendamm, and to completely forgive the young man's unfortunate Eastern origins. And because he had risen to the rank of captain, had a good bearing, and was a proper German officer and gentleman, the haughty young Jewish ladies of West Berlin were even willing to forgive his Semitic features, black eyes, and black hair, attributes they normally disdained.

David Carnovsky, himself an immigrant, felt very flattered and eager for this chance to gain entrance into the old established families of the Berlin Jewish community. Besides wanting the best possible future for his son, he also was thinking of himself. Since the war had ended, his business had suffered badly. His father-in-law in Melnitz was no longer alive and it had become progressively more difficult for David to earn a living. He had a daughter to raise and to marry off. He wanted Georg to enter high society not only for the advantages that would accrue to both of them, but also to improve Rebecca's chances of finding a wealthy husband.

"Do you hear, Leah?" he said to his wife with pride. "They're offering our boy the cream of Berlin society. I only pray that he has the sense to make the wisest choice."

"God be willing," Leah replied and raised her eyes piously to the ceiling.

Her husband's calculations aside, she yearned to see her son under a wedding canopy. She still burned with a passion for children, and although it was too late for her to have any more of her own, she looked forward to a brood of grandchildren from her son and from Rebecca.

One Saturday, instead of discussing the customary matches, Dr. Lippman told David Carnovsky about the gentile nurse Georg was seeing.

Carnovsky stopped and looked him over from his silk hat to his patent-leather shoes. "Impossible, Herr Lippman," he said, neglecting in his agitation to use the title "Doktor." "This is pure slander!"

Dr. Lippman laughed at someone daring to question his infallible knowledge of the comings and goings of Berlin's young Jewry.

"With a *shiksa* he's running around as God is my judge," he said with malice, shaking his shoulder-length curls. "What do you think of that, my dear Herr Carnovsky?"

Hurt and bewildered, David Carnovsky rushed home to share the terrible news with Leah. "A great satisfaction we've lived to enjoy from your son!" he blurted out the moment he had crossed the threshold and mumbled the customary "Good Sabbath." "He's gone and picked himself a *shiksa,* your darling little boy."

As usual, he stressed the fact that it was *her* son whenever the boy did something to upset him. And as usual when he was angry, he forgot his grammatical German and reverted to homely Melnitz

Yiddish. Leah tried to console him and herself as well. "It's nothing but a passing fancy. Can't a young man have a little fun? As soon as the right match comes along he'll drop her. Mark my words."

But her husband wasn't satisfied. "I've always had trouble from that boy and I always will," he said. "I know him too well."

Never had David Carnovsky complained about his Sabbath meal as he did that day. The fish was too peppery, the chicken too tough, and the tea smelled like the Melnitz bathhouse.

"Fetch me the ablution water," he snapped, leaving his food.

Immediately after the ceremony of ushering out the Sabbath and without even changing to his weekday costume, he went to his son's bachelor apartment near Kaiserallee to thrash things out. Not finding him at home, he went on to the clinic and paced for hours in the quiet street until he saw him coming out hand in hand with a young woman who barely reached his shoulder. David's heart began to race. No, Lippman had not deceived him. For a moment he studied the young woman at Georg's side. He was anxious to see what charms she possessed to cause his son to abandon both this world and the world to come. She had nothing of the great beauty about her, neither the charm, the grace, nor even the carriage that would lead a young man astray. And finding her so plain and colorless, David grew even more angry and disgusted.

"Georg!" he called out sharply.

Georg turned and saw his father standing in an agitated state and wearing his Sabbath outfit. "Is anything wrong with Mother?" he asked anxiously.

David Carnovsky nodded curtly to Georg's companion and in his finest German explained that his mother was well, but that he had a most urgent matter to discuss with his son and hoped the esteemed lady would excuse him for taking him away. Georg remembered that he had not introduced the two and proceeded to do so. David Carnovsky barely heard the girl's name and quickly mumbled, "Very nice to meet you. Good night."

"Good night, Herr Carnovsky," Teresa said apprehensively.

For a long time the father and son walked silently along the broad, deserted sidewalk. David Carnovsky kept reminding himself to be calm—above all to control his temper, as the sages advised in the holy books that regulated his existence. But with the very first word he forgot all his good intentions and felt the blood mount to his head. His rage showed in his blazing eyes and jutting, patrician Carnovsky nose.

"Tell me one thing. Is that the *shiksa* with whom you've been running around all over town?" he asked through clenched lips.

Georg felt his cheeks burn at the word.

"Father, let's not talk about it in the street," he said. "And please keep calm. I don't see any reason for you to be so upset."

"Maybe you don't," Carnovsky shouted, "but I do!"

Georg saw that it was up to him to remain calm and reasonable. But he and his father were too much alike. The moment he started talking, he too lost control and soon they were locked face to face like images in a mirror, despising in each other what they despised in themselves.

"Don't talk to me in that tone of voice, Father," Georg said. "You seem to forget I'm no longer a boy. I'm a doctor!"

"I'm not impressed with the quacks you work with!" David Carnovsky said.

When they walked into Georg's apartment and David Carnovsky saw the girls's photograph next to his Leah's, he exploded.

"Has it reached the point where you put that *shiksa* on the same level with your mother?" he screamed.

For two whole hours they wrangled bitterly, neither giving an inch. David Carnovsky demanded his son's promise to break off with the nurse. Excellent matches with girls from the best homes in West Berlin had been proposed. He, David, had spent a fortune to educate him and he wouldn't allow Georg to ruin his parents, his sister's chances for the future, and his own career because of some *goyish* bedpan-handler. If he were involved in an affair with the wench, he should break it off and behave like a son of David Carnovsky's should. "The devil wouldn't take her," Carnovsky said. "She'll find some other idiot to bleed! She's not worth sacrificing both this world and the next."

Georg was furious. Pacing through his apartment, he saw signs of Teresa everywhere—her photographs, the cushions she had sewn for him, the curtains and the tablecloths. He glared at his father with undisguised resentment. He wouldn't allow anyone, not anyone, to dictate his private life, to marry him off for cash. If it were a matter of money, he would see to it that his father got back every pfennig he had laid out for his education. But he would not allow himself to be bullied. And he certainly would not allow his girl to be insulted.

David rose to his full height to appear even more formidable. "And what do you intend to do about it? Slap me? Throw me out of the house?"

At midnight, when Georg still refused to promise to do as his father asked, David Carnovsky took his coat and got ready to leave. "In that case, choose between the *shiksa* and your father," he said. "It's either she or I."

He would not allow his son to help him into his coat, even though he was too excited to get his arms into the sleeves. "Make up your mind! Make up your mind!" he growled, and stomped out.

When he reached Grosse Hamburger Strasse he stopped to look at the sculptured features of his idol, Moses Mendelssohn. "Rabbi Moshe," he said to him silently, "our children are going away from us . . . and their way leads to apostasy. . . ."

The philosopher looked back at him with a wise, mournful face while drops of rain ran like tears down his chin and stooped shoulders.

19

The first person to come to Widow Holbeck's mind when her Teresa told her that she loved a Jew was the optician, Max Drechsler.

To her, he represented the whole species: dark, nervous, talkative, clever, and sinister. One night, when the young doctor unexpectedly brought Teresa home, Frau Holbeck's first glance bore out her preconceived impression of him and his kind. The thing that struck her light blue eyes first was an overpowering blackness. The hair, the brows, the lashes, the mustache, above all, the large and burning eyes, introduced an exotic kind of swarthiness into a house accustomed to pallid people. The fact that Georg was an obstetrician and looked at her so piercingly embarrassed her further and she imagined herself standing naked before him, looking like the wax dummy in Herr Drechsler's window; and for no appreciable reason she crossed her arms in front of herself to hide her sagging, cushiony breasts. What also concerned her was that he had come on the day she regularly did her heavy cleaning. She was so upset that the pince-nez kept slipping from her nose and she had to keep readjusting it. Suddenly it occurred to her that she hadn't greeted her guest properly. "I am pleased to make your acquaintance, Herr Doktor," she said, and held her hand out for him to kiss. But Dr. Carnovsky merely shook it. She asked politely, "It looks like it will be clearing after the terrible weather, don't you think, Herr Doktor?"

She waited for his response so that she could get on with serving the refreshments, but he was too busy reading the inscriptions sewn into a tablecloth. Finally she decided that she would serve the refreshments anyway.

Setting out her very best china, she launched a discussion about the ersatz coffee and the poor quality of pastry, but again Dr. Carnovsky did not respond. He greedily drank the coffee, chewed the cake with gusto, and wiped his black mustache and lips on the embroidered napkin. Widow Holbeck was horrified.

Finally she decided to talk about his profession. "Herr Doktor's practice is large?" she asked diffidently, hoping that this time he would answer.

He spun around quickly. "I work like a horse. It seems that all Berlin is making babies. They're speeding up the production that lagged during the war. But the product is a poor one, a cheap imitation of the real thing."

Georg's description of matters sacred to her made Frau Holbeck blush, and Teresa's eyes beseeched him to behave more prudently. He stopped smoking furiously and spoke about infant mortality, birth control, the venereal diseases the returning veterans had brought back, and even about the high rate of illegitimate children born while the men were away at the front.

"Oh, dear God!" Frau Holbeck kept saying in embarrassment.

Without knowing why, she led him into the hall to a large photograph of an elderly man in a carved gilt frame. "My late husband, Herr Doktor," she said, sighing heavily.

Georg looked at a stout *Bürger* with a round face whose every last wrinkle and blemish had been touched out by the photographer. In his high-collared shirt and Sunday coat he looked very solid and respectable. His bulging eyes stared out with bovine earnestness. Frau Holbeck stood back with folded arms awaiting some comment, but Georg only mumbled, "Very nice. . . ."

Actually, he was disturbed that Teresa's father should look so much like a cow. Frau Holbeck was relieved to hear a dog's bark followed by a man's sharp whistle. "That will be Hugo coming back from his walk," she announced and rushed out to meet her son.

Georg heard their voices in the hall arguing, hers pleading, his stubbornly resistant. It was impossible to make out the words but Georg guessed that he was the cause of the argument.

Soon a shepherd dog came loping in and sprang with great joy first at Teresa, than at Georg. His master followed, without any joy whatever—a tall, gaunt, colorless scarecrow.

"Oberleutnant Hugo Holbeck," he drawled, clicking his heels.

"Dr. Carnovsky," Georg said without clicking his heels.

They looked each other over, hated each other on sight, and each knew that the feeling was mutual.

"It looks like we'll be having some decent weather at last, *nicht wahr?*" Hugo said in a Prussian accent, but Georg ignored him and the situation grew more strained.

"Dr. Carnovsky was a captain," Teresa said, trying to make Georg seem more palatable.

Hugo clicked his heels again as was proper when meeting a fellow officer. "So?" he mumbled.

Of course it was a trifle better than meeting civilian scum, but to a line officer a military doctor, no matter of what rank, was no better than a chaplain. Only a stupid girl could get excited about some enema-giver. He wouldn't call him *Kapitän,* damned if he would. When Georg added that he had served on the Eastern Front, Hugo lost all desire to talk to him. Like most veterans of the Western Front, he considered the Eastern campaign a picnic.

His poker face showed a trace of life when Georg offered him a cigarette. He bent stiffly, accepted the cigarette, and was as effusive with his thanks as if the cigarette were some kind of treasure.

"Egyptian," he said authoritatively after one puff.

"The only kind I smoke," Georg said pointedly.

"A German Oberleutnant can't afford Egyptian cigarettes these days," Hugo said just as pointedly and stretched out a long, booted leg.

The pungent smoke cheered him somewhat and he began to describe a town in France that his company had taken in such a hurry that the inhabitants had fled, leaving everything behind. In one abandoned house he had found a whole pack of Egyptian cigarettes and cigars. Havanas they had been! . . . He had had a goddamn good time with those Egyptian cigarettes!

He rambled on in his Prussian accent and laughed often at things that weren't in the least funny. His language was dry and colorless.

Each time a word failed him he cursed. Georg smoked impatiently and stared at Hugo's stiff legs.

"Excuse me, Herr Holbeck," he said, interrupting the interminable story about the Egyptian cigarettes. "It looks as if you've picked up a nasty case of sciatica at the front. In the left leg, isn't it?"

Hugo's pale face flushed crimson. He hated to be reminded of this inglorious souvenir of his years in the trenches. The fact that the swarthy, sharp-eyed kike had diagnosed his condition so quickly enraged him. Besides, he didn't like his war stories interrupted. Instead of listening, this snot-nosed Christ-killer was trying to impress everybody with his goddamn medical knowledge.

"Ach, it's nothing!" he said bravely. "It doesn't pay to talk about it."

But Georg preferred to talk about it instead of the front. "I often found cases of this in the field," he said with a purely professional interest. "And I must say I've had pretty good results treating the condition."

Hugo was sure that this Jew was only looking for a patient and he let him know in advance that he was wasting his time. "A German Oberleutnant is lucky if he has enough for a pack of lousy cigarettes these days," he said, "let alone for doctors."

He awaited Georg's reaction. But Georg lashed out suddenly at the Oberleutnant's left leg and struck him sharply between the knee and the pelvis.

Hugo Holbeck screamed out in pain. *"Donnerwetter!"*

"That's what it is," Georg said, "and it's badly neglected too. It's a thing you can't neglect for too long."

For a moment Hugo considered punching Georg in the mouth, but the doctor seemed much too bulky and sure of himself. *"Quatsch!"* he finally growled. "Forget the whole thing!"

Georg ignored him and spoke directly to Teresa and her mother. Frau Holbeck would be able to treat her son at home with the medicine that he prescribed and Teresa could also massage the leg, which would be very beneficial. For the first time Widow Holbeck felt a semblance of warmth toward the young Jewish doctor. The fact that he had diagnosed her son's condition so quickly impressed her greatly.

"Herr Doktor is so kind," she said.

As soon as he left with Teresa she cleared the table and thriftily gathered the crumbs that she lifted to her lips with a finger tip. From a mother's ever practical viewpoint she knew that her daughter would have a good and secure future with this quick and clever Jew, and she decided to make the best of it.

"A nice young man," she remarked to Hugo. "Don't you think so?"

"A lousy kike," he said and turned back to his dog.

Although she was amazed that her daughter would even consider defiling a bloodline that went back for generations, her always practical side took over. Like most Berliners she had a high opinion of Jewish doctors. She was also sure that like all Jews he made a lot of money. Naturally, she would have felt differently if her husband were still alive and if a dowry were available for Teresa. But under the circumstances, Teresa was quite lucky to become a doctor's wife, even though the doctor was a Jew.

She also knew that Jewish husbands were generous, did not beat their wives, didn't drink or run around. In such bad times, when most of Germany's young men were out of work, like her Hugo, Georg Carnovsky's virtues outweighed his faults, which really boiled down to the fact that he was Jewish. Having accepted the inevitable, she also tried to win over her son. "Consider our situation, Hugo," she said. "We don't have a dowry and he doesn't care about one. Would you want your sister to give up her chance for a good life just because you didn't like her husband?"

"In these goddamn times a German Oberleutnant can't make demands," he said. "A German officer can only look, listen, and keep his mouth shut."

His face was as pale and expressionless as a mask. His light blue eyes did not flicker and only a thin whistling gave indication that he was alive.

20

Despite David Carnovsky's strict warnings, Leah went to see her son and his new bride in their first week of married life.

Although she was angry with him for the sorrow he had caused her and her David, although she could not forgive him for denying her the pleasure of seeing him under the wedding canopy at the synagogue, how could she turn her back on her own flesh and blood?

She knew that she was not the only one in the city with this problem. Some children had even gone so far as to convert. But despite what her David said, she didn't equate what Georg did with outright conversion. And parents had no right to renounce a child, no matter what. This only made matters worse.

Therefore she waited until David went to Hamburg on business and, swearing Rebecca to secrecy, made ready to visit Georg's new apartment. Rebecca fairly wriggled with anticipation.

Energetic and temperamental like all the Carnovskys and with a strong sentimental streak besides, Rebecca was thrilled both at the prospect of seeing Georg and of disobeying her stern father, particularly with her mother's collusion.

Leah, as usual, felt nervous at the prospect of meeting a stranger. She couldn't imagine being close with a gentile daughter-in-law. With a heavy heart she rang Georg's doorbell. *Should she say Mazeltov?* . . . She nervously pressed the bouquet of flowers to her breast. But the moment she opened the door and the light-eyed girl inside sprang at her with cries of love and affection, tears of relief began to run down Leah's cheeks.

"Mother!" Teresa cried, and embraced her.

Rebecca kissed her brother and sister-in-law. "Call me Sister, Teresa," she begged. "I never had a sister and now you'll be mine."

From then on Leah visited the young couple at every opportunity. Rebecca was even more enthralled with Teresa than was her mother. She needed an outlet for her passionate nature, for the love that nearly consumed her. Her outbursts of passion grew so violent that at times Teresa became frightened by them.

When Teresa became pregnant, Rebecca identified so closely with her sister-in-law's symptoms she seemed ready to give birth herself.

Each time David Carnovsky learned of his wife's latest visit to the couple he grew more enraged that his orders should be so flagrantly disobeyed. Leah told him how good and sweet the girl was and how she followed the customs of Israel, but he would not listen to her. "All these things have no bearing on it!" he roared. "It's the principle of the thing! What he has done is only the beginning, the first step to complete conversion!"

"Bite your tongue!" Leah cried. "Don't let such words even pass your lips!"

"The future is no mystery to the scholar," he said smugly. "Your female mind can't conceive of what's going on, but it's no secret to me."

Seeing that she could not sway him, Leah appealed to his friends. She complained to Dr. Speier about how wrong it was for a father to renounce his only son, and he agreed with her. "My dear Herr Carnovsky, that's life," he said to David after the Sabbath services. "You are not the only one in Berlin with this problem. The best thing is to accept it philosophically."

But David no longer believed in wise men in top hats. Since Dr. Speier had failed him during a time of crisis, he had lost all faith in him both as a person and as a man of God. He often thought these days about the Melnitz rabbi who had been responsible for his leaving Poland for the light and wisdom of Berlin. He was not so positive now about the vileness of Melnitz and the spirituality of Berlin.

Deeply hurt by the "enlightened" Jews of Berlin, David Carnovsky was even more disappointed by its gentiles. During the war and now in the postwar period he had suffered much degradation at their hands, even though he spoke the purest German and kept himself immaculate. He was often mocked and insulted, particularly when he went around collecting rents from his tenants in Neukölln.

Lawless bands of youths now roamed the capital's streets screaming for Jewish blood. They included not only the usual loafers and street brawlers but also university students from good German homes. They swarmed over streets named for Kant and Leibnitz and promised dire revenge against the traitors to the *Vaterland*.

David Carnovsky felt deceived by the city of his idol, Moses Mendelssohn. The Melnitz rabbi had been right after all. The ways of the philosopher led only to evil. It began with enlightenment and involvement in the gentiles' world; it ended with apostasy. As it had happened with Moses Mendelssohn's descendants, it was happening with his. If Georg would not himself convert, his children surely would. Perhaps they would even become anti-Semites, as converts often did.

He was even more worried about Rebecca, who now spent all her time with her gentile sister-in-law. Contemptuous of female reasoning in general, he was deeply concerned that his daughter might be tempted to emulate her brother. "I don't want her to go there!" he shouted to his wife, pounding his fist on the table. "She is an impressionable child. She's sure to stray from the path of righteousness and become a gentile too!"

Leah begged him to be easier on their children. She reminded him of how Ruth the Moabite had become a good Jewess but David was in no mood for parables. "Woman! Ruth went from Moab to Israel. Today, Israel goes to Moab! Do you understand?"

She did not understand and David Carnovsky bore his grief alone. They were all leaving him, his friends, his children, all those dear to him. Sitting alone in his large book-lined study, he realized that he was the last of a generation. No one would bother with the vast library he had so painfully accumulated. The whole great Jewish world that had taken thousands of years to evolve, the Torah, the

wisdom, the customs, the scholarship for which countless Jews had
bled and sacrificed their lives, all would be forgotten and wiped away.
After he died his treasures would be sold to a junk dealer or burned.
Brooding these dark thoughts, he became terribly afraid.

His grief drove him to visit Ephraim Walder. The old man was
already well up in his eighties. His skin was like the parchment
upon which he eternally scribbled. His hands seemed covered with
moss. But the mind was as keen and alert as ever and he greeted
David Carnovsky warmly. "Welcome, Reb Carnovsky, welcome!
What's new in the outside world?"

"Nothing good, Reb Ephraim. It's a sorry world out there these
days."

"It never was a better one, Reb Carnovsky," Reb Ephraim mumbled from out of a beard now almost green with age.

David disagreed. In his day, children respected their elders. Today
a father was little more than a clown.

Reb Ephraim chuckled. "Fathers have never been satisfied with
their children. It's a long time since I was a boy and I recall how my
father, may he rest in peace, used to tell me how disrespectful I was
and how in *his* day things had been different. Even the Prophet
Isaiah complained about it: 'I have raised them and they have sinned
against me. . . .' "

From rebellious children Carnovsky turned to the bad times that
prevailed, the privation, the hunger, the unrest that was sweeping
the land, and the hatred, particularly against the Jew. Reb Ephraim
was not surprised. He had lived through many such periods. So had
it been, so it was, so it would always be.

But David Carnovsky could not accept his disappointments so
calmly and philosophically, nor could he make peace with the fact
that his only son had exchanged him for a gentile slut. Reb Ephraim
remained unruffled.

"You are not alone, Reb Carnovsky. Consider my daughter. She
sits all day with her nose buried in those trashy novels. She suffers,
but she does not even know why. Nor did Rabbi Moshe of Dessau
derive any satisfaction from his own children. They were the first to
abandon the faith."

David sighed heavily. Perhaps the Hasidim were right in denouncing German enlightenment? Maybe the Melnitz rabbi was more exalted than Rabbi Moshe? It was easy to see what the "enlightened" brand of Torah had created in *this* country.

Reb Ephraim waved a frail hand. "Life is a terrible prankster, Reb Carnovsky. It loves to play tricks on people. German Jews wanted to be Jews in the house and gentiles in the street but life turned this ambition completely topsy-turvy. The fact is that we have become gentiles in the house and Jews in the street."

"Then perhaps Rabbi Moshe Mendelssohn is the guilty one?"

Reb Ephraim would not agree. The rabble always corrupted the ideas of a saint.

"No, Reb Carnovsky," he concluded, "the sage must remain a sage and the fool a fool. I wrote about this very thing in great detail and if you have a moment, I'll read it to you from my manuscript."

With boyish agility he scampered up the ladder, leafed through the notebooks lying on the top shelf, and located the exact pages he wanted. "Those rogues!" he scolded the mice that were chewing up his manuscripts. "There is no protection against them!"

"But you have a cat, Reb Ephraim," Carnovsky said, pointing to the feline curled up on a chair, her ears cocked as if listening to her master.

"Since Methuselah, may he rest in peace, passed away I can't get my hands on a decent cat," the old man sighed. "Even though he was old and blind he showed those scoundrels no mercy. He was a saint, the way he sacrificed himself in behalf of my books!"

Although parts were missing from the manuscripts, devoured by the "scoundrels," Reb Ephraim read the missing sections from memory.

"What do you say to that, Reb Carnovsky?"

Carnovsky had no argument with the old man's logic, but he seriously doubted that his writings could effect a truce between gentile and Jew. His, David's, outlook was more practical than that of Reb Ephraim, who isolated himself in the house. He had seen them, the gentiles, in war and in peace, in all their cruelty and ferocity, and they were filled with a thirst for blood—especially for that of the

Jews. And this did not only include the lower classes but students and educated people as well. But why even speak of gentiles when one's own children made no effort to understand their parents? Of what value were these manuscripts into which Reb Ephraim had poured so much effort and scholarship and years of arduous labor? " 'For whom do I toil?' " Carnovsky quoted.

Outside, Dragonerstrasse boiled liked a cauldron. Adding to the already crowded conditions were the thousands of homeless and exiled Jews from the other side of the border. They had come here from Galicia, having lost their precious King Franz Josef; from Poland, Rumania, Russia—from wherever the war and the carnage had driven them. Many Jewish prisoners of war from the Russian army had remained, having no place to which to return. Polish Jews bound for Palestine but unable to obtain visas had stayed on. Deserted wives seeking to rejoin husbands in America but lacking the fare had remained. They all somehow eked out a living, crowded the small kosher restaurants and every inch of the neighborhood's living space. The police made frequent raids, seeking persons without proper credentials, and the old quarter throbbed with hustle, bustle, and strife. Brokers arranged deals, peddlers bickered, beggars clamored for donations, policemen blew whistles, money-changers bartered foreign currencies, and pious Jews prayed with fervor. The phonograph in the bookstore downstairs wailed the latest tunes from America, blending cantorial chants, theater melodies, and cloying duets. But Reb Ephraim heard nothing, saw nothing, and remained completely aloof. He read page after page to David Carnovsky. The cat ignored the mice busily gnawing away at the books and listened avidly. Each time Reb Ephraim came to some favorite interpretation, a particularly novel and ingenious one, his face lit up, his eyes sparkled, and the years seemed to fall away, leaving an eager schoolboy.

"Remarkable . . . Truly remarkable," David Carnovsky said with genuine awe.

When Teresa felt her pains coming regularly, she checked into Professor Halevy's clinic where her husband himself prepared to deliver their baby. The members of the staff were shocked. "Aren't you afraid, Teresa?" the nurses asked. "Usually women don't trust their husbands in such cases."

"Well, I do!" she said, indignant at the thought that she lacked faith in her own husband.

The other doctors huddled around Dr. Carnovsky. "Are you sure you won't get nervous?" they asked, with the intention of making their overconfident associate exactly that.

"I'm sure," Dr. Carnovsky said.

Resentful of his assurance, they shrugged with an air of impending disaster. But old Professor Halevy rebuked them. "A doctor who lacks the confidence to care for the lives of his dearest ones has no right to care for that of strangers," he said. "Consider that, my young colleagues . . ."

Georg grew nervous only after he had safely delivered Teresa of a boy. Like most fathers, he was pleased that his first-born had been a son. His only concern was for his parents, particularly his mother. Although she was overjoyed to again have a baby to hold and to fondle, she began to look into her son's eyes with silent entreaty.

On the first day he was sure that he could hold out forever. He would not allow a barbaric ceremony to be performed on his son just because thousands of years before Abraham had promised his God to circumcise all his male offspring. What possible connection could there be between himself, a doctor in the heart of Western Europe, and a patriarch with his ancient customs and blood rites?

On the second day he was less adamant and more perturbed by his mother's searching eyes, but he still refused to give in. If the baby were Jewish on both sides, perhaps he would agree. But in this case there was the other side to consider. True, Teresa would have said nothing. She loved him and would never say anything to contradict his wishes. But he refused to place her in such a position. Just because he was a Jew and she a Christian he refused to force his will on her and her family.

On the third day Georg could no longer avoid Leah's face. Although she said nothing, her eyes spoke volumes. "It's in your hands," they seemed to say. "You can either make your mother happy or shorten her years."

He was worried about her. Perhaps she would not be able to bear the disappointment? And if he had a responsibility toward his wife, he surely had one toward his mother. True, the situation was an unpleasant one because it ranged Jew against gentile. But it also had to do with the fact that he wanted to court favor with his gentile wife and her family, and this too smacked of Jewish submissiveness and sense of racial inferiority that a truly free person must avoid.

On the fourth day a new concern entered Georg's mind besides the one about his mother's health. Now a father himself, he began to see his own father in a different light. Sentiment struggled with cold reason. Although his father had treated him unfairly and renounced him, it had not been from bad intent but because he was a stubborn and old-fashioned man and he, Georg, had to make an effort to understand him better. The little ceremony that, incidentally, was medically beneficial, might serve to win over his father and lead to a reconciliation. He would show him that a younger man could be more sensible and tractable, and that an egg could indeed be wiser than the hen.

On the fifth day he even considered going to his father and inviting him to the circumcision. This would disarm the old man completely. But now the Carnovsky stubborn streak asserted itself. No, this was too much. It wasn't he who had instituted the quarrel. Besides, he was the host and it was up to his father to come and offer his congratulations. If he did come, he, Georg, was prepared to give in to him on everything and to make him happy. If he did not come, then that would be that.

For two more days he tortured himself. Would his father come or wouldn't he? On the eighth day, when his father still gave no sign of coming, Georg circumcised the child himself without a rabbi, a quorum, or a celebration.

"Poor baby," Head Nurse Hilda said as she brought the screaming infant to Teresa's bed. "How did you ever have the heart to do it, Herr Doktor?"

"It didn't hurt him," Georg snapped. "I managed pretty well with it!" Filled with self-contempt because he had given in, he took his anger out on Head Nurse Hilda.

Now when Leah Carnovsky fondled the infant she felt a true sense of possession. She begged her husband to reconsider. "Stubborn man, what else do you want from the boy? He did it for you, after all!"

David Carnovsky knew that she was right but he could not bring himself to give in. The very fact that he was in the wrong kept him from admitting it.

To compensate Teresa for having made a Jew of her son, Georg named the boy Joachim, after her father. Teresa added the middle name of Georg, and, just like his names, the boy seemed a mixture of his two strains. His eyes were blue and his complexion fair like the Holbecks, but his brows and hair were raven black and the nose prominent and stubborn like a true Carnovsky.

21

The large Berlin hotels patronized by princes, diplomats, and opera stars for generations began to cater to a new breed of guests—Americans who kept their hats on in the lobbies and were not above dropping a friendly arm around a bellman's epauleted and gold-embroidered shoulder. It amused these tourists to exchange a single dollar bill for millions of marks and to flip them casually to servants, messenger boys, and waiters, each of whom outshone the other in the splendor of their uniforms. It also amused them to sleep and to make love in beds previously occupied by princes, princesses, and world-famous opera stars.

The smaller hotels were occupied by other foreigners—ruddy-cheeked, corpulent Dutchmen; elegant, swarthy Rumanians; huge Letts; fair-haired Czechs, Estonians, and Poles; boorish Russian commissars; and darting, black-eyed Jews. They all came with one purpose—to take advantage of a city whose currency had lost all value. Mostly the strangers bought houses—massive, solid buildings that had been constructed to stand for centuries.

The most crowded of all the hotels was the Franz Josef, owned by Reb Herzele Vishniak of Brod, which stood in the old secondhand clothes dealers' quarter. Here several guests were assigned to each room, even two strangers to a single bed. Immigrants from Galicia and Poland stopped here; Jews in short coats and in not-so-short coats, all eager to catch a bargain in a city gone economically mad. Although hotel rates were cheap all over town, they preferred Reb

Hertzele Vishniak's strictly kosher establishment where they felt so completely at home.

Among those who sold their houses was Widow Holbeck. The money she collected for rent was absolutely worthless. She could not even do a day's shopping with a month's rent receipts and she would come home from market with a light basket and a heavy heart. At first she sold her household possessions to keep going. Her oldest steins with the cleverest inscriptions, her collection of colored glass, her crystal—everything ended up in the antique shops that seemed to spring up like mushrooms throughout the city. When the food ran out and Hugo demanded money for cigarettes—several packs daily—she found a buyer and for two thousand American dollars in cash she sold her houses with all the columns, towers, cornices, angels, balconies, and carvings; houses that her husband had erected to serve the Holbeck families forever. She cried when she signed the sales contract. "If your late departed father only knew . . ." she wailed to her son.

Hugo remained as apathetic as ever. He only wanted a dollar from his mother, a single banknote that he promptly exchanged for a pile of marks in the street and used to have a rousing good time for the next twenty-four hours. For the single dollar he drank wine in a tavern, bought good cigarettes, shot targets in a shooting gallery, rented a saddle horse, and later even picked up a lady on Kurfürstenstrasse and took her to a hotel. The last of the money he gave to the taxi driver who brought him home dead drunk. The only thing besides the army for which he now had respect was the green American dollar that could provide a man with so much happiness.

Also among those who sold their houses was David Carnovsky. His tenants would not even hand over the worthless marks for the rent. The only one who paid now as Dr. Landau. The others merely sneered at the bearded landlord who spoke the overly precise German of a foreigner. "We aren't speculators and profiteers!" they said, implying that he and his kind were.

It became a painful task for David to take care of the house; outside of humiliation it brought him nothing. Nor was his lumber business doing any better, and for the first time money became a problem in the house. Each time Georg sent an envelope filled with money, David Carnovsky returned it unopened. "I don't sell *my* birthright for a mess of pottage!" he shouted.

When, week after week, he found himself short of money, David located a foreign buyer and sold his house for currency that still had value. He sighed deeply when he surrendered for a pittance property into which he had sunk such a fortune.

Although he had good reason to do so, Solomon Burak did not complain about the hard times.

He sold his goods for money that was worthless, money he did not even bother to count; but what motivated him was not the thought of profits but the hustle and bustle, the excitement of moving merchandise and keeping things humming. It amused him to watch the women tearing the goods from one another's hands, goods they did not even need. Each time she rang up a sale Yetta sighed heavily. "Solomon, we're giving away goods that are worth something for junk. Soon we'll be left with empty shelves and a bale of toilet paper."

"Don't fret, Yettele," he said, "as long as there's action I'm happy. . . ."

He had little choice but to sell like all the other merchants; but rather than complain about it he took pleasure in the atmosphere of frenzy, like a small boy who enjoys the excitement of a fire. Just as before the war, when he had entertained his relatives from Melnitz, he now addressed his Yiddish aphorisms to his gentile help, who were already accustomed to his humor. "A million more, a million less," he said, wryly dismissing the chaotic conditions with a quip.

"How much?" a customer would ask, fingering a corner of the goods.

"Five," Solomon Burak would say, lazily omitting to add "million."

"How much did you say?"

"Ten!"

"I thought you said five."

"Fifteen!" Solomon would say.

Actually, it did not matter, but it irked him to have to haggle

with people for money that had no value. At other times he urged
customers to buy shrouds. "Take it, my dear lady," he would say to
a bewildered housewife. "Soon they'll be going up in price. . . ."
He did it to entertain his sales force but the women would take
him seriously and buy the shrouds.

Yetta could not stand his antics. "Your father is crazy!" she said
to Ruth, who stood by the register and helped her mother take in the
worthless money.

Ruth did not even hear her. Although she was already married to
a man whom her father had selected and was herself a mother, she
still suffered the pangs of rejection and unrequited love. She knew
that her husband was a decent man who deserved her love and she
even tried to force some sort of response, but it was an impossible
effort. She existed in a kind of mist. She did not know what she
still expected—perhaps some sort of miracle. Her father often
chided her gently when she grew preoccupied and stared into space
as if communicating with invisible phantoms.

"Cockadoodledoo, Ruth, where are you?" he would crow to rouse
her from her reverie.

She did not hear him nor did she always hear when her husband
spoke to her.

Squat, stolid, and completely attuned to the world, Jonas Zielonek
was the exact opposite of Ruth's father. The son of a merchant from
Posen, he had charted his life with deliberation and followed this
blueprint with dogged determination. He had saved a great deal of
money; he had avoided the follies and excesses of youth; he had
indicated his precise choice of a wealthy and respectable bride to the
matchmaker, and just as deliberately entered into a partnership with
his father-in-law. His domestic life followed the pattern of his conduct at the store. He did not care for his father-in-law's crude remarks in Yiddish to the German salesgirls, nor did he allow any
familiarity from those who tried to draw him into a flirtation to
advance their positions. Like a good husband, he tried to discuss with
his wife every detail of conditions at the store and in the business
world in general. He expressed his concern over all the money he
had invested, including his sizable dowry, going down the drain in

the perilous times that prevailed. Ruth heard him out without comprehension.

"What did you say?" she would ask, lost in her musings.

Jonas Zielonek felt that it would be better if his wife took more of an interest in affairs that concerned them both, but he said nothing. He knew that when things could not be helped it did no good to talk about them. Nor did he respond when his father-in-law played the fool and carried on in the store. Not being an especially pious man, he attended synagogue only on the Days of Awe, but he fervently begged the Almighty to keep him from poverty and ruin.

Only God, Jonas had calculated after much deliberation, could save him now from disaster.

22

As usual when a serious operation was scheduled, the atmosphere in Professor Halevy's Maternity Clinic was charged with tension. Doctors and nurses in crisp white uniforms swarmed through the corridors, careful to walk on tiptoe. Orderlies silently wheeled patients on stretchers. Maids scrubbed the linoleum floors without making a sound. Women in labor, sensing the tension, asked nurses its cause, but the well-trained nurses did not reply—the rules strictly forbade any discussion of hospital affairs with patients.

The strained atmosphere even affected the elderly uniformed doorman and the reception clerk.

The excitement was highest in Professor Halevy's office, which adjoined the operating room. Head Nurse Hilda, her ripe curves nearly bursting from the uniform, knocked timidly on the professor's door and waited until it had opened a crack. The old man glared at her with his bulging black eyes. "For God's sake, I told you not to disturb me!"

Almost in tears, Head Nurse Hilda wrung her hands. "I beg your pardon a thousand times, Herr Professor, but it's His Excellency himself, Herr Ambassador. He begs a word with Herr Professor. . . ."

"Excellency or no Excellency, I can't see anybody now," the old man growled. It was his custom, once the family had agreed to an operation, to keep everyone out, even the patient's husband. From that moment on the patient belonged only to him, her physician.

"That idiot!" he raged about Head Nurse Hilda. "That stupid cow."

"It's not worth getting upset about, Herr Professor," Dr. Carnovsky said.

"Who said I was upset?" Professor Halevy demanded. "I am always calm! Especially before an operation!"

But he was far from calm and he knew it. And the knowledge of it upset him even more.

For the past twenty-four hours the patient, whose first pregnancy this was, had been unable to be delivered of her child. Not that this was the first such case in Professor Halevy's career. In more than fifty years of practice he had encountered just about every kind of situation. But this case was unusual in that the woman was the only daughter of an ambassador from a major power, and the professor felt a double responsibility—not only for his own medical reputation but for that of the *Vaterland*. Besides, he felt a particular fondness for the patient, as if she were his own daughter.

Young and fragile, with slim, delicate hands, a freckled face, and ringlets, she was more a hoydenish schoolgirl than a woman. Even in her final months of pregnancy she had behaved like a frivolous child, expressed her affection for the old man and kissed his cheek, leaving upon it the mark of her lipstick.

But small as she was, her belly was distended and Professor Halevy grew progressively more concerned as the pregnancy developed. The final twenty-four hours made him extremely anxious and his staff loyally shared his anxiety, especially Georg Carnovsky, who had been assigned to the case and who had not left the patient's side and had done everything to ease her agony.

"Doctor, am I going to die?" she asked Georg each time the pain subsided and she was able to speak again.

"Everything is coming along fine. You'll only have to suffer a little more pain," he said, gently.

"Don't let me die, Doctor!" she said, smiling through her pain and clasping his hand as if trying to hold on to life.

She reached for him convulsively each time the pain returned. "God!" she screamed in the first great suffering of her pampered existence.

When, after twenty-four hours, she still would not give up the child, Professor Halevy summoned Georg to his office. "We can't get by without a Caesarean," he said angrily, as if it were somehow Georg's fault. "And without delay! We can't afford to wait another second. . . ."

"Unfortunately not, Herr Professor," Georg agreed.

As usual, Professor Halevy took a long time to arrive at a decision, but once having made it he put it into effect with an energy that belied his years. Nurses boiled instruments, sterilized bandages and cotton. Doctors scrubbed up, put on gowns, caps, masks, and gloves. Everyone worked with silent, nervous dispatch. Georg prepared the patient for the operation.

"Doctor, is my condition serious?" she asked, frightened at all the preparations. "Am I going to be put to sleep?"

"Calm yourself, my dear, calm yourself," he said and again checked her heart and pulse.

Professor Halevy issued order after order. "See to it that everything is just so," he warned his assistants. "It must be done calmly and quickly! Above all, calmness must prevail!"

Professor Halevy insisted that calmness was the prime factor during an operation but this time he disobeyed his own edict. For some time now he had been feeling a weakness in his body, a sense of debilitation, and a kind of dizziness. For a while Professor Halevy had thought to consult his old schoolmate, Professor Bart, about these symptoms, but he was reluctant to divulge his condition to his friend.

They had never been more acute than during the twenty-four-hour period of the ambassador's daughter's confinement. The dizzy spells came one after another; the silver streaks plunged him into a terrifying darkness; the drawing in his temples gripped him like a vise, and his fingers cramped repeatedly.

Professor Halevy experienced trying moments during the preparations. He washed briskly and splashed cold water on his face. He also secretly took a pill for his nerves. He summoned Head Nurse Hilda to help him with the gown and the scrubbing up. When everything was ready, he glanced up at the picture of his father, the rabbi, as if beseeching him to stand by him in his hour of need. Then, walking with a firm, quick stride, he marched into the operating room. With a nod of the head he inquired of Georg if everything was in order. With a nod of his head Georg indicated that it was. The professor looked around. Everything seemed right—the doctors, the nurses, the instruments, the balloon filled with oxygen, the blood donor standing by in case a transfusion was needed. The patient lay under a mask, anesthetized.

With extraordinary effort to keep calm, Professor Halevy picked up the scalpel, the familiar old knife that had served him so well through the years, and prepared to make the Caesarean incision for which he was famous. But just then he felt a drawing in his right temple, a cramp as painful as if a vise were crushing his skull, and at the same time a brilliant flash blinded him and plunged him into total darkness.

The first to recover was Georg Carnovsky. Like an officer assuming command in the field, he took charge. "Carry him to his office and call Professor Bart!"

Several of the doctors caught Professor Halevy and carried him out.

"Watch her heart!" Georg told a doctor, indicating the patient. The doctor took over Georg's place; Georg moved up to operate. "Nurse Hilda, remain in place and stay alert!"

With a slight movement of her starched, fleshy body, Head Nurse Hilda acknowledged that she was awaiting orders.

"Calmly and quickly!" Georg said, quoting Professor Halevy's familiar admonition, and he picked up the scalpel.

Soon the baby's first squeals were heard and Dr. Carnovsky's bloodshot eyes blinked with relief.

When he came out of the operating room and Head Nurse Hilda stripped off his rubber gloves and mask, great drops of sweat dripped from his nose and chin. "Wipe my face, will you? I'm completely drenched," he said, and walked into Professor Halevy's office where Professor Bart sat by his friend's side, stroking his hands. "Lie still, you old fire-eater!" he said when the old man started to get up. "Don't you dare move!"

Georg quickly reported the success of the operation and Professor
Halevy smiled crookedly. Georg noticed that the right side of his
face seemed slack and covered with drool.

Although the staff tried to suppress the news, it leaked out, and
the newspapers described the dramatic moment when Professor
Halevy suffered his stroke and Dr. Carnovsky took over the operation. Reporters and photographers beleaguered the clinic and clamored for stories and pictures.

Professor Halevy was taken to Professor Bart's clinic. He never
resumed his practice and Georg Carnovsky took his place. His name
became known in the most important homes in the capital, particularly among the wives of the foreign diplomats. "He's simply divine!" the mother of the young woman who had been saved gushed
to her friends.

"And what an attractive man," the bored young wives agreed,
looking at his picture. "With a doctor like that it would be a pleasure to get sick."

"He looks too Oriental," the older and more jaded matrons said
sourly.

Among those who sent their congratulations was Dr. Elsa Landau. She wrote a brief note on a sheet of paper bearing the Reichstag
letterhead. Georg Carnovsky tore open the envelope with shaking
fingers. *So she's finally recognized me!* he exulted as he read and reread the strong masculine script. And the old longing for her came
surging back more strongly than ever.

23

Little Joachim Georg, who was called Jegor for short, a contraction of his two given names, stood in the garden of his father's house in Grunewald and sprayed the neat lawn and the rounded beds of flowers bordered by a small white fence. The short, evenly trimmed grass that looked like Karl the gardener's military haircut was already soaked and the excess water spilled out into the street. Teresa Carnovsky's Teutonic mind could not stand the disorder and she begged the boy to stop watering.

"Jegor, you're making puddles in the street!"

"Jegor, you'll snap the flowers!"

"Jegor, you'll get your feet wet and catch cold! You just got out of sick bed. Don't you remember how easily you catch cold, Jegorchen?"

Jegorchen remembered but he kept on soaking the lawn. Although he did not like being sick, he slopped his feet in the puddles to spite his mother. Teresa looked anxiously at the boy. He was tall, much too tall for five, and too thin. His long legs were mere bones, his neck too slight to support the heavy head. He caught colds easily and was always the first to come down with the childhood diseases. He had had them all already. No one could understand why he was so prone to sickness. The house stood in the finest section of town and was isolated from all sources of bacteria and infection. The family enjoyed every comfort. As soon as Dr. Carnovsky's practice had begun to boom and he started earning important money, the first thing he had done was to buy a house in Grunewald, a large house

with many windows and a garden surrounded by a picket fence.
Teresa Carnovsky had a maid and a handyman who took care
of repairs and of the garden and drove the family car. He also sold
his blood when Dr. Carnovsky needed it for transfusions. Little
Jegor had all the sunshine and fresh air a boy needed. He seldom
came near other children because he was timid and shy. His mother
raised him according to all the rules of scientific child-rearing. She
gave him the exact amount of milk and vegetables prescribed
in the manuals—not one ounce more or less. She also kept him
out in the fresh air as indicated and put him to sleep at the precisely appointed time. His father examined him often and kept a
close watch over him. He washed his hands thoroughly after leaving
his patients and checked his son over while playing with him to
conceal the reason for poking and tapping. Neither of the parents
could understand how the boy caught diseases that were usually confined to the workers' quarter in Neukölln. As is common in such
circumstances, each side blamed the other for the boy's delicate condition. Dr. Carnovsky was convinced that his son's susceptibility to
infection was inherited from the mother. It had been his professional
experience that people with thin skins and pale complexions were
more prone to sickness. Hugo Holbeck was just as thoroughly convinced that the boy's frailness was inherited from the Jews who,
although they might be excellent physicians, were weak and sickly
and could not bear hardships or heavy work.

"What else can you expect when you cross a pure-blooded Holbeck with a goddamn Carnovsky?" he said in his bored, apathetic
tone to his mother.

But she was confused. "Look at Georg. He is as strong and
healthy as a peasant."

Hugo tried to educate his mother. "It has nothing to do with him,
it's his race," and he repeated for her some theories he had recently
picked up in Schmidt's Bavarian Brauhaus on Potsdamer Brücke
where ex-officers and university students congregated. And if she
needed further proof, he told her about the only Jew in his company
during the war. He was a funny little runt with glasses, fat and
completely inept. "They are all alike, those stinking Jews," he assured her.

Frau Holbeck thought about Georg, who was tall and husky and had eyes like an eagle, and she was puzzled.

The only one who did not blame anybody for her son's delicate constitution was his mother. She knew that it was the war that was responsible. She had lived through many trying times while it had lasted and often did not have enough to eat at a time when she needed it most, during her adolescence. The years afterward were just as critical and she knew from the other mothers that postwar German children tended to be sickly and anemic and prone to infection. She poured gallons of cod-liver oil down the boy's throat to give him strength but little Jegor spat it out all over the costly Persian rug in the dining room. He also spat out any medicine his mother gave him and the milk she tried to force him to drink. He was able to vomit at will, even things he had eaten hours before.

"Mutti, I'll throw up!" he threatened whenever she refused to give in to one of his tantrums.

He was afraid to go quite that far with his father, but he did not allow him to force his will upon him either. He would not swallow the medicines his father prescribed or accept the spoon he was constantly attempting to force down his throat during his interminable bouts of sickness.

"Say ah, Jegorchen," Dr. Carnovsky urged.

"Mooooo!" the boy said spitefully, and kept his lips clenched.

He also loved to spite Grandmother Carnovsky when she came to visit. She leaped at him with hot maternal passion, kissed and embraced him, kept him prisoner on her lap, and enumerated the things a good boy must do. He must eat a lot, drink plenty of milk, and not be such a stick of macaroni, so green and pale, but be round and rosy as an apple.

"Joy, gold, diamond, little swallow, treasure!" she panted in her ripe Melnitz Yiddish.

Although he did not understand, the boy was amused by these endearments as he was by her broken German.

"*Schwelbele, feigele,*" he imitated her, ". . . *oy-tzer!*"

Teresa could not stand his impudence ."Ach, dear God! How can you make fun of your own grandmother? Excuse yourself, Jegorchen!"

But Jegorchen did not want to excuse himself and went to a corner of the courtyard where Karl the gardener sat and repaired things. He was forever fixing something—the car, or the wiring, or a piece of furniture. His shirt sleeves were always rolled so that his muscular tattooed forearms were exposed. The pockets of his brown velvet trousers were filled with hammers, pliers, and screw drivers and his cheeks held nails that he passed out one at a time and hammered into things.

"Good day, Karl!" Jegor greeted him each time they met, although it might be dozens of times daily.

"*Guten Tag,* Jegorchen!" Karl said, his mouth full of tacks, and pounded his hammer as if keeping time with some secret drumbeat.

His Neukölln-accented speech was sprinkled with juicy slang words that delighted Jegor. Because his mother specifically forbade him to use them, they held a special appeal for him. He also loved to watch Karl's brawny arms, to see the large veins and supple muscles twist and leap with every movement, like things with a life of their own. There was no end to the questions Jegor wanted to have answered. "Karl, why do you have a scar across your eyebrow?"

"Because a goddamn Frenchman bayoneted me during the war," Karl said with his mouth full of nails.

"Why?"

"Because there was a war, *nicht wahr?* We were fighting."

"And did you bleed?" Jegorchen asked timidly. He was terrified by the sight of blood.

"Bleed? Not half I didn't!" Karl said carelessly. "But that's nothing. I shoved my bayonet in his belly and laid him out like a stuck pig."

Jegorchen gasped, his large blue eyes drawn up in horror. "Oh, that must have hurt!" he cried.

Karl waved his tattooed arm. "One mustn't be afraid of blood," he said. "Otherwise how can you become a soldier and serve the *Vaterland* when you grow up?"

"Of course," the boy said proudly, "and I'll carry a sword, like Uncle Hugo."

Next to Karl, Jegor liked Grandmother Holbeck best. She came

from time to time and took him out for a few hours. She did not
speak so strangely as Grandmother Carnovsky did nor did she kiss
him so hotly and fuss over him. On the way to her house she took
him into a church, knelt, and told him to kneel too. The church was
a pretty place with colored windows and statues and when one spoke
the words echoed back from all the columns and carvings.

Jegorchen liked his Uncle Hugo too. To begin with, he was tall,
even taller than Father. And he let him look through his field
glasses, through which things could be made bigger or smaller. He
also let him play with his revolver that shot real bullets and told
him stories about the front.

It was then that Hugo came to life. His eyes blazed, his cheeks
colored. He got so excited that he forgot he was talking to a
child and mentioned things no small boy should hear. Like most
weak boys, Jegor loved to hear tales of strength, fighting, and heroism. He enjoyed looking at the photographs of Uncle Hugo in his
uniform, high boots, epaulets, and spiked helmet. Jegorchen bragged
about his father who was an officer in the war too, but Uncle Hugo
was disdainful. "*Quatsch*. What does being an army doctor mean?"
Jegorchen was disappointed in his father, who was not a real officer,
and grew prouder than ever of his Uncle Hugo.

"Why don't you still wear the spiked helmet and carry the sword,
Uncle Hugo?" he asked.

He had touched on Hugo's sensitive spot and the tall man became
apoplectic. "On account of the goddamn, hook-nosed—"

He suddenly remembered that he was talking to a child, and to
Teresa's child at that. He also reminded himself of his own status
and he declined to give his nephew an explanation. "You're too
young to understand, boy. You'll find out all about it when you grow
up."

Jegorchen was eager to grow up so that he might understand all
the things he was too young to know. But now he wanted to know
only one thing more—would Uncle Hugo ever again carry a sword
and wear a spiked helmet?

"It's hard to tell when, but the day will come. It surely will
come!" Uncle Hugo said, his eyes far away.

Jegorchen was glad that someday Uncle Hugo would again be an Oberleutnant. "I'll be a lieutenant too, Uncle Hugo," he said with pride, "just like you!"

"Not a doctor like your father?"

Jegorchen grimaced. To him there was nothing more repugnant than being a doctor. Everything seemed like more fun—to be a chauffeur, a messenger boy, even a chimney sweep. How disgusting to push spoons down people's throats and to give out horrible-tasting medicines like his father!

Uncle Hugo smiled at the boy and cautioned him not to reveal any of their conversations to his father.

"Of course not," Jegorchen said, proud to share a secret with his uncle. Grandmother Holbeck also warned him to say nothing about the church visit. "Why not?" he asked. "Doesn't Mutti want me to go to church?"

"Oh, yes. But your father might become angry about it."

"Why?"

"Because he may not like it."

"Why wouldn't Papa like it?"

Grandmother Holbeck started to reply, checked herself, and took the same way out as did all adults. "You'll understand when you grow up. In any case, you mustn't tell anyone about it."

Jegor said nothing, although he would have liked to. But he thought about it after his mother had put him to bed. He did not understand adults. He knew that he had a grandfather in the city; he had seen his picture in his father's office. But he had never seen him in person.

"Why doesn't Grandfather Carnovsky ever come to see me?" he asked his father.

"You'll see him after you grow up," his father said.

But Grandmother Carnovsky came often. She brought very sweet cookies baked with raisins and almonds. But how funny she talked! And she made him say such queer things before he could take a bite. He said them but he did not understand why. She told him that he would after he grew up. At the same time she also warned him not to say anything about it to his parents.

Indeed, Jegor wanted to grow up quickly. He stretched his legs as

far as he could in his bed as his mother had told him so that he
might grow up in a hurry. But no matter how much he stretched, he
remained a little boy. His father was seldom at home. He left for the
clinic early in the morning and afterward visited patients. Often he
did not come home at night and Mutti told Jegor that he was with a
sick lady. When he did come, he played with him, lifted him high,
and rode him piggyback on his shoulders.

But this did not happen often. The worst of it was that he was
always trying to examine him and look down his throat. In the middle of a game he would suddenly hold him in his lap, look into his
eyes, his ears, feel his neck and every bone in his body separately,
and order him to show his tongue.

Jegor hated to have his father poke things down his throat and
to look into his eyes and ears. What did he see there? His father
ran his fingers down his ribs a few more times and suddenly put
him down.

"Go for more walks with Mother and play with children instead
of hanging around in the garage with Karl," he said. "You hear me,
Greenworm?"

Jegor did not like to be called Greenworm, nor did he enjoy playing with other children. All they wanted to do was run around and
chase one another. He could not keep up because he tired too easily.
They also made fun of him and called him "Stork." Others called
him "Gipsy" because of his black hair. He was bashful, distrustful,
and even afraid of them. He refused to shake hands with the boys
and girls in the park when his mother urged him to join in their
games.

"Be friendly, Jegorchen," she told him. "A child must be with
other children."

"No," he said, although he would have liked very much to play.

Something kept him back, restrained him from going to them.
The children sensed this and avoided him. He watched them from a
distance and was envious, and this made him hate them. Best of all
he liked to be with adults, especially with the servants. He liked to
visit Liesechen, the maid in the kitchen, but his real favorite was
Karl. Karl knew lots of stories, especially about the sea and ships
that he had sailed in his youth as a stoker. Jegorchen could not sit

still during lunch. He was eager to run outside to Karl. He even
wanted to go to him after dinner, but his mother would not allow it.
She insisted that a little boy must get plenty of sleep and she put him
to bed. And Jegorchen lay there in the dark and was afraid.

He imagined all kinds of figures, horned devils that Liesechen had
described to him, long-haired witches with pointed chins who rode
on brooms, sorceresses in red cowls who slid down chimneys during
the night. He closed his eyes to avoid seeing the terrible creatures
but the tighter he squeezed his lids, the thicker they came charging
at him. They danced and caroused and ran in and out of the iron
oven door. On this door were carved figures of chimney sweeps, one
with a ladder, another with a coil of rope and a broom. Jegorchen
watched them come to life, climb down from the door, and cavort in
a frenzied dance. They laughed aloud and stuck out their tongues at
him—long scarlet tongues. He drew the blanket over his head to
hide from them, but they tore at the blanket and clawed at his
shoulders with sooty hands. He screamed, "Mutti! Mutti!"

When his mother came in he was completely drenched. He threw
his arms around her and held her close. "Mutti! Mutti! They wanted
to put me in a sack!"

Teresa wiped away the sweat from his face and comforted him. A
smart boy must sleep, not lie awake imagining all kinds of foolishness. A smart boy was not afraid because there were no such things
as witches and devils. She would put on the light and show him that
there was nothing there. And it was just as silly to be afraid of an
oven door. Let him watch as she opened it. Inside, it was black, but
that was as it should be because smoke made things black. Only a
foolish boy would believe that spirits flew in and out of a chimney.
A smart boy went to sleep as soon as he was put to bed and was not
afraid. He could look for himself and see that there was nothing
there. "Isn't that so, Jegorchen?"

"Yes, Mutti," he said. "When the light is on I don't see anything,
but as soon as it's out I see all kinds of things."

Teresa laughed. That did not make sense. It was just the other
way round. When it was light you could see things, when it was dark
you could not. That was why lights were used in the first place. She
tried to prove with logic that there was nothing to fear in the dark.

She covered him carefully, kissed his eyes, and quietly left, putting out the lights.

"Sleep, sleep, go right to sleep!" she said firmly. "Good night!"

"Good night, Mutti," Jegorchen said, watching the last rays of light vanish. As soon as they faded, the terrible figures came back. The shapes on the carved ceiling came to life and began to dance. Although the lamp had been turned off, it continued to give off fiery rays of light. Circles whirled in front of his eyes—big circles, small circles, tiny ones. They spun so fast that they seemed to be playing tag. Jegor was ashamed to call his mother again but he was terrified of the darkness that was so full of sounds and movement. His fear finally put him to sleep curled up in a ball and with the blankets drawn over his head. But even in his sleep the figures kept coming from every corner of the room, every crack in the door. All the dead soldiers about whom Uncle Hugo talked came together with torn, bloody bodies, without heads or legs. They swarmed around his bed. Now he was fully grown, like his Uncle Hugo. He wore high boots, a spiked helmet, and carried a sword. He was taller than everybody else and a lieutenant. The goddamn Frenchmen charged him, each of them a freak, a monster. He led his company in an attack and wreaked terrible havoc with his sword. They fell, one by one. But suddenly one leaped at him, a black man from Africa, the kind Uncle Hugo had described to him. He rolled the whites of his eyes, held a giant knife between his teeth, and leaped at him. Jegorchen held up his sword but the Negro caught the blade in his bare hands and snapped it. He took the knife from between his teeth and tore at Jegorchen's throat. "Yah!" he screamed like the wind whistling through the chimney.

Jegorchen sprang out from under the blanket, threw open the door, and bolted into his parents' bedroom. "Mutti!" he shrieked. "Papa! Help! It's so dark!"

This was now an old story to his parents. They switched on the lights in their room and Teresa smoothed the fear from the boy's face. Georg took Jegor into his bed and berated Teresa for allowing their son to listen to stories about devils and evil spirits. He was always busy and did not have time to supervise the boy, but she should have taken care of these matters and cautioned the servants to watch their tongues. He did not want this kind of rot discussed in his house. If he heard one more word of it, if Liesechen ever again so much as mentioned Satan and imps, he would send her packing. Putting on all the lights in the house, he took his son's hand and led him from corner to corner, demanding to see the evil spirits that Jegorchen claimed were everywhere. If he would show him just one, he would grab it and cut off its tail. Jegorchen laughed at his father but would not go back to his bedroom. He would rather sleep in a corner of his parents' bedroom, even on the floor if need be, but he would not go back to his room because he was afraid the terrible black soldier would come back to get him. It was only this night that he wanted to spend here—only this one.

Dr. Carnovsky put him down beside Teresa and the boy fell asleep immediately.

"Poor child," Teresa murmured, watching her son's bony arms stretched out on the blanket.

"It's those bloody war stories Hugo tells him," Georg said. "How many times have I told you to keep the boy away from that numskull!"

"Oh, dear Jesus!" Teresa sighed, and put out the light.

The couple lay silent but did not sleep. They were terribly worried about the child. They knew that he was not thriving, but neither would admit it. They each felt that, considering their age and physical condition, they should have had a much healthier, brighter child. They could not understand why Jegor was so restless, jittery, and obsessed with fantasies. Naturally, each blamed the other. Teresa was resentful because Georg did not spend enough time with the boy. A child needed to be with a father, especially such a sensitive child as Jegor. He did not obey her but he would listen to his father. Being a doctor, Georg should also consult his colleagues about the boy, famous child specialists whom he knew. She would have done it herself but she was afraid that he would be offended at her lack of faith in his own ability. She also believed that Grandmother Carnovsky's passionate embraces and frenzied devotion harmed the boy. She taught him all sorts of outlandish Hebrew prayers and expressions and stuffed him with cookies and candy between meals, disrupting the schedule that she, Teresa, had laid down according to the latest discoveries in scientific child-rearing. No matter how diplomatic she was, she could not stop her mother-in-law from pressing sweets on the child. She had even considered discussing it with Georg but she held back in fear that he would misinterpret her motives.

Georg also lay there with his eyes open and brooded on the differences between his son and himself. Although he had not been scientifically brought up or watched every minute, he had grown up healthy and happy and afraid of nothing. All the boy's fears had been put into his head by Liesechen with her devils, Hugo with his war stories, and Grandmother Holbeck with her saints and miracles. Although it was supposed to be a secret, he knew that Grandmother Holbeck took the boy to church and filled his head with religious nonsense. This made a strong impression on a sensitive child and helped to bring on nightmares. More than once he had vowed to speak to Teresa about it but he hesitated because he was afraid she would misinterpret his motives. He had warned his own mother not to fill the boy's head with Hebrew prayers because he did not believe in such things. She was angry with him, but he had not been afraid to speak up because she was his mother. It was different with his mother-in-law. She was a stranger to him and it was up to Teresa to tell her.

The devil take it, a man can't be free even when he knows how, Georg mused angrily. One was always saddled with annoyances, unwelcome relatives, strange superstitions, customs, and traditions. The heritage of generations trailed behind one like rags one could not cast off. A father could not be the master of his own child. He could not protect it from its family, its environment, its heritage. No matter how diligent one was in driving superstitions and taboos from the house, they sifted back through the doors, the windows, the chimney. From thoughts of environment Georg's thoughts drifted to those of heredity. It was obvious that Jegorchen took after his mother more than after him. Although he had the black Carnovsky hair, his skin was pale and translucent and quick to blush, like Teresa's. His height and gawkiness were also Holbeck traits and Georg was skeptical about these characteristics. He found people of this type not only sickly and of poor recuperative powers, but oddly prone to fantasy, superstition, and romanticism.

He looked at the sleeping boy. His lids were closed, his wasted arms awkwardly sprawled over the blanket, his forehead beneath the lank, dark hair was pale and lined with bluish veins. A wave of pity came over Georg. What was his son thinking? What went on in that childish brain? What visions appeared there when he was asleep? What fears haunted him? As a surgeon, Georg knew every tissue and cell of the human brain. But what was it actually, that small pile of matter, blood, and veins? Why did it differ so radically from person to person, encompassing every degree of brilliance and stupidity, coarseness and spirituality? Why did it bring joy and fulfillment to one, fear and torment to another? There lay his son, his own flesh and blood. Although he was a mere baby he was already burdened with dark thoughts and morbid fears. Whose blood called out within him in the night? Whose torment disturbed his sleep? Maybe it was some distant ancestor of the Holbecks, a serf punished by his master, a knight, or a mercenary who had fought for wages in foreign lands? Or perhaps it all came from his side, the Carnovskys? A leaseholder on whom the Polish squire had set his dogs, a rabbi who lived in fear of Gehenna? . . . Heredity was a mighty force, Georg knew. Often traits cropped up many generations apart. Sometimes they even stemmed from a distant branch of the family—a brother or a sister of a great-great-grandparent. Man's semen was full of hidden forces—good and evil, wisdom and stupidity, cruelty and mercy, health and sickness, joy and sorrow, genius and insanity, ugliness and beauty—all borne along in a tiny drop of liquid propelled by some mysterious force. This was nature, his colleagues explained, but what did it actually mean, this word? He picked out a book that claimed to explain the mystery of life. He was eager to know what Mendel had to say on the subject. It was years since he had read him. The monk's brilliant interpretations, accompanied by accurate proofs, fascinated Georg but did not explain the basic riddle. Nor were the philosophical books that he kept in the bedroom any more helpful. They did not provide clues as to what went on in the mind of a five-year-old boy who was afraid of the dark.

Georg laid aside the books and felt a deep compassion for his sleeping son who had cuddled up to his mother for protection. A vague apprehension about the boy's future aroused his paternal concern. He lay awake into the early hours of the morning, worrying and seeking possible answers and solutions.

24

The drawing room of the newspaper publisher, Rudolf Moser, on the West Side of Berlin was filled with the city's cultural and social elite—modern poets, internationally famed film and stage stars, correspondents of foreign publications, Reichstag deputies, musicians, artists—anyone currently in the public eye. The guest list almost always included some exotic personality—a dusky prince anxious to learn European customs, an Indian dancer, a wild-haired theosophist or notorious sorcerer. One of the regular guests at the weekly Saturday-night gatherings was Dr. Georg Carnovsky, whose attendance was assured by his dramatic rescue of the ambassador's daughter. Each time Frau Moser introduced him she made the same joke. "Meet Dr. Carnovsky, Berlin's best-known lady cutter."

Stout, middle-aged husbands of gay young wives who were customarily suspicious of women's doctors, particularly young and handsome ones, felt somehow ridiculous shaking Dr. Carnovsky's powerful hand. "An honor to make your acquaintance, Herr Doktor," they said with false cordiality.

Their pretty, sleek wives were delighted at the famous doctor's youthful appearance. Giggling prettily and batting their eyelashes, they shrieked, "How charming! We expected a much older man!"

"With a huge belly and a long beard, no doubt?" Georg prompted, his admiring eyes darting over the powdered and perfumed flesh.

"Precisely, Herr Doktor!"

"That will come later with the rheumatism and the title of 'Professor,' " he said, flashing his uneven but dazzling white teeth beneath the sharply trimmed mustache. "And this is my wife, Frau Carnovsky."

"Oh, how rude of me!" Frau Moser cried, and kissed Teresa as if she were a neglected child. "You will forgive me, won't you, my dear?"

"Think nothing of it, dear Frau Moser," Teresa whispered, blushing furiously.

She was used to being overlooked in a crowd. Usually people did not realize she was present until later. And although she insisted that she did not care, she felt deeply hurt. And no matter how hard she tried to hide her blushes with face powder, they could always be seen, to everyone's great amusement.

She grew completely flustered when the dancing began. The standards in the Moser household were less rigid than in other important salons. Here everyone was free to dress and behave as he pleased. Men in formal wear and stiff shirts rubbed elbows with artists in wrinkled velvet jackets. The American correspondents often came wearing colored shirts and light suits. Among the women in evening gowns and jewelry moved a female modern painter in a mannish gray shirt and tie and flat shoes with anklet socks. The guests also sat wherever they chose, some in the modern easy chairs, some on cushions, some on the rug, others on the broad staircase. They ate just as informally and took drinks from the elegant servants without being asked. Someone was always playing the piano, and wherever there was room couples danced the tango, the fox trot, and the Charleston, which was the latest dance from America. Frau Moser saw to it that all her guests felt unrestrained. She herself did not wait to be asked but selected her own dance partners and always made sure to dance often with Dr. Carnovsky. "If my blonde angel won't be jealous of an ugly, old woman, I'll ask your husband to dance with me," she said, and before Teresa could respond, she rested her hand possessively on Dr. Carnovsky's shoulder and pressed her whole body against him.

Nor did Teresa want for dancing partners. She was the only woman in the room whose hair was not bobbed and was worn in two round braids over her ears. The golden hair, milk-white complexion, and gentle curve of her neck brought to mind the Teutonic women in ancient prints, and the artists in the room were enthralled and eagerly sought her company. But she felt uneasy in the arms of strange men, particularly when they tried to dance the modern dances with her. She blushed each time her partner thrust his leg between hers and held her close. She grew even more disturbed when the men spoke to her insinuatingly and used the dance as an excuse to be familiar. Although she did not complain because it was impossible for her to make a scene, she despised such liberties taken with her body and at the very first opportunity she left the floor. "Thank you, but I'm tired," she begged off and fanned her flaming face.

Dr. Carnovsky saw over Frau Moser's shoulder that his wife was alone. He danced up to her, excused himself, and took Teresa out on the floor. Dancing with her Georg, Teresa lay her white hand on his shoulder and blissfully rested her face on his chest. Her neck was bent in a gesture of surrender. Georg pulled her to him roughly but there was neither resentment nor fire in her response. Her body was better than those of most of the females he saw in his practice but she was completely lacking in feminine wiles, the perversity and unpredictability that added so much spice to the game of sex. She did not even resist when he grew angry with her without reason or when, just as mysteriously, he later made up. From his long association with women, Georg knew that the periods of reconciliation could be among the best in a couple's relationship, able to forge stronger bonds of intimacy between husband and wife. Making love at such times assumed a particular perfection and became a matchless experience for jaded married couples. But Teresa was immune to all extremes of emotion. She did not become furious when he mistreated her or ecstatic when he made up. She was always humble and grateful for his love and he was bored to death with her. Even now, when they danced, she had no small talk and her responses were brief, timid, and unprovocative.

"Why don't you say something?" he said rather spitefully. "Don't you feel well?"

"I'm fine, Georg. I'm just so happy that you're dancing with me," she said and blushed like a schoolgirl.

"Angel," he sighed, and felt affection for her but as for a child rather than a woman.

His blood began to race when Frau Moser came back to claim him. She was not good-looking, far less attractive than Teresa. Her nape was straight as a man's, her hair was severely cut, her eyes feline and full of malice, and her mouth bitter and resolute. Her body was unsymmetrical too, the legs too muscular from exercise and horseback riding. But a wild kind of fire seemed to exude from her. With the cunning of the practiced voluptuary, she managed to instill all her sexuality into the dance and, now pressing close, now withdrawing, now coming nearer again, expertly tantalized Georg. Her gray cat eyes bored into his burning black ones. Through her tightly clenched lips she adroitly whispered the foulest words into his ear. Her tongue was as provocative as her body—she was always in the center of all discussions in her salon. She spoke knowingly about current books and paintings; kept up with the latest scandals, quarrels, affairs, and divorces. But what fascinated her most were the political machinations, intrigues, and conspiracies that decided the fate of the nation.

Born in Vienna, it was not a coincidence that her husband was the country's most influential publisher, or that the nation's most important leaders attended her soirees.

Men admired her, women envied her; most of all, Teresa Carnovsky, who felt lost in this highly sophisticated atmosphere. She knew that Frau Moser was stealing her husband. She also knew there was nothing she could do about it. And she left early.

Frau Moser took Georg's arm and led him to the fireplace where the scientists and politicians were gathered. She did this to keep him away from the gay young wives assembled at the other side of the salon and also because he enjoyed intellectual stimulation. Standing before the huge fireplace in which the curling bark of birch logs snapped and crackled, the men discussed world affairs, politics, philosophy, religion, and psychology. Typical of a country that had suffered a defeat, Berlin was full of revolutionists, seekers of faith, proponents of new ideologies, nature fanatics, prophets of doom, psychoanalysts, and mystics. Arguments flew back and forth, points of view were passionately espoused, bizarre concepts were scattered

recklessly. As usual, the most intriguing verbal duel took place between the two Siegfrieds—Dr. Siegfried Klein and Dr. Siegfried
Zerbe.

Former university colleagues, both doctors of philosophy, they had
started out together to be authors, poets, and playwrights, but neither had been able to achieve success. Aware of his shortcomings, Dr.
Klein had turned to writing for a humorous weekly and soon accumulated enough capital to publish his own humor magazine, which
immediately became a national success. Embittered over his failure
as a serious writer, full of resentment and envy, Dr. Klein vented his
spleen upon everyone.

And what he began with the word, his friend, Emil von Spahnsattel, finished with his caricatures. A product of the aristocracy and the
son of a general, Von Spahnsattel delighted in burlesquing German
militarism, the nobility, the clergy, and big business.

Prominent people lived in terror of the team of Klein and Von
Spahnsattel. They resented Von Spahnsattel even more than the
Jew, Klein. He was, after all, one of their own, a blue blood and a
Junker who had betrayed his own class. One of the most frequent
victims in Dr. Klein's magazine was Dr. Zerbe, his former class-
mate.

A failure at writing as was Klein, Dr. Zerbe had not given up. On
the contrary, the less success came his way, the stronger grew his
belief in his genius. He laid the blame squarely on the editors, theater directors, and critics who had formed a conspiracy against him
because they were mostly Jews without an understanding of the
German spirit and of his own mysticism. In his little publication
that hardly sold five hundred copies he vilified the cultural arbiters
of the nation who were either Jews, descendants of Jews, or their
lackeys. He excoriated the intellectuals, the liberals, and freethink-
ers. He advocated the revival of the ancient Teutonic love of war
and bloodshed. He ended his articles with his poems, obscure and
deeply mystical odes made of up lengthy, tangled sentences and long-
forgotten Germanic words.

But despite his conflict with Jews and liberals, he had no compunction about visiting the home of Rudolf Moser, the convert. Nor
could he stay away from his former friend Klein, also a Jew and

now his bitterest enemy. The son of a pastor and an intellectual to his finger tips, Zerbe personally could not abide the people he glorified—brutish martinets whose only interests were war, hunting, dogs, duels, and lechery. Slight and nearsighted, with the seedy look of a poor pastor's son, he despised the tall arrogant aristocrats who despised him even more. He enjoyed even less the company of the jackbooted young fanatics of the new National Socialist movement whom he proclaimed in his publication as the future saviors of the *Vaterland*. They flocked around him, the dedicated foe of the Jewish hierarchy, they bought his magazine and attended his lectures but he could not bear to be with them. He was repelled by their vulgarity, their sadistic animalism, by the slogans they chanted without comprehension. He felt at home in Rudolf Moser's salon where one could discuss philosophy, politics, theology, and world affairs and indulge in polemics without fear of being hit in the mouth. He never missed an opportunity to go where he was graciously accepted as merely another eccentric, although Herr Moser was a descendant of the very people whom Dr. Zerbe considered Germany's cancer. Like a moth seeking the flame, he was drawn to his sworn enemy, Dr. Klein, for the delicious pleasure of crossing verbal swords and trading insults.

Dr. Klein puffed happily on his cigar and blew smoke into Dr. Zerbe's face. Dr. Zerbe seethed. And when Von Spahnsattel drew a large caricature of him and passed it among the guests, he became almost apoplectic.

"This is going too far, my dear Von Spahnsattel," Rudolf Moser said. "Too extreme, if I may say so. After all, we are a people of culture."

Rudolf Moser was always diplomatic. This was probably the reason he had risen so high in his profession. His credo was compromise and moderation. His newspaper was fair to all political factions. He was so liberal that he did not even harbor a grudge against Dr. Zerbe for his attacks against those who, like himself, had converted. In fact, he lent Dr. Zerbe money each time the doctor's publication was in trouble, which, until recently, it had always been.

Von Spahnsattel drank another glass of wine. "Who says that we are a cultured people? We are savages, robber barons. But, rather than suffer our shame, we wear army breeches, and instead of spears we carry machine guns. Like our ancestors, the barbarians, who hated Rome because they resented its culture, we resent Paris, the cradle of ancient knowledge and art. We envy everybody, the French, the English, the Jews, anyone who is in some goddamn way superior."

Rudolf Moser was uneasy that such seditious opinions should be expressed in his house. Von Spahnsattel came from an excellent family and could afford to say what he pleased, but he, a convert and the publisher of a respected German newspaper, must be more careful. He would have liked to smooth things over and ease the tension but Dr. Zerbe would not let him. With flourish and hyperbole he spoke of the dangerous bacterium that the French conqueror had visited upon Germany and that had wormed its way into the bloodstream of the German people. The Bacillus Intellectualus or Bacillus Judaeus, he called it, and its mission was to ravage the healthy German body. But the awakening had come in time. The youth of the land had been alerted. It had shaken off foreign influences and would not allow itself to be sidetracked from fulfilling its destiny by Jewish secondhand goods. Germany was on the verge of a mass movement back to ancient Teutonism, glory, and purity of blood and race.

"Beware, you blind intellectuals who would deny the inevitability of the cleansing blood bath!" he thundered in unconscious imitation of his father, the pastor.

The host grew more uncomfortable. There was menace in the little man's threats, even though the others laughed at him openly. Such statements were heard often these days, far too often for comfort. Although Rudolf Moser felt that common sense, compromise, and the golden mean must prevail, although the entire topic was unpleasant to even think about, he felt a momentary qualm. Frau Moser, however, treated the matter lightly. "I do hope you won't let them harm me, Dr. Zerbe," she said coyly.

"For a beautiful woman I am always prepared to go through fire and water," Dr. Zerbe said gallantly and kissed her hand.

The crowd dispersed. Frau Moser put on her cape and prepared to leave. "Dr. Carnovsky has kindly offered to escort me to Wannsee," she said to her husband. "Good night, dear. Don't work too hard."

"Good night, darling," Rudolf Moser said and kissed her on her forehead.

She frequently spent Sundays at their summer house in Wannsee while he stayed behind and worked. Although he resented the fact that Dr. Carnovsky was with his wife, he raised no objections. Was he not a modern man who must look at things objectively and philosophically? . . . Graciously he bade Dr. Carnovsky adieu, thanked him for escorting his wife, and asked him to come again.

When Georg drove away with Frau Moser, he passed Dr. Zerbe trudging along in his cheap topcoat that had shrunk and grown shiny with the years and looked even worse against the black trouser legs of the tuxedo. Dr. Zerbe tipped his frayed hat to the occupants of the gleaming automobile and glared after them.

"A funny little man," Frau Moser observed. "Quite pathetic."

"On the contrary, he is someone who can prove extremely dangerous and cruel," Georg said. "He belongs to those hysterics who feel they have been slighted. They suffer from a delusion of grandeur and a persecution complex simultaneously. In times of upheaval they make the very worst kinds of brutes."

"Do you think so, my lover?" she asked, cuddling up to him and running her hand up his thigh.

"Hysterics who feel they have been insulted are more vicious than wolves. I saw madness in his eyes tonight," Georg added.

This gave Frau Moser the opportunity to discuss psychoanalysis, which was currently very much in fashion, as well as hysteria and inferiority complexes. Dr. Carnovsky was impressed with her knowledge. She spoke with the clarity and logic of a man. But the moment they went into the house she discarded her intellect along with her clothes and restraint. She knew how to exploit every nuance of love. She was submissive, violent, brazen, and inventive to such a point that even he, a woman's doctor, was astounded. Along with lyric and exotic endearments she uttered vulgar, coarse expressions in all languages and Georg was deeply repelled while he was also highly stimulated.

"You talk like a whore!" he said.

"Beat me, lover, call me whore! Do everything to me!" she moaned, writhing with passion.

When he started back to the city he was completely spent. He felt regret, contentment, and self-revulsion. He thought about Teresa lying alone in bed and he could not understand what drew him to this wild and perverted woman. She was not at all attractive. Her legs were too thick and muscular, her neck was mannish, her mouth was thin and vicious. He met hundreds of more desirable women in his practice. Many of them showed their interest and came to him just to undress before him and to feel his hands on their bodies. Since he had become famous he received letters from women by the dozens. Those who wrote included famous beauties from the best homes in Berlin. He could not understand what drew him to Herta Moser's bed. Driving through the cool night, he vowed to end the affair. He felt deeply ashamed and guilty about betraying Teresa. But after several days passed he grew restless again and missed the strange combination of instinct, intellect, and eroticism that made up this woman of the world and lowest kind of alley slut.

25

In the years following the war Hugo Holbeck tried a number of occupations. He sold vacuum cleaners, he sold shoes, he was an agent for hunting guns and held other jobs, none of which he was able to keep.

The one time he grew enthusiastic about a venture was shortly after his mother had sold the Holbeck apartment houses. Over a beer with a riding master, a former captain, Hugo mentioned the American dollars his mother had received in payment. The ex-captain, eagerly beating his crop against his high yellow riding boots, immediately proposed that they become partners in a riding academy. They were sure to make a fortune because the city was full of foreigners, especially American millionairesses looking for fun, who flung their money around as if it grew on trees. They also loved handsome young officers and would swoon over Oberleutnant Holbeck, the captain solemnly assured Hugo.

Hugo's pale face grew animated, as if he were being exhorted to lead an attack at the front. He agreed with the captain that this was probably the only decent occupation left to a German ex-officer. For once abandoning his taciturn, phlegmatic manner, he began to harass his mother to give him the money he needed. He promised her fabulous returns, kissed her hand, raged, even threatened to put a bullet into his brain if she refused him. The old woman could not stand up under the onslaught and with trembling hands turned over to him all the money she had left in the world.

Hugo was like a new man. He bought horses and expensive saddles. He hired stable boys, put advertisements in the newspapers, and waited for the Americans to come and fling their money around as if it grew on trees. He dreamed grandiose dreams. The novels that he occasionally read described many such meetings between noble but impoverished officers and American heiresses who gave their sweethearts not only their love but their fathers' millions as well. There was no reason such a thing could not happen to him too. Studying his image in the mirror, he was pleased by what he saw. The military tunic fitted snugly and was cinched in at the waist. The high boots gleamed. The smooth thick blond hair framed the narrow thin-featured face. He was an Oberleutnant from head to toe, a man equally at home in the trench and in the boudoir.

He waited for the American ladies to come. He waited. But just as unexpectedly as the inflation had begun, so unexpectedly did it end—almost overnight German marks regained their value and the hotels emptied of foreign speculators. No place was more deserted than ex-Oberleutnant Hugo Holbeck's Imperial Riding Academy. He came out of the debacle with only his riding breeches and crop. From then on he lost all interest in a world that had no place for a German officer.

His mother rented out part of their apartment and lived on the money that Teresa gave her. Hugo smoked cigarettes, played with the dog, and looked off into the distance through his field glasses. When he could no longer stand the house and felt a pressing urge to have a drink, to talk to ex-comrades, or to shoot in a gallery, he went to his sister for a loan.

There the food was always better and richer than at home. Carnovsky also stocked a large supply of wines, liqueurs, and cognacs, not only domestic but imported as well, and Hugo relished a glass of French cognac for which he had developed a taste at the front. He also took a handful of cigarettes from his brother-in-law's box, and as he drew in the rich aroma of the Egyptian cigarettes he brooded over the injustice that allowed a long-nosed enema-giver to live like a prince while he, a German Oberleutnant, must grovel in the dirt.

Donnervetter, what fine cigarettes that sheeny smokes, he thought, and went out to the garage where the family car was kept. The odor of gasoline was like perfume to him. Before the war he had loved racing a motorcycle. And at the front he had had many occasions to drive a car. He had not been able to pass one since without a twinge of envy.

Karl the chauffeur let him get behind the wheel and start the engine. The engine raced and Hugo listened to it as if it were music. It reminded him so much of the good, familiar sound of machine guns.

"A damned fine machine, Karl!" he said.

"*Jawohl,* Herr Oberleutnant!" Karl barked, just as he had been taught to address his superiors in the army.

When Jegorchen came home from school and saw his Uncle Hugo in the yard he beamed with delight. "Uncle Hugo!" he cried. "Uncle Hugo!"

"How goes it, boy?" Hugo asked grandly.

It felt good to be so warmly greeted in a household where neither his sister nor his brother-in-law thought much of him. He spoke to the boy as to an equal and Jegorchen squirmed with pride. Uncle Hugo showed him the inner workings of the engine, let him depress the pedals, hold the steering wheel, and step on the accelerator. When they were through playing with the car, he taught Jegor the proper military way to handle his air gun. Uncle Hugo was an expert shot. He could pick a bird off a branch of the acacia tree that stood in the yard. As usual, Jegorchen persuaded his mother to let Uncle Hugo take him for a ride, although Teresa was loath to give permission. She knew that her husband did not like it. However, she was too timid to stand up to her brother and she gave in. She did, however, make one request.

"For heaven's sake, Hugo, don't speed!"

"*Quatsch!*" he said scornfully, and as soon as they were out of sight he pressed the gas pedal to the floor. It reminded him of the good old days when he raced his motorcycle, with a girl hanging on behind for dear life. Jegorchen loved the ride. "Father never drives so fast!" he said.

"You call him a driver? It's a shame for him to own such a fine car," Hugo said and went even faster.

His pale, masklike face was flushed, he felt alive; the world was again a fit place in which to live. Like most timid people, Jegorchen nursed a secret love for recklessness. "Can you go any faster?" he asked.

"Of course, but the damned police are liable to stop us and then your papa will be angry."

Jegorchen looked at his uncle with large, admiring eyes and felt the urge to unburden himself to him.

Normally reticent, especially with his parents, he had no compunctions about telling his uncle everything. He knew that he came from a mixed household. He knew that his parents were somehow unusual, that his two grandmothers were very much unlike. He knew that he was not like the other children in school. Although his parents skirted the subject when he tried to ask about it, he knew that he was different and that this difference was not something to be proud of. The professor who taught religion did not treat him as he did the other children. Sometimes he let him remain during the lesson, sometimes he made him leave. The boys did not always treat him the same either. Usually they let him play, but when a fight broke out they called him "Jew." He insisted that his uncle tell him something—was he a German or was he not?

"*Ach, Gott,* of course you are a German on the Holbeck side!" Hugo said.

"Then why do the boys say that I'm not?"

"Because on your father's side you're a Carnovsky, and those snotnoses don't know the difference."

Jegorchen smiled at his uncle's description of his schoolmates. That's just what they were, snotnoses. But he still was not completely satisfied. What, exactly, was he?

"Isn't Papa a German?" he asked. "Mama says he is. Besides, he was a captain in the war."

Hugo smiled at his sister's conception of a German officer. What did a stupid female know about such things? But he said nothing to the boy whose feelings he could not bring himself to hurt. "Of course your papa is a German. Wasn't he born in this country? But he isn't completely a German, because he was born a Jew, *nicht wahr?* But it has nothing to do with you, lad. You're a pure German, a Holbeck."

Jegorchen was still confused. He thought seriously about the matter." What is a Jew, Uncle Hugo?" he asked.

"A Jew?" Hugo repeated. He stopped to think. It wasn't that he did not know. A Jew was a funny, black little creature with a hooked nose. He was rich and pushy and, according to the speakers in the beer halls, the one who betrayed the *Vaterland* during the war by thrusting a dagger into the army's back. Otherwise the German army would never have surrendered to the syphilitic frog-eaters. But he could not say all these things to the boy.

"A Jew is one who does not go to a church but goes to a synagogue," he said finally.

"But Papa never goes to a synagogue."

Hugo had nothing to say to this. "It's all a lot of *Quatsch,* boy," he said, "and you're too young to think about it."

But Jegorchen wanted to think about it. "Why didn't Mama marry a real German instead of Papa?" he asked. This was something that had been disturbing him for a long time and something no one would explain to him.

Hugo wanted to say that Teresa was a fool who fell in love, like any stupid female, but he told him only that women are a funny lot and of no concern to a real man. He, Jegorchen, would do better to learn how to shoot, ride a motorcycle, ride horseback, and fence so that he could grow up to be a good soldier.

Jegorchen was glad to hear these things but he was puzzled, because Grandmother Carnovsky had told him that since the war had ended the army no longer needed men. What did Uncle Hugo say to that?

"Quatsch!" he roared. What did an old Jewess know about such things? All that the German people had to do was bide their time and remain in readiness. Presently, things would be just like during the good old days. He, Hugo Holbeck, would put on his old uniform; there would be an army, and discipline, and orders, and war—the good old war. And the best thing for Jegorchen would be to keep away from the old Jew-woman who only looked to wrap him in a gaberdine such as they wore in Jewish Switzerland.

In his excitement he talked to the boy as if he were a pure Holbeck; but soon he remembered that he might have gone too far.

"Naturally, you'll tell no one what we've discussed," he warned the boy. "It's nobody's business what men talk about among themselves."

"How would I dare do such a thing?" Jegor said indignantly.

"Spoken like a man!" Hugo said, and stepped on the gas to bring the car back before his brother-in-law came home.

He was careful to avoid an argument with Carnovsky. For all his contempt for the sheeny enema-giver, he grew tongue-tied in his presence. Like most physicians, Dr. Carnovsky was patronizing toward laymen. His attitude implied that their future depended upon his ability to keep them alive.

"And how are things going with the Oberleutnant?" he asked.

Hugo Holbeck was annoyed by his brother-in-law's allusion to his rank. Although it sounded so right coming from Karl and other menials, it somehow sounded degrading when Dr. Carnovsky said it. "What can a German officer expect in these goddamn times?" Hugo replied, intimating that for the present, at least, it was the time for the Carnovskys to crow and the Holbecks to be quiet.

"These so-called 'goddamn times' will go on for a long time, Herr Oberleutnant," Dr. Carnovsky said pointedly. "And until they change, you can rid yourself of the romantic notion that the only choice for you is to behave like a general without an army."

"I have a different opinion, Herr Doktor," Hugo said.

"Well, be that as it may, let us in the meantime have lunch. I'm hungry as a bear," Georg said, and led Hugo and Jegorchen into the large dining room where the table had been set with a wide variety of good food. Teresa tied a napkin around Jegorchen's neck and called to her sister-in-law, Rebecca, who was visiting, to join them.

"Becca!" she called her as Rebecca had requested—Rebecca sounded too Jewish.

Rebecca came in from the garden with a bunch of cut flowers and walked up to the table in her rather heavy-footed fashion. "Ah, Herr Hugo!" she exclaimed in surprise.

Hugo sprang from the table and clicked his heels smartly. "Good day, Fräulein Becca," he said, kissing her hand.

Rebecca's black eyes sparkled. If only her former schoolmates could see her now, being paid court by a blond Oberleutnant!

He held her chair out for her with excessive gallantry and she sat down next to him. "Extremely kind of you, Herr Oberleutnant," she said, excited by the proximity of their knees under the table. He gave off a tantalizing aroma of tobacco, leather, shaving soap, and masculinity.

She suddenly felt a surge of love for her sister-in-law and kissed her extravagantly. Teresa blushed and straightened Rebecca's coiffure, which no matter how often it was fixed, remained disarrayed.

Dr. Carnovsky watched the little scene. "When a young woman kisses her sister-in-law too passionately, the psychologists would say she is thinking of her sister-in-law's brother," he commented wryly.

The others blushed and Rebecca looked at him hatefully. "You're a cynic, like all obstetricians," she said, furious because he had guessed her feelings.

Georg laughed and began to talk about the hysterical women in his care. Rebecca did not want to hear about such things. She was the sentimental type and her disheveled head was filled with thoughts of flowers, books, music, and fantasy. She could not bear her brother's mocking references to her sex. "I'd rather hear something from you, Herr Oberleutnant, something more pleasant."

Hugo Holbeck was embarrassed. He had never been much of a conversationalist. But Rebecca was looking at him with such passionately admiring eyes that he could not disappoint her, and he began spinning an involved story about some incident at the front. Feeling constrained because he could not resort to his normal soldier's jargon in front of the ladies, he stopped often to find the proper substitute expression. Rebecca was enthralled by the sheer glory of it all. "Ach, dear God!" she exclaimed again and again.

Georg snickered. His recollection of the front was somewhat different. "Well, and how about dysentery? Didn't anyone you know ever get the runs, Herr Oberleutnant?" he asked, pouring himself a glass of wine.

Rebecca glared at her brother. He was a hopeless cynic, as was everyone else these days, with no regard for chivalry.

"That's the goddamn postwar times," Hugo said. "Without the army life lacks all romance."

"Words of wisdom, Herr Hugo," Rebecca agreed. "Everything these days is so drab and calculated and practical!"

This was her chief complaint—that the men of postwar Germany were entirely too materialistic. They wanted only big dowries, and love was the last thing in their minds. She would not even look at the list of bachelors Dr. Lippman submitted to her. As is the custom among Jews to attribute all human flaws to their own faith, she was convinced that it was the young men's Jewish origin that made them consider everything from a materialistic standpoint—even love. She was enchanted by the tall blond officer who was so elegant, knightly, and gallant. Even his inability to find himself seemed so romantic and tragic. "He is like a big baby . . . so artless in a naïve, Christianlike way," she whispered to Teresa.

Teresa did not share her sister-in-law's opinion of Hugo but she remained silent. Rebecca accompanied Hugo into the garden and led him to a stone bench near the flower beds, her favorite spot. She talked about books and the theater with her usual passion. Hugo sat next to her with his long legs extended and listened more than he talked. He knew little about such things. He was bewildered when she quoted modern poets to him and astonished that a female could be so intellectual. He knew only two kinds of girls—the seamstresses with whom he slept but would not take out in public, and the girls from decent homes who let him do all the talking and laughed at the appropriate time.

"Very nice!" he remarked, although the poems made no sense to him. They did not even rhyme.

His helplessness stirred Rebecca. She combined her father's drive and zeal and her mother's sense of sacrifice and devotion to those weaker than she. Her feelings for men were as for children. She was not attracted to those who were worldly and adjusted but to the timid ones whom she could mother and mold into something worthwhile. The tall, gangling Hugo Holbeck stirred within her the urge to manage, to guide, and to mother.

"Ach, you're nothing but a big baby, Herr Oberleutnant," she chided maternally when he offered some of his quixotic opinions.

Hugo did not quite know how to behave in her presence. She intrigued him with her fervor and her sparkling black eyes and hair. She was not as simple and open as the blond girls he knew, but exuded a kind of female complexity. Although he had never had anything to do with Jewish women, his friends had assured him that they were full of the devil and marvelous lovers. Still, he was sure he would not want one for a wife—he resented their superior attitude.

He breathed easier once he left the house. As usual, it took him a long time to say good-by. He shuffled his feet, blushed, and smoked one cigarette after another. Dr. Carnovsky knew the reason for his brother-in-law's discomfort and dealt with it in his usual blunt fashion. "How much?" he asked, staring into the weak, shifty eyes.

"Twenty-five marks, if it's possible," Hugo said, shamefaced. "As soon as I begin my job I'll pay back everything. On my word of honor as an officer."

Dr. Carnovsky knew the story by heart. "What do you say to fifteen?" he asked mockingly, holding out the money.

Hugo accepted it and ran outside. *That shithead,* he said to himself, angry because he had to ask his brother-in-law for money and angrier still because Carnovsky bargained him down like the cheap Jew he was.

In Schmidt's Bavarian Brauhaus on Potsdamer Brücke he felt like himself again. Here many ex-officers gathered, along with university students and their girls. The beer was good, the sausages tasty, and the sauerkraut sour and salty. His comrades greeted him properly, with a click of the heels, and the waitresses smiled at him coquettishly.

When the students finished drinking and began their discussions, the atmosphere grew lively and spirited. The men here were mostly of the new breed. They spoke of the struggle for an aroused Germany, of revenge on France and on the traitors from West Berlin, the Jewish money-bags who so treacherously had thrust a dagger into the back of the brave army. Although Hugo did not take part in the discussions, he enjoyed the brave talk.

"Prosit!" he saluted his comrades and downed stein after stein of the foamy brew.

Later he went home with one of the waitresses whose caresses made him feel like a whole man again, not a parasite. If there was anything left from the money Georg had given him, he went to a shooting gallery the following morning and, if he was lucky, won a pack of cigarettes for hitting the bull's-eye.

26

Each day brought new troubles for Dr. Elsa Landau, North Berlin's representative in the great Reichstag.

"Go back to Dragonerstrasse!" the deputies of the New Order shouted. "Back to Jewish Switzerland with your Galician friends, the profiteers, counterfeiters, speculators, and Bolsheviks!"

Others dispatched her even farther. "Go back to Jerusalem! No Jews in a German Reichstag!"

Elsa Landau fought back. She told the world who the real profiteers, counterfeiters, and speculators were. She was privy to all the secrets of the enemy camp and with deadly, incriminating detail she outlined the whole sordid history of their rise to power. She documented all her accusations and provided facts and figures, but no logic could prevail against the ever rising chorus of jeers, insults, and mocking laughter. She wore herself ragged trying to stem the opposition. She grew hoarse, lost her patience, and occasionally even became hysterical, to the great delight of her enemies.

She got an even worse reception when she addressed workers' groups in the provinces.

Students, veterans, unemployed workers, street loafers, drifters, Gymnasium graduates too lazy to look for jobs, and all kinds of rowdies sent by the New Order whistled, brayed, hooted, and heckled her, threw rotten eggs and stench bombs. At times someone would even fire a revolver in the hall. Besides her Semitic origin, the youths in boots also attacked Dr. Landau's virtue. "Red Jew-whore!" they chorused, drowning out her words.

Although the other accusations meant nothing to her, she was terribly hurt by this epithet. It humiliated the woman in her. She who had sacrificed everything for the Cause; she who had sublimated all her womanly feelings and lived the life of a nun, to be called a whore! The worst of it was that the mob seized on the name and made it popular. Wherever she went it was hurled at her, stimulating the audiences far more than did her logic and statistics. Flushed with success, the youths in boots openly threatened to shoot her down like a dog if she dared to speak in German towns.

But she knew the smell of gunpowder from the days following the war and she was not afraid. The more threatening the letters she received, the farther she extended her activities, covering every sleepy village that the bullies of the New Order held in complete power. She prodded the dozing proletariat to stand up to its enemies in the mighty struggle that threatened to destroy all Germany. She restored defunct workers' organizations and fanned the sparks of revolutionary fires that had blazed so brightly just after the war. At the same time she noticed with great alarm the mounting strength of the New Order. Not only had it won over the small-town people and the farmers, it was also attracting increasingly growing numbers of workers.

They were tired of unemployment and false promises. They demanded action from the leaders in the capital. Elsa appealed to their reason and quoted from Party manifestoes, but the time for words had passed.

"We're tired of talk," the more outspoken among them said. "We want only bread and work!"

To this reasonable demand Elsa Landau had no answer. She saw the calamity that hovered over Germany with greater perception than did any of her fellow Party leaders. They kept up their constant doctrinal hairsplitting, avoided any contact with the working masses, and maintained an eternal optimism. Things would eventually improve, they said. But she knew better. She was out in the field almost constantly. She visited workers' homes in every part of the country. She ate at their tables and spoke with their wives. She saw the terrible privation that gripped Germany and, what was even worse, the apathy that prevailed everywhere. She warned the Party leaders and urged them to take steps, but she was a voice in the wilderness.

"Too pessimistic, Comrade Elsa," they condemned her with mild reproof. Secretly, they attributed her apprehensions to an inherent Semitic cowardice.

But she refused to be tranquilized. Her mind filled with dread when she lay awake in some provincial hotel room, unable to sleep. As long as she kept busy speaking and attending workers' celebrations, sports events, and parades, she was able to forget her personal problems and to devote herself fully to the class struggle. But when she was left alone in the hotel rooms that all seemed to look alike— the upholstered furniture, prints of castles and battles, wide bed, and heavily draped window—loneliness and anxiety would come over her and leave her weak and trembling.

She felt terribly alone and forsaken this night in particular. The wide double bed seemed to mock the slight body lost in its vastness. Through the walls she could sometimes hear the sounds of couples laughing and whispering and an occasional moan. She was seized by a sharp longing and tears came to her eyes. She tried to drive away these feelings with the iron discipline she had imposed upon herself through the years. What did the sounds of cheap sex mean to her, a fighter in the glorious cause of freedom and justice? But the feelings came crowding back, like insects drawn to a porch light. She recalled her father's words with a terrible clarity. "Someday you will regret your choice, but by then it will be too late. . . ."

She had laughed at him then but now, in the sleepless night, the words did not seem so funny. From her father, her thoughts strayed to Georg Carnovsky. She recalled another hotel room in another town—a room not much different from the one she was in now. The rain had been falling on the roof—yes, the rain . . . how long ago was it? Years and years, but she recalled every detail. He had loved her then. He had aroused in her a passion she never knew she possessed. And she had loved him too, loved him desperately. But she had exchanged him for the Party, for the thrill of the struggle, but above all—for glory. No, she had no delusions about herself. For all her idealism, she was consumed by personal ambition, by the need to be admired and the urge to show men that she was in every way their equal if not their superior. She had attained her goal. She was important. Men listened to her. Newspapers gave her reams of space. Even her enemies grudgingly acknowledged her abilities. How many women had told her they would do anything to trade places with her? . . . Was she happy? During the day she buried herself in her work, but the nights were long and lonely and brought out all her womanly doubts and feelings of inadequacy. She thought about a home and comforts, the luxury of idleness and of love. She could not put Georg out of her mind. He already had a wife, a child, a home. It was years since she had seen him, but she had kept up with his career. How good it would be to be with him, to be his devoted and obedient wife, yes, even to submit to him! Anything would be better than this gnawing, haunting loneliness.

From the darkness outside came the sound of a crying child and the mother's sleepy voice lulling it back to sleep. Elsa listened intently. She envied the woman whose baby had awakened her.

Her father had warned her of what happened to a woman who shunned the natural course of marriage and motherhood. She had scoffed at him then, but it seemed that he knew life better than she. The wives of the workers whose homes she visited seemed to lead lives of fulfillment. Their days were taken up with their children and their household tasks. She herself was delighted when a chubby, friendly child plunked itself on her lap. How delicate and sweet were the little fingers that clung to her neck and cheeks! How did all her triumphs and fame measure up against the thrill of motherhood?

She had traded away her chance for happiness. Others beside Georg had offered love and marriage, but she had rejected them all for an alleged independence. Why, then, did she not feel free now? . . . She had wasted away her youth and although men still complimented her on her figure, she didn't deceive herself. The years had left their mark. She frequently felt the need to rest and to restore her energy. These were the first signs of age, she knew. She also suffered headaches and various vague female complaints brought on by spinsterhood and the passing of youth.

Pulling back her blanket, she looked at her body and was filled with self-pity and remorse for the lost years. She knew she would never experience the joy of birth; that her meager breasts would never suckle an infant. Now she was still active and vigorous, but all too soon she would be middle-aged, and in no time she would be old. How empty and useless was the life of a woman alone in her old age!

She took a pill to quiet her nerves and to help her sleep, but the brooding thoughts were stronger than the chemical. Everything seemed hard and unyielding—the soft mattress, the downy pillows were crushing her. She could not get comfortable. All kinds of sounds came drifting out from the dark stillness—the gay laughter of a couple saying their interminable good-bys under her window, the slurred singing of a drunk, the cry of a child. The city clocks announced the time every quarter of the hour. Their bells filled the night with forlorn, drawn-out echoes. They seemed to sound a kind of ominous fear, an unrest and sense of foreboding, as if warning of the terrible events drawing ever closer. Elsa buried her face in the pillow and cried the desperate tears of a woman alone and abandoned in a hotel room in the middle of the night.

27

A mood of lawlessness, expectation, anxiety, and vague promise prevailed over the capital on the day the men in boots took over its streets and avenues.

They were everywhere in their drab, brown uniforms: racing around in cars and on motorcycles, carrying torches, playing martial music, clicking heels, and marching—constantly marching, marching.

The pounding of their hobnailed boots stirred and aroused the people. No one quite knew what the New Order would bring; but whatever it was, the citizens of Berlin awaited it with impatient, good-natured anticipation.

Just as in wartime, the crowds surged aimlessly in search of excitement. Louder than in the other sections, the boots of the storm troopers resounded through the streets of West Berlin: across the Kurfürstendamm, Tauntzienstrasse, past the luxurious homes of the black-eyed and black-haired merchant princes, professors, theater directors, lawyers, doctors, and bankers. The verse, *Wenn vom Judenblut das Messer spritzt dann geht's noch mal so gut, so gut,* rang out loud and clear, as if to make certain the words penetrated deep inside the houses.

They heard them, those who were meant to hear them; heard them in their shops and in the cafés where they lingered over their eternal coffees and newspapers. They felt somewhat uneasy, a little ashamed and embarrassed perhaps, but no one took the words to heart. How could sophisticated people become concerned over the lyrics of some

silly ballad? Nor were the merchants on Friedrichstrasse and Alexanderplatz overly disturbed. Business was good, better than usual.
The people gathered in the streets; they were festive and unusually
free with their money, in contrast with their usual stinginess. The
waiters kept serving their regular black-haired customers their customary coffee and apple cake; they brought them the newspapers
from all over the world and addressed them as Herr Doktor whether
they deserved the title or not. No one believed that the good life
would end. No one wanted to believe it. If anything did come of the
change, it would happen to others, people comforted themselves as
people will during any catastrophe.

Rudolph Moser, the publisher, drove up to the huge building that
housed his publication and went to work as usual. As unpleasant as
it was to hear songs about Jewish blood spilling, he never for a
moment considered that his own life was in danger. Although a
descendant of Jews, he was, after all, a convert, married to a Christian wife and even a trustee of the Gedächtnis Kirche, the oldest
church in Berlin. The most important government leaders visited his
home, even the members of the right-wing parties. What more
could be expected of him? He even entertained and subsidized one
of their own people, Dr. Zerbe. Whatever happened to the Jews
would certainly not affect him, a highly respected Christian.

Neither would the department store tycoons, the bankers, merchants, theater directors, playwrights, artists, and professors whose
names were world famous but who had remained part of the Jewish
community believe that the blood that would spray from the knives
would be their blood. Admittedly they were Jews, but this was a
mere technicality. They owed their allegiance only to Germany and
were firmly rooted in the cultural life of their beloved *Vaterland.*
They had contributed so much to it. Most had served at the front,
many with distinction. If anyone would be affected, it would be the
Jews who had clung fanatically to their orthodox habits, their Semitic culture, and even spoke about emigrating to Asia, of all places.

Neither did Dr. Speier believe that the warnings were intended
for him. Was he not a member of a family that had lived in Germany for generations? Did he not employ the most elegant German
in his sermons and quote from Goethe, Lessing, Schiller, and Kant?

Had he not urged his congregation to rise to his country's defense during the war and to shed its blood for the *Vaterland?* No, if there was any basis for complaint—and Dr. Speier had to admit that there *was* legitimate reason for the German people to be resentful—it was against the strangers, the newcomers to the country. Again, as during the war, he began to avoid his friend, David Carnovsky. In times of stress it paid to stay clear of a stranger, an immigrant. A man was foolish to place himself in a compromising situation. Was it not written, *He who remains constantly afraid is a sage?*

Dr. Georg Carnovsky followed his usual routine at the clinic. He was not particularly concerned about the threats the brown-shirted men shouted against Jewish doctors in the aroused Germany. What rot! He was a native German; he had studied at a German university; he had even earned a medal at the front and attained the rank of captain. His wife was a Christian, the daughter of an ancient and honorable German family. If he was at all apprehensive, it was about his parents, who were aliens. They were liable to suffer under the new regime.

Neither did David Carnovsky really believe that he would be persecuted in a land in which he had lived and prospered for so many years. Had he not sent his only son to the front? Did he not conduct his business in such an honest and ethical manner that all the Christian Germans who dealt with him praised him? Besides, he had taken special pains to familiarize himself with the language and customs and to rid himself of every trace of his Eastern background. If any danger threatened, it would be to those who had migrated after the war and settled on Dragonerstrasse. For all that he pitied them in a time of trouble, David Carnovsky also nursed a secret grudge against the Jews from the Quarter. They were too shifty, they capitalized on people's troubles by buying up property for next to nothing, and generally behaved in a sly and shady fashion. He was also secretly repelled by the large number of Jews in earlocks and caftans who had infiltrated the city—all kinds of alleged ecclesiastics whose presence shocked his sensibilities when he encountered them pushing their way onto trolleys and subways. Some of them had even penetrated West Berlin in their eternal quest for contributions. They did Berlin's Jewry no credit with their exotic appearance and execrable manners. He himself could not bear their ways—was it any wonder they provoked resentment among the gentiles? True enough, there were some decent and learned people among them, Talmudic scholars and sages like Reb Ephraim Walder. But mostly they were an irritant and it was possible that the new rulers would harass those of them who lacked proper credentials.

The inhabitants of Dragonerstrasse also made distinctions among themselves. The proprietor of the Franz Josef Hotel, Reb Herzele Vishniak, was as sure as two plus two equaled four that he and the other Austrian Jews would not be bothered. After all, had not Austria been Germany's strongest ally during the war? Had they not fought side by side against a common enemy? True, the section from which he came, Galicia, was now ruled by Poland, but its roots were inexorably bound to Germany. It was incredible to think that former soldiers would be persecuted by their comrades. If anyone would suffer, it would be the Russians, the refugees who had drifted into the Quarter after the war.

The Russian Jews made further distinctions—between those who had proper papers and those whose credentials were in doubt. Even those in the latter category were not too perturbed. After all, there were consuls here from their native lands. This was the twentieth century. Law and order would prevail.

"Things will get better," they comforted one another. "More than one barbarian has tried to wipe out our people and Jews have remained Jews. Come what may, God will look after us." And everyone kept to his ways, hustled, schemed, bought, sold, and somehow scratched out a living.

Business had never been better in Solomon Burak's Discount Store. Although the youths in boots harangued the shoppers to boycott the swindlers and profiteers, the women flocked to Solomon Burak's store to snatch up bargains. Jew or not, they were anxious to stock their homes with things of substance instead of the paper money that was liable to become worthless again as it had after the war. Solomon Burak darted through his store like an eel. He had lost none of his penchant for jokes. Neither the years nor the harsh times could change him.

"The latest Haman model à la Pharaoh's plagues, dear lady," he would say to the thick-set housewives who took his words literally.

His wife Yetta tried to restrain him. "Solomon, don't talk so much! Shlomele, even the walls have ears!"

His son-in-law, Jonas Zielonek, was scandalized. Not that he felt any concern for himself. He was from Posen, a German through and through and a veteran besides. But he was worried about his father-in-law, the immigrant from Melnitz. He could never stand his jokes and use of Hebrew expressions. Now he especially deplored this habit of drawing attention to their Jewishness. "For God's sake, let me take care of the customers," he pleaded. "It would be better at this time if you stayed away from the store altogether."

"What's the matter, just because you're from Posen you think they'll treat you any different? We'll swing side by side, Jonas, my boy," Solomon said.

Nor did he cease teasing his neighbors, the German Jews, with whom he had been feuding for years. Most of all he loved to torment his next-door competitor, Ludwig Kadish, who daily reassured himself that he would be safe from all harassment. First, Kadish pinned to his lapel the Iron Cross that he had been awarded for losing an eye at the front. He would stand with his chest puffed out to better display the medal. He also hung his army uniform in his window to show the German people that he at least was not one of those who had stabbed the army in the back. He felt that the uniform would deter the bullies from smashing the window as they already had in many Jewish shops. Some of Kadish's Christian neighbors had put crosses in their windows to show that the shops were owned by gentiles. Perhaps the Iron Cross would serve the same purpose. But Solomon Burak would not let him find comfort in it. "This *mezuzah* won't help you here, Herr Kadish," he said. "Haman the Wicked doesn't fear *mezuzoth*. . . ."

He goaded Ludwig Kadish into blurting out all the resentment he had stored up against his neighbor through the years. The troubles that he now had to suffer were the fault of Burak and his kind from the other side of the border. He, Kadish, and the other Germans of Mosaic faith had always lived in peace with their Christian neighbors. Things would have remained the same but for the Polish and Russian Jews who had overrun the country. It was they, with their swinish antics, the exaggerated Jewishness that they literally pushed down the gentiles' throats, their speech and their manners, who had fanned the sparks of latent anti-Semitism—they, with their Jewish Switzerland, their long caftans, their Yiddish jargon, their Zionism, Socialism, peddling, profiteering, forged passports, and shady business methods. They manipulated prices, they sold shoddy goods, and they hurt the decent tradesman, the Christian as well as the Jew. If at least they confined themselves to Dragonerstrasse. But no! They had to infiltrate pure German streets like Landsberger Allee! . . . But now all this would be changed. They would be driven back across the border where they belonged. And the ones who remained would be those who had been in the country for generations, those who had been able to adjust to life in a civilized community.

Solomon Burak laughed sarcastically. A typical kraut like all the krauts. Oh no, when the time came to crack skulls, his would be cracked just like everyone's else's. The *goyim* were only concerned with the material aspects of the matter. How did the saying go? "Ludwig or Schlomo—they hate the Jew but love his mazumah" . . .

Ludwig Kadish bristled with indignation. "I forbid you to speak to me this way, Herr Burak. I am a pure, one-hundred-percent German national!"

Even the glass eye that he wore in place of the one he had sacrificed for the *Vaterland* glistened with hate for Solomon Burak.

Solomon Burak was neither intimidated by his neighbor's anger nor worried about his own fate. He knew that evil times were coming but he felt no fear, only the same impatience that gripped all Berliners. Something surely was about to happen; what would it be?

The one most affected by the uncertainty and excitement was young Joachim Georg Carnovsky.

Although nothing had outwardly changed in the school he attended, a sort of laxity had settled over the institution and affected all its activities. The lessons seemed to have lost all purpose and meaning. The teachers were disorganized and confused. The strict discipline that had kept the school functioning was replaced by a mood of rebelliousness that stirred the boys' young hearts and hinted vague promises. It was the streets of the capital that drew them now and offered all kinds of seductive blandishments.

Jegor Carnovsky spent all his time in the streets. He stayed out of school and roamed through the city aimlessly, drinking in the sounds, sights, and smells of the great upheaval sweeping the nation. He wandered from Kurfürstendamm to Unter den Linden. He let himself be carried by the surging mobs from Alexanderplatz to the farthest reaches of North Berlin. He rode the subway, the trolleys, and the buses, not caring where he was headed. He fell in with the mood of disorder that gripped the city's inhabitants. No one now was where he was supposed to be. The police, the famous *Schupos* in their great helmets who customarily seemed so formidable and sure of themselves, wandered about as if lost and uncertain of their authority. The bus drivers were not sure whether to follow their routes. The only ones who seemed to act with purpose were the marching young men in boots.

Tall and gangly, his blue eyes shining with patriotism, Jegor let himself be swept along by the crowds frantically searching for thrills and excitement. The blaring music fired his young spirit; the beat of the marching feet exhilarated him. Like all those around him, he thrust his arm stiffly upward each time a company of men strode by. He yelled and chanted slogans. He bought the small insignia that represented the New Order from a street vendor for a few pfennigs and stuck it in his lapel. When he grew hungry, he went into a beer hall for the first time in his life and ordered beer and pig sausage like the others. He chewed the fat sausage with relish and gulped down the beer that was raw and bitter but at the same time contained the delicious flavor of forbidden adult pleasures. He listened to the coarse talk of the patrons and their cheap, pungent cigars irritated his eyes and stimulated him.

He made no connection between the Jewish blood the marching troopers sang of spilling and the Jewish blood that ran in his veins. He heard only the melody, not the lyrics. Like the words of any hymn, they were to him, as to the other Jews in Berlin, merely an accompaniment to the music. Besides, what did they have to do with him? Was he not a pure Holbeck, one of the millions who marched to fulfill Germany's destiny of victory and revenge? It had come about just as Uncle Hugo had predicted. His uncle was not the fool his mother and father made him out to be. Jegor no longer felt his usual listless and apathetic self; now he felt full of energy. He found himself near the Reichstag. The broad square was alive with flags, torches, noise, and marching men. From open touring cars the nation's new leaders exhorted the screaming mobs. The people bellowed, thrust out arms, and screamed hysterically. Jegor felt the blood rush to his head. He found himself cheering and repeating the short, ugly slogans in fanatical chorus with the inflamed thousands. For the first time he felt that life was good and had purpose. He knew he would never again be the same.

28

The youths in boots had meant it when they sang in the streets about spilling Jewish blood. To them, these were not mere lyrics, as the inhabitants of West Berlin had assumed. With each passing day more blood dripped from their daggers—drop after drop after drop.

Late one night they rapped on the door of Dr. Siegfried Klein, the editor of the satiric weekly, and dragged him from his warm bed in his luxurious apartment on Rankestrasse to the cellar of Schmidt's Bavarian beer hall on Potsdamer Brücke. As he was hustled along, Dr. Klein demanded of passing policemen, with the indignation only a liberal can summon, that they protect him from hooligans who had no authority to arrest him. But the police politely pointed out that they could not interfere.

"And what do you say to that, Herr Editor?" the youths asked tauntingly.

He retained his ability to counter with a quip until they led him down a narrow stone stairway to the cellar and the sour smell of yeast, hops, dampness, mold, and mice droppings assailed his nostrils.

"Remove the jacket and collar!" the leader of the gang ordered.

Dr. Klein gaped at him through his thick lenses. He could not understand why he must undress.

The leader enlightened him. "We only wish to shave Herr Editor and for that one must remove the jacket and collar to be more comfortable, *nicht wahr?*"

His comrades laughed coarsely and all at once Dr. Klein got the point. In his magazine he had called the leader of the New Order a barber and Von Spahnsattel had drawn him with a razor in hand and smirking with a fatuous pomposity. The caricature had created a minor sensation. Dr. Klein would be the first to concede that his magazine was cruel and malicious, but he could not see anything illegal or even unethical in satire. His opponents treated him just as unkindly. They portrayed him as a kinky-haired devil with a tremendous nose and the thick lips of a Zulu, although his nose was small, his lips thin, and his hair was straight. But this was all part of the game and he accepted it good-naturedly. What was the function of a humorous magazine if not to exaggerate? But the youths in boots obviously did not share his viewpoint. When he did not immediately respond to the command to undress, the leader hit the fat little editor in the eye. Dr. Klein fell, his head draped over a beer keg. It was the first time in his adult life that he had been struck and the experience upended him not only physically but emotionally. He was convinced that his end had come. The youths began to beat him coldly and methodically. The longer the beating kept up, the more intense grew Dr. Klein's attachment to life and, along with it, the bitter realization that a human body could withstand untold pain and punishment. Each time he fell, one of the youths would right him and the fists, belt buckles, truncheons, and boots would begin to descend again with monotonous regularity.

"Shoot me!" Dr. Klein pleaded.

The men burst out laughing. Shoot him? There was plenty of time for that. Now they only wanted to "barber" him a little. They would even stop beating him if he would tell them where his associate, the Jew-slave Von Spahnsattel, was hiding.

Through all his pain Dr. Klein felt a twinge of regret when they mentioned his friend's name. Days before, when conditions were still unsettled, Von Spahnsattel had offered to take him along in his sports car to Paris. But Dr. Klein had refused to flee. He conceded that the New Order might conceivably force him to cease publication, but he did not believe that any physical harm would befall him. How could he be legally prosecuted for making fun of people? Von Spahnsattel had looked at him with steely eyes filled with anger and contempt. "You Jews still don't know us Germans. You keep on seeing us through your Semitic eyes. But I know my own people only too well because I am one of them. *Zum Wiedersehen,* Klein. God have mercy on you." And Von Spahnsattel had vanished in a cloud of exhaust. Dr. Klein bitterly recalled the conversation between the strokes of the rubber truncheons on his pink belly and groin.

He swore that his friend had fled to Paris but they did not believe him. During the clear spells that alternated with periods of unconsciousness Dr. Klein reflected with a kind of amazed detachment on how remarkable it was that his soft body could absorb so much punishment. The beating went on and on through the endless night and as the hours passed the youths began to apply certain refinements, until Dr. Klein's agony grew as exquisite as death itself.

To Herr Rudolf Moser came not common street bullies but ranking Party officials equipped with the proper documents and orders. Nor was he beaten or humiliated—only jailed with common thieves and drunks to protect him from the "aroused mobs who sought his death as a traitor to the *Vaterland.*"

Rudolf Moser argued that he had nothing to fear from anyone and that he would personally accept all responsibility for his own safety. Besides, if necessary he would go abroad. He was given permission to leave the country, but only after he had agreed to sign over his newspaper and the entire publishing plant to the government. Frau Moser tried to see Dr. Zerbe, who had risen to a position of great importance in the New Order. He now prominently displayed the Party insignia on his sleeve and had taken over Rudolf Moser's position as head of the newspaper—even his office with the huge mahogany desk.

"Regretfully, Madame, Dr. Zerbe is unable to see you," Rudolf Moser's shamefaced servant told his former master's wife.

Neither did Dr. Zerbe find time for the wife of his former friend, Dr. Klein, who had not seen her husband since the night he had been torn from her side.

The windows of Dr. Fritz Landau's apartment in Neukölln were marked with red paint announcing that he was a Jew and could only treat his fellow Jews. No more would he be granted the privilege of running his fat Jewish hands over pure Aryan women's bodies, of violating little girls, and of sapping the blood of German workers. All Aryans were forbidden to enter his pigsty of an office. The youths in boots harangued old Johanna to leave the doctor. It wasn't fitting that she, an Aryan, serve a filthy Jew. But the old woman, almost bent in half from age, chased the youths from the house and announced in a voice loud enough for everyone to hear that no snotnose hooligans would drive her from the home of Herr Doktor. The youths called her a Jew-whore and let her be.

They were more conscientious in ferreting out Dr. Landau's daughter, that redheaded hellion and enemy of the Reich. They turned the city upside down looking for her. They raided workers' homes in Neukölln and each night converged on her father's house, hoping she would show up. They searched the apartment time and again, smashing jars and wrecking the laboratory. When she still did not come, they arrested the doctor and held him hostage until she had no choice but to surrender. He was released and spent his days tramping through the streets, his beard now white, a heavy cane in his hand, his head bared as always. He no longer stopped children and told them how to breathe properly but kept his eyes on the ground and abruptly responded to the few greetings his more courageous neighbors still ventured to make to him. *"Morgen, Morgen,"* he mumbled without looking up.

If a mother tried to describe her child's symptoms to him he would quickly stop her. "No talking to Aryans!" he would growl. *"Verboten, verboten, verboten. . . ."*

In the old, secondhand-clothes dealers' quarter, the youths painted *Jude* on every shop window, although all the stores here were Jewish. They even wrote it, rather superfluously, on kosher butcher shops, on synagogues, and on Reb Ephraim Walder's bookstore. They demanded a mark from each storekeeper to cover the cost of the paint and the labor. On Grosse Hamburger Strasse they smeared the word *Jude* not only on doors and show windows but also on the monument of Moses Mendelssohn. The philosopher's sad eyes looked down with tolerant understanding at the bloody stain defacing his torso. A large crowd of the curious gathered on Landsberger Allee to watch the fun when the youths in boots converged on Solomon Burak's Discount Store. Here they not only painted the word *Jude* on the gleaming windows but added a clumsy Star of David. When the youths were through, they went inside to collect their tribute. As usual, Solomon Burak had to have his little joke. "How much do I owe the gentlemen? For each window separately or for the whole job together?" he asked, playing the fool.

Yetta trembled. "Shlomele, don't talk! Solomon!"

But he kept it up. "The gentlemen also drew some very lovely stars. Surely there must be an extra charge for them?"

With exaggerated courtesy he paid out the money, but still the youths did not go away.

Jonas Zielonek now felt obliged to speak up. After all, he was a native of Posen and a veteran of the war and his German was faultless. "How can I best serve you, gentlemen?" he asked politely.

Solomon Burak pushed him aside and addressed himself to the leader. "I believe you gentlemen would be more comfortable in my office. Please be good enough to follow me."

The "gentlemen" followed him into the cubicle that he called his office. He got down to business immediately. He knew that he had many enemies in the neighborhood, people against whom he had preferred charges for being late with their installments, and he had no urge to be taken into "protective custody." He had planned how to deal with this situation days before.

"Live and let live, gentlemen," he said, "that is my motto."

The grinning youths heartily concurred. With a skill born of generations of bribing anti-Semites, Solomon Burak settled a hefty sum on the "gentlemen" and innocently suggested that they send their wives and sweethearts to him to select nice things from his stock.

"It would please me no end, gentlemen," he simpered, still playing the fool. "I've reserved the finest Angel of Death models for your lady friends."

They promised to send their wives and sweethearts to be fitted for the whatever-they-were-called models and marched out heroically.

"Hush," Solomon Burak said to his weeping wife and protesting

son-in-law, "a ducat less, a ducat more. God is our father. One time
He provides good furtune; another, a boil on one's behind."

The youths did not fare so well with Solomon Burak's neighbor,
Ludwig Kadish. Thrusting his Iron Cross into their faces, he would
not allow them to paint the word *Jude* on his windows. "I am a
soldier who served at the front and won an Iron Cross, gentlemen!"
he cried. "I was in the trenches for four years! There is my uniform
with the bullet holes still in it!"

"More likely moth holes," a storm trooper quipped.

But the mob was sobered by the sight of the well-known medal
and uniform. The youths in boots scoffed. *"Quatsch!* Any Jew can go
out and buy an Iron Cross and a uniform. . . ."

Suddenly Ludwig Kadish tore the glass eye from the socket and
dramatically held it up for everyone to see. "And did I buy this too,
gentlemen?"

The mood of the mob changed. Seeing looks of resentment on
many faces, the leader of the gang acted swiftly. *Resisting authority,
inciting to riot, and spouting anti-German propaganda.* This arrogant Jew bastard needed to be taught a lesson. Iron Cross or no, he
was a traitor and a bloodsucker, and he had to be dealt with severely.
They marked his window with not only the word *Jude* but *Saujude*
as well. Then they tore the Iron Cross from his breast because it was
a sacrilege for a sheeny to wear it and ordered him to take the uniform out of the window. As they led him away to be "interrogated,"
Ludwig Kadish wept. Even his hollow eye socket dripped tears.
"Four years in the trenches," he sobbed. "An Iron Cross, first
class. . . ."

Solomon Burak stepped in. Whatever Kadish was, he still was a
fellow Jew and Solomon could not stand by and see him taken away
by the *goyim.* With his consummate ability to deal with bullies, he
winked at the leader of the gang, who promptly remanded his order.
"Here, you! Pay ten marks for every window and you can stay!" he
ruled.

Before Kadish could gather his wits, Solomon Burak counted out
the required amount and with another wink indicated that the whole
matter could easily be settled out of court. He was anxious for the
gang to leave the neighborhood as quickly as possible. Ludwig Ka-

dish wiped off his glass eye and wrung his hands. "The things I've lived to see," he lamented. "Paint on my clean show windows. . . ."

Nor was Dr. Carnovsky arrested; he was simply forbidden to treat Christian women. He consoled himself with the fact that he could still practice among the diplomatic set, but soon he was ordered to stop this as well. Dr. Carnovsky could not maintain his clinic. A group of Christian physicians offered to take it lock, stock, and barrel off his hands for a pittance and he had no choice but to accept their offer. Only a short time before, he had completely renovated the clinic, installing the latest medical equipment and new furniture. He sold it for a tenth of its true value. All he had to show for his years of toil and dedication was a slim packet of money that he really did not know what to do with. He was afraid to keep it in the house and just as afraid to put it in the bank, where all kinds of frauds were being perpetrated against Jewish property.

He was also eager to sell his expensive automobile for which he now had no use, but his brother-in-law, Hugo Holbeck, made that impossible.

Hugo was now a respected member of the New Order. He had inveigled himself into the Party's good graces during his frequent drinking bouts, financed by his brother-in-law, at Schmidt's Bavarian beer hall on Potsdamer Brücke. As a former Oberleutnant he had been assigned an important task—to teach young comrades who had never done military service to march, shoot, and use a bayonet. He had performed these duties in secret locations on the outskirts of the city, and although the pay had been meager, he had enjoyed his work. It was good to issue orders again, to lead a company of men, to drill, and to inhale the good smell of gunpowder. Once the Party took over officially, he put on his officer's boots, the brown shirt, and the insignia of the storm trooper on his sleeve. He even came home in his uniform but made sure to stay away from his brother-in-law's house.

He no longer needed to come to him for the French cognac, the Egyptian cigarettes, and the "loans." He had everything now—all the marches, parades, salutes, and boots he wanted, as well as the

authority to wear his revolver proudly and openly. There was no
further reason to face that arrogant, hook-nosed enema-giver and
take his insults. Nor was he anxious to meet the doctor's frizzy-
haired bitch of a Jew sister, with her ridiculous poems and books;
nor even his own sister, that traitor to her race. He did think about
Jegor from time to time with mixed feelings of guilt and regret, but
he quickly erased such emotions from his mind. He was too busy
now, too important to care about the whole pack of mongrels. The
only thing that drew him there was the car.

For years he had been envious of his brother-in-law's procession
of fancy automobiles. He could forgive Georg everything—the elegant home, the clinic, the women who threw themselves at him, the
Egyptian cigarettes, and the French cognac—but never the car. He
used to gag over the injustice of it—that a Jew who couldn't drive
and never went over sixty should own such a fine machine while he,
who knew the car like his own ten fingers, was forced to walk. It was
nothing less than criminal. Now more than ever he felt the need of a
car. For one, it suited his new position. Besides, he was now very
popular with the ladies and he needed a car to drive them around.
His brother-in-law's car was a gleaming new Mercedes that he had
bought only recently, and Hugo racked his brain trying to think up
the least embarrassing way of commandeering it.

At first he could not bring himself to face his brother-in-law in
his uniform, but gradually this shame wore off. He knew that the car
would eventually be confiscated—all Jewish property was being
taken away these days. If he did not take the car, someone else surely
would. Was it fair that a stranger should take what was rightfully
his? Whatever else he might be, he was still Teresa's brother and he
had the strongest claim to it. Besides, there was nothing to be
ashamed of. That lousy Jew had sucked enough money out of the
German people. He had even managed to avoid action at the front
and had malingered in back of the lines in army field hospitals,
sleeping with all the nurses who in the old days threw themselves at
the Jews. He had even had the effrontery to sully the name of an
ancient and honorable German family and to pollute pure Aryan
blood. No! There was no reason to feel sorry for that thick-lipped
pig! He had swilled the finest wines and smoked the best cigarettes

while a German Oberleutnant who had been wounded at the front
(well, almost) went around without so much as a pfennig in his
pocket. Now justice had triumphed and he would be damned if he
would let a stranger steal the car that was rightfully his from under
his nose!

One evening, after much hesitation as to whether to wear his uniform, which he finally decided to leave on, he started off to his
brother-in-law's house. His hobnailed boots pounding the pavement,
he walked swiftly through the deserted streets of Grunewald. But
near the garden that surrounded the house his courage suddenly left
him. He looked up to Jegor's room, ashamed to let the boy see him.
Seeing that the boy was apparently asleep, he lost some of his anxiety. He looked at Teresa's room. The lights were still on. Hugo
paced back and forth for a long time, cursing his own timidity that
hardly seemed fitting for a member of the New Reich. Finally the
light in Teresa's room went out and Hugo walked up to the front
door and quickly rang the bell. Much of his bravado came back
when he saw the frightened look on his brother-in-law's face. He
partly raised his arm and greeted Dr. Carnovsky with a half-hearted
"Heil!" There was no response. Hugo coughed, cleared his throat,
and shifted from foot to foot. "Looks like it'll be clearing up soon,"
he mumbled as his voice broke, to his deep disgust.

Dr. Carnovsky merely looked at him. Hugo began to blink and
haltingly communicated the fact that he had come to borrow the car
for a few days. Dr. Carnovsky did not need it at present, *nicht wahr?*
And it would come in very handy at this time for him, Hugo, because
he had to take a very important trip, *nicht wahr?*

He smiled fatuously and waited for some sort of reaction from the
burly figure lost in the shadows. Anything would have been better
than the brooding silence that filled every corner of the darkened
house. But his brother-in-law simply ran his eyes slowly from the
bristly, short-cropped blond thatch down to the tips of the gleaming
boots and up again. Hugo Holbeck flushed a deep crimson. Dr. Carnovsky took the keys from his pocket and laid them on the table in
front of him.

"I hope Herr Doktor doesn't take this too badly," Hugo offered lamely. He began to mumble something about duty and country but Dr. Carnovsky turned his back and left the room.

Hugo felt small and debased. But as soon as he took the wheel of the car, he forgot everything and breathed in the good stench of gasoline. "That arrogant sheeny bastard," he consoled himself, furious because his brother-in-law had not effected the transfer more graciously.

The next day Dr. Carnovsky took the bus to his father's house. David Carnovsky was amazed to see his son, whom he had not seen in years. He stood there awkwardly and stared at him. Georg threw his arms around his father. "No more reason to be angry, Father," he said with an ironic smile. "Now we are all Jews alike."

David Carnovsky stroked his son's cheeks as if he were a repentant child.

"Be of courage, my son, as I am and as are all the men of our generation. We have borne persecution since the beginning of time and we shall continue to bear it, as Jews always have."

29

Dr. Kirchenmeier, the newly appointed principal of the Goethe Gymnasium effected many changes upon taking over. The first thing he ordered Herman, the school janitor, to do was replace the portrait of the great writer for whom the school was named with one of the scowling little man with the slack mouth and the mad, baggy eyes. Then he issued a directive that all teachers and students use the official greeting and gesture instead of the traditional "Good morning." Next he ordered that Jegor Carnovsky be isolated from the rest of the pupils and informed in no uncertain terms of his status under the New Order. Dr. Kirchenmeier also retained his position as biology teacher. He did this because he enjoyed teaching and also because he coveted the extra pay. When he came into the classroom for the first time after assuming his new duties and thrust out his arm, Jegor Carnovsky responded with the rest of the class. But Dr. Kirchenmeier made him lower his arm. "You may only say 'Good morning,' Carnovsky," he said righteously, at the same time looking conspiratorially at the others.

On that day Jegor would not eat his lunch nor would he tell his mother what was bothering him. He never told his parents when he was disturbed. When his father tried to take his pulse, he flew into a rage. "I'm not sick!" he screamed. "Let me alone!"

Teresa blushed. "Jegorchen! How can you speak that way to your father?"

Jegor fled to his room. Dr. Carnovsky realized that his son was suffering because of the difficult times and he was anxious to console him. Actually, there was nothing he could do. He couldn't very well apply the same palliatives his own father had to him.

With each passing day Dr. Kirchenmeier let Pupil Carnovsky know more emphatically where he stood under the New Order. As far as the principal was concerned, the boy was not the Holbeck he pretended to be but a Carnovsky, the only one in school with such a foreign, outlandish name. His place was apart from the others not only during religious instruction but always. He belonged on the last bench with the worst students. But even they refused to sit with him. Maybe they were stupid, but they *were* Aryans.

Standing alone and watching his classmates march across the schoolyard, Jegor felt like the lepers he had learned about in history. The other boys looked at him with scorn. Their heads held high they marched in their uniforms, saluted one another, and accepted the admiration of the schoolgirls. They were allowed to handle real guns and taught the manual of arms by the physical education teacher. It was too much for Jegor to bear to see them in all their splendor. The worst of it was that he didn't even know why he was being discriminated against.

It was true that Dr. Kirchenmeier often spoke about a mysterious "they" who had betrayed the nation, who had stabbed the army in the back, and who were about to receive their due punishment. Whenever he said this, the other boys turned and looked meaningfully at the last bench. But Jegor could not feel any guilt for crimes against the *Vaterland,* nor had he ever stabbed anyone in the back. On the other hand, he could not believe that everything Dr. Kirchenmeier and the newspapers were saying these days was lies, and he was anxious to discuss this contradiction with someone wiser. But there was no one in whom to confide. His mother did not understand him. No matter how often he told her about the military drills from which he was excluded, she made nothing of it and, like a typical female, told him that it was a good thing anyway because such drills could be bad for his health.

"What *Quatsch* you talk!" he would say rudely, stung by any reference to his delicate constitution.

He certainly could not discuss it with his father. He always felt uneasy in his presence, as he did around the other Carnovskys. But

Dr. Carnovsky did not wait for his son to come to him. He knew what the boy was going through and he tried to minimize the effect of the times. He made fun of the madmen who ruled the nation and told Jegor to ignore their preachings, to reject them as he did. To hell with stupid drilling and marching; he would do better to read some worthwhile books or to study.

His father's advice only made Jegor angrier, partly because he hated to study and partly because his father and all the Carnovskys made too much fuss about education. His misery drove him to his Uncle Hugo. Although his father was contemptuous of Hugo, called him an idiot in boots, and accused him of stealing the family car, Jegor felt closer to his uncle than to his parents.

After many tries, he found him at home one evening. Jegor nearly trembled from joy. "Uncle Hugo!" he cried and stretched to his full, gawky height.

Hugo hung back, cold and distant. Although he was fond of his nephew, he wasn't sure whether it was proper for a storm trooper to be so intimate with a half-breed. "How goes it, boy?" he asked cautiously.

"Just fair, Uncle," Jegor said with a bashful smile. Soon he poured out all his troubles, all the shame and humiliation he had been forced to endure at school.

Hugo sprawled in the low easy chair, his long legs extended, and cleaned his revolver. "That *Schweinhund!*" he growled when Jegor told him about Dr. Kirchenmeier. "That lousy shithead!"

He was furious. How dared that man insult his sister's child, a Holbeck? That other people were being persecuted did not concern him—he thought no more about it than one does about the thousands of animals slaughtered each day for meat. But that some *Scheiskopf* should dare to harass a relative of *his,* this was intolerable!

For a moment he considered grabbing the old goat by his neck and in plain storm-trooper language telling him to lay off or else. But soon he reconsidered and his military training took over. It was firm in his mind that those of higher rank must issue orders and those below must obey and remain silent about things that were not their concern. He had no business sticking his nose into a dispute between a racially impure boy, even if the boy was his nephew, and a perhaps overzealous school principal who was only following orders.

Having made this decision, Hugo Holbeck ceased to have any interest in the matter. Still, he felt that he owed the boy some explanation.

Of course it was rot to imply that Jegor had stabbed the army in the back. And it must have been damned frustrating for him, a Holbeck, to be kept out of military drills. But he, Jegor, must understand that he was suffering on account of his father's blood. In life, as in war, the innocent had to pay for the sins of the guilty. And this was something irrevocable, something that could never be changed.

Highly pleased with himself over this logical interpretation, Hugo rose from the low easy chair and with a great show of concentration began to shuffle his papers to indicate that the conversation was over and that he, Storm Trooper Holbeck, had more important things to do. For a moment he considered giving Jegor a lift home in his car but he soon thought better of it. Would it be wise to be seen in public with a mongrel? Granted, the boy did not look Semitic— his eyes were blue and his bearing was erect and un-Jewish. If not for the black hair, he could easily pass for a Holbeck. Still, it paid to be careful. One could never tell these days.

"Unfortunately very busy at this time, *Junge*," he mumbled and, touching Jegor's hand, raced down the stairs.

Riding home on the bus, Jegor felt even more depressed. There was no one else to whom to turn, no one who would stand up for him. He cowered in the corner of the bus and looked around with half-mad eyes. He almost believed that the mark of his tainted blood was visible on his face and that at any moment he would be publicly denounced for being a racial cripple.

He felt as if he were some horrible freak, a Quasimodo. Along with the shame, he nursed a growing resentment against his father, the cause of all his anguish.

He scowled at him when he came in to say good night.

"Where have you been keeping yourself, boy?" Dr. Carnovsky asked with concern.

"I was watching a parade," Jegor said innocently. "It was so nice, with all the torches and flags and marching men."

Dr. Carnovsky's eyes filled with pain and Jegor felt a momentary thrill of revenge.

At the Gymnasium, Dr. Kirchenmeier pushed ahead with his changes. He enforced his authority severely, especially over Pupil Carnovsky, the lone black sheep in the flock.

Sly and pedantic, with a face the color of congealed fish broth, bulging eyes, and bristly, rust-colored hair, Dr. Kirchenmeier had been unpopular wherever he had taught. His every effort to gain his students' respect had failed. They had made his life miserable, played pranks on him, and rebelled against him with such enthusiasm that he had often been forced to call in the principal to restore order. But rather than discipline the boys, the principal would demand from Dr. Kirchenmeier the reason he could not control the class.

"What can I do if they won't behave, Herr Direktor?" Dr. Kirchenmeier would ask, close to tears.

"How come other teachers are able to control their classes, Herr Doktor?" was the inevitable answer.

Not that Dr. Kirchenmeier had not done everything he knew to win his students over. He tried being lenient, he tried being strict, he even tried to tell jokes to alleviate the difficult subject he taught. But as if through conspiracy, the boys resisted his jokes and only started laughing when he became serious. They preferred to laugh at him rather than his jokes.

When, in the early years following the war, the disgruntled veterans began to mumble about traitors and oppressors of the German people, they found a sympathetic ear in Dr. Kirchenmeier.

Their race theories bored him. As a qualified biologist he knew that racial purity was poppycock. Neither was he happy with the grammar and syntax of the street speakers. The obvious crudity of their approach often made him wince. But Dr. Kirchenmeier had lost all his savings during the inflation. All the hard-earned money that he had managed to eke out from his salary by cutting corners and accepting second-best was dissipated in the frenzied days that followed the war. This had become the greatest tragedy of his life. He had thought of all the good things he could have enjoyed with the money and the more he had thought, the more bitter he had

become. Abandoning his usual logic, he had forced himself to believe that it was indeed the international bankers, that pack of swindlers and manipulators from West Berlin, who had cost him his
savings. His money had helped to buy their mansions and to drape
diamonds around their fat wives' necks. He closed his eyes to the
race theories and the other pseudoscientific nonsense that the men in
boots were propounding and became their strong sympathizer. What
attracted him to them most was the intensity of their rage and the
bitter sensation of always being wronged and victimized, the same
feelings that had consumed him for as long as he could remember.

While they had remained in the minority, Dr. Kirchenmeier had
kept his sympathies secret. As he liked to tell himself, *when in
Rome do as the Romans do.* When the movement began to gain
momentum and to score impressive victories, Dr. Kirchenmeier became a member of the Party. He had done this in secret, however,
because one could never tell which way the wind would blow.
When the New Order finally became established, Dr. Kirchenmeier
was rewarded with the post of principal of the school in which he
had been considered such a failure.

The day he assumed the position was the greatest in Dr. Kirchenmeier's life. He, the eternal victim, now sat behind the huge mahogany desk and watched the teachers line up before him to await his
orders. And he issued these orders one after the other.

When, at his command, Herman the janitor took down Goethe's
portrait, Dr. Kirchenmeier's hands trembled. He felt as if he were
committing a desecration. But he struck to his decision, although no
directive regarding portraits had come down from his superiors. He
wanted to demonstrate his complete fealty to the New Order that
had recognized his value as a human being and as an educator and
had made his life bearable again. The more changes he effected, the
less his conscience troubled him, and soon he began to believe in
many of the things he had previously considered pure drivel.

No one laughed now at Dr. Kirchenmeier when he strode by in
his old green jacket with the dread insignia on the sleeve. No one
would dare laugh at the sign of the New Order. To show his gratitude to the students who for the first time in his career hung on his
every word, Dr. Kirchenmeier behaved with admirable magnanim-

ity. He permitted the students to participate in countless parades and allotted them ample time for military training. He organized them into youth groups and taught them the new race theories. He really won them over with his treatment of Pupil Carnovsky. His knowledge of psychology told him that nothing gratified a person more than feeling superior to someone else, and he provided the boys with the most likely victim. Actually, he had always thought rather well of Carnovsky, who had never shown him any disrespect and who was always polite and attentive. But personalities did not enter into the rebuilding of a New Germany. Not only did he place Pupil Carnovsky in the last row, but he always found new ways with which to torment him each time he called on him. No matter how Jegor replied, Dr. Kirchenmeier was sarcastic. Daily he created fresh opportunities to inject the racial theories into the lessons that caused the pupils to look back at the thin nervous boy who sat alone on the rear bench.

Nothing delighted the youngsters more than Dr. Kirchenmeier's habit of rolling the "r" in "Carnovsky," thus giving the name an even more exotic and mock-Yiddish connotation. This trick he had borrowed from a comedian he had once heard in a cabaret, and he used it time after time.

One rainy night when his rheumatism kept him from sleeping, Dr. Kirchenmeier suddenly had a brilliant idea. What a splendid thing it would be to demonstrate the race theory before the entire school with a live model! It would undoubtedly cause a sensation in pedagogic circles; it might even be picked up by the newspapers! Who could tell how far it might carry his name? Perhaps to the Führer himself? . . . The idea promptly negated the doctor's pains and he fell asleep like a baby.

The following morning he began to make preparations. He invited a number of the highest officials from the Ministry of Education to attend the lecture, as well as a reporter from the Party organ. Several days later, the lecture was held in the auditorium before the entire student body. Dr. Kirchenmeier had issued a directive requiring everyone to attend. Jegor Carnovsky took a seat in the last row of the auditorium without being told.

It was the first time in his life that Dr. Kirchenmeier had faced such a large audience, and he was ecstatic. He had prepared the lecture carefully and was able to infuse it with much pseudoscientific authority. Since most of his audience did not understand what he was saying anyway, they were all the more impressed by the quotations and examples Dr. Kirchenmeier so liberally included in his discourse. As half-educated people will when confronted with a subject that transcends their intelligence, they leaned forward and with rigid attentiveness listened to the doctor expound the complicated racial theories manufactured by German writers and philosophers through the ages. They nodded wisely and awaited further developments. Dr. Kirchenmeier carefully polished his eyeglasses, drank a glass of water, and called out: "Carnovsky, up on the platform!"

All eyes immediately turned to the last row and the boys picked up a chant that swelled through the auditorium. "Carnovsky! Carnovsky! Carnovsky!"

In a state of near shock, Jegor did not stir from his seat.

Finally he stood and shakily began to walk forward. He stopped in front of the platform. Dr. Kirchenmeier sharply ordered him to come up and to stand beside the blackboard that was scribbled with various signs and symbols.

He roughly grasped the boy's head and turned it so that it faced the audience. "So!" he said.

The touch of the principal's clammy hand on his hot cheek made Jegor's heart trip quickly. He did not know what was coming, but he knew somehow that it would be something unbearably evil. The worst part of it was facing the audience. He had never been stared at by so many people at one time. His knees began to tremble and he was afraid he would faint. A low murmur swept through the auditorium and Dr. Kirchenmeier raised his hand for silence. "Gentlemen, we will now illustrate our theories with a live demonstration. I urge that you remain perfectly quiet and pay strict attention to the subject of our lecture."

First, Dr. Kirchenmeier used a compass and calipers to measure the length and width of Jegor Carnovsky's skull and he wrote the figures on the blackboard. With scientific precision he measured the distance from ear to ear, from the top of the head to the chin, the area between the eyes, the length of the nose, as well as every plane of the boy's face. At each touch of Dr. Kirchenmeier's cold, damp fingers Jegor cringed anew.

Then Dr. Kirchenmeier delivered a long and impassioned dissertation. "The audience will see from the figures on the blackboard the difference between the structure of the Nordic dolichocephalic skull —the long and handsome head that projects racial beauty and superiority—and that of the Negroid-Semitic, brachycephalic skull—the stubby and blunted head that resembles that of an ape and typifies racial deformity and inferiority. But in the case of our subject, it is particularly interesting to note the influence of the Negroid-Semitic strain on the Nordic. As you can clearly observe, the mixture has created a kind of freak. It may occur at first glance that the subject resembles the Nordic type, but this impression is strictly illusory. From the anthropological viewpoint one soon realizes that the Negroid-Semitic strain, which is always predominant in cases of mongrelization, has very subtly allowed the Nordic strain to dominate the external appearance in order to mask its own insidious influences. But this can be ascertained from the subject's eyes, which, although they may appear blue, lack the purity and clarity of classic Nordic eyes and are full of the nigrification and obfuscation of the African jungle and the Asiatic desert. You will also note that the hair, which may seem straight, contains Negro blackness and a hint of inherent woolliness. The prominence of the ears, nose, and lips clearly demonstrates the inferior racial strain."

To verify his conclusions, Dr. Kirchenmeier marked down a whole series of dots, dashes, and markings on the blackboard and offered for the audience's edification a large selection of quotations from various ethnic researchers and anthropologists, employing in the process a string of Latin and other foreign expressions. The distinguished visitors and the students were not only entertained by the demonstration but deeply impressed by Dr. Kirchenmeier's scientific knowledge. When he was completely finished probing Jegor Carnovsky's head, Dr. Kirchenmeier said coldly: "The subject of today's demonstration will disrobe."

Jegor Carnovsky did not move. Dr. Kirchenmeier flew into a controlled rage. "I distinctly stated that the subject will remove his clothes so that the audience may get a better understanding of the lesson!'"

Again Jegor Carnovsky did not move, and a nervous rustling swept through the hall. Dr. Kirchenmeier held up his hand for silence and called the school janitor, who now wore the uniform of the storm trooper. "Storm Trooper Herman, you will remove the subject and bring it back completely bare."

"*Jawohl,* Kamerad Direktor!" Storm Trooper Herman said, and hustled Jegor into a small room off the auditorium.

Jegor resisted with all his strength. "No!" he screamed in his voice that unexpectedly alternated between a baritone and a falsetto.

"Be smart, boy, or I'll have to use force on you!" said Herman, who in the past had collected huge tips from Dr. Carnovsky.

Jegor kept on struggling. He had already begun to mature and this made him especially bashful about his body, as boys usually are during the period of puberty. The thought of revealing his nudity terrified him. Besides, he was very sensitive about being circumcised. The mark of inferiority that his father had imposed upon him had always revolted him. When he was small, children had twitted him about it and nicknamed him "Damaged Goods." Since then he had always avoided undressing in front of others.

"No!" he screamed, feeling his strength waning. "No! No!"

Herman angrily tore the clothes from the squirming boy. He no longer had to be servile to the son of the Jew, Carnovsky. He was now a storm trooper and even the Direktor called him Kamerad. Jegor's struggles aroused his cruelty and sadism, along with vague sexual feelings. One by one he stripped the garments from the girlish body. When he came to the last garment, the desperate boy sank his teeth into Herman's tattooed wrist.

The sight of his blood drove Herman into a frenzy. "You *Saujude,* so you'd bite a storm trooper, would you?" he snarled, and gave Jegor a healthy swipe.

The punch, the first one in his life, drained the last of Jegor's resistance. Storm Trooper Herman lifted him by the scruff of his neck and half dragged him back onto the platform.

"Stand still and don't squirm!" he growled as Jegor's knees buck-

led. For an instant, raucous laughter and coarse advice rang through
the hall. The mark of the Semite struck the youngsters and the distinguished visitors as something highly amusing. Dr. Kirchenmeier
magnanimously allowed the laughter to go on for a while to further
ingratiate himself with the audience, but soon he signaled an end
to the frivolity.

Now everything proceeded without delay. Dr. Kirchenmeier
pointed out the marks of the inferior strain in the rib structure and
in the lock of the elbows. He even called attention to the genitalia,
whose premature development emphasized the degenerate sexuality
of the Semitic race. At this, the boys began to snicker but Dr.
Kirchenmeier quickly put a stop to it. Such a serious scientific subject as racial inferiority deserved the grave and mature consideration
of all who would participate in the building of a New Germany.

He would have liked to elaborate on many more aspects of the
topic but Jegor's legs could no longer support him and he collapsed.
Dr. Kirchenmeier ordered Storm Trooper Herman to take the subject into the side room, to let it dress, and to send it home.

That very same day's late edition of the Party organ carried a long
story about the remarkable lecture Dr. Kirchenmeier had delivered
at the Goethe Gymnasium on the degrading influences of Negroid-
Semitic blood on Nordic in mixed marriages. Dr. Kirchenmeier was
lauded not only for his scientific conclusions, but also for his imagi-
native application of progressive educational methods that should
serve to inspire all school principals in the nation. Despite his aversion to spending, Dr. Kirchenmeier bought numerous copies of the
newspaper and read each one separately to his wife. That night he
even tried to make love to her, but the long years of abstinence had
left him impotent.

In Dr. Carnovsky's house his son lay on his bed with his face
toward the wall and flatly refused to tell his parents what had happened. "Don't come near me!" he shrieked hysterically.

Late that night he developed a fever. Dr. Carnovsky applied ice
packs to his son's burning brow and checked his pulse and heart.

"What happened, son?" he pleaded with the boy.

"I want to die," Jegor said. He had suddenly developed a stammer.

Dr. Carnovsky was terribly concerned about this development, as he was about the boy's high fever. But what was most frightening was the madness that now emanated from his son's eyes.

30

A strange, brooding laxness settled over the Carnovsky household, the disruption of routine and order that accompanies a serious illness. Doors were left ajar, drapes were undrawn, floors were unswept, and the stink of vomit and medicine hung in the air.

Dr. Carnovsky did not leave his son's bedside and Teresa again put on her nurse's uniform and attended to Jegor's needs, alert to every sound he uttered in his delirium. When she could no longer stay on her feet, Rebecca Carnovsky relieved her. In the large dining room now not in use, since everyone ate at different times, David Carnovsky wandered about, his ears cocked to every sound from upstairs.

"Help us, oh Lord. Take pity on the poor innocent child," he prayed, not in German but in good, homely Yiddish.

He no longer felt resentment toward his son. The troubles that had descended on the family had dispelled all animosity. Now that his grandson was so desperately ill, David Carnovsky had no reservations about visiting a house he had sworn never to enter. For lack of anything better to do, he wound all the clocks in the house, a task he assumed everyone else had forgotten. When he was finished, he culled from his memory every prayer he had ever known to offer in his grandson's behalf. David had grown more devout since the bad times had come. He even recited his prayers in the chanting, Hasidic tone he had disdained during his involvement with enlightenment. Although it repelled him as would eating food that wasn't kosher, he even spoke the boy's mother's name as the Law prescribed, and repeated the prayers every day without fail.

Leah Carnovsky went up and down the stairs, thrust her head into the bedroom to check on Jegor's condition, and addressed herself to God in her intimate and overfamiliar fashion. "You can do it if you want to, dearest Papa," she whispered, her eyes cast heavenward. "Listen to me and let my words reach Your ears, sweet Father. . . ."

Grandmother Holbeck took over the kitchen and household duties. "Holy Mother and Jesus," she crooned to the religious pictures Liesechen the maid had abandoned on the kitchen wall along with the photographs of circus strongmen and acrobats.

She was forever fussing, cleaning, straightening, and brewing coffee for everybody. From time to time she brought some to David Carnovsky. "May I offer you a cup, Herr Carnovsky?" she would ask shyly.

"Than you so much, dear lady," he would say just as shyly and accept the cup from her trembling fingers.

It was the first time they had met and they were both deeply embarrassed by the years of mutual distrust and estrangement. David Carnovsky saw before him a kindly old lady with white hair and gentle eyes, a devoted grandmother with an obvious concern for her grandchild, although she was not as demonstrative in her grief as his Leah. The very act of bringing him coffee demonstrated a kind of womanly devotion and an acknowledgement of their kinship.

Despite David's outspoken opposition to the marriage, neither Teresa nor her mother displayed any resentment and he regretted the animosity he had nurtured for so long against these decent and gracious people to whom circumstances had bound him.

"Won't you have a seat, dear lady?" he said, holding out a chair for her. "It really disturbs me to have you fuss over me. . . ."

"It gives me great pleasure, Herr Carnovsky," she said truthfully.

She was impressed by his manners, his appearance, and his grammatical German that reminded her of her pastor's.

Although they tacitly avoided mention of the terrible times, the subject invariably crept into the conversation. As soon as it was polite, Frau Holbeck excused herself and fled into the kitchen.

She was ashamed of her country, of her people, of her son Hugo, who was part of the New Order, but especially of herself for having harbored hatred against the Carnovskys and their kind, although she would never allow herself to give voice to these feelings. In the excitement that had attended the elections, when the city had been full of music and proclamations and oratory, she had been hypnotized into following the trend in favor of the men in boots who had promised prosperity and the re-establishment of a strong and vigorous Germany.

Although her Jewish son-in-law was providing for her generously, she could not forget the loss of her beloved houses, Hugo's inability to find a job, and the terrible postwar years. The men in boots had promised to restore things to the way they had been before the war and her own son had assured her that once the traitors and speculators were eliminated, things would go back to normal.

And she had believed them and voted as they asked. Naturally, she had not considered her son-in-law one of the nation's enemies. He had provided her daughter with the best things in life, he had supported her and even her poor Hugo. And how could he be called a traitor when he had served at the front? No, the traitors were the others, the bankers from West Berlin whom the newspapers said robbed the poor and swindled people's houses away for pfennigs.

Yes, she had been tricked into voting for the New Order and she was ashamed. It even seemed to her that David Carnovsky's piercing black eyes somehow guessed her secret.

She had seen some ugly scenes in the streets lately. Young hoodlums attacked decent people, obviously not swindlers and speculators but respectable citizens, even elderly ones, and the police merely looked on. In the large shops and department stores where she had shopped for years with satisfaction, the windows had been marked with rude signs, the panes had been broken, and Aryans had been forbidden to enter. The famous doctors whom all Berlin had revered had been prohibited from practicing, her son-in-law among them. Her Hugo now ranted against everything, drank to excess, refused to give her money for household expenses, brought home all kinds of disreputable people—ruffians in hobnailed boots who in the old days would not have been permitted across the threshold and sometimes even cheap women.

She was greatly concerned about Hugo but she was even more worried about Teresa. Ever since the New Order had come to power, her daughter had been ostracized as if she were a leper. Frau Holbeck's oldest friends refused to come to her house, afraid of meeting Teresa there. Hugo wouldn't go near his own sister. He had even warned her, his mother, to stay away from the Jew-house, as he called it, because it might hurt his career. But she had not listened to him. Nothing, no one could keep her from her own flesh and blood! But it gave her little pleasure to visit Teresa these days. A kind of emptiness hung over the house, a self-imposed silence and sense of shame. Dr. Carnovsky did not go out and no one came to see him. Ever since he had been attacked by a gang of rowdies while walking with Teresa and she had been called a Jew-whore, he kept off the streets. Teresa also stayed mostly inside and felt terribly ashamed before her husband, as if she were somehow responsible for her countrymen's behavior. Frau Holbeck went through agony trying to get her daughter to go out for a few hours.

She was horrified by the terrible wrong that had been done her grandson. No one could convince her that her precious Jegorchen was inferior to other boys and deserved the contempt and torture he had suffered at school. And who had committed this injustice? Not common street bullies, but an educated man, a school principal!

Old age had brought Widow Holbeck little happiness. Looking at her husband's picture in the hall, the one in which he looked so solid and respectable in the high starched collar and the elegant jacket she had loved so well, she begged God to let her join her Joachim as quickly as possible. She prayed even harder before the Holy Mother's picture in the church where she always stopped for a few minutes before going on to Teresa's. Kneeling on the hard stone floor, she prayed for her poor tormented daughter, for her son who had strayed from the path of righteousness, for her Jewish son-in-law who deserved a better fate, and above all for the blameless child upon whom misguided people had vented so much unjustified evil.

"Holy Mother and Thy Son, Jesus," she whispered, her arms spread in supplication, "shield and protect this innocent child from all pain and evil. Send Thine angels to heal and comfort him, for he is young and pure and innocent as a lamb. . . ."

31

Although Jegor lay in bed only a few weeks, he underwent a great change in that short period.

He grew even taller and gawkier. His spindly arms now stretched far out of his sleeves. His voice changed completely. It lost its uncertainty and became deep and manly and sounded incongruous coming from the slender girlish body. The first dark fuzz began to color his cheeks and long dark hairs sprouted from pimples scattered on his pale body.

Because he was so gaunt now, his Carnovsky nose seemed even more prominent and the thick black eyebrows that met over its bridge only served to accentuate its size. A sharp knob also formed in his throat and bobbed up and down with every movement of his lips.

The first thing he asked for when he recovered consciousness was a mirror. He saw a face that reminded him of the typical *Itziks* caricatured in the newspapers. "God, how awful I look! So ugly and Jewish!" he cried and threw the mirror from him.

Teresa stroked her son's hair that had grown long and tangled during his illness. "What a terrible thing to say, Jegorchen. What if Papa heard you?"

He repeated the words, this time even louder.

Dr. Carnovsky made every effort to restore his son's health. He gave him all sorts of tonics to build him up and at the same time he tried to heal his soul.

During the whole time that Jegor had lain half-conscious, Dr.

Carnovsky had written down every word he had mumbled in his delirium. Alone, the words were garbled and meaningless, but bit by bit Dr. Carnovsky had fitted them together to reconstruct a picture of a crushing emotional experience.

He was even more interested in the boy's stammered words than the ones spoken clearly. While the stutter faded from day to day, it did not go away completely but came back each time Jegor became excited, which was often, since every little thing upset him. Dr. Carnovsky knew that the stutter was due to an emotional rather than a physical wound and he searched for a way to rid Jegor of his deepseated feelings of self-contempt and debasement.

He attacked the problem with his customary zeal. His well-stocked library contained many volumes on psychology and psychoanalysis, sciences that had never particularly interested him, a practicing surgeon more concerned with anatomy than with the psyche. Besides, he had never had the time to delve deeply into the books, which was the only way he knew to tackle a new subject. Actually he had bought them only because it had been the thing to do. Now he had both the need and the time to study them. Concepts that he had previously rejected because he had been in good health, secure, fulfilled, and invulnerable now seemed reasonable and appropriate, and he began to apply the methods that the books advocated in treating his son.

He regretted the years that he had neglected the boy because of his practice. Nothing remained now of the fame and the honors for which he had worked so hard. But he still had his son and he vowed to bestow upon him all of his future care and devotion. To send him back to that horror in school was unthinkable. He, his father, would become the boy's teacher, his mentor and guide; above all, his friend.

"Keep that chin up," he joshed Jegor in a mock-severe tone and playfully flicked his nose.

Jegor turned away and did not even smile back. "Leave my nose alone," he said. "It's big enough as it is."

Dr. Carnovsky dropped the frivolous tone. "Forget, my son," he pleaded. "They're scum. Despise them as I do. Wipe them from your mind. . . ."

Jegor smiled crookedly. Forget? He would never forget. He

couldn't. He racked his brain to recall every detail. Over and over he relived every exquisite moment of his torment and took perverse pleasure in its memory, like a child sucking its wound. Rather than hate his tormentors, he loathed himself. He even forgave Dr. Kirchenmeier for exposing his inferiority to the world. He could hardly blame him when he himself hated it so. Jegor Holbeck despised everything about Jegor Carnovsky—his black hair, his sharply etched brows, his arrogant nose.

When he confessed these feelings to his mother, she only laughed at him. Why, those were his best features, the very things that had attracted her to his father. . . .

What atrocious taste she has, Jegor thought. To him his father resembled a black tomcat, or maybe a toad. She was the one who was so beautiful, so fresh and fair and innocent-looking. His father's swarthiness only reiterated what Dr. Kirchenmeier had said about the nigrification and obfuscation of Africa and Asia.

But his mother's face was clear and open and shining. There were no shadows there, no dark pockets of cunning and cruelty. Everything was smooth and straight—the hair, the nose, the chin. That's how Uncle Hugo looked. That's how a German was supposed to look. If not for his father, he, Jegor, could look that way too.

All his troubles stemmed from his father and his kind. It was their fault that he was a poor runner, weak and sickly. Uncle Hugo had explained it to him over and over. The newspapers, the magazines, the artists, the speakers all said it too. They always showed the *Itziks* as weak, crippled dwarfs with frizzy hair and huge noses. Next to them real Germans looked trim and muscular. Had Dr. Kirchenmeier not proved it with his instruments? No, it couldn't all be make-believe, as his father claimed. It didn't make sense that a whole country should suddenly conspire to lie simultaneously. It was his father who was the liar. Jegor could even see the racial flaws in himself when he looked in the mirror. How horrible and disgusting he looked, so black and murky and big-nosed! He was so repelled by his appearance that he stopped going out of the house altogether. He was terrified of being publicly humiliated again.

Dr. Carnovsky was deeply disturbed by the boy's self-imposed isolation. From lack of fresh air and exercise Jegor had become sluggish and flabby. He lost his appetite, couldn't sleep, and stayed up late ruining his eyes over newspapers and magazines. He would oversleep, get up grouchy and sour, and later feel guilty and remorseful. He smelled of bedding and a kind of mustiness that disgusted his father. Dr. Carnovsky wanted to drag the boy out into the fresh air forcibly and to let the sun and wind purify him and wash him clean.

"Out of bed, lazybones!" he would chide him in the mornings, half in jest and careful not to antagonize him. "Splash some cold water on your face and let's take a walk, just the two of us!"

"What for?" Jegor would ask apathetically.

Dr. Carnovsky knew what kept his son inside. He was also apprehensive about going out but he would not give in to it. He'd be damned if he'd let that scum keep him in the house! After his first reaction to the New Order, when he had clung to the house to avoid the endless parades, demonstrations, and street gangs, out of pure rebelliousness Dr. Carnovsky began to go out even when he had no reason to do so. He walked briskly, holding his head high, and paced off the miles to purge himself of the sloth, struggling to control the depression that came over him. Some of his neighbors looked away when they saw him; others nodded. A few of the more daring even smiled and said good morning. Dr. Carnovsky kept his head even higher to show his indifference. He, Georg, was no one's inferior. . . .

He asked his son to join him on these walks, but Jegor would not show himself after his public disgrace, especially in the company of his obviously Jewish father. Nor would he cooperate when his father offered to tutor him. He wouldn't even go out into their own garden. Dr. Carnovsky now did all the work that Karl had once done. He hammered, sawed, mended, repaired. The physical exertion helped to dissipate some of his energy and made him feel less useless. He always asked Jegor to help him. "Let's see who can finish sawing first!" he would challenge him, knowing that boys enjoy a contest.

"I want to read the papers," Jegor yawned.

Dr. Carnovsky despised the publications that only slandered his kind. "Throw that filth out of the house!" he stormed.

But Jegor sprawled on the sofa and devoured the newspapers and

magazines. He kept the radio blaring all day and, knowing that it
drove his father mad, kept the volume turned up full blast.

He would have been glad to accompany his mother outside but
she seldom asked him to go with her. Whenever she did, he leaped
at the chance. She was so fair, so safe to be with. He couldn't hold a
grudge against his mother. The more he hated his father, the kind-
lier he felt toward her, the innocent victim of her husband's crimes.
He would kiss her passionately and brutally, leaving bruises on her
delicate skin. At times he went so far that Teresa became uneasy.

His face was sprinkled with acne. She had found some of the
illicit pictures he kept hidden in his room. Deprived of the compan-
ionship of girls his own age, he directed all his affection at his
mother. Teresa blushed furiously when he held her tight. "Enough
of that, silly boy!" she said. "Go out in the yard and help your father."

But Jegor did not want to help his father, who made him feel
even less worthy. Seeing him so tanned and vigorous and glowing
with the love of physical labor and a childish sense of accomplish-
ment only intensified Jegor's feelings of sloth and inertia. He was
sure that his father's dark eyes were mocking him, that the Carnovsky nose was scornful. Since the scorn was justifiable, Jegor was doubly annoyed. He was also terribly jealous of his mother, who each
night was taken from him by this dark and malevolent Jew.

He couldn't stand it when his father turned out the light in the
dining room and retired to the bedroom with her, slamming the
door in his face. She would then comb out her long flaxen hair and
put it up in braids. In her clinging nightgown she seemed to Jegor a
vision, a divine yet voluptuous idealization of the perfect Aryan
woman, the symbol of the New Order. He couldn't stand the lustful
and rapacious way his father looked at her. Jegor used every excuse
to disturb his parents in their bedroom and to keep them from being
together. The women in his sexual dreams always resembled his
mother and he often stayed in bed late to hide his shame from her
when she came in to change his sheets. His father's medical library
contained many volumes describing in clinical detail the sexual experience. There were books there on anatomy, on venereal disease,
on pathology, and on sexual aberration. Jegor studied these books

for hours, lying in his pajamas in his bedroom. The books aroused such emotions in him that he often didn't hear his mother call him to the table. His eyes shone with an unhealthy glow, his cheeks broke out in blotches. He made copies of the forbidden pictures as well as all kinds of fantastic drawings of naked female bodies. He also copied drawings from newspapers and magazines that ridiculed the Jews.

He hid these drawings carefully, but one day his father caught him at it. Jegor had drawn a blonde angel being raped by a fat curly-haired *Itzik*. Dr. Carnovsky looked at the crudely drawn cartoon with deep concentration.

"What is this supposed to mean?" he asked, although the answer was obvious.

Jegor didn't answer.

"Answer me, I'm talking to you!" his father said, his temper flaring.

Again Jegor didn't speak.

Dr. Carnovsky lost control and slapped his son's face hard.

Blood spurted from Jegor's nose. "Jew!" he screamed at his father, and burst out crying.

Dr. Carnovsky ran from the room. "God! What has become of us?" he cried, turning to the One in Whom he had never believed.

The next day, instead of his customary walk, he went to see about getting a visa out of the country.

Long rows of people stood in line before the consulates, people of every age and background: men of distinction from West Berlin next to peddlers from Dragonerstrasse; Jews in long beards and gaberdines and those who had severed all connections with the community but still were marked with the stigma of racial inferiority and damned for the sins of their fathers. They stood there reduced to the same level and waited for the huge consulate doors to swing open. Quietly, Dr. Carnovsky took his place among them. He would not rest until he had rescued his family, especially his only son in whom the ravages of self-hate had already wreaked irreparable damage.

32

Strangely enough, Rebecca Carnovsky had never been so happy as during the terrible times that threatened the lives of her family.

One day when, by sheer chance, she met Hugo Holbeck in the street in his brown shirt, high boots, and the dread insignia on his sleeve, the shock left her speechless. She looked at him with disbelief.

Hugo Holbeck shifted his weight in embarrassment and looked around to see if anyone were watching him fraternizing with a Jewess. "Good day, Fräulein Becca!" he said, smiling fatuously.

She only stared at him unblinkingly. Suddenly she felt her strength flowing back and half-raised her hand to slap his face, but she stopped it in midair and turned away. When she got home, she dashed into her room and settled down to cry. Her parents came in to see what was wrong but she wouldn't tell them. She only stopped to take a breath and went back to her crying.

She cried over her dashed hopes, over his duplicity and glib tongue, over the trust she had placed in this supposedly naïve individual. Like most oversentimental women, she exaggerated her disappointment. Like most such women, she quickly got it out of her system along with the tears.

She no longer felt anything toward him but a deep revulsion. He had given her a totally new insight into the brutal, blond military type that had so long intrigued her. She forced herself to readjust her attitude about the kind of man who previously had seemed so unattractive and in a very short time she fell in love with a typical example of the species.

David and Leah Carnovsky could not find the proper words when their daughter introduced them to the new man of her choice.

"Meet Rudolf Richard Landskroner," she said, pushing him forward. "Now you must love him as I do."

Her parents looked at each other in bewilderment and tried to appear pleased.

Despite his impressive name, Rebecca's sweetheart was an undersized, insipid little man, none too young, who carried a violin case that made him look like an itinerant fiddler.

The Carnovskys knew that he was not a fiddler but a concert violinist, an artist. Rebecca claimed that he was the greatest violinist alive. But even this did not alter their opinion of him. They did not, however, tell her how they felt. She was getting along in years and young men had never been much taken with her. Besides, most of them had already left the country and there was not even money for a dowry in case she did find somebody else. Rudolf Richard Landskroner was surely no prize catch, but whom did they have instead?

"Well, David, what do you think?" Leah asked when they were alone.

"At least he is a Jew," David said.

He was so disappointed in his daughter's choice that he did not even put on his Sabbath coat and silk hat for the quiet ceremony that was attended by only the prescribed quorum.

Rebecca did not need her parents' approval, their best wishes or receptions—she had her Rudi and this was enough for her.

Because he was so small and timid and soft, she loved him with a desperate intensity. She had always sought this quality in a man, the trait that would permit her to spoil, to dominate, and to fondle the object of her overpowering love. Before, she had seen this trait in the blond, soldierly young men. Now that one of them had deceived her, she had found it in her Rudi.

The very first time she saw him performing before a small Jewish audience, she knew that she loved him. He was smooth-faced and round-cheeked and his long silken hair hung to the collar of his jacket. Although he was forty, he had the plump, downy hands of a child prodigy. The audience was very warm to him and Rebecca clapped louder than anybody and led the chorus for encores. From that night on she attended all his concerts. Her adoration struck a responsive chord in him and he allowed himself to be completely taken over by her.

Once they were married, she took complete charge of his life. She carried his violin case, combed out his silken locks, dressed him for his appearances, and took off his shoes when he came home. She prepared all sorts of delicacies for him and forced him to eat even when he wasn't hungry. She performed every menial service— ran his errands, argued for bigger fees, praised him everywhere, and even helped him in and out of his overcoat, reversing their role as man and woman.

Rudolf Richard Landskroner accepted his wife's devotion like a capricious child who indulges his mother by allowing her to fuss over him.

When Rebecca became aware of changes within her body and knew that she was carrying Rudi's child, she nearly crushed her mother in a passionate embrace. David Carnovsky greeted the news with disgust. "This is no time to bring a Jewish child into the world," he grumbled.

Dr. Carnovsky almost lost his mind when he learned of his sister's condition. "Rebecca, your Rudi is an irresponsible idiot! Come to my house, I'll see what I can do to prevent this. It's a crime to bear a child these days!"

Rebecca would have clawed his eyes out. "No one is going to rob me of my happiness!" she hissed. "Not anyone!"

She flatly refused to apply for a visa, although her parents and friends pleaded with her. Rudi had elected to remain in the country; this was enough for her.

Never in his lack-luster career had Rudolf Richard Landskroner enjoyed such adulation. He had never been seriously regarded in the profession, but now that most of the famous concert artists had left the country he began to gain recognition by default, if nothing else. It was true that he could not demonstrate his artistry in the famous music halls to which he had always aspired, but he still was allowed to play for Jewish audiences and they, starved for any kind of entertainment, applauded him and cried for encores. Gushing matrons called him "Maestro," young girls pleaded for his autograph, and Rudolf Richard Landskroner was deliriously happy. He thought about his father, a musician in a restaurant, who had believed in his son's genius and had named him Richard in memory of the immortal Wagner. If only he could see him now, Rudi lamented, if only he could share his triumphs. . . .

Although life in Berlin was not without danger for those of his faith, he had accepted the inconveniences as one becomes reconciled to every evil. Naturally he avoided going out into the street unless it was absolutely necessary. He knew better than to sit on a park bench when he was tired and his eyes dropped automatically when a blonde woman approached. But otherwise life was sweet. His recognition made up for everything and Rebecca basked in his glory. She turned a deaf ear to her parents, to her brother, to her friends and acquaintances. She would not even accompany her family to the port of embarkation when, after years of waiting, they finally obtained their exit papers, because she refused to leave her two babies alone for even a single day—her Rudi and the child she had borne him.

"She's lost her mind altogether," Leah Carnovsky complained.

"Female sense," David grunted, and went to Dragonerstrasse to bid farewell to Reb Ephraim Walder.

"Did you know, Reb Ephraim, that the villains have destroyed Rabbi Moses Mendelssohn's monument on Grosse Hamburger Strasse?" he said indignantly.

"What is a monument after all, Reb Carnovsky?" the old man said calmly. "A pile of stone and metal. His spirit shall live on."

David Carnovsky felt guilty about going away and leaving the old scholar behind. "If with God's help we make it safely to the other side, I'll send papers for you too, Reb Ephraim," he said. "I won't rest until I get you out!"

"I am too old to be moved, Reb Carnovsky," the patriarch said slowly. "If you will manage to save my manuscripts, however, you will be performing a great service for humanity. The books and my daughter. Isn't that so, Yentl?"

Janet lifted her weak black eyes from her latest French novel and shook her frizzy head that was now more gray than black. "What are you suggesting?" she asked. "That I would leave you alone at your age?"

She didn't know exactly how old her father was—he might have been a hundred or even more. But she did know that he was nothing but a bundle of dry bones that could disintegrate at any moment.

Like an ancient tree that is ready to crumble, the old man had turned into a hoary ruin. His withered, brownish-blue skin had been squeezed dry of all juices and had peeled like bark. His long beard had turned green as moss. His eyebrows and the tufts of hair that sprouted from his ears were prickly and stiff as dried pine needles. His skeletal fleshless hands could no longer serve the body and Janet had to dress and undress him, to feed him, and even to help him dispose of his wastes. Although she herself was well into her sixties, her spinsterish soul made her cringe at the thought of sharing such intimacies with a male, even though he was her father.

Only the patriarch's brain continued to function as keenly and lucidly as ever. The older it grew, the more it rejected all human frailties—envy, passion, ambition, and greed—and enhanced its capacity for pure logic. The old man's vision and hearing also remained intact, and now that he spent most of his time in bed, he watched with resentment the movement of every mouse toward his beloved books and manuscripts. His keen ears also heard every sound from the bookstore below. "Yentl? What's going on down there?" he would call out frequently.

His daughter had little with which to cheer him. Hardly anyone came these days to make a purchase. The only ones who showed up with mounting regularity were the youths in boots demanding "contributions," and rampaging street gangs.

"Father," she would complain, "the bad boys have thrown a cat into the store!"

"What's a cat?" the old man would chuckle. "It's merely another of God's creatures."

"But it's dead!" she would cry.

"What of it?" he would observe. Nothing surprised him. He accepted all things and events as merely further manifestations of the divinity—whether they were a pebble, a human being, or a dead cat.

With similar equanimity he greeted David Carnovsky's passionate description of the outrages being perpetrated upon their people. "An old story, Reb Carnovsky," he said in the vigorous voice that belied the incredibly fragile body from which it issued. "An old, familiar story. It was ever thus—in Speyer, in Prague, in Cracow, Paris, Rome, and Padua. Since Jews have been Jews mobs have burned their books, forced them to wear identifying patches, driven them from their homes, and persecuted their sages. Still, Jewry has prevailed. Incidentally, the mobs have not only persecuted Jewish sages but their own as well. Wise men will always be hated for their insight and perception. Socrates was forced to drink hemlock. Akiba was flayed alive. But what has remained has been not the mobs but the teachings of Socrates and Akiba. Because the spirit can no more be destroyed than can the deity. . . ."

David Carnovsky could not stand the patriarch's calm appraisal of the desperate situation, but the old man would not give him a chance to protest.

"Be so kind, Reb Carnovsky, as to climb up to the bookcase and fetch down my manuscripts. They're on the top shelf. I wouldn't trouble you, but I'm not as agile as I used to be," he added wryly.

David got down the two bulky manuscripts—the Hebrew one for the Jews and the German one for the gentiles.

With trembling hands Reb Ephraim brushed away the spider webs and began to read to his visitor his most recent additions and notations.

As he read, however, new avenues of thought opened up and in order not to forget them he scribbled them on the margins. Although he could otherwise barely move his hands, they seemed to gain strength when wrapped around a goose quill. The trembling fingers clung lovingly to the pen like an old warrior's wielding his favorite sword. Although his mind was far away and he was in no mood for philosophical dissertations, David Carnovsky listened to Reb Ephraim out of his great respect for the old scholar. But Janet could not stand any more of her father's calm observations and said spitefully: "Father, you'll drip ink on the bed. Besides, you're not allowed to strain yourself. You must rest."

"I'll rest in my grave already, Yentl," her father said indulgently. "So long as my eyes still serve me, I'll do what I can."

Janet waved her hand disparagingly as one does over a dotard who has grown too senile to reason with. "Oy, Papa, Papa," she wailed, and bit her tongue to keep from saying what was really on her mind.

Reb Ephraim, who was sensitive to everything around him, smiled over Janet's pique. "She thinks that because I'm old I don't know what's going on. I know, I know everything, Reb Carnovsky, but still I continue to do what I must because that is the duty of the scholar. . . ."

Janet, who was cooking their supper in a tiny saucepan on the stove that she now kept going with old books instead of wood, was irked by her father's imperturbability. With each passing day she saw the tragedy coming closer. Dragonerstrasse grew more deserted and most of the stores were boarded up and bolted. At night the houses were shuttered. Only the sounds of speeding cars, gentile laughter, and Jewish lament gave evidence that someone else had been taken away after dark. The ghetto street, now vulnerable to murder and every outrage, filled her with a terrible dread.

"Father," she interrupted, "why must we endure so much suffering?"

Reb Ephraim showed his gums in a toothless smile. "That's a question as old as suffering itself," he said. "Our minds are too limited to cope with it, but there must be a reason for it as there is a reason for everything else. Otherwise why would these things be?"

This explanation was too ambiguous for Janet and she grew even more depressed. "Why must God mete out so much punishment?" she demanded passionately. "Why does He cause so much pain when He is able to provide only good?"

Again Reb Ephraim tried to answer her with logic. Only fools resented God for the evil they must bear and praised Him for the good He provided. This kind of reasoning was obviously fallacious, since all things had a place in the divinity. Nothing could be removed from it and treated as a separate experience. All things—all animals, plants, humans, and stars, everything that existed, that had existed, and what would exist—all so-called good and evil and happiness and suffering were part of this all-encompassing scheme.

Janet was scandalized to hear such a description of God—a God to Whom one could not complain; a God Who did not repay good with good and evil with evil; a God without mercy or justice. She yearned for the old God she had known and loved—One to Whom she could offer benedictions, call Sweet Papa, and complain to if necessary. Her father's interpretation of the higher world filled her with a sense of hopelessness. She could see no meaning at all to the virtuous life she had led if there were no reward for her goodness and morality in the other world. And she began to cry, although there was a stranger present.

"Don't cry, Yentl," her father said. "Nothing is served by crying." But she only cried harder.

David Carnovsky stroked her hand paternally, as if she were a little girl. "Don't cry, Yentl," he said. "As soon as we get to the other side, God willing, I'll send for you and your father and his books as well."

She dabbed at her eyes with a corner of her apron. Although she knew that her father was too old to travel and she herself was too set in her ways to begin life in a new country, she was relieved to hear a man's voice and to feel his comforting hand on her shoulder. She smiled up at him with moist, myopic eyes. Suddenly she realized that her father was lying motionless with his eyes closed and she ran to his side. "Papa! Papa!" she screamed hysterically.

The old man opened his eyes and smiled at her slyly. "What did you think, Yentl, that Satan had already come for your old father?" He laughed, showing his gums. "No. I'll manage to keep him at arm's length for a while yet. . . ."

David Carnovsky got up to go. He squeezed Reb Ephraim's trembling, icy fingers. "Keep well, Reb Ephraim," he said with a catch in his throat. "I have a feeling that somewhere, someday, we will talk and study together. . . ."

"I'll miss you, Reb Carnovsky," the old man said. "I'll have no one now to whom to read my manuscripts. . . ."

A few hours before leaving the country Teresa Carnovsky made a final visit to her mother's house. She wanted to see once more the place where she had been born and raised. She went into her old room, looked fondly at her old bed and at every familiar piece of furniture, at the embroidered towels and every knickknack. She studied her father's portrait in the hall, and she cried along with her mother over the life that might have been. Hugo slouched in the low easy chair, his long legs stretched out before him. He was disgusted by the women's tears. Although it was not easy, he tried to act brotherly toward his sister on her last day home.

In his exaggerated Prussian accent and curt manner he told her how he felt about her leaving the country. It was not right that she, a Holbeck, should desert the *Vaterland* at a time when it needed all its sons and daughters. And on whose account? A lousy Carnovsky. It still was not too late to get a divorce and to rid herself of this weight around her neck. She could be a human being again, live among human beings, and associate with her own kind and no one would ostracize her.

"But you know that Teresa loves Georg. And there is always Jegorchen to consider," his mother said.

Hugo had a solution for this as well. He knew important people, people who could get things done. He would take care of everything. There were many German women who had discarded their *Itzik* husbands and had their children certified as racially pure. It was a mere formality, a detail. All it required was an affadavit asserting that the boy had been sired by an Aryan lover, *nicht wahr?* He, Hugo, would take care of all the details. He would supply the witness, the alleged father, and everything would come off like clockwork.

During the whole time that her brother was speaking the blood kept mounting to Teresa's face. Finally she could no longer control herself. "You filthy dog," she said in quiet fury, "how dare you make me such a proposition? You swine! You snotnose! You pimp!"

Frau Holbeck stood as if transfixed. "Teresa, daughter, how could you?"

But Teresa would not be silenced. This was the ultimate insult to her womanhood. She abused her brother with words she had never before used in her life. She called him and his ilk bums, hooligans, offal, and sons of bitches.

Frau Holbeck was distraught. "Teresa," she pleaded, "O dear Jesus and Mary!"

But Teresa was beyond restraint. The bitterness that had festered within her for so long, the resentment over the evil done her husband, her child, and her dear ones spilled out of her like water from a broken dam. "I spit on your New Order!" she shrieked. "I spit on you too!" And she spat on his face and uniform.

Hugo turned as white as death and his jaws began to work spasmodically. As a soldier, he was less resentful of the spittle on his face than of that on his uniform, and all his instincts urged him to avenge this unspeakable slur. Teresa guessed what was going on in his mind. "Go ahead! Why don't you call the police?" she taunted him. "Go on, turn me over to your butchers! Denounce me, why don't you!"

He only took out his handkerchief and carefully wiped his uniform. "Jew-whore," he said dispassionately, as he had heard his comrades address blonde women who were in the company of dark men.

Frau Holbeck clenched the fingers of her half-paralyzed hands. "Holy Mother and Lord Jesus," she lamented. "What have I lived to see in my old age!"

Pale as a corpse and completely drained, Teresa fainted in her mother's arms.

BOOK THREE   *Jegor*

33

Temple Sha Mora on the Upper West Side of Manhattan was crowded again these days, not only on the Sabbaths but even during the week.

Since it had been built a few decades before, the large synagogue, which resembled a mosque, had seen good times, bad times, and disastrous times. In its first five years of existence it had been attended by the affluent, old-established Sephardic Jews who had settled in the luxurious apartment houses bordering the Hudson River. Swarthy, modish, exuding the exotic aroma of the oriental rugs, tobacco, and spices in which they dealt, they had calmly and haughtily taken their places in the synagogue and with the dignity of grandees indolently followed the monotonous chant of the hazzan intoning the prayers in Hebrew and Ladino. Their elegant wives, colorful in their silks and satins, gold and diamonds and costly mantillas, quietly joined in.

With equal pride and confidence in their status they listened to the sermons of their *hacheem,* Dr. Eusial de Alfasho, who, in his robe, high miter, and coal-black, curly beard, resembled the pictures of ancient Assyrian monarchs. When, prior to the reading, the *shammash* circulated through the synagogue and in an Arabic chant auctioned off the *mitzvoth* of being called up to the reading of the Law, the wealthy congregants vied with large sums for the honor.

Later, during World War I, when the Ashkenazi Jews, the Polish, Lithuanian, and Rumanian, prospered and fought their way up to the very summits of the Upper West Side, the haughty Sephardim disdainfully abandoned the section and, along with it, Temple Sha Mora. Instead of Sephardic hymns, Ashkenazi prayers and chants echoed through the mosquelike synagogue. Instead of the black-bearded *hacheem* who resembled an Assyrian king, the sermons were delivered by a young Ashkenazi rabbi who wore a thin blond mustache and who spoke in pedantic English, discussed the latest books, plays, charity drives, psychoanalysis, and birth control. After the war, when the bad times came back and the residents of Harlem, the Spanish, Irish, and Negroes, moved further uptown, Temple Sha Mora became as run-down as the rest of the neighborhood. The *nouveau riche* Ashkenazis were replaced by indigent shopkeepers and teamsters—unshaven, poorly dressed, and overworked men who for the most part stayed away from the handsome mosquelike structure.

With each succeeding Sabbath the congregation dwindled. The only time the synagogue was filled was during the Days of Awe, on the holidays, or during the memorial services for the dead. It became difficult to round up the necessary quorum not only on weekdays but even on Sabbath eve or on the Sabbath itself. The Hungarian beadle, Mr. Pitzeles, would stand for hours in the doorway, his black eyes alert for a stray Jewish male. He would be assisted in this by Walter, the German janitor, who from years of service in the synagogue had learned all the Jewish customs and spoke a Teutonic Yiddish that was no worse than the beadle's. With the pockets of his paint-smeared overalls bristling with hammers, screw drivers, and coils of wire, and with his eternal pipe clenched between his teeth, he would collar any passing Jew and urge him inside. "Hey, mister, you're needed inside for a *minyon.* Don't you know it's *shabbes* today, Mac?"

"Who's got the time for that?" the men would reply, rushing by, puffing on their cigars or cigarettes.

Walter also had to spend much of his time squabbling with the neighborhood children who had turned Temple Sha Mora into their own favorite playground. Swarthy Spaniards, fair-skinned Irish, black-thatched Jews, and dusky Negroes, they crowded around the synagogue, screaming and brawling. Adolescent girls liked to sit on the broad steps, whisper secrets to one another, and screech at the boys in the tattered sweatshirts who teased them. Little girls skipped rope, loudly reciting the alliterative chants handed down through generations. The boys were an even greater nuisance; they never stopped bouncing their balls against the walls of the synagogue, keeping up at the same time an apparently endless quarrel. In the evenings they lit fires in ash cans and burned scrap and paper that the wind carried in from the river. No matter how often Walter chased them, they always came back. The high walls and wide steps of Temple Sha Mora drew them like a magnet.

"Goddam little bastards!" Walter would spit out of his thin lips along with the pipe smoke, "Gethehelloutadere!"

What really made him angry was that even on the Sabbath they would crowd the steps and block the worshipers from coming and going. The two beadles, the Jewish and the gentile, were in a fury when they assembled the tiny band of congregants that seemed even smaller when drawn together in the vastness of the synagogue.

Within the past several years, however, Temple Sha Mora had again filled with worshipers, not only during the Days of Awe, the holidays, and memorial services, but even on the Sabbaths and weekdays.

These were the latest Jewish inhabitants of the neighborhood, the German refugees who had chosen the Upper West Side of Manhattan as their section and Temple Sha Mora as their house of worship.

When these newcomers first appeared in the synagogue, Mr. Pitzeles welcomed them with open arms. "Come in, good people, welcome!" he said in his Hungarian-accented German, rolling the "r's" extravagantly.

Walter, the janitor, was delighted to meet the people from *drüben* and grateful for the opportunity to practice the *Muttersprache*.

Standing on the stepladder and arranging the bulletin board that announced phonetically when *minchah, mariv,* and *haskorotneshamot* would be held, he engaged in polite conversation with the newcomers. *"Bitte schön, meine Herrschaften, sofort fangen wir schachres an,"* he would say. "Hurry, gentlemen!"

Mr. Pitzeles led the newcomers to the desirable pews and assigned them the honors of carrying the Holy Ark. He was amazed at the precision with which the newcomers recited the prayers and even

more astounded by their wives, who sat in the women's gallery upstairs. These refugee ladies came to services not only on Saturday
morning but on Friday evenings too, something rare indeed for
Temple Sha Mora. He was altogether enchanted with the youngsters. Scrubbed, combed, and neat in their high stockings and knee
pants, they presented a vivid contrast to the raggedy neighborhood
boys who raced through the streets like savages. The foreign youngsters behaved very correctly, minded their parents, and asked permission for the smallest thing. Mr. Pitzeles brought them the prayer
books in gratitude for their manners.

The congregation of Temple Sha Mora grew so quickly that soon
Mr. Pitzeles not only ran out of honors for the men but also out of
prayer books for the youngsters.

Within a short time the neighborhood around the Hudson River
was overrun by the newcomers. At first the old Jewish residents of
the area greeted them as warmly as had Mr. Pitzeles. It was easy to
tell the newcomers by the huge crates of furniture they brought from
the other side, crates that bore the stamped names of their ports of
origin—Hamburg and Bremen. The huge moving vans transporting
them could barely negotiate the narrow streets. The giant Negro
moving men cursed and sweated, trying to maneuver the oversized
pieces of furniture through the narrow doorways of the apartment
houses. The janitors of the houses, mostly Germans themselves, were
impressed by the expensive pieces but warned the newcomers that
they would have to leave their wardrobes in the streets because
American apartments had built-in closets. The gentile residents of
the area studied the newcomers and their abundant possessions with
silent hostility. Before the newcomers could decide what to do with
the pieces of furniture that they had struggled so hard to rescue, the
boys in the streets commandeered them for their own, bounced their
balls against them, and struck matches on the costly veneer. They set
fire to the dismantled crates and sometimes even to the furniture
itself.

The Jewish residents came forward to help the newcomers
make an adjustment to the new country and in a friendly and sympathetic way inquired about conditions on the other side. But the
newcomers ignored these overtures and remained aloof. They re-

fused to discuss the evil things going on in their Germany. The Polish and Lithuanian women tried to invoke a juicy Yiddish oath against the villains who were persecuting their people, but the newcomers would not utter a single bad word against their fellow Germans. They only grimaced with distaste and replied in a precise English that they did not understand the "jargon" in which the American Jews addressed them. After the initial rebuffs the Jewish residents avoided the strangers who behaved in such an arrogant and supercilious manner. Former immigrants themselves, they remembered when they had first arrived from the Russian and Polish villages with only their sacks on their backs instead of crates of expensive furniture. The only things they had brought with them had been their bedding, their Sabbath candlesticks, and their two sets of dishes, one for meat, the other for dairy. Nor had they immediately settled on the Upper West Side. They had been forced to move into the tiny garrets and basements of the Lower East Side. It had taken years of struggle and achievement to work their way up to the banks of the Hudson. They also felt a debt of gratitude to their Jewish neighbors who had welcomed them and advised them on how to get along in the new country. Now they began to express a strong resentment against the newcomers for their expensive clothes, their knowledge of English, their material wealth, and, above all, for their refusal to blame those who had driven them out and for their contempt for the Yiddish language and customs.

The Jewish grocers had no patience with the refugee customers who haggled over every penny and watched the scales as if expecting to be cheated. The kosher butchers were enraged. "How do you like that—we're not kosher enough for these *Yekes!*" they complained as they honed their knives on the whetstones.

The newcomers did not utter a word in their own defense. They had avoided all contact with the Eastern Jews in their old country; they would avoid it here as well. They kept to themselves and created their own little Reich.

At first, Herr Gottlieb Reicher, the former pork dealer from Munich, opened his own butcher shop in the neighborhood. The shop was spotless and antiseptic as an operating room. A former owner of a chain of pork shops that were known throughout Germany, Herr

Reicher now had a large "Kosher" painted in gold letters next to his name on the window of his store. At his side stood his son, a former optometrist, who wore his medical smock to work, the only thing he had left from his profession.

The refugee housewives forgot their troubles momentarily when they walked into the surgically clean shop for their meager portions of meat and the former optometrist waited on them. They addressed him as Herr Doktor and he, in turn, called them by their proper titles, remembering precisely who had been Frau Direktor, who Frau Professor, and who Frau Kommerzienrat. Any housewife who lacked a title he diplomatically addressed as "gnädige Frau." And the women no longer felt any apprehension about the meat being kosher, since Dr. Speier himself, the former rabbi of the Berlin synagogue, gave it his unqualified approval on a sign printed in German in Herr Reicher's window. Nor did they worry about the scale, since Herr Optiker Reicher weighed the meager purchases with scientific precision.

Following Herr Reicher's example, the matinee idol of the Berlin stage, Leonard Lessauer, opened a café—which he called Old Berlin —where one could drink coffee with whipped cream, eat apple cake, beer with frankfurters, and read German newspapers and magazines. At night Old Berlin became quite gay because Herr Lassauer would put on his old frock coat and starched shirt and declaim or act out little scenes from his repertoire. But in the daytime one could linger there for hours over a cup of coffee and be called Herr Doktor whether one deserved the title or not.

Following this, former Associate Professor Dr. Friedrich Kohn opened a cleaning store where garments were pressed while one waited, hats were blocked, and shoes were heeled and soled. Popular with his countrymen because he had taught philosophy on the other side and even more so because his father had been the famous Kommerzienrat Kohn who had been given the title by the Kaiser himself, Dr. Friedrich Kohn drew a large clientele to his cellar shop. Just like his late distinguished father, who had subsidized students from the East, Associate Professor Dr. Friedrich Kohn was a model of decorum and even wore the white mutton-chops that made him his father's image. He ironed garments with immense dignity and between soling one shoe and another peered nearsightedly into the Greek and Latin books that he kept on the shelf next to the old shoes.

Frau Doktor Klein, the widow of Dr. Siegfried Klein, the editor of the most popular satirical magazine in Germany of whom only a jar of ashes remained, then opened a dressmaking shop in her apartment where she not only sewed new dresses but also altered old ones. Her clients did not have to hide their frugality from her, since they were old friends and shared many memories. When they came to her apartment, they reminisced about the good old days, passed along greetings from the latest arrivals, and shed a tear or two over the jar of ashes that used to be Dr. Siegfried Klein.

Ludwig Kadish, Solomon Burak's neighbor from Landsberger Allee, was not able to open a store in the new country because, beside the Iron Cross that he had won for losing an eye for the *Vaterland,* he had not managed to save another blessed thing. He therefore was reduced to peddling ties in small Jewish restaurants. His daughters, who had operated a chemical laboratory on the other side, opened a small beauty parlor where for pennies they gave manicures and did hair dyeing. Middle-aged refugees tinted their hair to conceal their age while seeking jobs and dark-haired Jewish girls turned blonde to deceive employers who discriminated against their faith.

After a day of scratching for a living in the large friendless city, the newcomers liked to gather at the Old Berlin where, safe among their own kind, they could speak longingly of the good life *drüben.* Here one could always meet the newest arrivals and hear the latest news from home. Quietly and conspiratorially they inquired about friends and acquaintances, learned who was coming, who had been taken away in the middle of the night, who had died, and who had disappeared, leaving only a box of ashes.

They carried this same insulation over to Temple Sha Mora and little by little took over the congregation. First they erected an invisible barrier between themselves and the handful of old-time worshipers who still remained. When the others made friendly overtures in the spirit of true Jewishness, the *Yekes* snubbed them. They made no response whatever when the old congregants referred to the leaders of the New Order—this was a subject they would discuss only among themselves. The others took offense, felt like strangers in their own synagogue, and soon abandoned it altogether. Before Mr. Pitzeles knew what was happening, he was left without a quorum of the older congregants. And as they drifted away, the newcomers took control of the temple. When the last of the former congregants had gone, the newcomers turned Temple Sha Mora into an exact duplicate of their old synagogue *drüben*. They elected their own board of directors. The first to be named to it was Herr Reicher, the famous pork butcher who now ran a strictly kosher establishment. Then they changed the ritual of prayer to conform to that to which they had been accustomed on the other side. Walter, the janitor, now put up the announcements on the bulletin board not only in English but in German as well so that everyone could understand. Then they invited the celebrated opera star, Anton Karoly, a fellow refugee, to become the cantor of Temple Sha Mora. Karoly, the son of a cantor, wore a mop of bleached hair, a broad-brimmed hat and a monocle, and carried a briefcase full of yellowed clippings, letters from old admirers, faded photographs, and locks of hair. He organized a choir and performed with such gusto that the members of the congregation were enraptured. They also sent for Dr. Speier to become the new rabbi of Temple Sha Mora.

Cold and erect, his tiny pointed beard now turned gray from age and worry, Dr. Speier did not introduce a single new note into the sermons he preached in the new country. Just as in the good old days, he spoke about Israel, about the mission of the children of Abraham, Isaac, and Jacob, and about the codes and ethics of the Torah that God had issued through his deputy, Moses. Just as in the good old days he also quoted from German writers and philosophers and had the tact not to refer even once to conditions overseas. The women adored him, the men were enthralled. Even Ludwig Kadish's glass eye twinkled with animation at Dr. Speier's sermons. After a week of humiliation, anxiety, and frustration, it was good to relive the good old days when, in a top hat and frock coat, one slowly strolled the streets of Berlin on the way to Sabbath services.

There were only two people connected with Temple Sha Mora who were considered outsiders by the congregation. One, obviously, was the Hungarian beadle, Mr. Pitzeles.

Never, not even under the Kaiser, had the congregants felt anything but contempt for Hungarian Jews. Besides, Mr. Pitzeles wasn't even a Hungarian; he was a despised *Galitzianer*. They felt much closer to the janitor, Walter, who was, after all, a fellow German. The fact that a gentile, a pure Aryan, was their employee provided them a kind of perverse satisfaction after the years of abuse and humiliation on the other side.

The second outsider they were forced to put up with was Solomon Burak, who was not only on the temple's board of directors but also served as its president.

They had to tolerate him because he had worked his way up in the new country so rapidly that he was the only one in a position to contribute to the temple generously. Besides, most of the members of the congregation were dependent on Solomon Burak for credit and for the goods that they peddled from house to house.

Like their ancestors who had come to Germany with peddler's packs slung over their shoulders, the newcomers returned to the ancient trade of the uprooted Jew and subjected themselves to the mockery and contempt of the gentile world. The only difference was that they now carried suitcases instead of peddler's packs, but the doors were still slammed in their faces and the indignant residents could still vent their frustrations on these comical, pompous strangers with their square-cut, floor-length overcoats and overprecise English. After the years of prosperity, success, and contempt for the likes of Burak, the haughty Berliners were forced to seek out this very same upstart, to curry favors with him, and even to elect him president of their temple.

He had been among the first to emigrate to the new country. When the youths in boots began to visit him with increasing regularity, to harass him, and to send new men for bribes constantly, Solomon Burak decided to leave while there was still time. His neighbors, the *Yekes,* particularly Ludwig Kadish, were firmly convinced that conditions would soon improve because the *Vaterland* would not allow such evil to continue for long. No, they were not prepared to leave the land of their birth because of some temporary unpleasantness. But no one could change Solomon Burak's mind. He had no illusions about being a German, and he could evaluate the situation with an outsider's objectivity. Just as he had instinctively known the time to come to Germany, he knew the time to leave it. With bribes and chicanery be obtained the necessary papers for himself and his family, saved as much of his stock as possible and, with his wife, children, in-laws, and grandchildren, boarded the ship for America.

In the new country, with which he fell in love at first sight, he turned to his first occupation, peddling, just as he had done in Germany when he had first come from Melnitz. Again he stuffed his suitcases with all sorts of bargains to tempt the ladies and struck out to earn his living. But rather than travel country roads, he instinctively headed for the Jewish section near the East River.

Yetta Burak cried bitterly when she saw her husband going out into the street with a bulging suitcase in each hand. "What I've lived to see!" she wailed. "Oy, Shlomele!"

"That which I brought from Melnitz I still have in any case," he said lightly, "and now, let us have only luck and prosperity."

Just as in his younger days, he did not, like other refugee peddlers, court pity, did not whine or plead but, instead, quipped and joked and entertained the housewives. In a mixed German, Yiddish, Polish, and the first English words that he picked up in the streets, he enticed the women with his bargains until they could not resist. "A ducat more, a ducat less, live and let live, missus," he said and clapped his customer's palms with his own to signify that the matter was closed and the bargain sealed.

The women enjoyed his bargains almost as much as they did his unfailing good nature, his amusing sayings, and elaborate compliments. They laughed, but they were also delighted when he assured them how beautiful his goods would make them, so alluring that the men would swarm around them like bees around honey. On his very first evening Solomon Burak came home with empty suitcases and a pocketful of money. On the way home he stopped to purchase all kinds of delicacies—sour pickles, onion rolls, garlic salami, peppers, and smoked herring—and laid them out on the table of the tiny and cramped apartment that was filled mostly with goods. Although his bones ached from trudging the streets, from toting the heavy suitcases, and from climbing stairs, he did not utter a single word of complaint to Yetta and his family. "A plague on the enemies of Israel who will never enjoy such goodies as Solomon Burak has here," he quipped. "Don't keep your nose in the ground, Yettele, because if you do, I'll get me a new missus and you'll be left without a husband or a nose."

Yetta sighed. "All you can think about is nonsense, Shlomele," she said. "But I'm in no mood to laugh."

"The enemies of Israel won't live to see the day Solomon Burak cries," he said vindictively. "You'll yet stand behind a cash register and collect money like in the old days. This I promise you, Yetta darling!"

And, as usual, he kept his promise.

After several weeks of traipsing around and absorbing the rhythm of the city, its likes and dislikes, its way of doing business, its language and customs, Solomon Burak put his valises aside and bought himself a pushcart.

"Ladies, misses and mississes," he shouted through Orchard Street in a ripe Melnitz Yiddish garnished with Berlin German and topped with a measure of East Side English. "Yes, I've got them. Bargains, bargains, bargains. They're lovely, they're kosher, they're cheaper than borscht. . . . Grab them before it's too late, the end, the finish! Don't get shut out. . . . Hurry! Hurry! Hurry!"

The other peddlers tried to drive the *chutzpatig* greenhorn from the street but Solomon Burak was not one to be pushed around. Quipping, squabbling, pleading, even using his fists as a last resort, he defended his rights and did a brisk business. When sales lagged, he began to call down revenge on the enemies of Israel and abused them with such juicy oaths that his customers and even the other peddlers couldn't keep from laughing. But the one who enjoyed it most was Solomon Burak himself, who delighted in getting even with his enemies.

"Hey there, *madamele,* little lady, missus, may the anti-*Semiten* die a thousand different ways. Buy my bargains, cheap and pretty, a plague on all the Hamans, Amen!" he chanted in an affectedly pious tone.

Once he had attuned himself to the American way of doing business and accumulated several hundred of the most essential slang words, he left the pushcart leaning on its stand and bought a car, a battered wreck that somehow was still able to function. When it ran, all of its parts kept tune with its engine, the drooping fenders, the loose bumper, and the trailing exhaust pipe. While taking his test Solomon Burak broke every law of driving but, winking at the leather-jacketed examiner, he expressed his indignation at the miserly wages paid public servants and somehow or other managed to obtain his license. He painted the wreck a bilious green and upon it in screaming scarlet letters proclaimed to the whole world that the vehicle contained Solomon Burak's Berlin Discount Store. He loaded the car with his choicest goods and set out for the Catskill Mountains. He stopped at every hotel, from the largest to the smallest, and at most of his stops he did business. With a youthful vitality that belied his years, dressed in his flashy suits complete to a diamond stickpin and rings, he raced down highways and cowpaths at speeds of sixty and seventy miles an hour, and the clatter of his jalopy was matched only by his voice hawking his wares at every bungalow colony.

"A ducat more, a ducat less, live and let live," he would announce, then swiftly unpack his goods, count up the money, scatter a few well-chosen quips, and move on to a new location.

In a short time he traded in the wreck for a better car, opened a tiny store on the Lower East Side, and laid in a stock of cheaper goods, the kind with which he had had so much success on Landsberger Allee. Just as in Berlin, he was able to sniff out bargains— remnants, fire sales, bankruptcies, all kinds of seconds, thirds, and irregulars. Just as in Berlin, he quickly made friends with the wholesalers and jobbers, accepted cigars, distributed cigars, and did not let a bargain escape him. Again he began to sell on the installment plan and on credit. He had promised Yetta that she would again stand behind a cash register, and within a few short months he made good his promise. As soon as he earned a few extra dollars he began to bring over his and Yetta's relatives—just as he had brought them from Melnitz to Berlin. When they came, he sent them out to peddle or to collect installment payments. When business flourished he sent for more relatives, signing the required affidavits assuring their employment. In a short time he moved his business to a larger location on the Upper West Side and at the same time rented a spacious apartment that was strikingly similar to the one on Landsberger Allee.

Once again it was open house at the Buraks' for friends, relatives, strangers, and acquaintances, for anyone who needed financial assistance or a simple word of comfort. Again people slept everywhere, on upholstered chairs and sofas, on tables, on floors, wherever there was an inch of space. All day long food was prepared in the kitchen and the most recently arrived relatives made gefülte fish, put up preserves, baked the familiar almond cookies, rolls, and strudel, boiled noodles and fish broth. Again the phonograph blared cantorial chants and gay theater melodies. Immigrants came to spend a day and stayed for weeks. Again Solomon dubbed his apartment Hotel du Bedbug but, just as before, he said it in the spirit of fun, not in resentment. He helped everyone who asked him and in every way picked up the thread of life that he had abandoned in Berlin.

But now the ones who came to seek his help were not the inhabitants of the secondhand-clothes dealers' quarter but the former bankers, merchants, princes, and mainstays of the West Berlin Jewish community. They came to him although they despised him. One of the first to beg a favor was his former neighbor and competitor, Ludwig Kadish, who asked for goods on credit. The others soon followed. Solomon Burak turned no one away. He extended credit, lent money without interest, gave the choicest goods, co-signed loans, and helped bring their relatives into the country.

As president of Temple Sha Mora, he enjoyed accepting the traditional Sabbath greetings from his fellow worshipers. He knew that he would save time and money by joining another congregation, but it was worth everything to him to receive homage from the arrogant West Berlin aristocrats.

He was the only one to stand up for Mr. Pitzeles when the others treated the beadle with contempt. He would not even allow the beadle to address him in his broken German when he came to his house to discuss temple business.

"Yiddish, Mr. Pitzeles, good old Yiddish when you talk to me," he insisted, giving the beadle a glass of the Passover slivovitz that he liked to drink all year round. "We're two of a kind, you and I, and we understand each other."

Mr. Pitzeles looked gratefully at his employer and he poured out his heart. His livelihood was in jeopardy because some of the newcomers coveted his position. The one he feared most was the notorious Berlin match-maker, the spurious Dr. Lippman.

Dr. Lippman had not changed an article of his attire in the new country, to the great delight of the street urchins who loved to throw stones at the now green silk hat that he wore on all occasions. But there was no way of earning a living through matchmaking here and Dr. Lippman harangued his fellow refugees each time the name of Mr. Pitzeles came up. "It's outrageous that a lousy *Galitzianer* should hold down such a soft job while a man of my stature starves to death!" he raged. "A damn shame, that's what it is!"

He initiated a campaign to inveigle himself into Mr. Pitzeles' domain. He criticized his methods, interfered with his duties, mixed into community affairs, and had business cards printed that listed him as "Reverend" in addition to "Doctor" Lippman. He also trailed Solomon Burak around, brushed off his jacket, helped him into his coat, and flattered him outrageously at every opportunity. "You are our protector and our father, dear Herr President. First God and then you, Herr Doktor President."

"I'm no doctor, Herr Lippman," Solomon Burak would say, highly amused by Lippman's methods.

"Oh, yes you are! A doctor and a prince too," Dr. Lippman would insist. "An angel sent from heaven, that's what you are. . . ."

Mr. Pitzeles was afraid that in the end Dr. Lippman would persuade the congregation to make him the new beadle of Temple Sha Mora. But Solomon Burak clapped Mr. Pitzeles on the stooped shoulder that reflected so much concern and told him to stop worrying. "Don't let these *Yekes* give you even one moment of unrest. So long as I'm the head of this synagogue they won't touch a hair of your beard or my name isn't Solomon Burak. Here is my hand on it!"

34

A blazing sun baked the New York waterfront from which came drifting the acrid smells of fish, burning pitch, and rotten vegetables.

Spires of skyscrapers gleamed in the molten silver of sky. The Negro dockworkers had shed their shirts and the muscles of their arms and backs glistened wetly. The asphalt trembled under the huge trucks that rumbled by noisily with exhausts popping. They panted and seethed in a kind of frenzied fury and discharged clouds of smoke and fumes. From afar came the sound of elevated trains punctuated by the piercing shrillness of wheels biting into rails as they made hurried, sweeping turns. Echoes of traffic rumbling over bridges assailed the ear. Longshoremen, passengers, sailors, harbor officials, policemen, Western Union messengers, and cab drivers milled about, arguing, sweating, and jostling one another. A breeze suddenly blew in from the river. It stirred the oppressive atmosphere, hurled dust and paper scraps into dripping faces, and as unexpectedly as it had come it vanished. The humidity again embraced the people like a clinging towel, crept into every crevice of their weary bodies, and made breathing and walking an effort. Like a huge tidal wave it inundated the family Carnovsky that, after ten days of cool ocean air, landed abruptly in the seething hubbub of New York harbor. The green landing cards promptly became soggy rags between their fingers.

The first thing David Carnovsky did was moisten his hands at a drinking fountain and make a benediction over the new land to which God had brought him and his.

Dr. Carnovsky took off his hat and his eyes slowly took in every inch of the panorama before him, from the glowing tips of skyscrapers to the melting asphalt below. With the toe of his shoe he gingerly explored the ground, as if testing its firmness and stability. Suddenly he seized Teresa's arm and took her for a stroll along the harbor. No one even bothered to look at the tall black-haired man and the pale blonde woman at his side. The very idea that he could walk with his wife unmolested filled Dr. Carnovsky with a bursting joy.

"Teresa! This is America!" he exulted, sweeping the rather unlovely harbor view with his hand. "Aren't you even a little bit happy?" He hugged and kissed her.

"Yes, Georg," she said, embarrassed by such a display in public.

Dr. Carnovsky tried to pass his enthusiasm along to his son. "Well, boy, here we are at last!" he said, chucking his chin playfully. "Isn't it magnificent?"

Jegor grimaced. "Ach, what disgusting heat!" he said, and mopped his brow with disdain.

Like most boys, he resented it when his father acted without dignity, nor did he like to see him kiss his mother, least of all in public. He certainly could not understand why his father was so excited over a country that seemed hot, dirty, noisy, and full of all kinds of blacks and other racial inferiors.

He had hated it even before the ship had put into port, although the first sight of his new home from the ship's rail had been quite beautiful. The towering buildings seemed made of silver and shimmered with a magical sparkle. Sea gulls soared overhead like chips of shiny metal and the majestic Statue of Liberty seemed to cast rays of light from her uplifted torch. But the land onto which they disembarked bore little resemblance to the gleaming towers above it. It was soft from the heat, soggy, and littered with refuse—banana peels, cigar butts, candy wrappers, and cans. The air was heavy and limp as a dishrag. Newspapers and handbills clung to legs; once freed, they flew with a kind of insane frenzy to ensnare the next passerby. But even worse than the ground were the people who rushed over it, spitting and adding to the litter with an indifference that disturbed Jegor's Teutonic orderliness.

Half-naked longshoremen of every hue yelled, cursed, argued, and flung cigarette butts everywhere. Truck drivers unloaded their trucks and shoved whoever got in their way, displaying none of the servility with which workmen treated people of quality on the other side. The customs men wore drab uniforms and didn't maintain the dignity one would expect of uniformed officials. Jegor had already managed to have a run-in with one during the brief examination following landing. The inspector, whose uniform was open at the neck due to the heat, asked Jegor's name, age, country of origin, and religion. In his halting English that he had studied in school Jegor told him that he was a Holbeck and a Protestant. But the sweating black-haired inspector replied in a German that was more Yiddish that according to the papers Jegor's name was Carnovsky and that he was a Jew. He stamped the papers and told Jegor to move on. "Next!" he said gruffly. "Next!"

The longshoremen who carried their baggage didn't understand a word of Jegor's English nor did Jegor understand theirs. To add to his irritation, a wad of chewing gum had become attached to the sole of his shoe and no matter how hard he tried to dislodge it, it stuck there. "Goddamn filthy hellhole!" he screeched, aping Uncle Hugo's description of the foreign countries he had seen during the war.

As soon as the formalities of landing were finished, the Carnovskys were met by Leah's brother, Uncle Haskell Milner. Small, stooped, and lively, he dashed up to his sister whom he had not seen since childhood and embraced her warmly. "Leah! Leah! Do you recognize me?" he cried.

Before Leah could answer, he ran up to David, pumped his hand, kissed him, kissed his son Georg, and even Teresa. "Is that your daughter?" he asked Leah, after kissing the strange woman.

"No, Haskell, that's our daughter-in-law, Teresa, and this is my grandson."

"Well, a daughter-in-law is still a daughter-in-law," Uncle Haskell said and put his cheek up for Jegor to kiss.

"What's your name, kid?" he asked in his quick way. "Here they call me Harry. In Melnitz I was Haskell but here I am Harry, your Uncle Harry."

Jegor did not kiss the wrinkled cheek that the little Jew extended

toward him. Nor would he admit that he understood the jargon of
the old clothes dealers from Dragonerstrasse. After an uncle like
Hugo Holbeck, this ridiculous dwarf was an affront.

"I don't understand!" he said thickly and with unconcealed hostility.

"Ah, one has to speak German to this one!" Uncle Harry said
lightly, and laughed with good-natured mockery. "All right, Mister
German, German it will be—*Was ist dein Name, Herr Deutsch?*"

"Joachim Georg," Jegor enunciated carefully to accentuate the
little Jew's atrocious German.

Uncle Harry waved his hand. "Too long for America! Here they
like everything fast, quick, and to the point!"

As quickly as he spoke he also hastily pulled up his dusty Chev-
rolet and threw open its door. "Hop in!" he said unceremoniously.

Outside, the car was one cloud of dust; inside, it was full of screw
drivers, chisels, rulers, rags, cartons, and paint cans. Jegor was reluctant to step into the mess—he'd be damned if he would make things
easier for this alleged "uncle." But Uncle Harry ran up behind him
and pushed him inside with the agility of a subway platform guard
during the rush hour.

"Those are the tools of my trade," he explained. "I'm a contractor.
Sometimes I put up houses, sometimes I wreck them. Sometimes,
you might say, they wreck me . . . heh, heh, heh."

He rambled on in a mixture of Yiddish, English, Polish, Russian,
and German. Leah scolded him. Why hadn't he written in all these
years? She was also puzzled by his size. She remembered him as
being tall and husky. This shriveled, elderly man only reminded her
of her own advancing years. "Oy, Haskell, Haskell, Haskell," she
moaned. "I don't recognize you at all! Why didn't you at least send a
picture of yourself?"

"Never had the time, Leah, never had the time," he said, maneu-
vering the car through the midtown traffic.

As he drove, he spoke of the years that had gone by since he had
left Melnitz to avoid conscription in the Tsar's army. The things that
had happened to him! He had painted houses; gone on his own and
hired people to paint for him. He had moved up to building houses,
to wrecking houses. He had bought property and become wealthy.

During the war he had made thousands, then he had lost everything in the Crash and thought that he would have to go out painting again, but God had been good to him and his fortunes had turned once more. Now he was building again, wrecking again, and somehow managing to make a living.

He talked about his children and grandchildren. He asked Leah about herself and her family. Before she could answer his first question, he posed a second and a third. Life, he said, was not worth worrying about. He had been up and down, rich and poor. He had owned expensive limousines; now he was driving this old jalopy. Still, there was no reason to complain as long as one had one's health. And all the while he spoke, Uncle Harry didn't forget to sing the praises of his New York.

"Do you think it was always like this?" he asked, not waiting for an answer. "No, children. When I came here as a greenhorn, half of it wasn't here. We put it up afterwards. Some little town this New York, ain't it?"

His eyes glowed looking at his city that had grown before his eyes like a well-nourished infant. He loved not only the houses that he had put up himself but the whole concrete network of the sprawling metropolis.

"See that bridge there, kid?" he said, digging Jegor's ribs with a sharp elbow. "That was built when I came here. Some bridge, eh? Look at it. . . ."

Jegor had no interest in the bridge, the streets, or the houses. Although they were passing through a clean and wealthy section, he felt only contempt for the city. The fact that Uncle Harry loved it and was proud of it intensified his dislike. "My, my," he said, clicking his tongue at Uncle Harry's enthusiasm like an adult patronizing a child.

Dr. Carnovsky saw that Jegor's sarcasm was becoming too apparent and he tugged at his sleeve to warn him to behave.

But Jegor feigned innocence. "What's the matter?" he asked in a loud voice, fully aware that his father did not want attention drawn to himself.

When Uncle Harry turned into an obviously Jewish neighborhood, Jegor began to sniffle, to twitch his nose, and to cough pointedly. The sun-drenched streets were full of butcher shops on whose windows signs proudly announced that the meat inside was strictly kosher and painted chickens marched gaily off to be slaughtered. Synagogues, kosher restaurants, seedy movie theaters, delicatessens, funeral parlors, produce stores with outdoor stands, Yeshivoth bearing large Hebrew signs, bakeries, gasoline stations, barber shops, tombstone dealers—everything seemed indiscriminately thrown together into one garish, effluvious hodgepodge. Shingles announcing lawyers, matchmakers, rabbis, dentists, doctors, circumcisers, and caterers thrust out from ground-floor windows and doorways, and radios blared everywhere. On the sidewalks, behind parked cars of every make, shape, and color, young dark-haired mothers gathered in groups with children and baby carriages, talking, laughing, and rocking their little ones. On every stoop sat a bevy of stout women conversing, eating, fanning themselves, panting from the heat, and admonishing their children who played recklessly in the gutters.

"Sammy! Sylvia! Milty! Abe!" they screamed each time a car came hurtling toward the tightly packed clusters of children.

From balconies, fire escapes, garrets, and windows trailed lines of grayish, soggy wash. An occasional breeze from the ocean played havoc with voluminous ladies' underwear, mischievously ballooning the seats and ruffling shirts, brassieres, bathing suits, and girdles. Boys and girls lounged around corner candy stores eating ice cream, smoking, indulging in horseplay, and laughing. In the gutter, younger boys, bare-chested or in torn sweatshirts, threw balls with deadly precision and swung at them with cut-down broomsticks, arguing fiercely all the while. They feared nothing—no car, no truck, no force or authority. Bored policemen lounged against lampposts, yawning desperately and scratching. The clamor; the heat; the sound of voices praying, chanting, bargaining, and screaming; the wash flapping; the car engines roaring; the signs creaking; the dust and paper flying, all blended into one huge cacophonic whirlpool of life, movement, and vitality. David Carnovsky's eyes glistened. The throbbing, pulsating, frank Jewishness of the street filled him with joy and stirred long-stifled feelings of hope and pride. "Look, Leah! Jews, a world of Jews!" he thrilled like a long-lost wanderer come home.

"May the Evil Eye spare them all!" she intoned piously.

Dr. Carnovsky was appalled by the disorder, the congestion, the earthy slovenliness of the neighborhood. It wasn't only alien to him; it was, he was ashamed to confess, even repugnant. But after the years of guarded behavior, of fear and repression, it was a relief to see people who walked the streets relaxed and uninhibited. He threw back his deep chest and breathed in the hot, sticky air freely for the first time in years. "Look, Teresa, isn't it good?" he asked his wife, who looked with great staring eyes all around her.

He was most anxious to make his son aware of this freedom, to help him begin ridding himself of the sickness that had almost destroyed him.

"What do you think of it all?" he asked with feeling.

"One great big Dragonerstrasse," Jegor said. Like a liberated prisoner who longs for the security of confinement, he was appalled by the people who flaunted their Jewishness instead of keeping it hidden like the shameful affliction he knew it was. He equated it with the impudence of a cripple who waves his stump in the faces of men who are whole. He was distressed by their disregard for propriety. No one, not even the purest Aryans, dared act this boisterously on the other side!

His feelings toward this rabble were ambivalent. His Holbeck strain renounced all connection with it; his Carnovsky side made him feel guilty and ashamed, as if some particularly offensive relative were publicly misbehaving. He tried to be indifferent but he could not be. Their shame was his shame; their deformity, his deformity; their inferiority, his own.

He felt completely beaten when Uncle Harry pulled up before his house. It was a two-storied building near the seashore with a small garden, pillars, and balconies in front, and a large backyard where in garages and sheds were stored ladders, lumber, scrap metal, paint cans, tools, and other paraphernalia. It seemed incongruous that such a handsome house should belong to an Uncle Harry with his dusty car and his shirt sleeves rolled above the hairy arms.

Although it lacked its orderliness and cleanliness, the house reminded Jegor of his own house in Grunewald and he was seized with such a powerful yearning to return there that he had to force himself not to cry out in protest at his being a refugee in a strange land. That this ludicrous Jew should own such a magnificent home! . . .

He felt deceived as well. Riding through the grubby Jewish streets, he had fully expected to find Uncle Harry living in a filthy flat that smelled of garlic and curdled milk, and he would have enjoyed mocking it to his parents and making them feel guilty for having brought him there. Now he could only feel envious and humble.

His morale was not helped when Uncle Harry introduced his sons, who had come outside to welcome their new relatives. Towering muscular giants, they made Jegor feel even more useless and insignificant. Uncle Harry was proud yet ashamed of his strapping sons. He loved them, but he also realized what a ridilulous picture they presented next to him. To compensate, he made a show of parental authority and adopted a very sarcastic tone around them.

"American goods," he said wryly. Suddenly and without reason he became furious with them. "Don't stand there like a pack of dummies, say hello to your relatives!"

One by one the tanned, hard-faced youths shambled forward, showed incredibly white teeth in smiles, and said in a broken, American-accented Yiddish: "Hello Uncle, Aunt, Cousin . . . how are you?"

Awed by the sheer size of his cousins, Jegor tried to demonstrate his superior breeding. He drew himself up to his full height and barked his two names in clipped Teutonic accents. But the huge youths only winked at him and laughed. "Hey, Georgie," they said in their broken Yiddish, "relax and take it easy."

He was enraged. He tried to tell them not to speak to him in that disgusting jargon but in English, which he not only understood but was able to speak, probably better than they. They only laughed at him and stuck to the Yiddish one automatically used toward all greenhorns.

"How do you like New York?" they asked. "Great, isn't it?"

Jegor couldn't stand being patronized. "It's dirty and noisy!" he said, his blue eyes flashing.

His cousins could not have cared less. So secure was their faith in their America that nothing the effeminate boy said in his ridiculous English could disturb them. Their indifference completely unnerved Jegor. He became even more upset when Uncle Harry led the adults inside and left him alone with his sons.

"We're going inside to rest," he said. "You boys show your green-horn cousin a good time."

"We'll take him swimming, Pop," the boys said, and went into the garage to change.

Naked, they seemed even more powerful and invincible. Thick black hair matted their bodies from neck to ankle. Proud of their manhood they strutted around, wrestled, and laughed with animal gusto. Jegor quickly put on the oversized sandy trunks that they gave him and stood there, not knowing what to do. Ever since his playmates had laughed at his circumcised penis, he had been ashamed of his naked body. The incident at the Goethe School had only strengthened his feelings of self-revulsion. Even when he was alone he would look at his body with distaste, as if it were deformed. And although there was no reason to hide the stigma of Jewishness here, he cowered in the corner. The youths noticed it and laughed. "What are you ashamed of, greenhorn? You're among men!"

The beach was noisy and crowded. Swing music and voices of hysterical baseball announcers blared from portable radios. Girls squealed, children cried, boys wrestled. People of every size, shape, and color argued, laughed, gesticulated. The air stank of perspiration, tar, roasted nuts, and grilled frankfurters. Jegor was appalled.

"Hey, greenhorn!" his cousins called out. "Let's see who can swim faster, America or Germany?"

Jegor shrank back as if he were an outcast. He refused to sit, he refused to go into the water. His cousins teased him: "Come on, jump in! Sissy!"

Jegor didn't know exactly what the word meant, but he was sure it was not complimentary. He knew that his cousins were making fun of him and he hated them as he hated the whole noisy, screaming mob. Their every gesture was vulgar and uncouth. They reminded him of the caricatures drawn of the Jew on the other side; the dark, big-nosed, pushy degenerate. But what was perplexing was that these people seemed none the worse for belonging to an inferior race.

They were strong and tough; they boxed, wrestled, swam, and ran like athletes.

"Ach, what filth!" Jegor said to Uncle Harry's sons when they came out of the water and he pointed to the beach. "And your ocean is dirty too."

The youths shook themselves like jolly St. Bernards and did not bother to answer. Nothing could dampen their enjoyment of life.

Just as energetically as they had exercised, they now attacked the lunch their mother put out on the long dining-room table. They devoured the fruit, the vegetables, the crisp seeded rolls, the pickles, the fresh radishes—everything that was put before them. Aunt Rose, a stout, handsome matron with a great bosom, kept bringing to the table new dishes that the boys finished almost before she had set them down. Uncle Harry teased his boys and proudly called attention to their appetites. "How do you like the way they pack the food away?" he asked. "No wonder their papa is so small; his boys have eaten him up! Eh, heh, heh, heh. . . ."

"May the Evil Eye spare them!" their mother said reverently and beamed. "I love to see children eat!"

Busy serving and dealing out the portions, she spoke proudly of her sons. No harm should befall them, they were good boys. In the daytime they helped their father on the job—driving trucks, supervising the workers, even helping to paint walls when necessary. At night they attended college. They also helped around the house, tended to the furnace, cleaned the backyard, and watered the lawn. And obviously, it was no problem to feed them.

She was just as solicitous of Jegor as of her sons. "Eat, child, eat!" she urged him. "Don't be ashamed to take more. You see my boys, God bless them, aren't ashamed to take all they want. . . ."

Jegor felt drawn to the kind, motherly woman who seemed so concerned about him. But he also had to prove to everyone that he didn't approve of the greasy Jewish dishes she served, the noodles, chicken soup, pickles, onions, and stuffed intestine, and he pushed everything away with a loud show of disgust although his mouth watered for the delicacies. Let these muscle-bound louts slobber over the food; he, Joachim Georg Holbeck, would be above such gluttony! But neither the boys nor Uncle Harry paid the slightest attention to him. The boys kept on consuming everything in sight while Uncle Harry recalled the times he had gone through, the alternate periods of affluence and poverty.

"Hey now, you guys!" he shouted, suddenly recalling his parental role. "You've gobbled up enough. Into the kitchen with you and help Mama with the dishes!" He beamed at the idea of ordering around giants who sprang to obey him.

Everybody at the table, David, Leah, Georg, and Teresa, who understood perhaps one word out of ten that Uncle Harry said, was shocked at the thought of young men who were university students washing dishes. This was unthinkable on the other side! They congratulated Uncle Harry on having such fine and devoted sons.

Jegor squirmed in his seat when, from the kitchen, came the booming sound of the boys laughing and hooting. He was sure they were laughing at him. But soon he grew even more disconcerted when Uncle Harry's only daughter came running in, all out of breath.

Black-eyed and dark like her brothers, she was slim and lively as quicksilver and her curls and ringlets danced at every move of her body. Uncle Harry tried to bluster at her for coming home late but she soothed and kissed him, leaving a smear of raspberry tint on each withered cheek. She called him Sweetheart and Shrimp and Lollipop and Uncle Harry struggled to put on a severe expression. "You're lucky there are people here," he said, "or you'd get a good piece of my mind, you little *shikse.*"

She showed him the tip of her tongue. She took full advantage of being the only daughter. She left all the housework to her brothers, slept late, ate when she pleased, and took liberties with her father that her brothers would not have dared. All she had to do was sit in her daddy's lap, kiss him and call him funny names, and he would forgive her everything. She carried over this pampered attitude to everyone else, even to strangers who came to visit. She looked straight at her refugee cousin with her mischievous eyes and stretched out a soft hand to him. Unaccustomed to girls, Jegor felt his hand grow clammy against her warm, dry palm. Remembering Uncle Hugo's gallantry toward Aunt Rebecca, he stood behind his cousin's chair until she got ready to sit, then pulled the chair out for her. The boys burst out laughing. But what was worst of all was that she laughed right along with them.

"Call me Ethel," she said, dispensing with ceremony.

Jegor became all thumbs. Trying to serve her, he spilled the pitcher of water and spotted the tablecloth. The boys nearly choked with laughter. Convinced that it was her beauty that had befuddled her cousin, Ethel's eyes sparkled.

Jegor fidgeted. He felt stupid and clumsy. He was afraid to eat the roast chicken that Aunt Rose put in front of him. He was sure that he would have trouble handling the greasy, gravy-soaked fowl. He couldn't avoid looking at his uncle's boorish sons. Wherever his eyes strayed he saw one of them laughing at him. He felt spite and perversity come over him and he knew that soon he must do something to show that he, Joachim Georg Holbeck—yes, *Holbeck*—could not be laughed at by hook-nosed Jewish clods. He had to hurt someone. Because he knew how much it would disturb her, he refused even to taste Aunt Rose's chicken. Ethel, chewing vigorously on a wing, tried to change his mind. "Taste it, it's delicious," she urged. "Nobody makes roast chicken like Mama."

"Too spicy and greasy!" he snapped. "Besides, it's too damned hot in here. . . ."

Ethel licked her lips daintily with the tip of her pointed rosy tongue, which made Jegor think she was pointing it at him. "I'm not in the least hot," she said with unconcern.

Jegor's parents and grandparents looked at one another meaningfully. They all urged him to eat. But the more they insisted, the more obstinate he became. Finally Uncle Harry looked up. Staring at the boy who nervously shook off all attempts to placate him, he observed quietly: "I'm afraid that your *boyele* doesn't approve of us. . . . Not of us, not of our country, not of anything around here. Isn't that so, Mister German?"

"He may not like anyone else, but I bet he likes me," Ethel drawled. "Don't you, Cousin Jegor?"

"No!" he barked.

"Why not?" she asked in genuine surprise.

"Too black!" he said.

Rose made one last attempt to ease the tension. "It's all because he's such a delicate child. Look at him, he hardly eats at all," she said with the smugness of a mother of healthy, hungry children. And she dabbed at the large globules of sweat that had broken out on Jegor's brow.

Nothing she could have said would have incited Jegor more.

"I am healthy!" he screamed hysterically. "Goddamn healthy and I want to be left alone! That's all I ask, to be left alone!"

All the adults tried to calm him; only his cousins who had returned to the table continued to chew placidly, without so much as a glance in his direction.

"Jegor! Jegorchen . . ." Teresa pleaded. Her face had grown cinder-red.

Dr. Carnovsky took the boy's spindly arm firmly between his fingers and half led, half dragged him outside.

"I'll never come here again," Jegor cried. "I . . . h . . . hate them!"

After months of speaking properly, he had begun to stutter again.

"All right," his father said. "We won't come back, but get hold of yourself. Get hold of yourself, boy. . . ."

He interpreted the first day in the new country as an omen of the evil that hovered, ready to descend with all its fury on the family Carnovsky.

35

Solomon Burak did not keep his promise to Mr. Pitzeles that he would be kept on in his position as long as he, Solomon, remained president of Temple Sha Mora. During the whole time that the *Yekes* conspired against the Hungarian beadle, Solomon Burak had stood by him. In their animosity toward the beadle Solomon detected their hatred of him, a hatred they were afraid to express otherwise. But everything changed one Sabbath morning when he saw David Carnovsky enter the synagogue with his phylactery bag under his arm.

Solomon Burak was disturbed. He had never felt easy in the presence of the lordly Carnovsky. He vividly recalled how the other had humiliated him the last time they had met. He now turned to Mr. Pitzeles and began to discuss obscure synagogue matters to avoid a confrontation with Carnovsky.

But soon pride replaced humiliation. He, Solomon Burak, was no one's inferior, certainly no self-proclaimed *Yeke's.* If anyone had reason to hide, it certainly was not he. Sneaking sidelong glances at Carnovsky, who stood in a corner looking lost, grayer, and more stooped than he remembered him, Solomon Burak felt a surge of superiority and youthful vigor. *So there is a God after all,* he suddenly reminded himself, although he had never thought otherwise, *a God Who sees all and hears all and squares all accounts. . . .*

Wiping any traces of doubt from his still smooth and unlined face, Solomon Burak began to stroll sedately through his huge synagogue with the beadle trotting along behind. For a moment he considered ignoring Carnovsky altogether—he would repay arrogance with arrogance. Soon, however, he reconsidered. He, Solomon Burak, would be a bigger person. Now that he held the upper hand, he would be gracious and welcome the stranger to the synagogue— to *his* synagogue.

"*Sholom Aleichem*—peace be with you, neighbor," he said resonantly, and stretched out his hand to Carnovsky. "And how is your dear Leah?"

Although in the past they had always spoken German, Solomon now used a homely Yiddish to indicate that he considered Carnovsky a fellow townsman from Melnitz. He also asked about Leah first to show that it was on her account that he, Solomon, bothered to speak to him at all. He also mentioned Leah in case Carnovsky resorted to his customary trick of making believe he did not remember him. But David not only recognized him; he even remembered his full name.

"Herr Burak!" he cried, happily stretching out both his hands to grasp Solomon's. "Peace be with you, Reb Shlomo!"

Solomon Burak was thrilled to hear himself called Reb Shlomo. He had a fleeting suspicion that Carnovsky must be in dire circumstances indeed to greet him so warmly. But he quickly saw that the reaction was genuine, and the resentment melted in his heart. David Carnovsky looked down shamefaced. " 'A mountain does not meet with a mountain, but man meets with man,' " he quoted from the Gemara, something he would never have done before when speaking with an unlearned man. "I hope you bear me no grudge, Reb Shlomo."

This was enough to dissolve the last traces of Solomon Burak's resentment and to restore him to his usual merry self. He could never stay angry for long. Looking at the tortured face, he sensed that Carnovsky had already paid dearly for his sins. Relieved because no unpleasantness had marred the occasion, Solomon again extended his hand to Carnovsky to indicate that all bad feeling had been erased. "Forget everything that's happened, Reb David," he said warmly. "Instead, tell me your father's name so I can call you up to the Torah."

David was puzzled.

"I'm the president of the shul," Solomon explained, "and I'd like to extend this honor to you as befitting a distinguished guest."

He was completely won over to Carnovsky's side when, on the very next Sabbath, David became embroiled with the *Yekes* in the synagogue. After giving fervent thanks to the Almighty for rescuing him from the evildoers, David Carnovsky passionately began to assail those who had perpetrated such atrocities upon the children of Israel. Dr. Speier's icy face grew even more taut and rigid than usual hearing these thoughts expressed so openly by his old friend. After a sermon in which he had expounded lofty and ethereal concepts, he could not bear to listen to such mundane words. Besides, a man simply did not speak of such things in public, as one would not talk about a blemish on one's wife's body.

"The words of the wise are said quietly, my dear Carnovsky," he said, stroking his tiny beard. "What's the sense of talking about it, especially on the Sabbath?"

"I'm not discussing business matters, Rabbi Speier," David interrupted. "I'm talking about saving human life and this can be discussed even on the holiest of Yom Kippurs!"

And with even greater fervor he began to talk about rescuing the old sage and scholar, Reb Ephraim Walder.

Dr. Speier was irked by David's vehemence. "Your enthusiasm is very commendable, Herr Carnovsky," he said dryly, "but old Walder is not the only scholar who's been left behind. There are many more erudite men still there—we couldn't possibly bring them all here."

David Carnovsky could not bear to hear a disparaging word against his idol. "Lies!" he shouted. "There is only one Reb Ephraim Walder and there is no one like him anywhere!"

Dr. Speier felt insulted at this oblique aspersion on his own erudition, particularly in front of the entire congregation. But he managed to control himself as he always did and tried to make light of the incident. "Why all the heat, my dear Carnovsky?" he said. "Surely you must know that it is forbidden to light a fire on the Sabbath."

The others smiled at the rabbi's little joke but David Carnovsky would not let himself be turned aside so easily. "You're making jokes while a saint is being tortured by evildoers!" he cried accusingly.

Seeing that levity would not work, Dr. Speier resorted to the Torah. "'A word is worth a thaler and silence two,'" he quoted. "Surely a Talmudic scholar must know the value of silence—especially in the house of God."

David Carnovsky refused to be placated. For each quotation Dr. Speier offered he had ten in rebuttal. "The Scriptures also say that there is a time to be silent and a time to speak," he said. "This is the time to speak, even to shout, Rabbi Speier!"

Dr. Speier began to lose his composure under the steady barrage that David Carnovsky fired at him before the whole congregation. Now that humor and erudition had not had their effect, he attempted diplomacy. "Whatever the case may be, my most esteemed Herr Carnovsky, it must remain a private affair, not one to be dragged through the streets. And certainly not before strangers and outsiders."

He had a double purpose in saying this. One, to indicate that it was something not to be discussed in front of the Hungarian beadle, Pitzeles. Secondly, he wanted to let Carnovsky know that although he was an outsider too, he, Dr. Speier, was willing to accept him as a fellow German if he would abide by the rules.

But even this did no good. "We are all Jews here, Dr. Speier, regardless of whether we come from Frankfurt or Tarnopol!" David shouted. "A Jew is a Jew and persecution is nothing to be ashamed of!"

He vented his rage at the rabbi of Sha Mora just as he had once vented it at the rabbi of the synagogue in Melnitz. Dr. Speier realized that he could gain nothing by staying and he left the synagogue before his usual time, trailed by the sympathetic congregation. Solomon Burak felt so intoxicated by David Carnovsky's words—words that had needed to be said for a long time in Sha Mora—that he embraced him. "May you live to a hundred and twenty, Reb David, a blessing on your head! You really told those *Yekes* off, my dear friend."

From then on he would not leave David Carnovsky's presence. Although other matters required his attention, he pushed everything aside and asked David to accompany him to his house for the sanctification of the Sabbath. David was reluctant to go. Recalling the wrongs he had done Solomon Burak, he was ashamed to face his family. He, David, was not one to forget a transgression in a hurry, least of all his own. He was ashamed to face Yetta Burak, to whom he had been so unfriendly. Least of all did he want to see Ruth, whom he had so categorically rejected as a daughter-in-law. "Not today, Reb Shlomo," he begged off. "I don't have the heart to face your family just yet."

Solomon would not take no for an answer. "You just leave it to me, Reb David. My Yetta will be delighted to see you!"

David tried another tack. "My Leah will worry if I don't come straight home," he said. "After all, we've only just arrived. . . ."

But Solomon had a solution for this too. He would send the beadle to tell Leah that David was at his, Solomon's, house. What was he saying? He, Solomon, would go get her himself! Where was Carnovsky staying? They would pick up Leah and take her along. . . . In his confusion he ran to the corner where his car was parked, but he suddenly remembered that it was the Sabbath and they walked instead, Solomon trotting, David trailing helplessly behind.

Just as they had on the other side, Leah Carnovsky and Yetta Burak embraced, burst out crying, giggled like young girls, embraced again, kissed, and began talking at the same time. Torrents of words poured from the two old friends. Yetta had set her usual bountiful table. It was stacked with all kinds of Melnitz delicacies— bread, preserves, strudel, and almond cookies. Solomon kept filling the glasses with Passover slivovitz.

"A long life, Reb David," he toasted, clinking glasses after each round. "May all Jews prosper and their enemies be destroyed. Drink up, Reb David, make yourself right at home."

But no matter how he tried, David Carnovsky could not relax. Every member of the household reminded him of the wrongs he had done the family. Not that anyone gave him cause to feel guilty. Ruth served him refreshments and even asked about Georg. David averted his eyes. "Don't put yourself out, dear lady," he muttered in embarrassment. "Just don't bother about me."

Dunking cake in sweet brandy as if it were a celebration, the two older women looked at each other and burst out crying as women will at a time of rejoicing.

"I've grown old, Leahele," Yetta blurted, seeing her own advancing years in her friend's wrinkled face.

"What can I say, Yettele?" Leah cried and dabbed at her eyes.

Solomon Burak became disgusted by the endless weeping. "Why all these tears in the midst of the Sabbath? Instead let's have another drink and let there be only joy for Jews from now on. . . ."

Yetta could not bear to see the bottle emptying so quickly. "Shlomele, you're not a youngster any more," she chided her husband. "You're an old man, my husband, so take it easy or it's liable to hurt you!"

"I've never felt so young in my life!" Solomon boasted. "The older I get, the younger I feel . . . I could go out with the suitcase again, my legs feel so strong!"

"Bite your tongue," Yetta said. "Let the enemies of Israel go peddling. You've done more than your share of it!"

"Woman, I didn't mean it. I was only trying to prove a point," he said.

"Best say nothing and be quiet," she advised gently.

But Solomon Burak was in no mood to be silenced. Once he grew properly tipsy, everything he had bottled up inside him came pouring out.

"Reb David, today is like a holiday for me," he said with feeling. "When the mighty Herr Carnovsky himself makes the Sabbath benediction at the house of Shlomo Burak, it's a day to rejoice; it's *Simchas Torah!*"

Yetta saw immediately that her Shlomo was courting trouble and as usual she tried to restrain him. "Don't start wagging your tongue, Shlomele," she urged. "Why don't you go and lie down instead?"

"Yetta, let me speak!" he insisted. "I must have my say!"

He purged himself of all the resentment he had harbored against David Carnovsky through the years. When he came to the worst humiliation of all, the time that he had come to beg in his daughter's behalf and David Carnovsky had rejected him, Ruth Burak Zielonek ran from the room and Yetta clapped both her hands over her husband's mouth.

"Let him speak, Frau Burak. It's better that he does," David Carnovsky said.

He was anxious to hear his sins brought out into the open. The more Solomon Burak unburdened himself, the lighter David Carnovksy's spirit grew. He felt cleansed and relieved. "True, all true, Reb Shlomo," he repeated, "every word of it."

Once Solomon finished, his buoyant good nature was immediately restored. "I'm only an ignoramus who had to get things off his chest; but it had to be done—otherwise it would have choked me. Now I feel better, Reb David."

"I do too, Reb Shlomo," David Carnovsky said. "Now I can look you straight in the eye."

That very same evening Solomon Burak ran to the house of the strictly kosher butcher, Herr Gottlieb Reicher, and to the other members of the synagogue committee and insisted that David Carnovsky be appointed the beadle of Temple Sha Mora and that Mr. Pitzeles take over the duties of Walter, the janitor. The officers grumbled unhappily. As if it were not enough to put up with that Hungarian, with his atrocious German! If there had to be a change, they had enough applicants for the position among their own kind. People with titles, even. Nor were they anxious to fire Walter, to whom they felt much closer than they did to that filthy *Galitzianer,* Pitzeles.

"But our most esteemed Herr Burak, you're asking too much," they protested, "and that's not right. Ever the golden mean, we say."

But Solomon Burak would not yield. "Leave it to me," he assured the *Yekes.* "Whatever extra expenses come up, I'll take care of them. A ducat more, a ducat less, live and let live. . . ."

No one could say anything to this and David Carnovsky became the beadle of Temple Sha Mora.

Leah Carnovsky dabbed at her eyes when she heard the news. She felt no disgrace on her own account but her heart went out to her poor David, David the scholar and intellectual who in his old age was forced to become a beadle of a synagogue headed by Shlomo Burak. "What have we lived to endure, David?" she cried.

David would not let her go on. "We should give our thanks for every minute that God saved us from the evildoers," he said humbly.

"It isn't for me that I feel so bad, it's for you, David," she said.

"Let it be payment for my sins," David Carnovsky said righteously, "for all the grief I caused Shlomele, for my arrogance, false pride, and idolatry."

Leah could hardly believe her ears. Never in her life had she heard such words from her proud husband's lips.

36

To the family Carnovsky, America was like a new pair of shoes—a pleasure to put on, a pain to wear.

Oddly, it was the oldest members of the family who adjusted first. Although David Carnovsky was forced in his old age to become a beadle and to exist on a tiny salary, his wife Leah was happier than she had ever been on Oranienburger Strasse. After the years of estrangement and loneliness in the German city to which she could never adjust, she was again able to lead the type of easy and comfortable existence that she preferred. Unlike the other refugee women, she quickly made friends with the Jewish women in the neighborhood, particularly with those who had originally come from Poland. When her neighbors made overtures and asked about conditions on the other side, she did not withdraw as did the German women but discussed the matter freely and openly and with the indignation one would expect from a victim of persecution. She was grateful for the women's advice and suggestions on how to adjust to the new country and was promptly accepted as one of their own. She was delighted to be able to converse in a comfortable Melnitz Yiddish without the fear of sounding ignorant and ungrammatical. She could fondle strange children without being told how harmful and unhygienic it was. Here, the easygoing mothers considered her actions normal and were proud that she found their babies appealing. She quickly picked up the essential English words that the women interspersed with their Yiddish and grew accustomed to the

speech and habits of the neighborhood butchers, bakers, grocery-
men, and fishmongers. She enjoyed their jocular way of doing business and the merchants liked her as a customer. Quickly she sought
out her townsmen from Melnitz, of whom there were more in New
York than in the home town itself. They were scattered throughout
the city—in Brownsville, the Bronx, the Lower East Side, and Washington Heights—and Leah was delighted to spend time with them.
They all knew who she was, the daughter of Reb Leib Milner, and
she knew them as well. She was able to travel everywhere in the city
by simply asking directions in Yiddish. She renewed her ties with
her home town, learned all its gossip, passed along regards and accepted them.

David found the same kind of peace and contentment in the new
land. He spent all his spare time at homely synagogues and yeshivas,
where he sat with his new-found cronies and discussed the Torah
and wisdom. And just as Leah felt the strong urge to bring Rebecca
and their grandchildren to America, so was David obsessed with rescuing Reb Ephraim Walder and his precious collection of books and
manuscripts.

"Men, a veritable treasure hoard will be lost!" he harangued his
new friends, the Hebrew scholars and Judaists. "One of the sages of
Israel will expire among the wicked. . . ."

The younger members of the family Carnovsky were not able to
adapt to their new country as easily.

Following the first days of visiting relatives and friends came
long, dreary months in the small drab apartment on Manhattan's
Upper West Side. It was a particularly depressing time, following
as it did the gay, joyful days of arrival when they had been caught
up in the excitement of beginning a new existence in a strange country. The friendlessness and indifference of the alien city seemed to
shriek out of every wall of the crowded apartment. It penetrated
through the doors and windows and hovered overhead like a poison-
ous cloud. The main thing to which the Carnovskys could not adjust
was the noise—the eternal noise. After the years of quiet exist-

ence in Grunewald, where the loudest sound was the scrape of leaves against the pavement, their ears were especially vulnerable to every jarring note of the raucous, impudent city. They flinched at every blare of an automobile horn, every screech of a tire, every piercing siren of a passing ambulance or patrol car. Worst of all was the constant drone of the roller skates along the uneven sidewalk below. The neighborhood children were unusually noisy in their games that went on from early morning until long past a decent bedtime. They skated, threw balls, played tag, screamed and hooted, their shrill voices carrying to the sky. When they finally became quiet, a new distraction would begin. From every window came the sound of radios, each tuned to a different station. Fiery political speeches, cloying announcers hawking soap and cereals, swing music, the artificial laughter of audiences listening to comedians, the sermons of preachers and evangelists, staccato descriptions of fights and hockey games—the whole strident, discordant cacaphony blended into one tormenting, agonizing sound that pierced the brains and jarred the nerves of the Carnovskys. Teresa went around with a constant headache. Nor was she able to cope with the congested apartment.

Dr. Carnovsky had specifically warned her not to bring so many of their possessions to the new country, but she had disregarded his advice. Accustomed since childhood to frugality and to saving everything that was still serviceable, she had not been able to part with anything. Each item reminded her of some familiar and precious experience, especially the carved and costly pieces of furniture that Georg, in his urgency to leave them behind, had called junk. Although she had always been an obedient wife, this time she ignored her husband's orders and secretly added to the pile of things that were already jammed into the huge crate. She took along all their porcelain, crystal, rugs, linen, furniture, old clothes—everything that she had accumulated during the years of affluence and prosperity. It had cost a fortune to transport all these things and now they were completely worthless. There was no room for them in the tiny apartment and they required constant care and attention. Teresa spent all her time dusting, oiling, polishing.

In addition, Dr. Carovsky's instruments and machines occupied half of the apartment. He had managed to save a number of X-ray machines, heat lamps, diathermy machines, and all kinds of surgical equipment from the clinic. Although they symbolized the only hopeful aspects of the Carnovskys' new existence—the time when Dr. Carnovsky would again resume practice—their present uselessness cast a feeling of futility and gloom over the apartment, like the clothing and possessions of one recently deceased. No matter how often and carefully the instruments and machines were cleaned, they immediately became coated with a layer of dust, and Teresa felt terribly depressed each time she looked into their cold, metallic glitter.

She was just as upset by the street, the unfamiliar language, and the odd customs of the city. She was convinced that she would never be able to find her way around Manhattan or learn the weird, nasal speech of the Americans. Even the church where she dropped in for a moment of solace seemed alien and friendless. The services in the strange language were meaningless and of no comfort. She could not be sure that God heeded these unintelligible offerings. She would leave the church with a heavy spirit, carrying the straw basket with which she went marketing. With even heavier spirit she counted out the precious, dwindling dollar bills on which they were subsisting. Reluctantly she doled out the green pieces of paper, fingering each one several times before she passed it to the quick, grasping fingers of the storekeepers. She could not bear to see how negligently they totaled the bills, threw the food on the scales, snatched the food from the scales, and stuffed it into paper bags. She could not bear the indifference and wastefulness with which American women bought mounds of things they didn't need and threw out articles that were barely used—shoes, dresses, even furniture. She could not rid herself of her urge to repair and to salvage everything she owned. She wouldn't keep a lamp burning an extra second. She did all her own laundry to save a dollar. She didn't wear stockings in the house. She was forever darning, sewing, and repairing. But no matter how carefully she husbanded her resources, the dollar bills flew from her purse. Humbly and with her head hung low, she would go to her husband, as if it were somehow her fault that they were using up their small hoard of cash. "I'm ashamed to say that I need money for the house again," she would sigh. "You won't be angry with me, will you, Georg?"

"How can you even think of such a thing?" Dr. Carnovsky would say tenderly, pressing the bills into her hand.

He was just as distressed as she by the congested apartment, the noise from the street, and, most of all, the sight of his instruments hovering in the background like so many corpses. Cleaning and sharpening his tools, particularly the scalpels that had brought him so much fame and honor, he felt such a gnawing urge to do that for which he was trained and which he loved that he almost cried out in despair. The futility of his existence haunted him and gave him no rest, but he drove it from him as if with whips. One of the few things that he had brought from the other side was the proverb: *Gelt verloren, nichts verloren. Mut verloren, alles verloren,* and he struggled not to lose his courage. He stayed away from the house to avoid breathing the odor of rags and naphthalene and looking at his instruments.

On the other side, he had been accustomed to spending part of every day in a café, no matter how busy his schedule had been. But now he made sure to stay away from the Old Berlin. Although he was well known there and was respectfully called Herr Doktor, he refused to allow himself to take part in the eternal reminiscences about the good old days. As far as he was concerned, the old days were over and finished. Actually, he felt a strong affinity for the tough hard city that challenged one's determination, and he drove himself to marshal the necessary courage with which to come to grips with it and to conquer it.

Early in the morning, as soon as he had eaten, he went out for his daily walk. Striding firmly and bucking the strong winds that blew in from the green, mountainous banks across the Hudson, he cleansed his lungs of all the bedding, naphthalene, and fusty odors that filled his narrow apartment and burdened his spirit. The fresh air helped dispel doubt and melancholy. Although he took the same walk daily, he still enjoyed the feeling of the good free earth where one could hold one's head high and be completely ignored. He also went frequently to the seashore, something he had missed sorely in recent years after Jews had been prohibited from swimming in Wannsee. Lying on the sand and inhaling the smells of sun, salt water, fish, and seaweed, or digging out mussels and sea shells from the rocks, he felt marvelously relaxed and charged with an exhilarating sense of energy and vitality. Revived and invigorated, he would visit Uncle Harry and eat the tasty lunch that Aunt Rose set before him. And just as Aunt Rose enjoyed his appetite, his cousin Ethel was attracted to his virility, his tanned body, and the smell of salt, sun, and sea that he brought into the house. Often they went swimming together or raced along the shore and Dr. Carnovsky held his own with his young and athletic cousin.

The same energy with which he walked and played he applied to learning English, which was a requisite for the State Medical Board examination he would have to take before he could be licensed to practice in the new country.

Just as he had during his days at the Gymnasium, but with much more at stake, he sat at his bench and with his sharp black eyes followed every word that the teacher, Miss Doolittle, wrote on the blackboard. Like an eager schoolboy, he raised his hand high each time he knew the answer.

He was pleased that he was the best pupil in the class, which consisted mostly of stout, indifferent housewives. He enjoyed seeing Miss Doolittle mark his grades with her calligraphic handwriting. Above all, he enjoyed watching her blush when she marked his notebook.

A tall, gaunt spinster, Miss Doolittle had managed to maintain a pedantic, impersonal veneer until the tanned and husky doctor joined her class. For the first time in years she began to take special care with her appearance, to leave open an extra button on her blouse, and to dab rouge on her cheeks. Although she took extreme care to be discreet, the sharp-eyed doctor noticed the transformation —there was little about women that escaped him. Although he could not possibly work up a spark of enthusiasm for this old war horse, her awareness of him both gratified and amused him.

But most of the time he was obsessed by strong feelings of resentment and humiliation. After surviving the front and the difficult climb to fame and reputation, it irked him to sit like a schoolboy and recite simple words from a primer.

But as soon as the gloom settled over him, he would cast it off and force himself to feel optimistic. This was exactly what his enemies wanted—that he grow disheartened and give up. But this he would not allow himself to do.

"Keep your chin up, Tereschen," he consoled his wife. "Things will be good for us again. Let me just get past the examination."

As he had during their early courtship, he sat her on his lap and ran his fingers through her flaxen hair. "It's only because of me that you're suffering, little one," he said remorsefully.

"God, how can you say such a thing?" she raged. And although she loved being petted, she could not indulge herself in the pleasure of sitting on her husband's lap—her housework called out to her. But her husband would tear her away from her tasks by force and take her for a walk or to the movies.

"Listen to me, *Goyisher Kup!*" he would say with mock severity, and half drag her outside.

This was enough to chase away her depression. She loved to hear him call her by that name, an endearment from the days when they had first begun to go together. This was the only thing to which she could cling in the strange and frightening city—the thing that had been slipping from her on the other side. Although she had never spoken of it, she had been ridden with jealousy and resentment because of his neglect and his affairs. Since he had become famous, her nights had been long agonies of wakeful suspicion. She had felt that every woman in Berlin was laughing at her, Dr. Carnovsky's docile and stupid little wife. Now, after years of silently borne humiliation, she was again sure of his love. They walked together, went to the movies together, and held hands. He called her Tereschen, silly goose, and *Goyisher Kup.* This was almost sufficient reward for her wretchedness and loneliness and the constant headaches she suffered. It was easier to bear the drudgery knowing that Georg was sitting in the next room studying his English.

Once he even tried helping her with her housework, as he had seen American husbands do, but Teresa was scandalized and would not let him put his fingers in the water. She was a German *Hausfrau* and as far as she was concerned the husband was the lord and master of the house and must not lower himself to do woman's work. She shined his shoes, brushed his garments, and put on and took off his coat when he came in or went out. She even began to sing in the house, a thing she had not done in years, because when he kissed her now it was out of love, not duty.

Slowly and reluctantly she accustomed herself to the strange city, learned how to go from place to place, picked up some English words, even became used to the habits and customs that no longer seemed so offensive. She even began to like certain aspects of American life.

But none of this carried over to the youngest member of the family Carnovsky, Joachim Georg.

37

Like a rabid dog that, although mad with thirst, will not drink, Jegor Carnovsky longed to be with people, yet was deathly afraid to go near them.

Knowing his son's fears, Dr. Carnovsky did his best to help him. As a skilled physician he knew that often a contagious disease can be cured with a serum bearing its own organisms, and applying the same principle he strove to cure his son with the very thing he feared most. With characteristic Carnovsky obstinacy he tried to force the boy to participate in the vigorous life of the new land. With the same obstinacy Jegor resisted and cowered in his room like a mole in its subterranean lair.

At first Dr. Carnovsky tried kindness. He made every effort to ease Jegor's life in the strange city, to introduce him to the taste and rhythm of America as one spoon-feeds medicine to a stubborn child. He took him to zoos and amusement parks and to the finest neighborhoods. He invited him to go walking with him and to the beach. But Jegor turned his face to the wall and drew the blanket over his head. "Lazybones, the sun is shining!" his father would chide him good-naturedly.

"What do I care about the sun? I'm sleepy," Jegor would mutter from under the blanket.

"We'll rent a boat and go rowing."

For a moment Jegor would think it over. He had always been fond of ships and the water. But the pleasure of refusing his father outweighed the pleasures of boating.

"I couldn't sleep the whole night because of the noise in this goddamn city," he would grumble. "Let me go back to sleep."

The more his father praised New York, the more he would deride
it. He was even less tolerant than his parents of its noise, congestion,
and intolerable weather; nor could he stand the small and crowded
apartment and all the discomforts with which he had to put up. He
hated America. Everything about it irritated him—the disorder, the
lack of manners, the free and easy attitude Americans adopted toward strangers, the arrogance and rudeness of its public servants.
His frayed, tightly wound nerves were attuned to every jarring
sound and rustle. Passing cars woke him from his sleep. Needing
an outlet for his anger, he invaded his parents' bedroom to rage
against the city. "Goddamn sewer!" he half cried. "I'll go crazy in
this lousy pesthole!"

Dr. Carnovsky tried to reason with him. "Look here, son. The city
won't adjust to you—you'll just have to adjust to the city. That's
simple logic."

"You and your logic!" Jegor said, unable to come up with a sensible reply.

Logic proving useless, Teresa tried tenderness. "Be fair, child," she
pleaded. "You know we didn't come here on our account. It was for
you, all for you. . . ."

"That's what *you* say," Jegor sneered.

He would go to bed late and oversleep the next day, sometimes
into the afternoon. No matter how late he got up, he spent the rest
of his day in his pajamas and walked around rumpled and groggy
from too much sleep. He listened to the radio all day, eager for some
news from the old country. Although he had studied English and
was convinced that he knew the language, he could barely understand the announcer's rapid speech. He fiddled with the dial for
hours until he found an item of news about Germany.

He also avoided the screaming and rowdy boys and girls who
crowded the neighborhood streets. He sat for hours by the window
and watched them at their play. Teresa could not bear to see him
sitting there like an outcast and begged him to go downstairs. When
his father told him not to be afraid of the youngsters in the street,
Jegor became enraged. "Who's afraid?" he screamed, furious at his

father, who always managed to pinpoint his feeling correctly. "I'm not afraid of anyone!"

But he could not rid himself of his deadly fear of being ridiculed and belittled. Every time someone laughed, Jegor thought it was at him. To forestall possible humiliation, he erected a defense against all humanity, categorizing everyone as a potential enemy.

Realizing that logic and tenderness would not release Jegor from his self-imposed isolation, Dr. Carnovsky compelled his son to go outside. Jegor obeyed reluctantly, walking like a skater on thin ice.

"Here yawiththeball! Let's have it!" the boys screamed when the ball accidentally bounced near Jegor. All he had to do was intercept it and he would have immediately become part of the group, but this phrase was something he had never encountered in a textbook and he replied with the only appropriate response he knew for the occasion. "Begging your pardon, sir?"

The boys forgot about the ball and became hysterical "Katzenjammer!" one of them cried. "Vich is you, Hans or Fritz?"

Jegor fled back to his room. The thing he feared most had happened. From then on, he clung even more closely to the house and took extra pains to avoid the gang of sweating, screaming youngsters. He sat by the window and was delighted when one of them fell or threw the ball badly.

When autumn came and Dr. Carnovsky began to talk about school, Jegor felt panic rise up within him. This was what frightened him most—the thought of going to school. He lost his appetite, he could not sleep and fidgeted all night. On the morning that he was scheduled to begin school he came down with a high fever. Teresa became frightened and called her husband. He examined the boy and saw that he was not malingering, he really had a fever. But he also knew that it was not due to anything organic but to anxiety, and he ordered Jegor to get up and go to school.

Jegor looked at his father with hate. "It's all the same to me," he said, "but if I get sick, it'll be your fault."

Teresa was upset and looked pleadingly at her husband, but he would not relent. "He'll get used to the boys," he told her. "It will help cure him."

The fever subsided as Dr. Carnovsky had predicted, but Jegor did
not get used either to the school or to the boys. Because of his
awkward English, he was put into a lower grade. Gawky, easily
a head taller than his classmates, he was embarrassed about his
height and about being in the same class with younger children. He
was also anxious about his accent, which made the whole class laugh
the first time he answered a question. It reminded them of the German dialect comedians they were used to hearing on the radio. The
more the class laughed, the more embarrassed Jegor became and
finally he began to stutter. The boys and girls laughed even harder.

The English teacher, Mr. Barnett Levy, quickly put a stop to the
laughter. Tapping his pencil on the desk for silence, he deliberately
polished the lenses of his glasses and halted the lesson to lecture the
class in his deep baritone. His voice had always been his most effec-
tive teaching tool. A short, fat, kinky-haired man, he enjoyed little
popularity with the rowdy, racially mixed student body until he began to speak. But his dulcet soothing voice commanded instant attention and he would employ it like an instrument. He used it now
to stop the laughter. "Quiet, children, quiet," he said to the nearly
hysterical youngsters.

He didn't grow angry. Instead, he calmly pointed out the conditions that had caused the stranger to leave his native land and to
come to their country where the language and the customs were
unfamiliar to him. His explanation touched the children, particularly the girls, and they felt sorry for the tall and bashful boy.

Pleased by his sensible solution. Mr. Levy looked in Jegor Carnovsky's eyes to convey to the boy his personal sympathy and compassion. And to lighten the mood of the serious lecture that he had
imposed upon the class, he jokingly predicted that one day Jegor's
English would be better than his own and that Jegor too might become a teacher as had he, the son of an immigrant tailor.

With that, he winked at Jegor to affirm their kinship. But instead
of a grateful smile, the boy gave him a look of utter, icy contempt.
"I am no Jew!" he said sharply.

Mr. Levy was nonplussed. What had gone wrong? Like every
Jew, he felt that he could ferret out a fellow Jew in any gathering

and he was certain he had not been wrong this time. But he also knew that this was neither the time nor the place to settle the matter.

"We'll leave that to the race specialists on the other side," he said somewhat maliciously. "Whatever you may be, let us get back to our lesson."

From then on a quiet but deadly feud existed between teacher and pupil.

Jegor concentrated all his hate for teachers on the only one who had tried to defend him. He did this partly to curry favor with the Aryan-looking students in his class. Jegor separated his schoolmates, as he did all people, into two categories—those with blond hair and blue eyes whom he admired but feared, and the dark ones of whom he was not afraid but for whom he had contempt. He was overly drawn to the former and overly suspicious of the latter, and both these emotions were evident to all. Playing together, the boys often chided one another about their nationalities. The words "Guinea," "Mocky," and "Polack" were freely used but caused no grudges. But Jegor's posturings and conflicting emotions, his arrogance, submissiveness, pretentiousness, and hauteur struck a jarring note in the easy, good-natured relationships the boys enjoyed and they quickly learned to avoid him and to laugh at him behind his back. They loved to imitate his walk and stance and his frequent habit of stretching his shoulders stiffly. Jegor knew that everyone referred to him as Sauerkraut and Katzenjammer.

He tried to get back at them by making fun of their country and the other institutions they held dear. He praised everything German —its army, navy, sport champions, cars, and boats. He refused to participate in school athletics because he knew he wasn't good at sports and was deathly afraid of making a fool of himself. The boys challenged him to contests and to fights, but Jegor would not fight and the boys called him a pansy and yellow. Because school was such a torture, he often made believe he was sick, came in late, and did everything possible to avoid going to class. To spite Mr. Levy, he didn't learn his lessons and neglected his homework. Dr. Carnovsky was sure that his son was feigning his illnesses and told him so and Jegor felt a murderous hate toward his father for knowing him so

well. Nothing could be hidden from the black, piercing Carnovsky eyes and Jegor hated and feared them. He hated even more the
sharp, penetrating gaze of his grandfather, David, when he came to
visit.

In America, David had become the complete Jew. The tip of his
pointed, trimmed beard had blossomed into a full rabbinical growth.
He spoke a ripe Yiddish instead of the grammatical German he had
employed on the other side, and frequently interpolated Hebrew
similes into his conversation. He constantly exalted Judaism, the
holy teachings, the observance of the Sabbath, and other such foolishness that made Jegor wince. His grandfather's sudden transformation into a Biblical patriarch enraged Jegor. He was also disgusted
with Grandmother Carnovsky, who brought the stinks and sounds
of Dragonerstrasse into the house. She peered into pots, mumbled
about the observance of *Kashruth,* and babbled on in an unintelligible Melnitz jargon like some marketplace crone. The thing he
hated most was when they asked him about his progress in school.

"And are you studying hard?" David Carnovsky would ask in the
newly acquired singsong that made Jegor grit his teeth.

"No!" Jegor would shout.

David Carnovsky would bristle. "A shame!" he would cry. "Rabbi
Elisha Ben Abijah, a great Hebrew scholar, said that he who studies
can be compared to ink written on a crisp sheet of paper, while he
who does not, to ink written on a crumpled sheet!"

"It's all the same to me what some rabbi said or didn't say," Jegor
would reply in the most insolent tone he could manage.

The old man would seethe and predict a dire future for the boy. If
he didn't study, he would come to a bad end. He must decide now
what he wanted to be and grow up a learned and dedicated man as
had all the Carnovsky men.

Jegor would turn his back on his grandfather. "Who cares?" he
would say.

Leah would recall her husband from the boy's room before anything worse happened. With kindness and concern she tried to win
her grandson over and gently chided him for his lack of respect
toward his grandfather. Didn't he know that one must respect one's
elders? To palliate her lecture she would give him some sweet al-

mond cookies. "Eat, child," she would say, her voice quavering. "It's good for you, it will build you up. . . ."

But he rejected her cookies as he did her kind words and the boys she sent to keep him company. As the best influence on her rebellious grandson she had chosen Ruth and Jonas Zielonek's son, Marcus.

At seventeen, Marcus was a carbon copy of his mother, the favorite of the Burak family. Although he had been in the country only a short time, he had accumulated all kinds of academic medals and honors. His picture had even been published in the Yiddish newspaper, and Leah hoped that he would exert a steadying influence on Jegor and demonstrate to him the rewards of hewing to the path of righteousness.

Recalling past incidents between the families, Leah was not sure that Ruth would allow her son to come to Georg's apartment. But Ruth only embraced Leah and graciously said that a friendship between the boys would please her greatly. Leah Carnovsky arranged a meeting at her house. At first, Dr. Carnovsky and Ruth felt uneasy, meeting after so many years. In an overly solicitous tone he asked about her piano-playing at which she had once excelled; she, in turn, was too friendly toward Teresa and held her hands. Afterwards, the Carnovskys invited the Zieloneks to their house, along with their brilliant son, Marcus.

Never sure how his son would respond to strangers, Dr. Carnovsky led the boy to Jegor's room and made the introduction. "Marcus, meet Jegor," he said with an adult's condescension. "You two boys should be good friends." Then he slammed the door and left, as if the friendship were already an accomplished fact.

The boys looked at each other hesitantly. Marcus stuck out a soft downy hand that exuded warmth and amiability and acceptance of the world as it was. He had nothing of his grandfather Burak's quickness, tartness, and sharp Nordic features. He was plump, like his mother, with dark, gentle black eyes and a yielding, girlish body. "Hello, Jegor," he said in English, "pleased to meet you."

"Joachim Georg!" Jegor barked in German and clicked his heels. His icy blue eyes took in every detail of the other's face and body.

Marcus reminded him of a fat, placid sheep and Jegor began to treat him with an obvious and pointed contempt. But like many easy-going people, Marcus was immune to sarcasm. Jegor hated and envied Marcus' lust for life, his unfailing good nature, his obvious delight with himself. When Marcus showed Jegor the medals he had won at school, Jegor clicked his tongue. "Are these all?" he said with heavy sarcasm.

"I'll be getting some more soon," Marcus said with maddening self-assurance.

When they rejoined the adults and his parents began to praise Marcus openly, Jegor could not resist the opportunity to make scathing remarks about education, professors, and people who made such a fuss about books and learning. The Zieloneks, who were both completely devoid of humor, listened with open mouths. To avoid a scene, Dr. Carnovsky made light of the whole thing. "Don't listen to anything he says," he said easily. "It's only the blabberings of a half-grown show-off."

Jegor sat up sharply. "I'm old enough to know what I'm saying!" he spat out between clenched teeth. "And I don't like being gagged."

Abandoning all restraint, he launched a tirade against intellectuals and scholars, particularly those with curly hair and eyeglasses. He sounded exactly like the Party speakers on the other side.

A deathly silence followed. The one who took it hardest was Teresa Carnovsky. As the only gentile present, she felt doubly embarrassed hearing the race theories expounded by her son. "Oh, dear God!" she wailed, wringing her hands.

Dr. Carnovsky felt it was not yet too late to save the situation and tried to turn the whole incident into a joke. He gripped the boys by the shoulders and steered them toward the door. "No politics now!" he said lightly. "Outside with the two of you! A walk will do you both good!"

Although Marcus wanted to say something in rebuttal to Jegor's diatribe, he good-naturedly turned to obey Dr. Carnovsky; but Jegor would not go. He didn't want to be seen in the streets with such an obviously Semitic, four-eyed bookworm. And although Marcus remained blissfully unaware of Jegor's contempt, it had become pointedly clear to his mother and it aroused in her the old feelings of resentment against the arrogant Carnovskys. "Come, Marcus," she said. "You obviously aren't welcome in this house."

Teresa clutched her arm. "Please don't go—I beg you to stay!"

But Ruth was adamant. "Get my coat, Jonas," she said, cold with anger.

Dr. Carnovsky knew that he must maintain control and not do anything foolish, but his rage took hold of him. "Apologize to our guests!" he ordered his son. "Apologize this instant!"

As usual when he became upset, Jegor began to stutter. "N . . . n . . . no!" he shrieked and dashed to his room. He was terrified to have people hear him stutter. As long as he remained in the house with only his parents he was able to speak clearly, even eloquently. But with strangers it was another matter.

His stuttering was even worse when he met a girl or a woman and he became greatly disturbed when Uncle Harry's daughter Ethel came to call. She would often drop in on the Carnovskys, laughing, gay, and spirited, and just as abruptly rush away. She loved to flirt with Jegor. Because he was so stiff and curt toward her, she had great fun teasing him, telling him how much he appealed to her, and even trying to kiss him. "Don't you think I'm adorable, Jegor?" she would ask, cuddling up to him.

Despite the feelings her warm, young body aroused in him, he acted cold and unresponsive. But his palms would begin to perspire and he would have to thrust them into his pockets. For weeks after her visits he would recall the touch of her hands, have sexual dreams about her, and wake up feeling guilty and ashamed. She complimented him on his blue eyes but at the same time called him a clumsy, arrogant German lummox, an expression she had picked up from her parents. She would suddenly catch his hands and dance him around the room, but Jegor, his face blazing, would tear free.

Ethel would then run up to his father. "Surely you won't refuse me, Doctor?"

"I should say not!" Dr. Carnovsky would say gallantly and waltz her expertly across the floor.

"Watch your father, dope, and learn how to behave around a lady," Ethel would say to Jegor.

Jegor watched and burned with envy. He knew that his father was very attractive to women and he hated him for it. Even his mother, his fair, beautiful, pure Aryan mother, found this swarthy, saturnine Jew exciting. The more he compared himself to his father, the less confidence he felt in his own scrawny body. He raged inwardly against himself and recalled all the ridiculous and gauche things he had been provoked into saying to Ethel. He flagellated himself mercilessly, relishing the self-abasement.

Rather than continue torturing himself, he would suddenly experience great surges of self-pity. He would stop blaming himself, justify all his actions, and transfer the blame to others. Always he attributed most of the guilt to his father and his kind. All the world's evil stemmed from this source. That was what he had been told by Uncle Hugo, the teachers on the other side, the newspapers, the books, the radio commentators. Jews themselves said it.

He read with a particularly bittersweet relish many inflammatory attacks against Jewry written by Jewish renegades. It was a way of taking revenge on the Semitic strain that he hated so desperately. It was an avenue through which he could cleanse himself and vent all the guilt on his father, the Jew.

For his mother he felt only sorrow—she had no reason to suffer. She was an Aryan of the purest, most aristocratic background. What right did that black Jew have to involve her in this mess, to uproot her from the land of her ancestors?

"Why did you do it, Mutti? Why did you go with him?" he often asked her.

"*Him?* That's your father you're talking about! You have no right—"

"Oh, how I hate him!" Jegor cried. "And he hates me too!"

"What nonsense! Papa loves you more than anything in this world. . . ."

Jegor began to kiss his mother's hand. "Mutti! Let's go home . . . just you and me. . . ."

She hugged him as if he were a child. "We no longer have a home," she said sadly.

"I cannot live here. . . . I'll never get used to it!"

As much as she hated to discuss the humiliation he had suffered on the other side, Teresa felt impelled to remind him about it. "How can you talk of going back when those people hurt you so badly?"

"I don't care! Let's go back. Uncle Hugo will fix everything."

He had abandoned all reality and had begun to live in a dream world, to wish for things that his logic knew were impossible. The more he took refuge in the world of make-believe, the more credible his reveries seemed. In his dreams he saw himself on the other side, marching with the rest of the aroused nation. Women and blonde young maidens threw flower petals that he crushed beneath his hobnailed boots.

He would wake up in a daze when his mother shook him and said it was time for school. "Mutti, I don't want to go to school," he would bleat. "I want to go home to Grandma Holbeck's. Say we can go, Mutti."

"You know it cannot be, Jegor. I want you to stop talking this way."

"Oh, I know that I mean nothing to you," he would wail piteously. "*He* is the only one you care for."

Now that he saw that nothing would tear his mother away from his father, he began to long for the only thing that he thought would make her his alone—his father's death.

38

No matter how hard the booted youths of Neukölln tried to persuade old Johanna to leave the Jew, Landau, they could not manage it. They tried using reason, they insulted her, they even threatened her. It was unthinkable that she, a pure Aryan, should serve a Jewish bloodsucker and ravager of Christian women. But old Johanna would not be swayed. She publicly announced that she had no fears of being seduced by Dr. Landau. The people in the courtyard had a good laugh over this and the brown-shirted youths felt sheepish and somehow insulted. At the same time she called them snotnoses and unweaned pups, and other ripe Neukölln names. Whenever they came too close to her, she spat at them. She was too old to be removed by force and although Dr. Landau was no longer able to supply her with the meat that she liked so much and she was forced to share his "grass," she stayed on. Although she had never approved of his dietary habits or his method of collecting fees, she refused to abandon him to the mercy of the wicked men who ruled Germany.

Dr. Landau tried to drive her away on his own. "You foolish old woman, what's the point of starving to death here?" he raged. "Go among your own people, at least you'll get your meat and coffee there!"

"Bosh!" she cackled, as angry at him as ever. "You'd do better to clean the crumbs from your beard! Since they've taken Fraülein Elsa away, you go around like a tramp with your beard full of vegetables!"

One morning she did not get up at the crack of dawn as had been her custom all her life. Dr. Landau went into the kitchen where she lay on her high iron bed. "What is it, Johanna?" he asked.

"I'm dying," the old woman said calmly.

Dr. Landau pushed his beard aside and put his ear to her chest. "Don't be ashamed, you silly goose," he scolded her when she tried to hide her naked breast. "I'm not about to pollute your race, I only want to hear what's wrong. Breathe in and out!"

"Ach, the nonsense you prattle!" she said and did not do as he directed. "I'm old and it's my time to die. I don't want a doctor, I want a pastor."

Dr. Landau felt her pulse. It was beating weakly. He knew that Johanna was not deceiving herself and he put her hand back under the blanket. "All right, Johanna, I'll get you a pastor."

All the wrinkles and folds in the old woman's face melted in a beatific smile. "Go quickly, Doctor," she said, "soon it will be too late."

Himself a heretic who sneered at the rites of religion, Dr. Landau hurried to get the pastor so that the old woman could receive the last rites she so desperately wanted. He also saw to it that the janitress, Frau Kruppa, called in the elderly women who because of their age were allowed to enter a Jew's house, so that they could prepare the body for burial according to the dictates of Johanna's faith. With his last few marks he paid for her funeral. He was its only mourner, walking behind the hearse until it turned into the cemetery at Friedhof, and he also tipped the gravediggers. With his head sunk low, he returned to his empty apartment to clean up and to prepare his meager dinner. It would be the first time he would make his own meal in years.

But when he came home, he found the place freshly scrubbed and everything in order. The beds were made, the floor was still damp from mopping, the table was cleared, everything had been put away. Dr. Landau tugged at his beard several times, disturbed by the miracle. His amazement mounted when he stumbled over Johanna's shopping basket and found it full of his favorite foods—carrots, beets, and potatoes, and even a bottle of fresh milk. For a moment Dr. Landau was furious. He was not accustomed to being given things, *he* was the one who did the giving. But soon he grew ashamed of his pride and became angry at himself for being irked at people's generosity. He sat down at his bare table, ate the vegetables, and drank the milk. From that day on he frequently found his apartment cleaned when he came home from his long walks. He also found food packages at his door—sometimes some green peas, sometimes a cheese or a bottle of milk. He no longer felt so wretched and alone when he sat down to eat. The thought that Neukölln had not forgotten his long years of sacrifice, that people took the dangerous chance of helping a Jew out of gratitude, gave him a feeling that all was not wrong in the world.

"*Morgen, Morgen, Morgen!*" he responded heartily when the more daring of his neighbors greeted him in the street during his early-morning walks.

The friendliest of all was the elderly postman, Herr Kohlemann, who occasionally had a letter for Dr. Landau stamped with the dreaded mark of the concentration camp. Herr Kohlemann, who knew everything and everybody in the neighborhood, knew who had sent these letters and, although they came rather infrequently, he always made a great show of searching carefully in his pouch when he met Dr. Landau. This gave him the opportunity to exchange a few words with the doctor.

"A letter, Herr Kohlemann?" Dr. Landau would ask impatiently each time he saw the postman.

"Unfortunately not today, Herr Doktor, but it will come, it will come," the old man would say sympathetically. "Perhaps one day soon Fraülein Doktor herself will be coming."

"I've already lost all hope, Herr Kohlemann," Dr. Landau would reply, shaking his head ruefully.

"Don't lose courage, Herr Doktor, even if these are bad times," the old man would whisper, looking around to see if anyone was listening.

His words proved prophetic. One evening as Dr. Landau was standing by the black iron stove fixing his dinner, the front door swung open and Elsa came in. Dr. Landau stood rooted, the kitchen knife still gripped in his hand. He barely recognized his daughter. Her body was gnarled and withered, her once coppery hair had turned a dull gray. The only thing that was familiar were her eyes, although they were now full of pain and mistrust. Everything about her seemed shriveled and shrunken—her coat, her shoes, even the satchel she carried. Still holding his knife, he ran up to her.

Elsa was as calm and deliberate as ever. "Watch the knife, Papa," she said. She took it from his hand as if he were a child and with her lips searched for his mouth in the thickets of beard and mustache. *"Papachen, dear, sweet Papachen!"* she said over and over.

"Poor child," the old man crooned, stroking her drab, bristly hair and recalling how glossy and brilliant it had been just a few short years before.

Although Elsa had been careful to slip in quietly, the next morning there were two bottles of milk outside the door and, in addition, a small bouquet of flowers. Elsa's eyes grew misty when her father gave her the pathetic bunch of flowers to which was attached a small piece of paper with the scribbled words: "Welcome from Neukölln." But she did not allow the tears to flow past her lids—she had learned how to control them. In the concentration camp she had become even more disciplined and calculating. There was not one torture or indignation to which her body had not been subjected; it had been broken and violated beyond repair. But her spirit had grown even more tenacious. Energetically she managed to sell the few possessions that still remained in the house. With equal determination she went from consulate to consulate until she got visas for herself and for her father. Dr. Landau felt that it would be easier for his daughter to leave the country alone and he urged her to save herself and to forget about him. He was old; he would finish out his life where he was; the good people of Neukölln would not let him starve. But Elsa ordered him to do only what he was told and not to interfere. She treated him with the blend of tenderness and firmness one applies to a child.

Carrying only the barest minimum of personal belongings— the doctor's instruments, the tray for fees, and the biggest bouquet Neukölln could manage at the last moment—the father and daughter left the workers' quarter that had been their home for so long and took the train to Hamburg and the ship that would take them to America. During the entire trip Elsa never let go of the pocketbook that contained their passports with the stamped "J's" to indicate that she and her father were Jews—she needed physical reassurance that she had actually managed to leave the inferno that had been her beloved Germany. Just as carefully she guarded the small packet of marks that remained after the train fare, boat tickets, visas, and various levies had been paid. It came to all of forty marks—a person leaving the Third Reich was permitted to take out only twenty marks.

When they arrived in New York they sought out the same kind of section in which they had lived in Berlin, a grim and grubby block on the edge of Harlem where for a few dollars they rented a room in a decrepit hotel and located a cheap vegetarian restaurant where they could eat their nourishing meals for pennies. Dr. Landau was like a child in the great, strange, noisy city, but Elsa quickly learned how to get around. She had not used her time behind barbed wire idly but had read all that she could find about America—its habits, customs, history, geography, and economy. She had studied the language, reading a dictionary page by page, along with every English-language book that existed in the prison library, including the Bible. Dr. Landau was amazed to hear his daughter speaking so fluently with Americans. He was astounded when, a mere week after their arrival in the strange country, she led him to a large, crowded hall filled with people who had come to hear Dr. Elsa Landau, former deputy of the Reichstag and noted Party leader.

Again there was applause and spotlights and newspaper photographers. People cheered, bands played. Dr. Landau could not believe his eyes. Elsa was back in her element. She acted as if nothing had happened to interrupt one of her customary campaigns. In a clear, commanding voice she urged her American comrades to keep up the struggle that one day would be won. The audience roared and would not let her leave the stage. On the following day Elsa's picture was in all the newspapers. Reporters flocked to the small hotel to interview her. Elsa spoke to them fluently in their own language. Many calls started coming in for Dr. Elsa Landau on the small hotel switchboard. Women's committees, societies, and organizations invited her to address them. Elsa began to order eggs and more elaborate dairy dishes for her father along with the meager vegetable soups. She found a better hotel and rented two rooms there, one for each of them. After they finished their meals at the vegetarian restaurant she would playfully pluck the crumbs from her father's now all-white beard and mustache.

"Don't sulk, funny old *Papachen,*" she would chide him. "Give your little Elsa a smile!"

But Dr. Landau was in no mood to smile. Just as he had hated the furor over his daughter on the other side, he hated it in the new country too. He could not bear the fiery speeches, the noise, the fuss made over her. Elsa was rarely at home any more—just as in the old days, she traveled all over making speeches and organizing anti-fascist activities. She was away for weeks at a time. Dr. Landau felt wretched and alone in the large city where he did not know the language and always got lost. He wanted to be with his daughter. He still hoped that she would return to medicine and that they could practice somewhere together. Walking through the congested streets filled with raggedy Negro, Puerto Rican, and Italian children, he felt an urge to rent a street-level apartment, to put his collection tray on a table in the waiting room, and to thrust his thermometer under children's tongues and lecture them on hygiene.

"Elsa, you haven't learned a damned thing!" he scolded his daughter. "Instead of trying to help millions, why don't you try helping a hundred? Give up your idiotic Party and let's open an office together. From what I can see, the neighborhood could use a couple of doctors. Besides, medicine is your true calling, not politics."

"No, *Papachen,*" she said firmly. "There are plenty of doctors but few fighters. I must do what I have to do."

Seeing that she was adamant, he began to seek means of returning to practice himself. Carrying his ancient, oversized diploma, he went from institution to institution looking for some sort of job. But everywhere he went he was told he needed a state medical license and a knowledge of English. Dr. Landau grew despondent. He knew that he could never master the language. He did not know enough of it to order a plate of beans at the restaurant when he went there without Elsa.

His daughter urged him to forget his aspirations. She would support him; he deserved to retire after his long years of hard work and to spend his time walking and relaxing. If he was lonely, she could arrange to board him with a refugee family where he would feel more at home. They would prepare the kind of dishes he liked and he would have company and a chance to rest.

"I'm not ready yet to be put out to pasture like some old nag!" he roared. "I'm a doctor and I want to work!"

"*Papachen,* don't get so excited!" Elsa cooed. "It isn't good for you!"

"The egg must not teach the hen!" Dr. Landau stormed, stomping his cane for emphasis. "I know better what is good for me!"

Finally, in one office where he sought employment, they showed a mite of interest. "What do you know about chickens, Doctor?" they asked.

He hesitated. "Not too much, but I've always been very interested in animals. I used to treat them in Neukölln often. They would bring me sick dogs, cats, rabbits, and birds and I made them well."

The men looked at each other. "We need somebody for a chicken farm," they said, "but we don't know if you can handle the job at your age."

Dr. Landau's face turned slightly purple, as it always did at mention of his age. "Give me your hand, *Mein Herr,*" he said to the head man of the committee.

The man was puzzled. "My hand?"

"Don't be afraid, I'm not going to take your pulse," Dr. Landau snorted. "Simply shake hands with me."

The official stuck out his hand gingerly, as if Dr. Landau were some kind of witch doctor.

Dr. Landau took the hand and squeezed it so vigorously that the startled committeeman cried out in pain.

"Well, am I too old?" Dr. Landau demanded.

"I believe we'll give you a chance, Doctor," the official grinned, rubbing his aching fingers.

Nothing Elsa could say could deter her father from accepting the job. She was forced to stand by while he packed his things in a valise and went off to his chickens. He put on the velvet trousers that he had not worn in years, the thick-soled walking shoes, a rough work-ingman's shirt, and walked vigorously toward the battered coupé that would take him to his new place of work.

"Gimme your hand, Grandpa, I'll help you," the leather-jacketed young driver said indifferently.

"I don't need your hand, young man," Dr. Landau growled and gracefully vaulted into the car.

"Pop, you've got lots of pep in you yet," the driver said admiringly.

Dr. Landau beamed at the compliment. As soon as they drove out of the city and the country breeze began to ruffle his beard, he felt revived and as vigorous as a buck. The first group of fat cows grazing on a sloping meadow filled him with an indescribable joy. He no longer felt like a stranger in the alien land; every low, whinny, and bleat was dear and familiar to him. The craggy hills and boulders breathed the agelessness of creation. Dr. Landau sensed their voice, their force, and their eternal mystery and he began to sing an ancient mountaineer's ballad he remembered from his student days. At the first sight of light the following morning, he threw himself into his work. His hair and beard white as snow, he hopped jubilantly among the white chickens and in a minimum of time he learned to differentiate between a sick and a healthy bird.

With great gusto he ate his vegetables and eggs and drank glasses of fresh water from the well. In the evenings he lay on the cot in his room above the garage and read books about poultry-breeding that Elsa brought him. He applied himself to the subject of chickens as assiduously as a young man beginning a career. With each passing day he learned more about his birds. Just as he had come to love his human patients, he grew inordinately fond of his feathered ones, picking out those that were ailing with a single glance and nursing them back to health in the little "hospital" he had set up.

"Don't peck each other, *Dummköpfe!*" he scolded the fighters among them. "There is enough corn for everybody!"

He hated the dealers who came to take the chickens to the slaughterhouses that supplied the area's summer hotels. The terrified clucking of the young white pullets tugged at his heart as if they were the cries of his own children. But it was a treat for him when Elsa came on Sundays to visit. Just as in the old days, they went hiking through the countryside, up hills and down valleys. Elsa tried to hold her father back. "Slowly, *Papachen*," she cautioned him.

"The egg does not teach the hen!" the old man raged. "And don't breathe through the mouth, damn it, through the nose, the nose, the nose!"

Elsa recalled the times when Georg Carnovsky had walked beside her and spoken of his love and a deep sigh escaped her tightly set lips.

"What is it, Elsa?" her father asked.

"It's nothing, *Papachen*," she whispered, and to conceal her emotion she began telling him of her travels and triumphs throughout America.

Her father refused to listen. "You'd do better to settle here on the farm with me," he said.

"With chickens?" she asked mockingly.

"Yes, with chickens! They aren't as simple as you think. They're a lot more interesting than people."

She picked the crumbs from his beard. "You'll never learn to keep your whiskers clean," she said severely, and wiped away a vagrant tear.

39

With each day the rift between Jegor Carnovsky and Barnett Levy grew wider.

Like a good educator, Mr. Levy tried to conceal any antipathy he might have felt, but Jegor was quite frank in his distaste and badgered the teacher at every opportunity. He never responded in a straightforward manner but always with sarcasm and an infuriating insolence. He averted his eyes when he addressed Mr. Levy and a vicious little smile played on his lips. His schoolwork was sloppy and indifferent. But Mr. Levy kept his patience until one day Jegor forced his hand and he had to act to retain his authority.

The inevitable clash occurred during a class dealing with the war. With immense enthusiasm, Mr. Levy described the battle of the Argonne Forest—the triumphant attacking American troops and the fleeing, demoralized Germans. Mr. Levy felt particularly close to this battle since he himself had been in it. He often wore his overseas cap, battle ribbons, and the uniform that threatened to burst from the stout little body and had seen so many American Legion conventions. He never tired of discussing every detail of his months at the front. His voice mellow as a cello, he described the glorious charge of his company and the utter rout and confusion of the enemy. His vibrant tones infuriated Jegor Carnovsky like the scraping of a dull saw. He had heard a quite different version of the same battle from another participant, Oberleutnant Hugo Holbeck. This particular defeat had long rankled Uncle Hugo and he blamed it squarely on

the profiteers and slackers who had plunged the knife into the back
of the heroic German troops in the trenches. . . . At last Jegor
could not stand any more of Levy's boasting and he stood up. "Sir!"
he interrupted the teacher in the middle of a sentence. "It wasn't the
German troops who lost the battle, it was the traitors at home who
stabbed the army in the back!"

Normally, Mr. Levy encouraged interruptions because he felt that
differences of opinion stimulated class interest. But this time he was
too deeply involved in the subject to be objective. "Who were these
traitors, Carnovsky?" he asked sarcastically.

"All the enemies of the country," Jegor said heatedly. "If not for
them, the German army would have won!"

"If a ram had an udder it would give milk," Mr. Levy said.

The class, which usually sided with a student who baited the
teacher, this time was entirely on Mr. Levy's side and jeered Jegor.
As usual when people laughed at him, Jegor became upset. "I'm
talking seriously and you're making jokes!" he shouted.

Mr. Levy restored order and struggled to remain calm. Knowing
that youngsters liked to identify with athletes, he began to describe a
bout between a skilled boxer and a poor one. The good boxer scored
points while the poor one complained that he had been fouled, that
the referee was prejudiced, and that he had been threatened so as to
make him throw the fight. But the important thing was the outcome,
not the "ifs," "buts," and excuses. Did the class agree?

"Yes, sir!" they bellowed in unison and looked triumphantly at
the foreigner.

Mr. Levy rapped for order with his pencil and went back to the
lesson.

Jegor knew he could not win the argument—there were too
many things stacked against him: his poor command of the language, his inability to remain calm, and his stutter. But, propelled by
the perversity that dictated his whole existence, he plunged in as he
always did, knowing full well that he would be hurt in the end.

Mr. Levy went on to discuss the present conditions in Germany,
its leaders, and the changes they had effected. Jegor knew that he was
telling the truth—had he not personally suffered persecution under

the New Order? But he resented these facts being mentioned by a Levy. It was enough to push him over the brink. "Sir!" he warned. "You must not say such things about my country!"

Mr. Levy lost his patience. "Carnovsky! You are here! *This* is your country!"

The blood rushed to Jegor's face and he plunged into the abyss. "Once a German, always a German!" he blurted out.

Mr. Levy reacted like any Jew toward a coreligionist who conceals his faith. "I believe the authorities had a different opinion of your origins, Carnovsky," he said. "Otherwise they wouldn't have kicked you out of the country."

"*I* am no Jew, Mr. *Levy!*" he said, accentuating the Hebraic name to point up the difference between them.

"That is of absolutely no concern to the school," Mr. Levy said. "All we are interested in are a pupil's learning ability and his conduct. Sit down!"

Jegor began to make some insolent remark but Mr. Levy would not allow him to finish. "Leave the room!" he ordered. "And the first thing tomorrow morning, report to the principal."

That night Jegor lay awake. He was both eager and apprehensive about meeting the principal to whom he had never spoken but for whom he felt a great admiration. A tall, burly man with a ruddy face burned a deep red by the sun and wind, he had the light blue eyes of the seafarer and fair, straw-colored hair that belied his fifty-odd years. In fact, he looked more like a Viking sea captain than a school principal and Jegor liked everything about him, down to the curved pipe he was never without. After Levy's swarthy, fuzzy-haired corpulence it was a pleasure to look at Mr. Van Loben, who looked like the posters of the Aryans on the other side. Jegor felt that they would get along well.

At the threshold of Mr. Van Loben's office, he drew himself up tautly and clicked his heels together. He was anxious to show that he could be respectful when dealing with those of proper origin. "Joachim Georg Holbeck Carnovsky," he bawled. "It is a pleasure to be at your service, sir."

But Mr. Van Loben was not impressed. "We don't go in for all that nonsense here, young man," he said. "Sit down and give me just one name I can remember."

Jegor became confused by the unexpected rebuff and remained standing, but Mr. Van Loben jumped up and with a meaty hand on each of Jegor's spindly shoulders rammed him firmly into the chair. "Like this," he said amiably, and vaulted into his own chair so that it groaned beneath his bulk. Stretching his legs lazily so that the golden, downy shins could be seen above the drooping socks, he glanced at the papers on his desk and lit his pipe.

"What's the idea of giving Mr. Levy a bad time?" he asked.

Jegor cleared his throat and launched into a complicated defense. His sentences were long, with endless asides, digressions, frequent "sirs" and circuities. Mr. Van Loben puffed on his pipe vigorously to conceal his boredom. Although he was a noted educator, he hated to deal with problem students. He could get along well with those who were merely mischievous—boys who had thrown a paper wad at a teacher or perhaps disrupted the class with a joke—and he was even able to handle students who had committed more serious offenses such as fighting or stealing. Basically a man of action, he was able to reach such boys with his earthy language and his knowledge of the ethics of the street, and to exert the kind of forceful yet tolerant authority with which they could make peace. But he hated to deal with real problem children. Above all, he hated whiners and cry babies.

"Get on with it," he urged Jegor, who was in the throes of a passionate appeal for justice. "Get to the point, boy!"

Jegor could only reiterate his violent attack against Mr. Levy. He hated everything about him, he told the principal, who looked at him with level, unblinking eyes—his conduct, his looks, his . . . his . . .

He stopped and looked at Mr. Van Loben for some sign of agreement or sympathy but he saw nothing except a blank, neutral coldness that only intensified his uncertainty. He plunged on. Perhaps he had not been lucid enough. Perhaps he was obliged to make his meanings clearer. He, Mr. Van Loben, surely understood what he meant. They were, after all, two of a kind.

"It's merely a matter of blood," he concluded in the high soprano that often erupted from him in moments of stress. "I assume we understand each other perfectly?"

Mr. Van Loben quickly tapped the slag from his pipe and said one blunt word: "Crap!"

Jegor remained sitting as if petrified. This was hardly a word he had expected from a school principal.

Mr. Van Loben tamped his pipe with the strong navy tobacco to which he was addicted and lit it. "Yes sir," he said, "that's just what it is, a whole lot of crap and I won't swallow any of it."

He suddenly pulled his wastebasket closer with his huge feet, took out a bunch of leaflets, and threw them in front of Jegor. "Look at this garbage they send me just because my name begins with a 'Van.' And you see what I do with it!" He picked up the papers and flung them violently into the wastebasket.

Jegor looked down at his hands. Suddenly the huge blond man smiled like a child. "Listen to me," he said in a fatherly tone. "I want to talk things over with you, but I like people to look me in the eye when I speak to them. Raise your head!"

Jegor braced himself for a long, drawn-out lecture, but Mr. Van Loben began to ask questions that only a doctor would. "How old are you?"

"Eighteen."

"Show me your arm."

Jegor was confused. Mr. Van Loben picked up the arm and felt it. "That's a girl's arm, not a man's."

Suddenly he put his head close to Jegor. "Tell me, kid, how often do you do it?"

Jegor blushed and looked down, but Mr. Van Loben stuck a thumb under his chin and raised his head up. "Look at me. . . . You know I could transfer you to a different class where you'd have another teacher, but I'm not going to."

"Why not, sir?" Jegor asked forlornly.

"First, because Mr. Levy is a good teacher; and second, just because you hate him so much it will do you good to stay with him until you cure yourself of that racial nonsense your head is stuffed with."

Jegor wanted to pursue the subject further, but Mr. Van Loben looked at his watch to indicate that the interview was over. "I'll square things with Mr. Levy and we'll forget the whole thing," he said. "But I want you to take a note home to your father. There are a few things I want to discuss with him."

Jegor began to sputter. He wanted to ask Mr. Van Loben not to involve his father but again the principal cut him short and walked him to the door.

Jegor walked out of the office completely distraught. Nothing had changed except that now his father was involved. Shakily, he walked to the subway and boarded a train. A blind man worked his way through the car jingling coins in a cup, but Jegor could see nothing but his own despair. At first the car was filled with black-haired Jewish men and women; a few stations later, blond men in overalls and women in curlers, carrying shopping bags, came on; later, Negroes of every size and hue. A drunken, almost blue-black man came staggering along. "Le's shake hands, my white friend," he said to Jegor, extending a huge, pink-palmed hand.

Jegor shrank back. He was sure that the Negro had selected him because he had detected his inferior strain. Soon the train again began to fill with fair and blue-eyed people: matrons with large purses, gawky, flaxen-haired boys with closely shorn temples, and stolid men carrying tool boxes. German could be heard along with English. A round-faced woman who was knitting with Teutonic precision pulled at her daughter's flaxen pigtail and exclaimed sharply in a pure Berlin German: *"Sei doch artig, Trudl!"*

Jegor suddenly felt as if he had taken a drink of cool water after a long spell in the desert. Although he had no business in the neighborhood, he got out at the next station.

Outside, stout housewives sat on steps of old houses and gossiped in a mixture of German and English. One after another they called to the children playing in the street, "Hans! Lieschen! Karl! Clara! Fritz!"

The windows of the beer halls, candy stores, and restaurants displayed familiar foods and pastries. German signs advertised rooms for rent. A funeral parlor sequestered among the taverns and bakeries proudly proclaimed its century-old existence, its tradition of courteous, reliant service, and its reasonable fees. Wherever there was a bare spot—on a wall, a dusty show window of an empty store, or a fence—swastikas had been chalked and, very, very rarely, a hammer and sickle. Near a neighborhood Democratic club where men in rolled-up sleeves played pool, a row of associations with long German names was concentrated along with loan companies, commission agencies, and currency exchange offices that offered to send money and packages to the Old Country. Ground-floor windows displayed shingles whose gilded Gothic letters advertised doctors, dentists, lawyers, business representatives, insurance and real estate agents. Bookstores displayed all kinds of colorful pictures and posters from the other side. From behind an open window a phonograph played a rousing military air.

Jegor suddenly felt alive. He looked all around, listened to every sound, inhaled every aroma. The wide doors of a church stood invitingly open. Above them an inscription was carved in Gothic letters, *"Ein fester Burg ist unser Gott."*

He suddenly thought about Grandmother Holbeck who used to take him to church, and he went inside. Soon he came out again. Across the street a theater marquee announced a new film from the other side. Jegor looked in his wallet. He had a five-dollar bill his mother had given him to pay the electric and gas bills, and some change. He went up to the cashier's booth. The girl inside was as pink and blonde as the girls on the posters. In his most elegant German he asked whether it would be too much trouble to take the fifty-cent ticket out of the five-dollar bill. "Unfortunately, Fräulein, I'm out of change," he said with the insouciance of one to whom a five-dollar bill was a trifle.

Counting out his change, the cashier treated him to a dazzling smile and complimented his German.

"Just recently arrived from the other side, Fräulein," he said. "I'm here on a pleasure trip."

"I noticed at once that you were from Germany," she said, dimpling prettily.

Proud to be mistaken for a German, Jegor walked into the theater. Perhaps he did not resemble his father as much as he feared. The lights went out and on the screen flashed familiar scenes of parades, war planes flying in formation, troops drilling and marching past

cheering crowds. With a catch in his throat Jegor recognized familiar streets and landmarks. When the picture ended, the audience applauded fervently. Jegor kept it up longest and looked around to see
if any one was watching.

When he came out of the theater it was already dark. He knew
that his parents must be worried but he made no move to go home.
In a restaurant window a fat, jolly dwarf was sitting astride a beer
barrel and from inside issued tantalizing odors of pork and sauerkraut. Jegor was starving. He had not eaten the whole day. He
walked inside, intending to have something at the counter before
heading home. So far he had spent only fifty cents of the five dollars
his mother had given him. But suddenly a blonde, buxom beauty in
a brief Bavarian costume accosted him and sweetly asked for his
coat. Jegor was so dazed that he handed over the worn raincoat with
a quarter tip in advance.

"*Danke schön, gnädiger Herr,*" she said, smiling sweetly.

"Ach, don't mention it!" he said grandly, as if quarters were beneath his notice.

He was watching her round, rotating buttocks recede into her
booth when an older woman, quite stout and respectable, took his
arm and led him to a table decorated with flowers.

"I hope you will find this table satisfactory, sir," she said with a
graciousness befitting her age and station. "Shall I send the waiter
now or is the gentleman expecting someone?"

"No, I'm quite alone today," Jegor said with the jaded air of the
man-about-town.

The stout lady sprang into immediate action. She snapped her
finger imperiously at a husky, totally bald waiter in Bavarian leather
shorts and an embroidered vest.

Jegor felt a twinge of panic. He knew that he was squandering
money that was scarce in the house and worrying his parents by not
coming home but by now it was too late. And even as he felt
uneasy, he also felt a kind of spiteful pride in doing things that were
forbidden.

"A stein of beer, *gnädiger Herr?*" the waiter suggested rather
than asked.

"Naturally," Jegor said.

With obvious pride in his work, the waiter balanced a brimming porcelain stein of beer and set a full plate of food before Jegor. He was also persuaded to buy a cigar from the cigarette girl and he smoked it although it made him choke. He pushed back the change from the dollar bill, smiling.

"How come the young gentleman is alone?" she asked.

"Would you care to keep me company, sweetheart?" he asked.

"I'm on duty now," she said. "It's not permitted."

"But a stein of beer you can surely share with me, *nicht wahr?*"

"Could you make it cognac instead?" she asked sweetly, remembering her arrangement with the restaurant.

Presently a violinist walked down from the bandstand and began to serenade them. Tears came to Jegor's eyes. It was the first time in his life he had been so royally treated.

He still had momentary qualms about the anxiety he was causing his parents and the money he was squandering so recklessly, but he was caught up in a state of exhilaration. He was surrounded by people at other tables who raised glasses to him, wished him a long life, and accompanied him in rowdy German tavern songs.

He was the last one to leave the restaurant. He was still singing when he came out on the deserted street but he soon stopped and felt in his pockets for the few coins remaining there, a total of three nickels and a penny. He sobered instantly. His head felt dull, leaden. His thoughts were just as oppressive. He walked down into the subway. A derelict was blacking in the center tooth of a model demonstrating tooth paste on a large poster. "How is that?" he asked Jegor, breathing the rankness of the sewer into his face.

Jegor drew back.

"Give us a dime for a flop, Mac!" the bum said aggressively.

Frightened, Jegor handed over two of his last three nickels and envied the bum who could sleep where he pleased without accounting to anyone.

Broodingly, he stepped into the subway car. The ride seemed to last forever. He got out at his stop and climbed the stairs to the street. The closer he came to home, the slower his pace became. He lingered before the shop windows studying the naked mannequins and listened to small groups arguing baseball. He walked past his house

and looked up. All the windows in the apartment were lit. He knew
how worried his mother must be if she had neglected to put out the
lights that normally she watched so carefully. He debated whether
to go up, but at that moment the window flew open and his mother's
voice rang out through the deserted street. "Jegor! Jegorchen!"

He went upstairs. His mother was standing in the doorway wearing his father's overcoat over her nightgown. She looked vulnerable
and very fragile inside the bulky garment. "Jegor, are you all right?"
she asked, although he obviously was.

Jegor felt a great wave of pity for her but he was too ridden with
guilt to show it and he reacted with his usual arrogance. *"Quatsch!*
Why didn't you go to sleep?"

Teresa smoothed her disarrayed hair. "Papa is at the police station! We thought something terrible had happened to you!"

Suddenly she smelled the alcohol on his breath. "Where have you
been, child?" she asked with concern.

Jegor said nothing. He ran to his room, slamming the door behind him. He wanted to barricade himself against his father, who
would be back at any moment. He dropped onto his bed with all his
clothes on, fell asleep, awoke, and slept again. He rose early in the
morning the following day before his father's customary knock on
the door. But this morning his father did not knock.

Rather than send his son to school, Dr. Carnovsky went himself,
having received the note from the principal asking him to come. Although he had slept only a few hours, he rose at his usual time, took
his customary cold shower, did his customary calisthenics, and went
to the school, using the long distance to advantage for his usual
morning walk. Striding along briskly, he took pleasure in the exercise, as he always did. He was not overly concerned about Jegor's
staying out; he remembered when he had been young and had
spent night after night carousing. He understood the boy's need for
some rowdy fun and diversion. He couldn't have cared less that his
son had been drinking or even that he might have been with a pros-
titute. At Jegor's age he had done worse things. In fact, he hoped
that the spree would help assuage the boy's loneliness, give him assurance, and help make him into a man.

Nor did the letter from school overly upset him. He smiled, recalling the time his father had been summoned to school by Professor Kneitel. He was glad that he was able to treat the matter more lightly than had his father. Like most middle-aged people, he was also struck by the swift passage of time. How long was it since he himself had been bickering with his father? With a philosophical smile he mused about the evanescence of life.

Mr. Van Loben greeted Dr. Carnovsky effusively. Dr. Carnovsky felt a warmth emanating from the principal that was communicated through his firm handshake. The two men felt a sudden affinity. The doctor's appearance clearly refuted Jegor's racial pretensions. Mr. Van Loben lit his pipe and offered Dr. Carnovsky a cigar. Puffing thoughtfully on his pipe, the principal tried to find some diplomatic means of bringing up the subject of racism without resorting to the word *Jew,* which, like most gentiles, he was most reluctant to use to a Jew. But he soon grew tired of subterfuge and in his usual blunt manner asked: "You'll pardon the question, Doctor—I'm not usually inclined to discuss a person's religion—but in this case it is quite pertinent. Do you happen to be Jewish?"

"I am and there is no need to apologize for the question," Dr. Carnovsky said easily but with a slightly strained smile. Like most Jews, he was proud of his faith, but also somewhat sensitive about it.

Mr. Van Loben exhaled a puff of smoke with relief. "One other thing, Doctor. Are you the boy's real father or his stepfather?"

"What are you thinking of, Mr. Van Loben?" Dr. Carnovsky asked with slight annoyance, sensing something wrong.

Mr. Van Loben smiled guiltily. "Your . . . your son has been expressing some very peculiar ideas. Very odd theories that have no place in an American school. That's why I asked you to come, Doctor, and I'm very happy that you decided to do so."

He relit Dr. Carnovsky's cigar and began to puff on his pipe with great energy. He told Dr. Carnovsky the whole story about Jegor and Mr. Levy. The longer Mr. Van Loben spoke, the lower Dr. Carnovsky's head sank. He was ashamed to look into the principal's eyes. "Unbelievable . . ." he mumbled.

Van Loben realized that the doctor was reacting too strongly and tried to minimize the incident. Laughing, he clapped Dr. Carnovsky

I.J. SINGER

Author of the modern classics,
"The Brothers Ashkenazi," "Yoshe Kalb," etc.
whose last great novel

THE FAMILY CARNOVSKY
has just been published by Vanguard Press

on the back and urged him to forget the whole thing. It was a mere
nonsense that irresponsible fools had drilled into the boy's head, the
obvious sort of hogwash he threw into his wastebasket daily. Dismissing the matter, altogether, he urged Dr. Carnovsky to do everything in his power as a physician to force the boy into some sort of
healthful activity. He was sure that everything would turn out well
in the end. "I have children too," he said, "and I've got plenty of
troubles with them. I am very glad for the opportunity to have met
you, Doctor. Send your boy back to school and don't take all this too
hard. Good-by!"

But Dr. Carnovsky did not follow Mr. Van Loben's advice. He
was livid with rage. His usually strong and steady legs trembled as
he walked down the front steps of the school. All the way home he
thought of one thing only, how to keep control of himself and remain calm and objective, as Mr. Van Loben had suggested. But the
moment he crossed his threshold the blood began to rush to his
brain.

Jegor heard his father's angry footsteps. They sounded grim, ominous. "I spent the five dollars Mutti gave me to pay the bills!" he
said defiantly to his father.

Dr. Carnovsky did not flick an eye. Jegor felt let down. "I drank
the money up," he said, "every last penny of it. . . ."

Again there was no response from his father. Jegor became more
fearful than resentful, but Teresa was relieved. Suddenly she saw
blood-red flecks on her husband's cheeks and she became terribly
afraid.

"I was at your school today," Dr. Carnovsky said with deadly
calm.

Jegor did not speak and his silence only fed his father's anger.
"You dared to defend our enemies?" Dr. Carnovsky asked incredu-
lously.

Jegor did not answer.

"You dared insult your teacher because he spoke the truth?"

Again, no answer.

"You dared talk to the principal about race theories?" Dr. Carnovsky said, coming a step closer.

He took hold of the boy's lapels and began to shake him like a dog. "I'm talking to you!" he said. Jegor looked at his father with insolence and without a trace of regret.

For the second time in his life Dr. Carnovsky slapped his son hard across the face. For a long while Jegor said nothing, stunned by something he no longer expected at his age. But suddenly he recovered. "Jew!" he screamed in a piercing, stammering voice. "Jew! Jew! Jew!"

Teresa could not even bring herself to step between them. "Dear God!" she moaned.

Jegor ran to his room, locked himself in, and fell on his bed. It grew dark outside but still he did not switch on the light. His mother knocked and begged to be let in—she had his dinner ready. But he kept the door closed. At first he thought of ways of avenging himself on his father for this latest humiliation. Never had he hated him as he did now. His face buried in the pillow, he felt violent urges to do terrible things to the one who had not only caused all his troubles but who still dared to lay his dirty Jewish hands on him. The fact that he could do nothing, his own helplessness, only fortified his will for revenge. His hands burned with the urge for patricide. When the rage against his father subsided from sheer impotence, Jegor began to consider suicide. He could not see a glimmer of hope for himself. He was a stranger in a friendless land, a weakling, a dupe, a victim of everyone's contempt. *Kill yourself!* a gnawing thought urged him. . . . He had been doomed from birth. A product of two conflicting strains, he was destined to suffer the rest of his life. He could expect nothing but failure and frustration. Suicide was the only way out. It would also be a perfect way of getting even with his father.

He closed his eyes and pictured his father coming in in the morning and finding him hanging with his tongue out. He relished his father's reaction. He even staged his own funeral and imagined his father walking behind the hearse, tormented with guilt. . . .

He sat at his desk and by the light from the street lamp began to compose the note he would leave behind. He wrote one after another, then tore them up. The more notes he wrote, the less he thought about doing himself harm. Soon he was filled with self-pity. He turned to the wall to avoid looking at the window sill to which he had been so strongly drawn a few short minutes before. No! Anything but that. . . . He suddenly became very conscious of the warmth of his own body, the inviting softness of the bed, a longing for food, and a sharp urge to see, hear, feel, taste, smell, and live. He even briefly considered putting on the light, opening the door, and demanding his dinner. But soon he became disgusted with his weakness and lack of character and again felt contempt for himself. He could not live, he could not die, he could not be with the people with whom fate brought him together or be without them. He was good for nothing; he was a misfit, a burden to himself and to others. This was the reason no one respected him; this was the reason everyone despised him. Even the principal had treated him not like a man but like a snot-nosed boy. No wonder his father felt free to hit him!

His mother knocked again. "Jegor! Jegor, open the door for just a minute. I just want to give you a glass of milk and make up the bed for you."

Jegor did not answer. Huddling in his blanket, he heard his mother and father talking on the other side of the door. "Georg, I'm worried about the boy. He doesn't answer," he heard his mother whisper.

"*Quatsch!*" his father said loudly. "Let him go hungry a day or two, it'll do him good. Don't go begging him to come out!"

Again the feeling of hate toward his father came over him. Mostly he hated him because his father knew him for what he was, a weakling and a coward. He seethed at his own helplessness. He would show his father what he was made of! But suicide? Never! All it would do would be to bear out his father's opinion of him and he would be pleased to have been proven right. No! It would be better to leave this house that had brought him so much unhappiness. He would cut the bonds with his family, with his name. He had nothing in common with the Carnovskys and their kind.

His energies restored, he rose and stretched vigorously to rid himself of fatigue and apathy. He glanced at his watch. It was very late. Carefully he opened the door and listened. His parents had obviously gone to sleep. He tiptoed into the bathroom and splashed cold water on his face. The water revived him and reminded him of how hungry he was. He went into the kitchen and took some food from the refrigerator. Once he was full, he began to prepare for the first positive act of his life.

He put underwear into a suitcase and took along one extra suit. He also took the Leica that his father had given him many years before. Then he packed all the photographs from Germany, including the one of Uncle Hugo in his uniform, and took his raincoat, the semimilitary one with the epaulets. In the pocket of the raincoat he found the movie ticket stub and a penny—not even enough for subway fare. But there was an envelope in his dresser drawer with ten dollars and some change. He flushed at the thought of taking his father's money but finally he put it in his pocket. The last thing he took was a photograph of his mother that he stripped from its frame on his father's desk. Instead of a suicide note he wrote a farewell letter addressed only to his mother. Although the note was full of self-recrimination for the grief he was causing her and the money he had taken, Jegor actually felt none of the things that he had expressed in the letter. He signed the note Joachim Georg Holbeck.

Afterward, he quietly opened the door and went down to the street, using the stairs instead of the elevator. At the corner he found a cab, its driver dozing.

"Yorkville," Jegor said.

A cool night breeze blew in through the open taxi window. Jegor took his apartment key and flung it into the street. This was his last act of defiance, a gesture calculated to sever all connections with his former life.

In the small hotel room for which he paid a dollar in advance the bed was invitingly made up but Jegor did not lie down. He was too stimulated to sleep. He looked at the pictures of Kaisers on the wall, the ancient battle prints, and a card listing the rules of the establishment. Suddenly he noticed an announcement from the German Consulate stating that all those wishing to conduct business there were to call between ten and two o'clock. The announcement was printed in German and the pointed seraphs of the characters penetrated like spears into Jegor's brain. A brilliant thought struck him. Although it was close to daybreak, he sat down at the small writing desk and by the thin light of a dark red bulb began to compose a letter. His introductory sentences were filled with the elaborate preliminaries prescribed by German protocol; they begged pardons and paid due respects. After a decent interval the language grew less flowery and more to the point. The letter evolved into a petition and, finally, a confession. Jegor's bitterness and frustration filled page after page. He described his troubles with the teacher, Levy. He drew heavily on his descent from the Holbeck family, with its distinguished record of loyal and devoted services to the *Vaterland,* including that of Storm Trooper Hugo Holbeck. He begged His Excellency The Consul's pardon and respectfully asked that he, Jegor, be allowed to return to his homeland where he was prepared to lay down his life for the Third Reich. Rewriting his long letter again and again, he finally arrived at a satisfactory version, signed it Joachim Georg Holbeck, and gave the return address of the hotel. He addressed the letter in his finest calligraphic German script that had been pounded into him by the teachers at the Gymnasium and went downstairs to post it.

As the first light of dawn began to brighten the deserted street, Jegor felt that his life was about to undergo a dramatic transformation.

40

Dr. Siegfried Zerbe, Chief of the Press Bureau of the German Diplomatic Corps, sat bored and disgusted at his large desk although the day had only begun. His large watery eyes, which always looked moist and turbid and as if they had just been crying, were bloodshot from lack of sleep. His wrinkles seemed especially deep this morning, full of shadows and sharply defined, particularly those creases that ran from his nose to his chin. The thick blue veins in his temples throbbed as they always did when he had a headache, which was often these days. Even aspirin did not help. Pressing his fingers to his temples so that he could actually feel the pain coursing through them, he looked with a jaded eye through the huge office window at the network of buildings, steeples, chimneys, roofs, and wires that made up the skyline of Manhattan. The city seemed petrified this morning, like a huge cemetery buried under an army of tombstones. Only a quiet drone rose up from it, like the buzzing of myriads of bees. Gazing at the concrete vastness, Dr. Zerbe felt a measure of relief. He wished the moment of tranquillity would last forever. But soon the telephone began to jangle insistently and its shrillness drilled sharply into him. Worst of all was the clicking of heels by his subordinates each time they entered or left his office. *"Heil,"* he would say halfheartedly.

Not that Dr. Zerbe was opposed to the New Order. On the contrary, he had been among the first intellectuals to join the movement, long before the Party had ascended to power. But he was very resentful that he had been given such an insignificant post as a reward.

At first he had been made editor-in-chief of the nation's largest and most influential newspaper. He had filled its pages with his deeply erudite articles and the mystical poems and epics that he had never been able to have published when the Jews had controlled the press. He also managed to stage his dramas, with their fantastic Germanic heroes spouting accolades to the Teutonic spirit and to national glory.

That had been the high point of Dr. Zerbe's existence. Critics had been generous with their praises and actresses had smiled at him and indicated their interest. Although he had not taken advantage of these invitations, since, as a true disciple of the Greek philosophy, he considered it demeaning to consort with the female sex, he had enjoyed the attention and admiration. And in gratitude for this belated renaissance of his talents he sought only to repay the masters of the New Order.

A dedicated foe of ignorance, sensuality, and vulgarity, he forced himself to compose epic poems about the leaders of the New Order and to deify them in stanzas that drew heavily upon Greek mythology and ancient Germanic Nibelungenlieder. He compared these leaders to mountains and giants and immortalized their murder and rapacity. His mystical dramas reflected his sexual fantasies. In them, half-naked blond satyrs wielding swords gamboled among caves and boulders and declaimed incredible speeches in a language they barely understood. The allegories were so abstruse that few in the audiences gathered their meaning. To compound the confusion, Greek choruses sang passionately and other abstract elements were introduced. The critics were effusive in their praises but Dr. Zerbe's ascent to fame was short-lived.

Although the audiences did not dare walk out, they yawned, coughed, and fidgeted while the ponderous sentences fell like dull shafts on a bed of cotton. People fell asleep in their seats and soon stopped coming altogether. Nor did Dr. Zerbe's symbolic poems and essays meet with greater success in the newspapers. Before he even had a chance to settle himself properly in Rudolf Moser's old office, he was replaced by a former reporter who did not have a degree in philosophy and had never seen the inside of a university.

In the theaters, the producers began to stage plays by authors who in Dr. Zerbe's opinion did not have an inkling of dramatic construction, lyrical rhythm, or command of the language. They introduced vulgarity, obscenity, and cheap bathroom humor—all the elements attributed to the Jewish directors in the past.

But most disconcerting of all was the fact that the audiences whinnied with delight at these offerings. The same critics who had decried the prostitution of the German theater by degenerate Jews now praised the new playwrights who went even further.

Dr. Zerbe did everything he knew to get back into favor. Although he despised coarseness, he decided to outdo all others in creating popular dirty comedies geared toward the lowest element of society. He did this because, despite all his devotion to philosophy and ethics, he was a pragmatist who always stood ready to serve those in power. He admired Socrates for choosing death because of principles, but he himself had no urge to emulate him. He lacked both the will and the courage to fight the world. He hated the rabble as one despises a mad beast but appeases it to survive. And if the rabble, that great scabby swine, would rather gorge on swill than spirituality, then he, Dr. Zerbe was ready to serve it up. With mixed feelings of zeal and revulsion he began to turn out the kind of filth they wanted. But no matter how low he stooped, they would not accept him.

He was weak where they were strong, spiritual where they were earthy. His theological heritage was too deeply ingrained to let him become one of them. He could not gorge himself as they did, guzzle to excess, smoke, brawl or carouse sufficiently to gain their approval. He had neither war experiences nor amatory conquests to brag of and he bored them almost as much as they bored him. He dampened their spirits with his pious manner and appearance. Making fun of intellectuals to curry favor with the vulgarians, he remained every inch the intellectual he could not help being.

He often longed for the old days when he could trade verbal shafts with his colleague, Dr. Klein, at Madame Moser's Saturday night soirées. But there was no going back, he knew. The Third Reich would endure for the next thousand years.

As soon as he had taken the first step, the slide downward was swift and deadly. First, he was made secretary of the newspaper of which he had been editor-in-chief. Its new editor, the former police reporter, became his superior and even rejected the articles that he still submitted from time to time. Later, he was relieved of even this demeaning position and given a job entailing more work and less responsibility—reporting on the marches, parades, and demonstrations held daily in the capital. Eventually he was assigned to minor spy work abroad.

Dr. Zerbe was not one to deceive himself. The title of Press Chief of the Diplomatic Corps meant nothing to him—he was merely one of a thousand minor agents in the vast international German spy network. He, the poet, scholar, and thinker, was forced to serve under a superior who patronized him, ordered him about, and watched him constantly, as if his loyalty to the *Vaterland* were suspect.

Just as he had been unable to win favor at home, he was unable to get into the good graces of his associates in the new land. Mostly they were upstarts without any knowledge of diplomatic procedure, Party hacks who strutted about arrogantly and managed to antagonize everyone. They looked down on Dr. Zerbe as an amusing anachronism and a nuisance. He, on the other hand, considered them brutes and barbarians. Their frequent *"Heils!"* deafened him; their clicking heels made him ill, their arms thrusting in and out like robots only intensified his revulsion. He was tired, frustrated, disappointed. He swallowed aspirin like candy but the headaches only intensified.

This morning he felt particularly disgruntled. A large pile of mail awaited his attention. It seldom contained anything useful. Mostly the letters were from misfits and social outcasts; accolades from hysterical spinsters; preposterous poems; accusations from paranoiacs; confidential information that was totally meaningless; military secrets of no value, and similar lunatic outpourings. Dr. Zerbe grimaced with distaste at the mixture of sentimental claptrap, prurience, and propaganda that flooded his desk. Reading one word out of ten, he would skim through the letters rapidly and cast them aside.

With the customary feeling of disgust he began to scan the letter signed by one Joachim Georg Holbeck. He was ready to fling it into the basket after reading the first few sentences of polite introduction when suddenly his experienced eye caught something out of the ordinary. He realized that he was not reading a letter but a confession —a desperate appeal for help. Although it was juvenile and full of self-pity, it expressed a tragic longing. Dr. Zerbe no longer scanned the pages, he read every word. Frequently he reread a line, and when he had read the letter through to the end he looked it over again.

It was not the author of the letter who intrigued Dr. Zerbe; he did not have the slightest interest in people. The only one in the world who mattered to him was Dr. Siegfried Zerbe. All others were classified merely as sources of pleasure or displeasure. As a philosopher by profession and inclination and an authority on history and natural science, he knew that murder and evil were old as the world itself. The strong always took advantage of the weak; they always had, they always would. He did not agree with Jewish historians who claimed that one day the lion would lie down with the lamb, but, like the Romans, he believed that people were like wolves. Naturally, the lamb was bound to protest when the wolf attacked it, but it was preposterous for a philosopher to attempt to change a wolf's nature. The world belonged to the strong; that was axiomatic. The law of natural selection was a scientific fact. It was the moralists' and preachers' business to shed tears about it; the philosopher was bound only to examine conditions intellectually, not try to do something about them.

Dr. Zerbe was persuaded that others cared as little about him as he did about them. When he tossed in his bed, unable to sleep, no one shared his torment. Neither did anyone care when he was sick, frustrated, or lonely. No, it was not someone named Joachim Georg Holbeck who intrigued Dr. Zerbe. Nor did the fact that Holbeck was partly Jewish influence Dr. Zerbe's feelings. As a trained scientist versed in ethnology, he dismissed theories of racial superiority as sheer poppycock and scoffed inwardly when earnest Party zealots sought to convince him of the inferiority of Jews. Dr. Zerbe knew better. If anyone was superior intellectually, it was the children of Zion. He still relished memories of dialectic jousts at Rudolf Moser's Saturday-night gatherings.

The only thing of interest about Joachim Georg Holbeck's letter was of what future use he could be in his schemes. His long experience told him that the writer of the letter was no ordinary person. He was either a zealot willing to die for an idea—if so, Dr. Zerbe had use for him—or he was a cunning counteragent in the employ of a foreign power, trying to get into his good graces for the purpose of sabotaging his effort. In either case, Dr. Zerbe was interested in meeting him. Rereading the letter, he tended to believe that its author was a fanatic of the kind not infrequently encountered among young Jewish refugees who had allowed the unusual circumstances of the times to undermine their reason. If this were the case, Dr. Zerbe had good use for such a renegade.

For a long time he had been seeking a defector from the enemy camp, preferably a Jew, to enlist in his network.

It would help his task enormously to know what was going on in the refugee world. Although the refugees were for the most part timid and frightened people who kept their promise not to discuss conditions at home—one of the requisites attending their departure —there were always recalcitrants, and it would pay to know who they were so that their relatives on the other side could be punished. Although Dr. Zerbe had several agents assigned to this task, they were outsiders. He needed a Jew with an easy access to the tight circle of refugees, one before whom the others would not be afraid to speak.

The prime culprit among those who dared break their vow of silence was the former Reichstag deputy, Dr. Elsa Landau. She alone caused Dr. Zerbe more grief than all the other refugees combined. Although she had also vowed to be silent before being permitted to leave, she had broken the promise immediately upon landing and, what was even more distressing, openly boasted of this act of defiance. She traveled throughout the country maligning Germany's leaders before packed audiences of impressionable Americans. She named names, she revealed secrets, she organized resistant groups of German-Americans, she even published a small but widely distrib-

uted anti-fascist weekly that printed details of German atrocities so
horrible yet so accurate that Dr. Zerbe was at a loss to understand
how she had been able to smuggle the information out of the country. She even managed to get hundreds of copies of her paper into
Germany.

But the most damaging thing she did was to select him, Dr.
Zerbe, as a special target for her abuse and to slander his name
among Americans of all denominations.

It was part of Dr. Zerbe's job to influence American public opinion; to make friends with the upper strata of intelligentsia, the
power structure, and all those who could help his country's cause; to
insert propaganda subtly into newspapers that were not alert to his
intentions, and to infiltrate church groups, teachers' associations, and
writers' and artists' circles. With charm, brilliance, and eloquence he
argued the case for the New Order and sought sympathy and understanding for the German people with every weapon in his intellectual arsenal. He had no compunction about quoting from the Bible
or the Talmud itself. He managed to win, if not sympathy, at least a
more conciliatory reaction to the horrors his countrymen were per-
petrating in the name of reform. The sheer magnitude of his intel-
lectualism impressed influential individuals and rendered them more
receptive to the New Order. Once again Dr. Zerbe savored the de-
lights of intellectual repartee at cocktail parties and gatherings of
Manhattan's elite. After dutiful evenings of carousing in Yorkville
beer halls with heel-clicking Party clods, it was exhilarating to cross
verbal swords with wrathful and indignant Jewish liberals. But always Dr. Elsa Landau's invisible presence took the edge off any
small victory Dr. Zerbe might achieve. His opponents quoted her at
length and repeated her slanders of his good name. She alerted all
the news media about the propaganda he tried to insert under the
guise of news. She wrote letters to those newspapers that did use the
material to pinpoint the lies and inaccuracies it contained. She informed the city's intelligentsia about his motives. With mounting
rage Dr. Zerbe read the frequent use of his name in Dr. Landau's
weekly. It reminded him of the old days in Berlin when Dr. Klein
had made him the butt of his scorn in his scurrilous scandal sheet.
He trembled with indignation when, week after week, Dr. Landau

exposed his every act to the American people with a wit and inci-
siveness he would never have attributed to a female. He was incensed when occasionally she even poked fun at his physical habits
and appearance. She labeled him not only a spiritual cripple but a
physical one as well, and made dark insinuations about his masculinity, hinting at dreadful sexual inclinations. Dr. Zerbe lost much
sleep because of Dr. Elsa Landau's attacks. Even his own colleagues
in the diplomatic corps took great delight in them and frequently let
him know just how funny they found them. Dr. Zerbe burned with
resentment and plotted all kinds of revenge. He sent agents to trail
Dr. Landau but she sniffed out their presence with an infallible
sense of self-preservation, rendering their efforts useless. He needed
someone of her own kind, a fellow Jew, to serve as his eyes and ears
in the enemy camp. He glanced down at the signature again:
Joachim Georg Holbeck. Was this the opportunity he had been
awaiting so long?

In his customary methodical fashion, he first made a thorough
search of his records; there was no dossier on any Holbeck. Dr.
Zerbe wrote, asking him to come.

Jegor Carnovsky's hand literally trembled when the letter with
the official stamp reached him at the small Yorkville hotel. Although it was curt and formal, just a few lines, he read and reread it
until he had memorized it. That night his impatience would not let
him sleep. The next morning he took special pains with his appearance and studied his image in the hotel mirror for a long time. At
first he saw nothing of his father's blood in his features. But soon his
assurance crumbled and doubts formed in his mind. The more he
searched for the Semitic strain, the more conspicuous it appeared to
him. Mostly he was offended by his hair—it was black as a crow's
wing. He went downstairs to a barbershop and asked for a short trim
with the temples and nape shaved in military style, which made him
appear more Germanic.

He started out early to allow himself plenty of time. When he
was ushered into Dr. Zerbe's office he did not know whether to
stretch out his arm stiffly, as was the custom, or whether this was
forbidden those who were racially tainted. To compensate, he clicked
his heels with extra vigor and barked with thunderous military pre-

cision: "Joachim Georg Holbeck, I beg to report, Your Excellency!"

Dr. Zerbe cringed inwardly at the despised heel-clicking and noisy greeting but he showed none of his displeasure. "Very pleased to know you, Herr Holbeck," he said. "Sit down, please."

Jegor remained rigidly at attention. "I wrote the letter to Your Excellency," he announced, "and Your Excellency was good enough to send for me!"

Dr. Zerbe's face creased with pleasure. No one ever called him "Excellency." He waved regally at the earnest young man. "Herr Doktor will do," he said magnanimously. "Sit down."

"*Jawohl,* Herr Doktor," Jegor barked and sat down on the edge of the chair.

For a long while neither spoke. Dr. Zerbe looked his visitor over carefully. He no longer had any doubts that he was facing a simple and artless neurotic and he turned on all his charm to further beguile the nervous young man. "You seem to be very young yet, Herr Holbeck," he said tactfully.

"I'm old enough!" Jegor said heatedly. "I'm eighteen!"

"Dear me, all of eighteen," Dr. Zerbe said with mild irony. "From your letter I would have guessed that you were a much older man. . . . Incidentally, your letter touched me deeply. Very, very deeply."

Jegor blushed. "Then dare I hope that Herr Doktor will give me some of his valuable time?"

"I am prepared to give you all the time you need, Herr Holbeck," Dr. Zerbe said graciously.

Jegor began to speak. His words flowed as if in a torrent. He wanted to say so much so quickly that he became incoherent. He broke out in a sweat and could not come to the point. But even then Dr. Zerbe did not interrupt. Although he was bored to distraction, not a trace of what he felt showed on his face.

"Do go on," he urged each time Jegor looked at him eagerly, uncertain whether to continue.

Dr. Zerbe knew that to reach a treasure one must dig through mounds of dirt and he had trained himself to listen carefully and to set aside for further consideration those points he considered impor-

tant. When Jegor blurted out the name of Carnovsky, Dr. Zerbe
cocked his ears alertly. The name struck a familiar note, dating back
to the Saturday-night gatherings at the Jew Moser's house. "Carnovsky, Carnovsky," he repeated. "Isn't your father a physician?"

"*Jawohl*, Herr Doktor," Jegor admitted. "He used to own a maternity clinic on Kaiserallee. We lived in Grunewald."

Dr. Zerbe no longer had any doubts about the youth's usefulness
to him and he became very pleased with himself. Jegor kept bab-
bling on until he grew exhausted. Dr. Zerbe smoothed the few remaining sandy hairs on his large dome and fell into deep thought.
He behaved like a noted specialist deliberating over a dying patient.
After a long pause he began to speak in a soft and calculated manner, weighing every word.

As usual, he had his speech carefully prepared. At first he com-
miserated with the tormented youth. Poor fellow! He, Dr. Zerbe,
knew exactly how he must feel. He knew the pangs of youth—the
longings, the frustration, the loneliness. He was particularly sympathetic to the problems of Germany's young people because he himself had described them in his poems and because they were so
deeply ingrained in German literature. He could understand the anguish of a young man torn like a flower from familiar ground and
replanted in a strange and alien earth.

Jegor's eyes filled with tears at Dr. Zerbe's analogy. "That's just
how it is, Herr Doktor," he breathed. "You've phrased it precisely."

Dr. Zerbe acknowledged the compliment graciously. The poetic
aspect of his dissertation concluded, he turned to historic considerations.

As a poet he could sympathize with a flower being uprooted. As a
scientist he knew that at times, for the good of the garden, plants
must be ruthlessly weeded out—those plants that mar the order and
harmony of the garden and damage the fruit. Not that he doubted
the young man's goodness and spirituality. Naturally he felt a deep
pity for him. But there were such things as historic justice and the
sins of fathers being visited upon the sons. As the son of a surgeon,
the young man could understand that proud flesh must be severed
from a body if the body was to survive.

Just as he had been touched by being compared to an uprooted flower, Jegor now hung his head upon being compared to proud flesh.

Dr. Zerbe patted his shoulder. The young man should not take these words personally because they were not intended to be literal, merely symbolic. There were, of course, people who *did* take them literally, but he, Dr. Zerbe, was far from taking such a crass approach to such a complicated problem. He placed it on a much higher level—one of historic expediency, the resurgence of national spirit and national glory that dictated a self-preservation and a climate of racial purity. Historic justice could not be manipulated to accommodate every individual but called for laws affecting large segments of the population. This, of course, compounded the tragedy of the innocent individual caught up in the sweeping movements of history. But it was an old story—the individual sacrificed for the good of the community; the son suffering for the sins of his elders. And in his, Jegor's, case, there was no alternative. According to the standards set up by the New Order he was a one-hundred-percent Jew. The laws were quite rigid and he knew what extraordinary measures it would entail to allow him to become a citizen of the New Germany.

In desperation Jegor began to stammer, "D . . . does this mean, Herr Doktor, that there is no w . . . way out for me?"

Dr. Zerbe leaned his elbows on the table. "If that were the case, young man, I would not have summoned you," he said judiciously. "When I sent for you, it was because of your letter. Seeing you, I am even more struck by your sensitivity. Now, I'm going to be extremely frank with you."

Red blotches broke out on Jegor's cheeks. Dr. Zerbe looked at him sternly. There *was* a way out, a very good way, but it involved sacrifice, hard work, infinite patience, and total obedience.

"Nothing would be too hard!" Jegor said passionately.

Dr. Zerbe waved aside the interruption and began to speak with uncharacteristic fervor. The New Germany was hard on its enemies, as implacable as a boulder, but it could also be soft and yielding as a mother's lap to those willing to sacrifice themselves in its behalf, to serve it with body, mind, and spirit. The *Vaterland* made provisions

for those who had sinned against it to redeem themselves through
sacrifice. The New Germany knew that blood was stronger than ink
and a way could be found to wash away the ink that wrote the decrees with the blood that was shed for the *Vaterland.*

Jegor sprang to his feet. "Herr Doktor, I am ready to lay down my
life for the *Vaterland* and to protect it with my body against its
enemies! If only I could go home again!"

Dr. Zerbe curbed Jegor's enthusiasm. It was very nice of him to
be willing to die for the *Vaterland,* but this was not a sacrifice—it
was a privilege, not open to everybody. But there were other than
the obvious battlefields. There were battles to be fought against hidden enemies too. Of course this kind of warfare was not as attractive
or dramatic—there were no helmets, no swords, just a quiet kind of
struggle that often was more trying and demanding than the other
kind. But the *Vaterland* also knew how to reward those who waged
this kind of struggle.

Jegor looked blank. Dr. Zerbe barely checked an urge to shout
"Stupid!" and forced himself to elaborate. The *Vaterland* was facing
difficult challenges all over the world and its enemies were everywhere—in newspaper offices, in salons where liberals and intellectuals gathered, in workers' organizations, in churches, banks, restaurants, clubs, and private homes. It was the duty of heroic soldiers to
seek out these enemies, to trace their every step and anticipate their
every plan. Thousands of loyal soldiers were serving on this unspec-
tacular front, some of the nation's bravest and most devoted sons.
Did he not want the honor of being one of them?

Jegor remained sitting in silence. Although Dr. Zerbe had
couched his appeal in glorious and poetic terms, he was not intrigued. To him, a soldier fought on a battlefield, like Uncle Hugo.
This business of spying and informing was alien and repugnant to
him. He had not told even his parents how Dr. Kirchenmeier had
humiliated him at school. He had always believed that it was evil to
inform. He looked down at the floor and did not reply. Dr. Zerbe
realized that the boy was reluctant and renewed his efforts. Of
course it was infinitely more romantic to strut about in a uniform, to
jingle spurs and be fawned over by *Fräuleins.* Certainly it was more
pleasant to remain in one's native land than to live among the bar-

baric Americans. Did he not consider that he, Dr. Zerbe, would have preferred to remain at home where he was an Aryan entitled to all the rights and privileges? And did he, Carnovsky, therefore imply that he was better than Dr. Zerbe? . . . His voice took on a slight edge and he used the name Carnovsky instead of Holbeck to let the young man know precisely who and what he was.

Dr. Zerbe's petulance distressed Jegor. "I beg your pardon a thousand times, Herr Doktor, I never said such a thing. I wouldn't dare even think it."

Dr. Zerbe realized that he had struck the proper note and went on. Carnovsky should realize that his, Dr. Zerbe's, time was extremely valuable. He had not summoned him merely to indulge in conversation. If he had shown him his merciful side it was only because of his earnest desire to help. He had offered him an opportunity, a rare opportunity to redeem himself from the stigma of mongrelization, a chance seldom granted others. If he carried out his work well, he would be absolved and proclaimed a true Aryan by the grateful *Vaterland*. If, however, he chose to be juvenile and selfish. . . . And Dr. Zerbe began to shuffle his papers to indicate how busy he was.

"Whatever you decide, Herr Holbeck," he warned, "you must understand that our conversation must remain strictly confidential."

His eyes bored into Jegor's with intensity. He was anxious to see how the boy reacted to pressure and he was not disappointed. Carnovsky sat there like a whipped cur, like a condemned prisoner bereft of all hope. Dr. Zerbe dropped his severe tone and resumed his previous charming manner. "You take things too hard, Herr Holbeck," he crooned. "To paraphrase the Americans, 'Take it easy!' "

Jegor tried to defend himself. "Herr Doktor must excuse me. It isn't easy to decide to become a . . . a. . . ." He could not bring himself to say it.

"A spy?" Dr. Zerbe said with amusement.

Jegor blushed.

Dr. Zerbe laughed urbanely. "Why call it by such a pompous name? All it is is gathering information."

Curtailing his laughter as if with an ax, he began to make light of the entire matter. The young man had obviously misunderstood. He had made a mountain out of a molehill, a big to-do out of a trifle. Did he actually think that he, Dr. Zerbe, was a spy? He was a poet, a thinker, a scholar. His task was to introduce Americans to the glorious traditions of German culture and to win friends for the new regime. But, regretfully, he was surrounded by enemies of the Reich who spread lies and made terrible accusations against the *Vaterland*. Was it wrong to resist these liars, Jews, and Communists? The worst of them was that bitch, Dr. Elsa Landau. This fiendish monster disseminated her despicable lies all over the country and millions of Americans were being poisoned by them. She was the one who had labeled him, Dr. Zerbe, a spy and a saboteur, and this was precisely the reason he needed an eye and ear in the enemy camp—so that he could continue his good and useful work unhampered. As it was written: "He who would a poet understand must first visit the poet's land." No, his intentions were quite innocent. All he wanted was a fighting chance, the opportunity to meet the enemies of the *Vaterland* on even terms. And the information he needed could easily be obtained by a young man with access to refugee circles.

Jegor wanted to dispute the point. "But I have nothing to do with these circles!" he cried. "They are not my kind and I want nothing to do with them. That's why I came to see Herr Doktor in the first place—to get away from them."

Dr. Zerbe laughed. "That's nonsense, young man, sheer nonsense."

For the very reason that he, Jegor, wanted to get away from these people he would have to force himself to remain with them a while longer. A brave soldier caught behind enemy lines did not run away but took advantage of his position and gathered valuable information for his side. A brave soldier did not even hesitate to put on an enemy uniform to help swing the tide of battle. And the *Vaterland* knew how to reward such loyal sons.

Jegor did not speak and Dr. Zerbe let him brood. He knew when it was time to be quiet. He passed a hand over his balding crown. "Would you care to join me for some lunch?" he asked the tortured youth.

His sudden changes of mood confused Jegor as they were intended to do. "You pay me too much honor, Herr Doktor," he objected.

Dr. Zerbe tucked a sheaf of papers into a yellow leather portfolio, placed a derby on his bulging skull, wrapped a white silk scarf around his neck, and struggled into an overcoat. Jegor sprang up to help him. "Very kind of you, Holbeck," he said. He picked up the portfolio and an ebony cane. He looked even scrawnier and less formidable in the coat with the velvet collar and the yellow spats over the patent-leather shoes—like a corpse dressed for its funeral.

Outside, a taxi was waiting. Dr. Zerbe climbed in and ordered the brooding young man to sit beside him. He made no further mention of their discussion but talked about the weather and the glorious sunshine.

He knew that an impressionable young person could better be persuaded in the friendly atmosphere of a home than in the grim offices of the Consulate. He ordered the taxi to stop before a florist shop and bought a bouquet of roses. "My old servant woman never sets flowers out on my table," he complained to Jegor as if he were an old friend. "I always have to remember to buy some on the way home."

After a long ride they came to a section of sparsely settled one-family homes surrounded by lawns and gardens. Jegor noted from signs on storefronts and service stations that they were somewhere in Long Island. The section reminded him of Grunewald. The taxi pulled into a dead-end street and stopped before an isolated house with lowered blinds and an iron picket fence. Dr. Zerbe asked Jegor to hold his portfolio while he opened the door with a small key.

Jegor stepped aside to let him in but Dr. Zerbe would not hear of it. "No, no! You are my guest. After you, my dear young fellow."

Jegor walked inside. The sudden transition from the sun-drenched street to the nearly total darkness inside made him open his eyes wide. Suddenly a shrill voice broke the oppressive silence. "Mealtime, Dr. Zerbe, mealtime!"

Startled, Jegor squinted and saw a parrot whose vivid greenness stood out starkly against the dark background. Soon other colors began to separate from the dark mass—the redness of a rug, the blackness of a piano, the spots of color from paintings on the wall. He felt a kind of uneasiness mingled with curiosity. Dr. Zerbe excused himself and went off somewhere, leaving him alone for what seemed a very long time. The parrot finally stopped shrieking its incessant cry. Soon an elderly woman padded in and opened the blinds of one window.

"Good day!" Jegor said and bowed slightly.

"Day," she responded crankily, and walked out as silently as she had come in.

The first thing the light from the window illuminated was the painting of a totally nude woman. Jegor turned away in embarrassment. Although it was allegedly a work of art, it seemed more pornographic than artistic. The subject was too voluptuous, too coy, too lascivious in her pose and attitude. He began to examine the other objects scattered throughout the room—carved furniture, vases, jugs, copper plates, bronze plaques, Japanese screens and engravings. The bookshelves held books bound in leather. Next to volumes of philosophy and the classics were books of erotica, tooled in gold and beautifully illustrated. In the corner surrounding the parrot's cage stood primitive African carvings of men and women with exaggerated sexual organs. Jegor's face glowed in the darkness.

He felt a hand on his shoulder. "What do you think of my things, young man?" Dr. Zerbe's smooth voice asked. He was wearing slippers and a silk dressing gown. Along with his clothes he seemed also to have shed his formal and rigid manner. He draped his arm around Jegor's waist in German fashion and led him to a table on which bottles of liquor were lined up. "Wine or whisky?" he asked.

"Anything will do, Herr Doktor," Jegor said.

"In that case, let us drink wine," Dr. Zerbe said, and led Jegor to the dining table where the old woman had set out platters of seafood and cold cuts. Dr. Zerbe dug out the lobster meat with clawlike fingers and chewed clumsily, sucking his teeth. He resembled some weak, frightened animal feeding hurriedly before a stronger beast took its food away. Jegor was too bashful to eat and Dr. Zerbe had to urge him repeatedly. "Shut up!" he screamed at the parrot, which did not cease its shrill chant. "Let others do some talking for a change!"

Pouring two fresh glasses of wine, he stopped to admire the brilliant color of the beverage reflected against the crystal of the glass. "May I call you by your given name?" he asked.

"I would consider it an honor, Herr Doktor," Jegor said.

"Well then, Joachim, why aren't you drinking your wine?" he asked.

"I'm not accustomed to drinking, Herr Doktor."

"Wine is a noble drink fit for poets and dreamers," Dr. Zerbe said, clinking glasses with Jegor. "Beer, on the other hand, is for clods. Don't you agree?"

"I don't know. But if Herr Doktor says so, it must be true."

To prove his contention, Dr. Zerbe drew on historical facts. Cultures thrived only in societies that venerated wine—Greece, Rome, Egypt, even Palestine. The ancient Hebrews contended that wine exalted the spirit of man. Did Joachim agree?

"I wouldn't know," Jegor mumbled, distressed at the turn of the conversation. "I don't really care."

"Shame on you, Joachim, shame!" Dr. Zerbe reproached him. "You're maligning a great culture. Although I am a disciple of Athens and Rome, one cannot dismiss the influence of Jerusalem as the racists would in their ignorance."

He filled Jegor's glass again and again, and soon the boy began to feel much more optimistic about things. Dr. Zerbe kept talking about erudite matters and the old woman brought coffee and cleared away the dishes. Dr. Zerbe told her to put the cups on a small coffee table in front of the sofa and asked Jegor to join him there. Sinking down into the softness of the cushions, he suddenly began to recite poems he had written in his early years, poems that had been rejected by the Jewish editors.

"How do you like that one?" he asked Jegor after each one.

"I am no judge of poetry, Herr Doktor, but to me they sound magnificent," Jegor said, his tongue thickening.

Dr. Zerbe's pallid face colored. "I thank you, my young friend," he mumbled, and suddenly kissed Jegor's cheek.

Instinctively, Jegor rubbed his face to wipe away the wetness of the slobbering old lips. Dr. Zerbe noted the look of disgust on Jegor's face and the color drained from his cheeks. "That was merely an expression of affection a father might show his son," he said resentfully. "The paternal feelings of a lonely man whom fate has denied the privilege of fatherhood. I'm sorry if my gesture offended you."

Jegor hung his head.

Without mentioning the services he expected in return, Dr. Zerbe placed a wad of money directly in Jegor's vest pocket. Jegor flushed. "Oh no, Herr Doktor!" he said, his voice suddenly breaking.

"Not another word!" Dr. Zerbe said. "I know that you haven't a penny and I would be highly insulted if you refused this small loan."

He was not too far wrong. Jegor was down to his last few cents and offered no further resistance. Dr. Zerbe led him to the front door. "Come and see me any time you feel sad and depressed," he said. "I will be happy to help you in any way I can, whether spiritually or materially."

It was not long before Jegor became sad and depressed and needed spiritual and material assistance from Dr. Zerbe. Without really knowing when or how, he became one of his paid informers.

41

During all the time Dr. Carnovsky was preparing for the test by the State Board of Medical Examiners he was anxious about only one part of the examination—the language. He was highly amused and not a little annoyed by the fact that he, a mature—even famous—surgeon, should have to submit to a test like some medical student. With most of his European colleagues he shared a generally low opinion of American doctors and medicine, and without knowing a single physician on the board, he was convinced that its total medical knowledge did not equal his. He resented the board members, but he had no idea how much more they resented him and his kind.

In the few years that the transatlantic ships had been transporting refugees from Germany, they had brought literally hordes of physicians. In the beginning, the local doctors had greeted their foreign colleagues graciously, especially those whose fame had preceded them. But as ship after ship disgorged specialist after specialist and one famous doctor after another, the local physicians' enthusiasm gradually turned to annoyance and, finally, to hate.

They had sufficient provocation. To begin with, the refugees were quick to show their contempt for the Americans. Secondly, they began to draw patients away from the local men. In addition, every refugee physician who stepped off the gangplank laid claim to fame—there seemingly was not an ordinary general practictioner among them. And with each day the rift between the two groups widened. Wherever the American doctors gathered, in clubs, at parties, or on golf courses, they complained about the newcomers, about their arrogance and superciliousness. In addition to legitimate complaints, the more hot-headed among the Americans even began to fabricate slanders and to level false accusations. The most vehement among them was a Dr. Alberti.

Dr. Alberti was a well-known figure in Manhattan's medical circles, but no one knew precisely how old he was or from where he had come.

For reasons unknown, he bore a murderous hatred against the refugee doctors. Each time he was called to serve on the Board of Examiners he took revenge upon them.

Without actually conspiring to do so, many of his colleagues also began to fail the foreigners who threatened their livelihood. Of the thousands of refugee doctors who took the tests, only a few were passed.

Dr. Alberti was enraptured each time he prevented some internationally famed physician from obtaining his license and he boasted of his feelings openly. His colleagues were less obvious about it but inwardly were just as delighted.

The rejected specialists and professors seethed with indignation, but to no avail. They either turned to other professions or began to study anew, like medical students.

No amount of seething helped Dr. Carnovsky when he was handed the sheet with the twelve questions, the answers to which would decide his future in the new land. Not that the subject was unfamiliar to him—there was not one aspect of medicine with which he was not familiar. It was the way the questions had been phrased that incensed him. They actually had nothing to do with medical knowledge, nor were they a fair test of a physician's ability, and he knew that he would not be able to answer them. For the life of him he could not remember the exact percentage of protein and sugar in spinal fluid.

As the minutes ticked by, Dr. Carnovsky grew more and more unsure of himself and committed flagrant errors in his English. Trying to correct them, he compounded them even further. He even began to waver in medical interpretation, something at which he had always been outstanding. He felt the same state of anxiety as during his first examination before Geheimrat Lentzbach. His normally dry, warm hands grew moist and unsteady and the pen wobbled in his fingers. He knew that he was putting down facts that were incorrect and this knowledge completely unnerved him. He watched the hands of the wrist watch that he had placed on the table move ahead with uncommon rapidity. The two hours allotted for the examination were almost up and, like one who no longer has anything to lose, he threw caution to the winds and wrote down whatever came to his head in order to finish the examination on time.

He failed, as he knew he would, and began to prepare for a new examination.

Although he knew that his failure had not been his fault, he was ashamed before Teresa, before Miss Doolittle who had worked so hard to help him, before his friends and family.

The whole effort of sitting on a school bench and repeating simple words, all the homework, preparations, and humiliation had been for nothing. He would have to begin all over again. At the same time he had no assurance that the second test would be any easier than the first, since it was no longer a matter of medical knowledge but of luck.

To top things off, all the money that they had struggled to bring to the new country, all the parsimony Teresa had been forced to practice, had not proven enough, and Dr. Carnovsky began to pawn things. First it was the gold watch, then the ring with the stone that Teresa had given him. Teresa began to pawn her own jewelry. When it was all gone, she took her precious possessions—the crystal, vases, ceramics, Brussels lace, Dresden china, and other assorted treasures—and sold them for pennies.

When there was nothing left to pawn or sell, Dr. Carnovsky began to bring prospective buyers for his X-ray machines. Bright-red blotches broke out on Teresa's cheeks. "No, Georg!" she cried. "I'll go to work. I'll be a maid! I'll take in washing! Only don't sell the machines!"

The look he gave her almost froze her. He had not sunk so low that his wife would have to support him. He felt a void in his heart when the machines were removed from the house, the kind of emptiness one feels after the body of a loved one has been carried out.

Teresa wept desperately and Dr. Carnovsky grew angry at her to hide his own anguish. "No crying, *Goyisher Kup!*" he growled.

For a while they existed on the money they had received for the machines. They lived as frugally and thriftily as possible in a new and even smaller apartment. Dr. Carnovsky practiced his English and read aloud to accustom himself to the language. He took long walks and did calisthenics to keep his emotions under control. When this money began to run out too and they faced the prospect of being left penniless in a strange land, he threw his books aside. For the first time in years he skipped his morning walk and calisthenics and, instead, took the subway to Uncle Harry's house. As he stood pressed among the sleepy people on their way to work he was prepared to do anything to support his family.

Uncle Harry, gulping down his breakfast in the same hurry that he did everything else, laughed when his nephew asked him for a job in construction work, house-wrecking, or whatever he had to offer. It was his impression that his nephew was a bit of a cut-up, a lighthearted fellow who liked to swim, run, and do acrobatics on the beach. He was sure that he had come to take his Ethel swimming and was simply having a little fun by asking for a job, and he chose to ignore him, since he was in a hurry to get to work. He went to wake his daughter, who had more time for such foolishness.

"Ethel, jump into your pants," he called to her. "Your cousin has come to take you swimming!"

But Dr. Carnovsky was in no mood for jokes. He fixed his large, slightly protruding eyes on his uncle and told him as seriously as he knew how that he was ready to do any kind of work—paint, carry lumber, sweep up—anything to earn a living. Uncle Harry looked up with a piece of bagel still in his mouth and stared with his darting, quick eyes at his nephew. "You must be joking. . . . You're a doctor!"

Dr. Carnovsky finally managed to convince him that he was serious and Uncle Harry's eyebrows shot up. "It's easy to talk about painting," he said, "but they'd rip off my head if I brought in a stranger!"

"I'm not a stranger!" Dr. Carnovsky said, puzzled and resentful.

"Even if my father, may he rest in peace, came to paint for me,

these union bums would chop me up in little pieces!" Uncle Harry
said with untypical anger.

Instead of a job, Uncle Harry offered his nephew coffee and cake,
but Dr. Carnovsky stormed out of the house. In desperation he went
to the last person he would have normally asked for help, Solomon
Burak, and told him that he wanted to become a peddler. Although
Solomon Burak had had all kinds of "aristocrats" from the other side
seek his assistance, he was embarrassed when the handsome and elegant Dr. Carnovsky asked for a peddler's valise.

"Herr Doktor, this is no work for you," he protested. "It's a degrading business. You won't be able to go through with it!"

"I'll have to go through with it," Dr. Carnovsky said with an
ironic smile.

"Herr Doktor, I'll advance you money until you're able to practice
again. Only please don't do this."

"Herr Burak, I don't want your money, only your goods," Dr.
Carnovsky insisted.

Solomon Burak took down a large valise from the top shelf, one
of the famous lucky pair with which he had launched his career in
the new country, and began to stuff it with all kinds of bargains—
hosiery, ties, shirts, and blouses. He tried to teach Dr. Carnovsky
some of the tricks of the trade. "The main thing in business, my
friend, is never take no for an answer. Just because the customer
won't buy, you must sell him. Once the door is opened, get your foot
inside and don't let him slam it in your face."

He glanced up at his pupil to see how he was absorbing the instruction and stopped in the middle. For all of his desperation to
make good, the doctor's burly frame reflected only rigid pride and
hauteur. Solomon Burak realized that his words would serve no purpose. "Herr Doktor, do me a favor and find something else to do," he
pleaded. "Take my word for it, you're not cut out for peddling."

"Peddling has been our people's occupation for generations, Herr
Burak," Dr. Carnovsky said with a bitter smile, "and one cannot
escape one's destiny."

42

A new life, completely free and unrestricted, began for Jegor Carnovsky who now called himself Jegor Holbeck.

After several days at the hotel, he rented a furnished room for ten dollars a month. Although the room was dark and small and several steps below street level, it suited his purposes perfectly.

He slept as late as he wanted in the mornings, making up for all the days he had been forced to get up early for school. No one woke him, no one asked whether he had done his homework. Frau Kaiser, the superintendent of the building, in whose apartment he lived, was very respectful toward him and minded her own business. The blonde waitresses in the Bavarian coffeehouses where he took his meals were just as polite. Their *danke vielmals* for his nickel tips were as sweet as the cakes they served. But the sweetest thing of all was to be rid of all responsibilities and obligations and of people who ordered him around.

He had time to spare now and he savored every golden moment of it. Instead of cramming his head with history and science, he attended German movies and sneaked into burlesque shows to watch women strip as they sang dirty songs. At first he felt ashamed, as if he were going to a brothel; but soon the noise, the music, the shouts of the hawkers, the coarse laughter, and the smell of lust and human flesh made him forget all reality and he roared with the other men when the girls took off their final garments. He was not daring enough to yell "Bay-bee!" as did the sailors or to make impossible anatomic suggestions. He only silently lusted for the voluptuous women and laughed at the obscenities that accompanied their every move.

He had even more fun in the German youth club to which a new friend brought him. They had met on the day Jegor moved in. A beefy fist pounded on his door and, before he could answer, a husky youth with ropy flaxen hair dangling over his face and a shirt open to the belly came in. "Ernst Kaiser!" he said, and stuck out a muscular hand that was too hard and powerful for his boyish face.

His chest was as incongruous as the beefy hands; it was broad and bulky and barely fitted into the nondescript colored shirt that could have been anything from a boy scout blouse to a storm trooper's brown tunic. Jegor clicked his heels and barked his three names, "Joachim Georg Holbeck!"

"Are you one of us?" the youth asked.

"*Jawohl!*" Jegor said, blushing at the lie.

"I figured as much," Ernst said.

He pulled a pack of cheap cigarettes from his pocket and offered one to Jegor, as if to seal their friendship. Jegor blew the smoke through his nostrils to show that he was a man of the world and looked happily at his first friend after the long years of solitude. He liked everything about Ernst, from the thick flaxen hair to the overdeveloped hands, barrel chest, and quasimilitary shirt.

"How about a beer?" he suggested.

"Let's go!" Ernst agreed.

Outside, Frau Kaiser was struggling with a huge sack of garbage that she was trying to hang on the tip of the iron fence that surrounded the cellar flat. "Ernst, hang the garbage for me," she told her son.

"Ach, let me alone! I'm going for a beer with my buddy," he said.

Frau Kaiser put her hands on her broad hips and leaned back on her heels. "Herr Holbeck, stay away from this good-for-nothing!" she said. "He's a bum and he'll make a bum out of you!"

"Shut up!" her son said, and flipped his cigarette butt at her feet.

The beer hall was decorated with posters of fat, jolly Germans quaffing beer and a large sign announcing that credit would be extended only to those over eighty who were accompanied by their grandparents. The room was full of laughter, loud talk, smoke, and the clinking of glasses.

"*Prosit!*" the men shouted after each round.

"*Prosit!*" Ernst said, clinking Jegor's glass.

"*Prosit!*" Jegor replied, drinking down the bock beer. He drank one glass after another and chain-smoked to keep up with his new friend. He also paid for all the drinks and cigarettes. From the tavern, Ernst took him to the Young Germans Club.

Down cellar steps they went, across winding corridors whose walls were covered with swastikas, pornographic drawings, dirty words, dates of meetings between boys and girls, painted hearts pierced by Cupid's arrows, and all kinds of sayings about Fritzes and Karls who loved Mitzis and Gretchens; past water pipes, boilers, electric installations, barrels, and all kinds of trash until they came to a door on which was printed in Gothic characters, "Young Germans Club." The big room inside was full of broken chairs and sofas that had been dragged in from the street, a greasy billiard table with a torn cloth, and an equally decrepit ping-pong table. Colored papers left over from a party trailed from lamps and fixtures. On the walls hung ancient proverbs, pictures of film stars and athletes, and photographs of soldiers and storm troopers. A young girl was sitting at a broken-down piano, energetically pounding out a waltz. Ernst Kaiser dug his hand into her shoulder. "Jegor Holbeck," he said, indicating Jegor.

She stood up and smiled, showing strong white teeth. Her snub nose was covered with freckles. Her firm, pointed breasts pushed against the canary yellow sweater. They jiggled with her every gesture. Jegor clicked his heels and barked his three names in a voice too loud with excitement. The girl in the yellow sweater was self-assurance itself. "Lotte," she said simply.

Ernst Kaiser took her place on the bench and began to beat out a heavy-handed waltz while Lotte's hips began to sway to the music.

"Dance, why don't you?" Ernst said.

Before Jegor knew what was happening, Lotte put her soft hand on his shoulder and thrust her incredible breasts against him. He felt himself grow warm.

Ernst continued to assault the keys. "Hey, hup, hey!" he sang hoarsely.

Lotte danced with her whole body. Her laughing mouth was opened wide and everything about her seemed to be laughing too, her eyes, teeth, hair, hips, and breasts—each nipple separately.

Soon other boys and girls began to drift in. As carefully made up and groomed as were the girls, so were the boys sloppy and informal, dressed in ragged sweaters and some even in overalls. Ernst Kaiser, with the ever present cigarette in his mouth, introduced each one separately to Jegor, who clicked his heels until his ankles stung. The din became unbearable. The girls laughed at everything the boys said. New people kept crowding their way inside. Some of the boys played billiards; card games sprang up here and there. The boys tested their strength as the girls shrieked their admiration. Ernst Kaiser was the strongest of all and Lotte beamed her approval. Soon someone began to play the piano again and couples danced. Lotte came dancing up to Jegor and again put her hand on his shoulder. He felt every curve of her body against his. She laughed and laughed and her joy was so infectious that he found himself laughing aloud, something he could not remember doing for years. When the dancing was over, the boys set up a target and began to fire at it with a rifle. The object was to hit the mouth of a carved figure of a devil with black curls, a hooked nose, and thick lips whom the boys called Uncle Moe. As each one fired, the crowd hooted: "Give it to him! Let him have it!"

Lotte laughed, showing her gums, and squeezed Jegor's hand sweating inside hers. "Isn't it hysterical?" she shrieked.

"Very," he admitted, and flinched inwardly each time the satanic Uncle Moe was hit. He felt an inexplicable kinship to this figure—it reminded him of Uncle Harry. To cover up his uneasiness, he laughed louder than anyone, almost to the point of hysteria. He felt better when the boys abandoned the game and began to drink from pocket flasks. Ernst brought over a flask for Lotte, Jegor, and himself, and Lotte took a long swig, just like a man. Jegor tried to outdo her. Suddenly someone turned off the lights, leaving only a small lamp covered with red tissue. Couples went off to corners, to sofas, to chairs, even to the floor. Jegor found himself in a corner with Lotte.

Inexperienced with girls, ashamed and thrilled to be near one, he merely held her hand. But she pressed up against him and whispered, *"Bube . . . my Schatz. . . ."*

Jegor, who had seen such things only in movies, could not believe that it was happening to him. His urge for love and a woman was so strong that he didn't dare take Lotte in his arms; he was like a starving man who won't eat the food placed before him. But she was skilled and experienced and knew what to do. "Kiss me," she whispered, and filled every void of his body with her own.

With each kiss Jegor felt his manliness expand within him. He suddenly felt confident and filled with a pride he had never known before. Lotte whispered endearments and offered samples of the pleasures hidden within a woman's body. *So this is love,* he exulted.

From then on Jegor did not leave his new friend's side. He went with him to bars and to pool halls, to movies and to meetings of the Young Germans Club. Lotte trailed along and Jegor paid for all three.

His services for Dr. Zerbe were not as pleasant. Although the doctor had taught him how to infiltrate the refugee circles, how to get on their committees, how to attend religious services and ferret out information, Jegor despised this work. Like one cripple who hates to be seen in the company of others, he avoided contact with those of his faith so as not be reminded of his own flaws. So long as he remained in Yorkville he felt every inch a Holbeck. Only infrequently now did he imagine that people glanced at him suspiciously when they first met. Generally he was accepted without question, particularly when in the company of such obvious Aryans as Ernst and Lotte. But among the black-haired and black-eyed people he felt his own inferiority keenly. They asked him who he was and from where he had come; what he was doing and what he intended to do, and he had to make up intricate lies, to tell fantastic stories and to act deceitfully—things that did not come easily to him. Nor was he good at extracting information; when the time came to report to Dr. Zerbe, he never had anything important to tell. He lived in constant terror of being found out in his dual existence. But fortunately his Yorkville friends had little contact with the refugees in Washington Heights. Even Dr. Zerbe did not reprove him for coming to him empty-handed; he merely encouraged him to continue his efforts. And each time they met he gave him a few more dollars.

Jegor no longer objected when the doctor gave him money. He had learned what it could buy and the pleasures it made possible, and he grew more and more dependent upon it. The first time he was unable to give the doctor any real information, he made up a story. He was worried that Dr. Zerbe would catch him in the lie but the doctor seized upon the bogus information with greater eagerness than he had accepted the truth. Thus encouraged, Jegor began to manufacture information. Not a liar by nature, he subconsciously came to enjoy the thrill of toying with danger. The fear of being caught in the web he had created was attractive. He began to lie to others, to Frau Kaiser, to Ernst, to Lotte, to everyone with whom he had contact.

He never saw his father, but he wrote several letters to his mother and even arranged to meet her secretly in the street. Teresa arrived all out of breath, as if afraid that he would no longer be waiting. She patted his face, held his hand, and felt his body to see if he had lost weight.

"Child," she wept, "foolish child. . . ."

"Mother, behave, for God's sake. I'm no longer a child," he said, and told her all sorts of fantastic lies about himself. One time he told her that he was a German interpreter; another, that he was working for a shipping company. Teresa never mentioned the inconsistencies in order not to embarrass him. She sensed that his life was not tranquil and urged him to come home. He would not have to go back to school, he could keep his job. She would not interfere in his life in any way and would even keep his father at a distance if only he would come back.

"Jegorchen, do it for me, for your Mutti!" she pleaded during one of their meetings.

Jegor refused even to consider it and told her more miracles about his successful career. In his determination to prove how well he was doing, he even tried to press some money on her. "Take it and buy yourself something nice to wear," he said with pride, relishing the thought that his father could not afford to be so generous.

Teresa did not accept the money and left full of worry and anxiety. Although she did not reach her son's shoulder and could not match his stride, she still thought of him as a child, her little Jegorchen whom she had raised according to all the rules of hygiene. When she made up the beds, she speculated whether his was being prepared with as much care. When she ate her meager meals, she wondered if he were eating on time and whether his meals were wholesome and nourishing. When it rained, she looked worriedly at the sky and wondered if he were wearing his raincoat and rubbers. When she tossed sleeplessly at night, she hoped he was not going with bad women and exposing himself to disease.

Her longing for him was most acute in the nights. She and Dr. Carnovsky would fall prey to the gloom of couples with no children to rear, who are left in a kind of brooding vacuum with nothing to say to each other.

"*Himmel,*" she would sigh quietly so that Georg should not hear. But he would also be lying awake and brooding silently.

He was not concerned because his son was out of the house and among strangers. This in itself was no tragedy. What worried him was the boy's future. Although he was not superstitious, he had strange misgivings about his son's fate. He had had these apprehensions while Jegor was still a child and had been overly afraid of the dark. He had continued to have them after the boy had grown into a moody and difficult youth. They had been intensified when Jegor had suffered his great humiliation at school. And he could not rid himself of the feeling that evil was somehow attracted to his son and that he was doomed.

Dr. Carnovsky knew that in addition to an instinct for life, man was also prone to wishes of death. He had seen it on the battlefield when soldiers raced to be killed not because of patriotism or bravery, as the chaplains and generals claimed, but from an urge for self-destruction. He had seen the same thing in patients who refused to be saved but sought death as if driven by some force. His colleagues had a term for such patients, called them insane or lacking the instinct for self-preservation, but these were labels. In time he had even learned to distinguish these characteristics in people and he knew that all medical efforts in their behalf were useless since they had a prearranged rendezvous with death. He had detected these same characteristics in Jegor, and he was afraid. Each time he came home he paused before crossing the threshold, expecting to hear about some catastrophe that had befallen his son.

Since the boy had left the house, Dr. Carnovsky's apprehension had grown even stronger. Every sound of hurrying footsteps outside in the night frightened him. Still, he refused to give in to Teresa, who urged him to be magnanimous and beg the boy to return. Although he knew that such obstinacy was childish, he clung to it and in an effort to justify himself said things he didn't mean. "Just leave him alone. He'll be back on his own," he assured Teresa. "Just let him get a taste of starvation and he'll come runing back like a scared pup."

But Jegor did not come back. With each passing day he savored his freedom more and in time forgot not only his father but his mother too. He now had another woman to love, his Lotte.

One evening when the air in the Young Germans Club grew so stuffy that even Lotte lost her urge to dance, Ernst Kaiser had a brilliant idea. Wouldn't it be *wunderbar* to take an excursion in the country?

Lotte clapped her hands with delight. "You'll come along, won't you, *Schatzi?*" she said teasingly to Jegor.

"I'll bring Rosalind," Ernst said, "and the four of us will have a goddamn good time together. . . . We'll go camping!"

Lotte laughed from the sheer joy of anticipation and for that laugh Jegor would have gone to the ends of the world. Early the next morning they tramped to the edge of the city. Ernst, still wearing his fading shirt, took huge strides and Rosalind almost had to run to keep up with him. She was a thin and angular girl, sour and pessimistic.

"Don't run," she pleaded. "I can't keep up with you."

"Ach, keep moving!" Ernst said, not even breaking stride.

Rosalind's pinched face grew even more spiteful, but she ran after the fast-moving youth. As usual, Lotte could not stop laughing as she watched the two figures trying to outdistance each other.

The foursome pushed on through the day. They walked part of the way and hitched rides whenever they were tired. When they were hungry they stopped at roadside stands for hot dogs and beer.

Jegor paid for everybody. At night they reached their destination, the camp.

The huge encampment surrounded by a barbed-wire fence reminded Jegor of the other side. On every building, every tent, every garage and fence hung signs in German announcing all kinds of rules and regulations. The street signs bore the names of old German kings, generals, and admirals as well as of the new leaders of the land. Among the quadrangle of tents laid out with mathematical precision young storm troopers raced about, drilling, exchanging stiff-armed salutes, and bustling about importantly. A brace of them stood guard before a group of booths, as if protecting some important military site. Stout burghers puffing on cigars came strolling out of bungalows accompanied by their equally fleshy wives. In the outdoor beer garden, red-faced men and women sat drinking steins of beer served by jolly waitresses in Bavarian costumes. The men laughed thunderously, the women knitted. Newspaper boys hawked newspapers and magazines from the other side. Ernst Kaiser kept greeting acquaintances and introducing Jegor, who kept barking his three names and clicking his heels. Although a Stars and Stripes fluttered from the huge flagpole in the encampment, Jegor felt completely at home.

When a uniformed youth blew retreat with exaggerated importance and an older storm trooper ran down the American flag and ran up a new one with a swastika on it, Jegor felt a tug of anxiety, as he always did when he remembered the false role he was playing. But he stretched out his arm along with all the others and sang with feeling. When he came to the stanza about Jewish blood dripping from knives, his throat grew somewhat dry and constricted, but he swallowed bravely and went on. The fact that no one had detected his lie and that he had been accepted restored his courage. He felt himself a Holbeck from head to foot, a direct descendant of ancient Teutonic warlords. He was back where he belonged, in his rightful environment from which he had been driven like a leper through no fault of his own. With mixed feelings of recklessness and anxiety he went through the entire ceremony along with the cheering, panting hundreds, their faces bathed in the light of the torches surrounding the flagpole. He did breathe easier once the rite was concluded and everyone sat down to the starchy supper to which a second bugle call summoned them. The meat was fatty, the sauerkraut salty, the beer ice cold, the smiles of the perspiring waitresses sweet as honey. Never in his entire life did Jegor recall eating so much at a single meal and laughing so heartily. Lotte's gaiety infected even the usually dour Rosalind. During the dancing that followed, Lotte put her hand not on Jegor's shoulder but around his neck, as did most of the women on the floor. "Sweet, precious *Bube*," she whispered into his ear.

Jegor could not believe that anyone would address such words to him—the ugliest and most repulsive creature alive. For the first time he felt that his life had meaning and purpose.

They went to look for a place to sleep. The night was dark and soft as velvet in the deep meadow between the towering mountains. From time to time fireflies lit up the darkness. The sounds of laughter, singing, the chirping of crickets, and the barking of dogs echoed and re-echoed through the valley. Wherever they turned they bumped into couples seeking love beneath the cover of darkness. From bungalows, tents, attic rooms, bushes, and pastures its whispers and sighs could be heard.

There didn't seem to be an empty space in the whole camp. Even the barns and garages were full. For the few dollars that Jegor had paid for everyone's admission they had been given a torn piece of canvas and some tent poles, along with several military blankets. Loaded down with this equipment, Ernst plunged farther and farther into the darkness.

"Where are we going?" Rosalind asked peevishly.

"What's the difference?" Ernst said and pushed on.

Suddenly he stopped and threw down his load. "I believe this will be a good spot to spend the night," he said with finality.

Like a trained soldier, he put the tent up in complete darkness. "Push away the stones and crawl in!" he ordered his girl friend. Rosalind obeyed silently. Lotte crept under the second blanket and laughed insanely.

"What are you laughing at?" Jegor asked.

"Nothing! Take off my shoes, *Bube*," she whispered, and laughed again. Then she grew quiet and began to whisper in his ear. "Cover me, I'm cold."

Crickets chirped incessantly in the night. An owl hooted, was still, then hooted again. "Why so quiet, *Bube?* Aren't you happy?" she asked.

He felt all the sweetness of life concentrated into the one, delirious moment of ecstacy. The great happiness that consumed him left him shaken and silent.

Through the torn canvas the stars blinked brilliantly in the deep blue sky and looked with neutral unconcern at the earth and mortals below.

43

Dr. Zerbe did not reward Jegor Carnovsky for his services as he had promised.

He neither restored him to the status of official Aryan nor made any further mention of ever doing so. He also stopped being generous with his money and paid only for specific information, and sparingly at that.

It was his practice to be very severe with the people he managed to ensnare into his service, especially those at the lowest level. Secret agents, he knew, were like seduced women. It was merely a matter of inducing them to sin the first time, and for this one required only time, energy, and money. Once they were trapped, with no way out, they sank lower and lower for less and less compensation. At this stage, the more brutally they were treated, the more abject and subservient they became. He had employed this method successfully on others; he used it now on Jegor Carnovsky.

He was greatly displeased with his latest hireling, particularly since he had entertained such high hopes for him because he was half Jewish.

He had always had a real regard for the intellectual capacity of Jews whom, although he had despised them, he also was forced to admire. He had noticed this superiority even during his student days when he had avoided the company of the roughnecks from the fraternities, the beer guzzlers, brawlers and skirtchasers, for that of Jewish bookworms and intellectuals. Afterward he had found himself gravitating toward Jewish literary salons. He hated and envied

Jews but he could not deny their cleverness, their ambition, and energy. The more he despised them, the higher grew his esteem for their abilities, until he acquired a kind of perversely exaggerated admiration of Jewish skill and talents, attributing it all to supernatural causes.

For all his erudition, Dr. Zerbe had never drifted far from the inherent mysticism that had been ingrained in him during his childhood years in the home of his father, the stern and fanatical village pastor. One of the earliest emotions that had remained with him was the primordial fear of the dark-eyed and dark-haired children of Israel who had murdered his Lord. In every Jew he saw the spawn of the ancient patriarchs; the heir to prophets; an eternal Wandering Ahasuerus who bore in his magic bag the ancient Jewish wisdom and treachery, the gift of prophecy, magical powers stolen from the Egyptians, and a treasure trove of knowledge accumulated through generations of roving. Meeting modern Jews, even those who had made strenuous efforts to become one-hundred-percent Germans, Dr. Zerbe detected in each the cunning and mystery of Biblical Hebrews. It intrigued him, this ancient and stiff-necked race that refused to be dominated by the world around it. Worse still, he was strongly attracted to it.

This was the reason he had been so thrilled to enlist Jegor in his service. The youth's letter had been rife with hidden and veiled connotations for Dr. Zerbe, who liked to give his own interpretations to everything he read or heard. That the boy was partly Jewish sufficed to imbue his confession with all kinds of dark and secret allusions.

From historical research Dr. Zerbe knew that Jews always served their masters well. They enjoyed wide experience as henchmen and agents for a variety of rulers, and as long as they were fairly decently treated their fealty was unshakable. Every ancient court and squire-archy had its Jew, whether he was an *Itzik* in a caftan and beard or a *Moritz* in a frock coat and sidewhiskers. Whether court attendant, agent, steward, or theater director, they brought to their task the typical Jewish energy, initiative, and cunning. And the slyest of all were the Jews who had turned renegade. History was replete with blood baths and revolutions these turncoats had fomented. And he, Dr. Zerbe, had wanted a court Jew of his own.

Jegor Carnovsky had proven a great disappointment. He had shown none of the typical racial drive and initiative. He was merely a soldier like his Uncle Hugo and could only obey orders, and badly at that. Dr. Zerbe had expected imagination and creativeness—he had enough clods to obey orders, good Aryans all, besides.

"No, boy, this won't do," he said coldly to Jegor when he brought him some inconsequential, totally worthless item of information.

Jegor was beside himself. "But Herr Doktor has been so pleased until now!" he whined. "You even told me how well I was doing. . . ."

Dr. Zerbe could not stand any more *Quatsch* and he let Jegor know exactly how things stood between them.

"Too naïve! Or to be more blunt about it—too stupid!" he said.

Jegor was crushed. He wanted to offer some sort of defense but Dr. Zerbe cut him short. He was an idiot if he thought he could pull the wool over his, Dr. Zerbe's, eyes. If he had shown Jegor sympathy and a fatherly concern it was not because he was easily taken in but to encourage Jegor to do better. But he would not allow himself to be misled by false information. He was not about to throw away the *Vaterland*'s good money to subsidize beer drinking and parties.

Jegor blushed and tried to answer, but again Dr. Zerbe silenced him. "It's no use, boy, I know everything. I am one person you can never fool," he said.

Jegor no longer tried to bluster; he merely hung his head. He knew that this wrinkled little man who knew everything, saw through all his motives, and from whom there was no escape had him under complete domination. The fact that he could only listen and obey and not offer even one word of protest crushed him. He felt humiliated and degraded. The knowledge of his position made him despise himself. He abandoned all shame and, weeping, promised to mend his ways and do better if only Herr Doktor would give him another chance. But could he have a few dollars in advance so that he could go on with his work? "I am penniless, Herr Doktor!" he cried piteously.

Dr. Zerbe remained unmoved. Instead of money, he offered Jegor an old anecdote from the past when he had been young and naïve and had asked editors for advances on poems he submitted. A wise and experienced editor, a Jew, naturally, had told him that the best way to help an artist was not to give him advances. And this principle applied to informers as well.

Seeing that it was useless to plead and demand, Jegor got busy and began to bring in information. When the truth seemed too gray and dull he also resorted to his old tricks and colored it with embellishments. But he could not fool the doctor again.

"No more lies," Dr. Zerbe sneered, the next time it happened.

Jegor flushed. "I never brought you lies!"

"That's the biggest lie of all," Dr. Zerbe said and laughed in his face contemptuously.

Jegor sagged. "Tell me what to do, Herr Doktor, and I'll do it," he whimpered. "I'll obey your every command!"

"That's the very thing that disturbs me," Dr. Zerbe said. "In this kind of work what's needed is not obedience but creativity—just like in poetry. You understand, boy?"

"*Jawohl*, Herr Doktor," Jegor cried, stretching himself erect to curry favor with his superior. But Dr. Zerbe grew even more disgusted. There was nothing he hated more than military heel-clicking —particularly by a Jew.

"Cut out all that nonsense," he growled. "I don't want a Prussian robot. I want brains; a head . . . a Jewish head. . . ."

Jegor bristled. "I am no damn Jew!" he cried, "Nor do I want to be one!"

"It would be better if you were," Dr. Zerbe observed sourly.

Jegor could think of nothing to say in his defense. He was convinced that Dr. Zerbe was persecuting him, but he could not determine why. He brooded over the injustice until it became his obsession. Dr. Zerbe's face, laughing mockingly, haunted him day and night. And what was worst of all—there was no one to whom he could unburden himself. In his despair he conceived the idea of making himself appear a martyr before the doctor. He had often thought about being arrested for his work, and in time the anxiety became a half reality and he actually felt that he was being followed and spied upon. He decided to inform the doctor about this situation. Hadn't Dr. Zerbe often said how much dedication and sacrifice were required to serve the *Vaterland?* By showing the doctor that he had not given anything away during the interrogation he would prove his loyalty to him and to the Cause. Maybe then the doctor would treat him kindly again? . . . Intrigued by this plan, he began to elaborate upon it. He wove such an intricate and detailed account that he came to half believe it had actually happened. His head held proudly high, he told the doctor about his ordeal. But Dr. Zerbe did not react as expected and, smiling ironically to show he did not believe any part of the story, he began to question Jegor closely. And although his disbelief was obvious, at the same time he solemnly informed Jegor that since he was now under suspicion his services as an agent would have to be terminated.

Jegor realized that his lie had only served to make things worse for him and he began to hedge about his story, but Dr. Zerbe was adamant. "My principle is caution, absolute caution," he said, smirking piously.

Jegor grew desperate and began to whine about being sent back to Germany now that his services were no longer needed. This had been the promise the doctor had made to him. He was anxious to go back and to lay down his life for the *Vaterland,* but Dr. Zerbe yawned in his face with unconcealed boredom. Even if he wanted to help Jegor, he could do nothing for him. But since the youth seemed prone to abnormal reactions, the doctor decided it would be politic to humor him. "We'll see," he said negligently. "Cultivate some patience, lad."

But Jegor was in no mood to be put off. He demanded that which he had been promised, and demanded it with uncharacteristic firmness and obstinacy. Dr. Zerbe rapidly began to tire of this dolt who took every remark so literally. To his philosophical viewpoint, nothing in the world remained constant—everything underwent change, even matter that was solid; to say nothing of such a temporal and vulnerable thing as human flesh.

"You take things too seriously, boy," he said. "Take it easy."

Jegor did not want to take it easy. He had nothing left now except Dr. Zerbe's promises. He demanded, positively demanded his due. He even threw back the few dollars Dr. Zerbe offered him. Dr. Zerbe felt a slight twinge of fear. The boy was a fanatic, completely unstable. If sufficiently provoked, he conceivably might be capable of violence. He sent him away but Jegor continued to call on him and to send long, demanding letters. Dr. Zerbe ignored the letters and left strict orders that Jegor be barred from his home and office.

Now Jegor was left with no future. All his plans had come to nothing. A deep and gnawing hatred against Dr. Zerbe began to fester within him. He walked the streets lost to everything around him, his lips moving in some secret colloquy. People looked and laughed smugly, as people will at one in greater torment than their own. Like other misfits, he presented himself at employment agencies whose cynical employees snickered at his gaunt and strained appearance.

"Joachim Georg Holbeck. Protestant!" he announced in a voice louder than necessary.

He had learned from watching the reception afforded others how important last names and religion were in seeking work. He saw it in the eyes of the girls who closely studied the applicants and from the embarrassed glances of the dark-haired Jews who spoke their names quietly and reluctantly, as if afraid to offend. The girls took his applications and told him he would be notified if anything came up. Like a wounded animal that must be alone in its agony, Jegor began to avoid all contact with people.

One morning as he was sleeping late Ernst Kaiser pulled him out of bed. "Let's go get a beer!" he said.

Jegor showed him his empty wallet.

As usual, Ernst laughed. He lit one of his cheap cigarettes, drew the smoke in deeply, and suddenly came up with the notion that they go seek work in the country, since there was no work in the damn Jew-run city. Jegor was intrigued by the idea. Ernst's burly frame exuded so much power and confidence that somehow Jegor felt secure in his presence, as if he were back under his mother's care. Ernst flung back the flaxen hair from his forehead as if it interfered with his thinking. "If we could get hold of a little car and get out on the highway, there'd be no problem getting work," he said. "There is always work in the country."

Jegor shook his change purse in which only a few pennies remained, but Ernst was not concerned. "What about your camera?" he said.

"I don't want to sell it."

"You don't have to sell it—hock it. Soon as we get a few bucks you'll take it out."

Jegor did not answer but Ernst bubbled with enthusiasm. "For fifteen bucks we can get a car—even for less!" he said. "We'll work a week in a place, then move on. We can sleep in barns or in the fields. We'll take the girls along too. It'll be swell!"

"Do you think Lotte will want to go?" Jegor asked.

"What girl wouldn't?" Ernst said. "Girls can always find housework to do."

Jegor gave his camera no more thought. In the mood he was in he would gladly have pawned the shirt off his back to get away.

With a spurt of energy Ernst began to lay plans for their great adventure. Draping the camera around his shoulder with a proprietary air, he led Jegor to the nearest pawnbroker, an elderly man with a hearing aid and leather elbow patches on his sweater. He offered them twenty dollars. Ernst countered with the filthiest curse he knew and stalked out. In the next place the bald young man behind the counter looked up with a jeweler's loupe screwed into his eye.

"It's a Leica," Jegor said proudly.

"Big deal! A Leica E with a 50 millimeter F/3.5 Elmar," the clerk said, hardly glancing at the camera. "Thirty dollars."

"Forty!" Ernst said.

"Thirty," the bald young man said, and turned back to his work. He looked up at Ernst and winked, the loupe still in his other eye. "Are you sure it's yours? We don't buy stolen goods, you know."

"It's mine," Jegor said, embarrassed. The young man studied him for a moment, then counted out the money into his palm.

They went directly from the pawnshop to a used-car lot where hundreds of washed, waxed, and polished models were lined up like orphans in an asylum trying to entice prospective foster parents. A large banner stated in screaming red letters that for the greatest bargains in the world one should consult Happy Jim.

"How can I make you happy today?" asked a theatrically dressed man who was somewhat less handsome and happy than his portrait on the banner indicated.

Ernst picked out the cheapest car in the lot, climbed behind the wheel, and raced its engine. "It stinks and it's noisy," he announced.

"If you had eighty thousand miles under your belt you'd stink too, brother," Happy Jim said, belching from a too hasty lunch. But soon he decided to live up to his nickname and slapped Ernst's shoulder good-naturedly.

"I'd love to sell you a new Caddy, kid," he said, "but for the money, this old baby will still give you miles of service. You can take Happy Jim's word for it."

After much banter, haggling, and bickering, Ernst bought the wreck for twenty dollars. For this Happy Jim threw in a foxtail to hang from the radiator as a good-luck charm.

Early the next morning they crossed the bridge out of town. The day was fair, with brilliant sunshine and a cloudless sky. Ernst drove, Jegor sat beside him, and Rosalind and Lotte occupied the creaking rumbleseat.

Once outside the city, all four piled into the front seat and Ernst drove with one hand, the other playing with his girl friend's garters. Lotte planted herself on Jegor's lap and nuzzled up to him. Ernst whipped the car around curves so recklessly that the other cars began to give them a wide berth. The girls squealed with delight.

When they grew hungry, they stopped for hot dogs dripping with mustard. Jegor treated everybody. Ernst suggested that Jegor drive for a while. Jegor was ashamed to confess that he did not know how. "I don't have a license," he said.

"Neither do I!" Ernst laughed. "Come on, don't be a sap!"

As Jegor took the wheel, they fell into a mood in which everything seemed funny. Each time Jegor did something wrong the girls grew more hysterical. Finally Ernst took the wheel back. He pushed the accelerator down to the floor and raced the old wreck as if chased by the Furies.

"Where are we going?" Jegor asked, anxiously watching the gasoline gauge go down.

"Who cares?" Ernst said and drove on.

"Aren't we going to look for work?" Jegor asked.

"Work? . . . Oh sure, we'll do that tomorrow. Right, girls?" The girls thought this was the funniest thing of all.

Jegor did not bother to ask again. That evening Ernst stopped the car at the very brink of a deep canyon and, with his hand shielding his pale eyes, studied the terrain. The sun had sunk halfway behind the dark purple mountaintops. Huge boulders loomed overhead as if eager to crush the intruders. The earth was strewn with pebbles and pine needles. A squirrel peered down from a giant hemlock. Ernst reconnoitered the area like a hunting dog and finally found a hollowed-out crevice beneath a boulder. Signs of previous occupants littered the ground—empty jelly jars, beer cans, and cigarette butts. Two charred pieces of wood lay over a pile of ashes. A foaming, bubbling stream raced mere yards away and cascaded down the mountainside in a sweeping arc. Ernst scrambled down to the stream and cupped his hands to drink.

"We'll spend the night here," he announced. "Girls, gather some wood. I'll build a fire."

Grouped around the fire, the girls kept taking out cans of foods that were eaten as quickly as they were opened. When it grew completely dark, the girls cleared the ground of pebbles and spread out the blankets. Lotte couldn't stop laughing. "Why are you sulking, you grouchy old bear," she chided Jegor. "Isn't this fun?"

But the mood changed noticeably the next day when they went looking for work. Ernst pulled up with a flourish before one gasoline station after another, but as soon as he asked for only water and work the attendants turned surly. "No work here," they said. "Try further on."

The farmers were even less cordial. "Try the hotels," they grumbled and turned back to their chores, jealous of the carefree young foursome.

Jegor kept opening his purse to pay for the gasoline that the ancient wreck guzzled with the thirst of an old sot. He also paid for the cheap cigarettes that Ernst consumed by the hundreds and the innumerable hot dogs they devoured. The lighter his purse grew, the less confidence he felt in Ernst's promises of employment. Ernst, however, maintained his optimism and Lotte did not stop laughing.

On the third day everything began to go wrong. It started with the car. Suddenly and without any apparent reason it refused to go up the road that led to their mountain retreat. Ernst stretched out underneath and poked and jabbed at its insides. He tried adjusting things under the hood. Finally he told the others to help him push. But even then the car refused to budge. Ernst left it and walked up the hill. The air that evening was humid and oppressive and flashes of lightning lit up the sticky darkness. Ernst took off all his clothes and without inhibition strolled into the stream. "Hey, girls, how about a swim?" he simpered in a shrill falsetto.

Rosalind hung back but Lotte did not hesitate for a moment. She peeled all the clothes from her superb body and waded in after Ernst. As usual, Rosalind trailed along. Nothing in the world could have induced Jegor to undress before the others. Lotte and Rosalind urged him while Ernst urged and taunted him at the same time. "What's the matter, *Fräulein* Gretel? Is it your time?"

Rosalind screamed with appreciation and Lotte laughed too, which enraged Jegor, but he would not take off his clothes. He sat down on a rock and brooded, deeply hurt and humiliated. Ernst swam away with Lotte, leaving Rosalind behind. She wasn't a good enough swimmer to keep up. "Ernst, I can't go out that far!" she screamed. "Ernst, come back!"

Ernst kept on swimming farther out, with Lotte close behind. They could no longer be seen but the sound of their laughter came drifting back through the sticky night air. Rosalind came stumbling out of the water blue with rage and indignation. "Don't you dare look at me!" she screamed at Jegor, and flounced off to get dressed. Jegor remained sitting, full of bitterness and resentment. From time to time he heard a distant splash and laughter. After a long time they appeared around the bend, Ernst in front, Lotte swimming sedately behind.

Jegor strayed off to a narrow path leading through the woods. He heard Lotte calling him from afar but he didn't answer. When he came back, Rosalind was sitting with her wet hair clinging to her face and crying. "Stop bawling, you silly ass," Ernst said. "We only swam up to the bushes."

Jegor saw a swift, knowing glance pass between Ernst and Lotte. Rosalind couldn't stop crying, but suddenly she leaped up and confronted Lotte. "Whore!" she screamed.

Lotte only laughed and her reaction cut through Jegor like a rusty saw. Only after Rosalind's pointed nails had raked her smooth face was Lotte provoked to grab a handful of Rosalind's stringy hair and punch her hard in the belly.

Ernst watched the girls fight over him with undisguised delight. "That's it!" he urged them on. "Hit her again!"

Jegor hated him then as he had never hated anyone.

The following morning a nagging, penetrating rain began to fall. There was no coffee left, no canned food, not even a slice of bread. Ernst gloomily collected stubs of cigarettes from the wet ground and Rosalind trailed behind him with the hangdog expression of a repentant hound. One by one and careful not to address one another, the foursome went down to the car. Again Ernst stretched out on the wet earth and poked around inside its entrails. He hammered, pushed, pulled, and heartily cursed Happy Jim. The car showed not a sign of life and Ernst spat into its cold and dirty engine. "I'm going to catch a ride back to the city," he announced, wiping his greasy hands on the wet grass. "There is nothing here in these goddamn mountains. Rosalind, get the blankets!"

"Yes, Ernst," she said obediently, looking at him submissively.

Lotte paused indecisively, looking from Ernst to Jegor. Then she laughed. "Spit on the lousy corpse and come along with us, Jegor," she said. "It'll be more fun together."

He pointed down the road. "Go!"

She shrugged and walked away. He watched the three of them growing smaller and smaller. The last thing he saw was the bright flash of color on Lotte's kerchief; then they were gone. It was hard to believe that this callous girl was the same warm, loving creature who had shared his bed under the pine boughs and stars. He looked at the car—lifeless, completely out of harmony with its surroundings. The foxtail good-luck piece drooped dispiritedly. Occasionally cars drove by but Jegor was too disheartened to flag them down. Finally a rangy, rawboned truck driver stopped. "What's the matter, sonny, having trouble?" he drawled. Without waiting for an answer, he ducked under the hood. The rain began to beat down furiously but he ignored it. He didn't get angry, curse, or spit but patiently inspected all the parts, cleaned them, dried them, and looked for further trouble. He fiddled around for a long time. Then the engine choked, sputtered, and caught and the truck driver came up looking proud. "Good luck!" he said, and vaulted into his cab.

Jegor took the wheel and tried to think what to do next. He had neither a license nor money nor friends nor a place to go. Without any conception of where he was headed, he began to drive the car unskillfully up the narrow, rain-slicked road that led straight into the mountains.

44

Like a lost dog that races along sniffing desperately for a familiar scent and is unable to hold his own among the tough street curs, Jegor Carnovsky roamed from town to town, buffeted and battered by his initial contact with hard life.

The first time he ran out of gas and money together he tried to persuade the service station attendant to lend him a few gallons until he could earn enough to pay him back. The attendant, wearing a black leather jacket with the name Johnny painted on it, did not even bother to look up but kept on polishing a car that had been muddied during the week-long rains. Jegor could have cheerfully killed the stupid-faced oaf with the tiny mustache that wound along his upper lip like an obscene snake. His urge was to spit and drive on, but how? He had to swallow his saliva along with his pride.

"I'll clean the car for you," he offered.

Again there was no response. Jegor saw that pleading was useless and he showed the attendant the expensive fountain pen his mother had given him, offering to exchange it for a tankful of gas. Still the man did not respond. Only when Jegor showed him his spare tire did he bother to look up. His lips opened a tiny crack and issued two words, "Two gallons."

Jegor was so taken aback he didn't even ask for a full tank as he had intended. "At least give me five, sir," he bleated.

Johnny turned back to his work and Jegor quickly agreed to the two gallons. "Take that crappy tire off and throw it in the corner," Johnny said.

The pump rang twice, then stopped abruptly as if mocking Jegor.

From then on the insults multiplied at every stop. As long as the two gallons lasted, Jegor kept stopping at farmhouses and in his awkward accent accompanied by frequent "sirs" politely asked for work. The farmers seldom bothered to answer and merely stared at the gawky youth who appeared never to have done a day's work in his life, until he turned away. Only one went so far as to ask Jegor to show him his hands. The farmer took them in his own. "I need a farmhand, not a college boy," he said.

"I am *not* a college boy, sir!" Jegor said.

"That's where you belong, boy," the farmer said.

Jegor drove on. The fountain pen that the gasoline station had spurned came in handy in Uncle Tom's Cabin, a fly-specked restaurant whose hairy-armed Greek proprietor gave him two hamburgers and a cup of coffee in exchange. Now that he was full, he again stopped at farmhouses and asked for work. But no work was available. In the last gasoline station to which he finally straggled with his tank completely empty he no longer tried to get fuel on credit. There wasn't anything left to strip from the car and Jegor offered the automobile itself. At first the owner informed him that he was in the gasoline business, not the junk business. Later, he relented and offered Jegor five dollars. Jegor told him he had paid twenty and the man laughed. "Then all I can say is, good for the dealer."

Jegor had no alternative but to abandon the car with the foxtail that was supposed to bring him luck and, with a suitcase in one hand, his oversized raincoat in the other, and the five dollars in his pocket, he struck out along the highway.

"A refugee?" asked those who gave him lifts.

"Certainly not!" he said. "A tourist!"

Nor did he give himself away in the Jewish summer hotels where he stopped to seek work and someone detected something familiar about him. He wandered ever farther and farther, wherever the cars happened to take him. And wherever he went, the degradation of a man without money in his pocket or authority in his fists followed.

As long as the weather stayed warm he stuck it out, accepting handouts and insults alike. He washed dishes in summer colonies, wallowing in grease and garbage from morning to night for a dollar a day and meals. But when it was discovered that he was too slow and broke too many dishes he was sent packing.

Another time, he was hired to pick apples that had fallen to the ground in an orchard. Although he was stiff and sore from the unaccustomed labor, he managed to hang on for a week, collecting his dollar a day. The other workers bullied him and made him the butt of their cruel jokes. His chief tormentor was an elderly tramp who demanded money from Jegor, ran his filthy hands over his body whenever he came close, and treated him like a lackey. Anxious to avoid trouble, Jegor even agreed to play cards with the old bum and lost half his week's wages to him. But this made the tramp behave even more brutally and finally he challenged him to a fight. The others were delighted and formed a circle, but Jegor was afraid of the vicious old man and he slunk away to a chorus of hoots and jeers. With his remaining few dollars he existed another week, eating hot dogs and sleeping wherever he could. Once he walked past a chicken farm where a white-haired and white-bearded old man who hopped among his birds like Santa Claus among his helpers waved to him good-naturedly. In the lonely nights he often took out his mother's picture and thought with remorse about how worried she must be. He vowed to himself to write to her, but he never got around to it. A feeling of total lethargy had come over him and become part of him. He drifted along aimlessly. His floor was the earth; his walls, the mountains; his roof, the sky.

The days began to grow shorter and the nights colder. The green of the trees turned a vivid saffron, scarlet, purple, and gold. The people began going back to the cities and one summer house after another was shuttered for the winter. Webs floated in the air and clung to everything. On scraggly dirt-poor farms in the rocky mountainous earth the clapboard houses and barns squatted silently, bathed in a mysterious mist like souls lost in limbo. The wire fences ringing them seemed intended to keep the inhabitants locked in rather than intruders out. The rains came and the winds tore the leaves from the trees and lashed the branches and trunks. Just as wild and untamed as the wind was Jegor Carnovsky now. His shoes were torn from scrambling over rocks, his clothes were foul, his hair was long and matted, his face sunburned, pitted, and raw. Farmers drove him off when he came close; women screamed at the apparition. Cruel people reveled in his appearance, atrocious accent, and preposterous blend of pride and servility. "Hey, bum, buy yourself some soap—you stink!" they called after him.

Respectable drivers were reluctant to pick him up and only an occasional truck driver, desperate for company, stopped for him and sometimes even offered him a cigarette. One dropped him off at the edge of the city to which Jegor had finally decided to return with the advent of cold weather. He found himself on the waterfront, near the fish market.

During the few days that Jegor spent around the waterfront he stripped himself of every vestige of his former existence. He sold his watch for a quarter that, because of his gnawing hunger, he spent all at once in an Italian restaurant patronized by longshoremen, sailors, and waterfront loafers. Then he sold his dirty shirts for a nickel each to an old-clothes dealer and, having no further use for the valise, he sold it too for a dime. Dressed in his oversized raincoat, he mingled with the dockworkers, sailors, fishermen, tramps, and truck drivers and inhaled the stink of rotting fish, putrid vegetables, smoke, oil, and gasoline. The whistles of the freighters seemed to be calling to him.

"Perhaps you have work for me on your ship, sir?" he asked the crew members loitering near the gangplanks.

The men puffed their pipes and looked past and through him and Jegor had the odd sensation that he somehow lacked substance. Borne along by his wretchedness, he wandered from pier to pier, spent nights in flophouses where for a dime he was provided with a bedbug-ridden cot and an orchestra of nocturnal inhuman noises. When he was stripped of everything worth trading, he abandoned the waterfront and drifted off to another part of the city.

For Jegor the sensation of being lost in some fantastic dimension became increasingly acute. It grew strongest one evening when the streets became lit by a mysterious glow. A championship bout was scheduled that night, the first major fight of the season, and thousands of people were hurrying home to their radios. The area around Madison Square Garden was jammed for blocks as taxis hurtled madly into the congestion of cars and people, their drivers leaning on horns and abusing everyone in sight. People pushed, yelled, argued, and laughed. Mounted and foot policemen made no effort to maintain order. Frenzy-eyed hawkers peddled souvenirs of the fight. The time for the main event drew nearer and from every car, store front, and ground-floor apartment radios blared hysterical accounts of pre-fight trivia. Clusters of gesticulating people gathered around the loudspeakers and talked of great fights of the past. When the first punches began to land, the whole city seemed to come to a sudden halt. Cars stopped in the middle of the street, traffic policemen abandoned their posts, youths of every size and color screamed and jigged with joy or disappointment. Just as soon as the fight ended, the streets grew deserted and inhospitable again, as if nothing of consequence had occurred only moments before. The only trace of the event was a gutter full of gum wrappers, fight programs, and newspapers. Soon a dreary rain compressed even these few remnants into the soggy, gray mass that is the undergrowth of the city.

Jegor reeled along, soaked to the skin. He shivered and sweated at the same time and felt himself grow groggy. He bent under the force of the rain, although he could have ducked into a subway entrance for protection. Somehow the night boded tragedy. The wail of ambulance sirens hurrying to some unknown disaster ripped through the darkness.

For a second Jegor considered going home to his parents. Hunger gnawed at his intestines. His wet clothes clung to every part of his stinking, sodden flesh and froze there. Tears ran from his eyes and mixed with the rain. The wetness dissolved all feelings of obstinacy, resentment, and pride and left him with a powerful urge for warmth, dryness, food, and sleep. He was ready to beg a nickel for the subway ride home and he approached the man in the booth who was stacking piles of nickels behind the iron grille of his cage. "Sir, I've lost all my money," he said, "and I have a long way to go."

"So?"

"Sir, I promise to bring the nickel back!"

"That's what all you bums say and I never got one nickel back yet," the man said and swept the piles into a canvas sack.

A wave of hot anger coursed through Jegor and warmed his congealed blood. It shook him out of his mood and he was furious with himself for his moment of weakness. When the man in the booth was temporarily occupied, Jegor impulsively vaulted over the turnstile and raced down the stairs. He did not even care if he was caught, but no one bothered to stop him. The small act of daring made him feel bold and adventurous. He boarded a train, not one heading toward his parents' house but in the opposite direction—toward Long Island.

A vagrant spark flickered in his muddled brain: *Dr. Zerbe.* . . .

He was the one responsible for all his grief; *he* was the one who had used, then discarded him; it was *his* fault that he had cut himself off from his home, his friends, and his family. Now it was time for a reckoning, for a squaring of accounts. He would demand what was coming to him—only that and nothing more. He would also prove of what stuff Joachim Georg Holbeck was made!

The clocks on the subway platforms indicated a late hour but Jegor did not even see them. His glazed, febrile eyes were fixed on his goal, on the great task before him.

Racing through the dark streets of Long Island, he gazed into windows where warm, respectable citizens enjoyed the peaceful sleep of the righteous. A passing car drenched him from head to foot. Almost lost in the hiss of rain and the creaking of tree branches came the sound of a distant piano playing *Liebestraum.* He ran until he reached the lonely house at the end of the street, guarded by the high picket fence. He climbed the front stairs and paused before the door, his finger poised on the bell. A stream of water from the roof drenched his collar and ran down his chest and back. He turned as if to go but instead he pressed the doorbell, becoming unaccountably frightened at the sound it made inside the house. He waited, tense from the cold and anxiety. After what seemed like eternities he heard a familiar dry cough inside. The door swung open, creaking from dampness, and Dr. Zerbe, wearing a dressing gown and slippers, put out a veiny, liver-spotted hand. "What is it, boy, a telegram or a registered letter?" he asked in his poor English.

"No, it's I, Herr Doktor!" Jegor said in German.

Dr. Zerbe peered into the darkness. For a while he did not recognize the figure in the doorway but soon his pale face grew taut with rage and indignation. "You?" he asked in disbelief. "You?"

Jegor began to stutter. "I had to see Herr Doktor. . . . A very urgent matter. . . ."

Dr. Zerbe became livid. "That is what my office is for!" he said between clenched lips. "My home is my castle, *donnervetter!*"

He was tempted to slam the door in the youth's face but Jegor had already stepped inside and stood there, resolute and immobile. Something about his eyes and manner gave Dr. Zerbe pause. "At least close the door," he grumbled, "it's blowing in. . . ."

Jegor took off his raincoat and left it on the stairs outside. He began to rub his soaking shoes against the mat with the *willkommen* inscribed upon it. "I've been walking in the rain," he explained lamely.

He took from his pocket a filthy newspaper that he had salvaged from a trash can and tried to wipe up the mess. But it was a hopeless task. He glanced at the doctor, whose disgusted eyes took in every stain on the floor and carpet. Jegor rose, his hate for the older man growing and expanding like a physical force. Dr. Zerbe walked into his study and Jegor followed. A small fire was burning in the fireplace and a platter of cake, along with several bottles of liquor, was standing on the table. The portrait of the naked courtesan on the wall was half bathed in shadow. The parrot began its hoarse refrain: "Mealtime, Herr Doktor, mealtime!"

"Shut your bill, chatterbox!" Dr. Zerbe screamed.

He sat down in a deep armchair and looked at the disheveled youth. "What possessed you to come here at this time of the night?"

"I came to get what was promised me!" Jegor said.

Dr. Zerbe exploded into a tantrum more simulated than real, hoping that it would frighten the obviously disturbed youth into leaving.

"For official business you see me at my office!" he shrieked. "This is my house, damn it, my house!"

"I went to your office many times but they wouldn't let me see you, Herr Doktor," Jegor said, shifting from foot to foot.

"That's no excuse for breaking in on me in the middle of the night!" Dr. Zerbe shouted. "In my free time I like to be left alone— quite alone!"

He watched to see if Jegor would make a move to go but the

youth merely repeated his demands for that which was due him. He ranted about duty and sacrifice and love of country until Dr. Zerbe lost his patience altogether. *"Quatsch!"* he roared. "I promised nothing and I don't want to hear another word about it!"

"Oh yes! Herr Doktor did promise and I demand what's coming to me!" Jegor insisted.

Dr. Zerbe's voice rose perceptibly. "Look here, if you need a few dollars, I'll give them to you, but this is no hotel for tramps. This is my home! You understand? My home!"

He pounded his puny fist on the table to convince Jegor of his determination but Jegor didn't seem in the least frightened. He did not stir and stared stubbornly back at him. His reaction disturbed Dr. Zerbe. He realized that the youth would not be frightened away and he decided to change his approach. He walked to the window and looked out. "A godawful night," he remarked, drawing his arms up into his sleeves. "It looks as if it will never stop pouring. . . ."

He strolled to the fireplace and motioned the silent youth to come closer. "Why are you standing there? Sit down by the fire and dry off."

Jegor came up to the fire and steam began to rise from his clothes. Dr. Zerbe wagged his head. "A dog wouldn't be out on a night like this." He walked to the table. "Which would you prefer, wine or whisky?"

Jegor did not answer and Dr. Zerbe filled two glasses. "I'll drink my customary wine. For you, I believe a glass of whisky would be better at this time."

He shoved the glass into Jegor's hand. "Well, drink up! Drink up!" he said with irritation, watching Jegor closely.

Jegor put the glass to his lips and drained it in one gulp. Dr. Zerbe nodded with relief. "Are you hungry?" he asked.

"No!" Jegor snapped, although hunger raked at his ribs.

"Of course you are!" Dr. Zerbe said and pushed the platter of cake toward him.

The smell of food on top of the whiskey on an empty stomach made Jegor groggy and he took a piece of cake in his dirty hand to allay his dizziness. He swallowed it in one bite. Soon he took more cake and although he felt that he was degrading himself, he gobbled up the whole plateful. Dr. Zerbe watched him with growing relief. He was sure now that the danger had passed and that Jegor would soon revert to his usual self. However, he still was careful not to arouse him. He wanted to render him completely harmless and he decided to do this not with force but with humilitation. "God, how filthy you are," he said with disgust.

"I've been on the road," Jegor said defensively.

"Why didn't you go home, stupid?"

"I couldn't go home after working for you," Jegor said.

"You take things too hard, much too hard," Dr. Zerbe sighed.

Again Jegor brought up his claims for payment for his services. Especially now that he had nothing else, he needed passage to the other side. But Dr. Zerbe curtailed his diatribe abruptly, feeling his control of the situation rapidly returning. "Put another log on the fire!" he ordered Jegor brusquely. *"Mach schnell!"*

Jegor put another log on the fire and Dr. Zerbe listened with enjoyment to the sound of the dry wood crackling and snapping. He sipped his wine calmly and meditated his next move. He suddenly rose, went into the bedroom, and came back carrying a pair of worn but serviceable patent-leather shoes.

"My maid will growl like a bear in the morning when she sees the mess," he said with a chuckle. "Here, put on these old shoes."

He threw them at Jegor. Again Jegor felt that he was degrading himself by accepting but he exchanged his wet shoes for the dry ones. "Aren't they too tight?" Dr. Zerbe asked.

"No," Jegor said, although they pinched his toes.

Dr. Zerbe studied his reflection in the wine beaker and poured more whisky into Jegor's glass. "I don't want any more," Jegor protested.

"Drink it down!" Dr. Zerbe ordered with complete authority.

Jegor drank. He knew that he shouldn't but he drank glass after glass.

The fire dried his clothes and filled the room with the smell of his unwashed body. Dr. Zerbe wrinkled his nose. "You could use a bath," he said.

Jegor flushed with shame. He began to say something but again

Dr. Zerbe cut him short. "Go upstairs and clean yourself up properly," he said. "I'll find you some clean underwear."

Again Jegor knew that he was acting against his better judgment. He had not come here for a handout but for payment of what was due him. But again he did as he was told and was enraged at himself for his timidity.

Dr. Zerbe hurled his final insult up the staircase. "Wash the tub after yourself and don't spare the water while you're at it!"

By the time Jegor came downstairs Dr. Zerbe was his usual insolent self. He had lost every trace of fear of the youth who had barged in on him so fiercely out of the night. Jegor's cleaned face looked boyishly innocent, his eyes were mild and tepid as ever. The borrowed clothes robbed him of whatever forcefulness and dignity he had displayed before and made him look foolish and inept. Dr. Zerbe struggled unsuccessfully not to laugh.

"Is Herr Doktor laughing at the way I look?" Jegor asked, although it was apparent.

Dr. Zerbe saw no reason to deny it. "Put more wood on the fire!" he ordered.

Jegor put more wood on the fire.

"Now pour me a glass of wine, and pour one for yourself as well."

"I don't want any more," Jegor said.

"Do as I tell you!" Dr. Zerbe said.

Jegor drank.

Suddenly Dr. Zerbe leaned toward Jegor and pinched his cheek. "You're a nice lad," he said, "only stupid."

Jegor was repelled by the touch of the slippery fingers and irked by the doctor's patronizing tone. "I'm goddamned old enough to know what's coming to me!" he said, attempting a tough manner, and he repeated his complaint about receiving what was due him. But Dr. Zerbe ignored him and reiterated his opinion of Jegor— nice but stupid. He, Dr. Zerbe, had assumed that he could use his services because Jegor stemmed from an intelligent race, and if he had succeeded he would have been amply rewarded. But he had made a grave mistake in engaging him, and now it was over.

"Understand this, boy. You're absolutely worthless and I can't use you," Dr. Zerbe said, throwing the insult in Jegor's face and looking at him mockingly. "What have you got to say about that?"

Jegor looked with amazement at the gnarled little man who dared to taunt him so flagrantly. Unexpectedly, Dr. Zerbe abandoned his malicious tone and began to speak softly and quietly, as one talks to a child after a spanking.

He, Jegor, must not think that he, Dr. Zerbe, was severe with him because he hated him. On the contrary, he had always considered Jegor a nice boy and felt sorry for him. If he had acted at all harshly it was because Jegor babbled such nonsense and made impossible demands. But he was prepared to forget everything and to begin from scratch. He would even give Jegor a job. Of course he could no longer use him in secret service because such work required perseverance, initiative, energy, and even imagination; in short, attributes that he, Jegor Carnovsky, could never acquire. Still, he would give him work—easy, uncomplicated work that he could do without trouble and even enjoy. He, Dr. Zerbe, had been trying for a long time to replace his old servant woman. She was a nasty old frump who minded his business, offered unsolicited advice, and was a general nuisance as were all women, with whom no civilized man could deal. He had given the problem much thought and if he, Jegor, promised to be humble and obedient he would gladly engage him as his personal body servant and provide him with room and board, clothes, and even a little spending money besides. "What do you say to that, boy?" he asked.

Jegor looked at him with glazed, staring eyes. Dr. Zerbe's voice grew silkier and more intimate. Jegor need not think that he, Dr. Zerbe, was anxious to degrade or humiliate him. He had to learn to accept things philosophically as he, Dr. Zerbe, accepted them; not to fight fate but to submit to it. Every intelligent person knew that since the beginning of time people had been divided into two categories— the masters and the servants. Only fuzzy-headed liberals thought it could be otherwise; thinkers and scholars accepted it as a natural law. He, Jegor, obviously did not belong to those destined to rule, since he was not endowed with leadership qualities. But since the gods had not chosen to favor him, he would do well to accept his lot. It behooved him to be humble and docile, and only then would his life be tranquil. "What do you think of that, boy?" he asked for the second time.

Jegor did not respond and Dr. Zerbe continued. He had always considered it in bad taste to engage women servants, a practice cultivated by priests and other fuddy-duddies but repugnant to a thinking man and an epicure. The ancient Greeks knew how to live. They never surrounded themselves with women but kept slave boys as body servants. They selected these lads from the best families of conquered races, the offspring of princes and noblemen. They also bought young Jewish princelings from Jerusalem and sold them as slaves or objects of pleasure to wealthy aristocrats and philosophers. He would also like to maintain a nice pure lad who would obey him and gratify all his wishes. "What do you think of that, boy?" he asked for the third time.

Jegor only stared at him through clouded eyes and Dr. Zerbe considered the matter closed. He poured two glasses of wine. "Here, let us drink to our new existence," he said, quaffed the wine in one swallow, and kissed Jegor full on the mouth.

Jegor felt so revolted by the wet slime that he recoiled. Dr. Zerbe moved after him. *"Bube!"* he panted through drooling lips. His gnarled face had turned an unhealthy blue. His eyes were like tarnished pieces of dirty glass. His weak, eager hands clawed at Jegor's garments.

Jegor's eyes opened wider and wider and suddenly saw double— two faces at once. One moment it was Dr. Zerbe's; the next, Dr. Kirchenmeier's. The wrinkles, the murky eyes and naked skulls, even the rasping voices seemed one and the same. He felt the tremendous surge of revulsion, hate, and strength that possesses one when facing a particularly loathsome reptile. From the bookshelf against which he cowered, an ebony statue of an African goddess with exaggerated breasts looked down on him. He gripped it in his hand and drove it with all his strength into the naked, sweating skull of the frantic little man before him.

The first to cry out was the parrot. "Mealtime, Herrrrrr Doktorrrrrrrr!" it croaked in its throaty voice. "Mealtime!"

At the same time it started the blood-curdling cackle of a madwoman. The laughter only served to fire Jegor's anger and he drove the statue repeatedly into the crumbling skull as the doctor's body sagged to the floor. Jegor stooped and kept pounding the skull until it was pulp. When the bird's laughter ceased, Jegor's arm stopped flailing. The bloody, staring eyes of the crumpled figure looked up at him blankly. Although he had never before seen a corpse, he knew that this was death and he took a fold of the dressing gown and covered the face to avoid seeing it. At that moment he realized that he was wearing the dead man's clothes and he tore them off hurriedly and put on his own things. He ran outside and pulled on the raincoat that he had left by the door. It had stopped raining and a thick yellow mist hung over everything. From the nearby ocean, foghorns warned mournfully of the dangers that lurked in the night. Nothing could be seen in the dense fog, no houses, trees, or bushes, and the only light, vague and indistinct, issued from the house he had just fled. Without knowing why, he went back inside to turn off the lights. The parrot began to laugh again. Jegor went around turning off the lights one by one. When he came to the green lamp above the desk, he found the drawer half open. He looked inside. It contained letters, papers, postage stamps, a few obscene photographs, a set of false teeth, gold cuff links, money, and a small pearl-handled pistol. Jegor took only one nickel and the pistol, something for which he had longed since childhood, when he had played with Uncle Hugo's army gun. Putting out the final light, he went outside and quietly closed the heavy warped door behind him as if afraid of waking someone inside. Through the foggy darkness he heard the laughter of the parrot mocking him. "Mealtime, Herrrrrrrr Doktorrrrrrrr, mealtime!"

He hurried to escape the terrible voice. The echo of his footsteps started him, as if someone were trailing him, and he began to run while his fear kept pace beside him.

45

Although it was the middle of the night when sleep is soundest, Dr. Carnovsky instantly heard the echo of a gunshot in the hall outside. For months his ears had been alerted for the bad tidings he knew must come.

Jegor was still holding the pearl-handled pistol when his father came running out into the hall in his pajamas. He was propped, half sitting, half lying against the wall, with a sickly grin on his face.

Dr. Carnovsky took his son's hand and forced the pistol loose from the fingers. "Open your hand, son," he said quietly. "Like so . . ."

Jegor kept smiling guiltily. "It's I, Father," he said. Although the words were choppy and rasping, they were full of the love Dr. Carnovsky had yearned for years to hear from his son.

The short, harsh breathing and hungry gasping for air told him that the bullet was lodged in the heart area. He pulled away the clothes from his son's chest with one hand and felt for the pulse with the other. It beat strongly. "Breathe, son," he told him.

"I can't, Father. It hurts too much," Jegor said, eagerly sucking for air.

There was no further doubt in Dr. Carnovsky's mind. From his experience at the front he knew precisely the kind of wound it was and he turned his attention to his son's wasted breastbone where a small charred hole showed just below the pink nipple. From the lip of the wound he ascertained in which direction the bullet had traveled.

"Put your arm around my neck, son," he said, carrying the boy lightly into the apartment.

Holding his father's strong, warm neck with both arms, Jegor began to tremble. "I beat him, Father!" he said haltingly, "I beat him to death! He insulted me . . . insulted me terribly . . . I'm so frightened! . . ."

"Try not to shake, son," his father said. "Gently, boy, gently. . . ."

Nothing would have surprised him, so certainly had his intuition foretold the calamity.

Jegor clasped his father's neck as he had when he was a child frightened by nightmares. "I'm so afraid!" he whispered.

"I am with you, boy," Dr. Carnovsky said.

Teresa Carnovsky went white with shock when she awoke from a deep sleep and saw her husband carrying their son to the bed; but Jegor's short, painful breathing quickly roused her from her lethargy. "Jegorchen!" she moaned and ran to the door to get help. But her husband stopped her.

"No noise!" he said. "Undress him. Quickly!"

His brisk, positive air dispelled her panic and she moved to obey as if they were again doctor and nurse. "Child, what have you done to yourself?" she asked, pulling the filthy clothes from her son's body.

Although he was weak from pain and talking was an effort, Jegor smiled wanly at his mother. "I had to do it, Mutti," he whispered. "I was insulted . . . terribly insulted. . . ."

Dr. Carnovsky lit every light in the house, moved tables together, and issued more orders. "Water and soap. Spread a clean sheet over the table and prepare alcohol, iodine, and ether."

As she smoothed the sheet over the table, Teresa was again seized with fear. "Georg, let me call an ambulance!" she said, remembering that he had no license to practice.

"Do as I tell you," he said. "Every second counts!"

She did not speak again but awaited further orders.

Everything was laid out in precise order in Dr. Carnovsky's cabinet, in the same sequence as in the clinic. Even the rubber gloves and surgical gown lay in place, washed and ready. Dr. Carnovsky asked

Teresa for only the most essential instruments and in order to save time did not even put on the gown or gloves.

With the rapid skill he had developed in the field, he prepared, omitting the embellishments attending a formal operation. He did not even wait to have Teresa sterilize the instruments—he was too afraid of a hemorrhage. With soap and cold water he washed his son's chest, sprinkled it with alcohol, then doused it with iodine. "Keep up your nerve, son," he said to Jegor, who was looking up at him with staring eyes.

Jegor took his father's hand and kissed it. The act of love spread a warm glow through Dr. Carnovsky and he took a moment off to kiss Jegor on the lips. Immediately afterwards he grew professionally detached and, holding a cloth to his son's sweat-drenched face, began to drip ether onto it, drop by drop.

He scrubbed his hands and told Teresa to pour alcohol over them. He took another look at the sleeping boy still smiling the guilty smile of the prodigal son, then at Teresa, whose pale face reflected the reddish glow of the strong lights centered around the table. His hands felt firm and steady and his mind was calm and controlled. He glanced for the last time at the unconscious boy so close to death, yet, in a way, completely cured, and he felt very proud of him.

"Calmly and deliberately," he said to Teresa, who stood by his side ready to obey his every command. He picked up the scalpel that Professor Halevy had passed on to him, the one that had served him so well through the years, and made the incision.

In the still night outside, a horse's slow hoofbeats echoed against the pavement and the familiar voice of the milkman carried through the cool, moist air. "Whoa, Mary, whoa. . . ."

The first light of dawn pierced the fog and bathed the room in a clear greenish glow.